PENGU

THE VIE

Malcolm Cowley grew up in Pittsburgh, Pennsylvania, and interrupted his undergraduate career at Harvard to drive an ambulance during World War I. He moved to New York City in 1919 and worked as an editor of *The New Republic* from 1929 to 1944. He served as president of the National Institute of Arts and Letters from 1956 to 1959 and from 1962 to 1965 and was chancellor of the American Academy of Arts and Letters from 1966 to 1976. Penguin Books also publishes Malcolm Cowley's *Exile's Return: A Literary Odyssey of the 1920s; The Faulkner-Cowley File: Letters and Memories, 1944–1962; A Second Flowering: Works and Days of the Lost Generation; —And I Worked at the Writer's Trade: Chapters of Literary History, 1918–1978*; and *The Dream of the Golden Mountains: Remembering the 1930s.* He is also the editor of *The Portable Faulkner* and *The Portable Hawthorne* and coeditor of *The Portable Emerson,* also published by Penguin. Among his many awards and honors are the Gold Medal for Belles Lettres and Criticism from the American Academy and Institute of Arts and Letters and the Hubbell Medal of the Modern Language Association for service to the study of American literature. Mr. Cowley's view of 80 is mostly from Sherman, Connecticut, where he lives with his wife, Muriel. Seven of his thirteen books have been published since he was seventy years old.

Also by Malcolm Cowley

EXILE'S RETURN

AFTER THE GENTEEL TRADITION
(with others)

THE LITERARY SITUATION

BLACK CARGOES
(with Daniel P. Mannix)

THE FAULKNER-COWLEY FILE

THINK BACK ON US . . .

BLUE JUNIATA: COLLECTED POEMS

A MANY-WINDOWED HOUSE

A SECOND FLOWERING

—AND I WORKED AT THE WRITER'S TRADE

THE DREAM OF THE GOLDEN MOUNTAINS

Malcolm Cowley

PENGUIN BOOKS

Penguin Books Ltd, Harmondsworth, Middlesex, England
Penguin Books, 625 Madison Avenue,
New York, New York 10022, U.S.A.
Penguin Books Australia Ltd, Ringwood, Victoria, Australia
Penguin Books Canada Limited, 2801 John Street,
Markham, Ontario, Canada L3R 1B4
Penguin Books (N.Z.) Ltd, 182–190 Wairau Road,
Auckland 10, New Zealand

First published in the United States of America by
The Viking Press 1980
Published in Penguin Books 1982

LIBRARY OF CONGRESS CATALOGING IN PUBLICATION DATA
Cowley, Malcolm, 1898–
The view from 80.
Originally published: New York: Viking Press, 1980.
1. Cowley, Malcolm, 1898– . 2. Aged—
United States—Biography. I. Title.
[HQ1061.C663 1982] 305.2′6′0924 81-13933
ISBN 0 14 00.6050 2 AACR2

Printed in the United States of America by
R. R. Donnelley & Sons Company, Harrisonburg, Virginia
Set in CRT Janson

A shorter version of *The View from 80* appeared originally in *Life* magazine; "The Red Wagon" in *The Sewanee Review*.

Grateful acknowledgment is made to the following for permission to reprint copyrighted material.

Farrar, Straus and Giroux, Inc.: Selection from *Maximum Security Ward* by Ramon Guthrie. Copyright © Ramon Guthrie, 1968, 1969, 1970.

Alfred A. Knopf, Inc.: Excerpts from *The Measure of My Days* by Florida Scott-Maxwell. Copyright © Florida Scott-Maxwell, 1968.

Macmillan Publishing Co., Inc., and A. P. Watt Ltd: Selection from "The Tower" from *Collected Poems* by William Butler Yeats. Copyright 1928 by Macmillan Publishing Co., Inc. Copyright renewed © Georgie Yeats, 1956. Selection from "The Spur" from *Collected Poems* by William Butler Yeats. Copyright 1940 by Georgie Yeats. Copyright renewed © Bertha Georgie Yeats, Michael Butler Yeats, and Anne Yeats, 1968.

A. P. Watt Ltd: Selection from a letter by William Butler Yeats to Lady Elizabeth Pelham from *Life of W. B. Yeats* by Joseph Hone (1943).

To the Class of '19

A FOREWORD

Early that summer, Byron Dobell, then senior editor of the new monthly *Life*, phoned and asked whether I would like to write an article about growing old. I said I would think about it. The more I thought and read, over a period of weeks, the more I was attracted by the notion. Apparently a great deal had been written about old age, but most of the authors who dealt with it were lads and lasses, as it seemed to me, in their late fifties or early sixties. They knew the literature, but not the life. Some of them had brought together statistics or pored over medical reports, while others had tracked down the aged with camera and tape recorder; what they didn't and couldn't know was how it feels to be old. I knew, close as I was to my 80th birthday, and I decided that there was still room for an honest personal report.

I set to work. In writing about age I was delayed by some of the infirmities that were part of my subject. Phlebitis was the unexpected one; it had me on my back for much of August; and also there was that 80th-birthday celebration. Nevertheless the article was finished in good time to be published in the December 1978 number of *Life.* The response over the next few months was surprising. "The View from 80" won various awards (if two can be called various), it was condensed in *Reader's Digest,* and it called forth what was to me an astounding number of letters from many parts of the country.

Almost all the letters were from men and women in their eighties who spoke frankly about their sorrows and satisfactions. They gave me credit for being equally frank. Many were struck by a list I had made of messages from the body that tell us we are old. Thus, V. Woods Bailey wrote from Iowa, "I was chagrined to find that you were onto many of the dark secrets of my more than 80 years—especially the row of little bottles on the shelf. I have never before in all my life resorted to *pills*—and now here stands that little row. But on one point I am ahead—all this came on me after I was 85, instead of after I was 80." Morton S. Enslin, a classmate of 82 whom I had mentioned by name, wrote from Pennsylvania, "Those lists of messages were rather more than guesswork. Nearly all were too truly mine. And a couple of them I read with distinct pleasure and relief, for I had been inclined to view them as peculiarly mine."

Another classmate of 82, George D. Flynn, Jr., wrote from Providence, "Well, *did* we go for that December *Life* story! . . . Dot and I read it a couple of times and have quoted from it often, especially that item about your agelessness when sitting in a chair, ruminating and remembering, and then, what happens when you decide to get up for a ramble in the woods with gun and rod, creaking to a plantigrade position and almost falling on your butt." Claire Whitehurst of Coral Gables had no time for sitting back in a chair. "Being one year less than 80 and a lady," she said, "I view the panorama of life a bit differently—always busy, always searching for the new, which keeps my daughter and granddaughters busy keeping up with my new friends." Several correspondents were proud of being physically active, none prouder than A. M. Botway, then 86, who wrote from Key West, "I'm afraid that my new country"—that of age—"is not new to me. At seven this morning I did what I've been doing for at least 15 years, ever since I had to slow down. When I opened my eyes I did my 20 sit-ups while still on my back, jumped out of bed, slipped into my swim trunks, jumped on my bike and headed the half mile to the Atlantic, where I first did the very same calisthenics we did in the army when Pershing went after Pancho Villa in 1916.

"After the work-out I swam around till I had enough, jumped on the bike, and at 7:30 was enjoying a hearty breakfast. . . . Ponce de Leon, here I come."

Several letters that gave me a pleasant feeling were from women I had known as girls and hadn't seen for half a century. Jean Miller Davis wrote from Pittsburgh, where she has spent her life, "I could not resist the urge to tell you how much I enjoyed sharing your view, as I am now 81. In Peabody High School I sat just across the aisle from you in several classes and thought you were very smart. My life has been quite a happy one and I am the grandmother of 12. . . . *P.S.* I no longer have red hair—it is mostly gray now and my eyes are very poor." Mary Mardis Davis wrote me from Ohio. Nine years older than I, she was the daughter of a prosperous farmer; I knew her when she was the prettiest girl in our little Pennsylvania village. Once when she was 20 and came to dinner, she so embarrassed me with her good looks that I crawled under the dining-room table, among all those feet.

Mary became a nurse and married a Kentucky doctor. While her husband was in the army during World War I, she ran an emergency hospital with 150 beds and no other nurses to help her. She has spent most of her life taking care of other people. In 1945, when her husband died of a heart attack, the other doctors in the county—there weren't many of them—persuaded her to keep his office open and take care of the patients—"as I had been doing," she says. "They checked all the medicines and said they would stand back of me. After two years, making calls at night way out in the country was too much for me and I sold my home." She now lives with a daughter near Columbus and she writes, "I am 89 and you really hit the nail on the head. I can't hear. I don't use a cane, but should. I read all the time and I'm not seeing too well. But I am with my daughter and she allows me to do as I please, and I am getting along fine." Mary has started to put her memories on tape.

Lois Blair Jensen is also older than I. In school days my friend was her younger sister Mary Blair, who became a leading lady on Broadway and died of TB. Lois is now in a Pennsylvania nursing home. "After lunch," she writes, "nephew Kenneth Blair brought me a copy of *Life* and read a part aloud to me. My eyes are not good. I enjoyed the photos. May I congratulate you on being 80. I am 86. Before lunch I had told the visiting doctor that I consider Golden Age as Yuk." She was not the only correspondent who objected to the phrase Golden Age. On a related topic, Dorothy Shelmire, 83, was rather heavily ironic. "Maybe—just *maybe*—" she wrote from a town near Philadelphia, "I might in the future *profit* from your article and learn to *appreciate* the pleasures (?) of being past 80!?"

A letter signed only "Gracie"—it must have

been from Gracie Carlisle, whom I haven't seen since the 1930s—berated me for being a slippered pantaloon. She said, "This is in commiseration of your 'Creaking Age Speaks.' You're as old as you FEEL. Old age is just a rumor." Gracie has often shown her spunk, and I bowed my head to her rebuke. I was flattered, though, by a letter from Ida Carey, who wrote from Mt. Pleasant, Michigan, "I *love* your article, which 'hits the nail on the head' for me. I find, in these last several months, that it takes sheer *will power* to get up from a sitting position. Once up, I walk around these rooms bent forward (due to arthritis) till I must resemble that slouch that Groucho Marx used to assume. At 90, my contemporaries are gone, but having lived in this community for 70 years, I have many good friends. Have my own teeth (a few missing molars) and can recite *reams* of poetry. . . . You have inspired me to begin writing a sort of memoir of my life—something my elder daughter, Pat, had asked me many times to do."

There should be more, many more, of such memoirs. Each of the letters that came to me—and I might have quoted from dozens of others—somehow asserted a different personality, and many of them gave hints of lifetimes rich in adventures. Rereading the letters after several months, I felt a burst of affection for those in my age group; for all my coevals, to use a word from "the literature." Each of them has found his or her own sort of wisdom, an individual way of adjusting to circumstances, and some have displayed a courage that puts me to shame. We octogenarians form a loose and large secret order, with many members in each city and with representatives in almost every village. I have to say members and representatives, not chapters, for most of us are comparatively isolated (except for our families, if we are lucky enough to have them). I should like to establish communication and to be, in some measure, a spokesman for others. If I had time I should enjoy writing a long letter to each of the volunteer correspondents, and to many more besides. But after 80 there is never time enough.

Instead of writing letters, I set to work on this little book. I planned to include in it everything said in the article, besides much else for which I hadn't found space. Still other reflections, examples, anecdotes crowded in on me as I worked ahead. The manuscript grew longer, but without going beyond the modest limits I had set for it. Here is the book, and I hope it will serve as a personal message to each of my comrades in age.

M.C.

THE VIEW FROM 80

1

They gave me a party on my 80th birthday in August 1978. First there were cards, letters, telegrams, even a cable of congratulation or condolence; then there were gifts, mostly bottles; there was catered food and finally a big cake with, for some reason, two candles (had I gone back to very early childhood?). I blew the candles out a little unsteadily. Amid the applause and clatter I thought about a former custom of the Northern Ojibwas when they lived on the shores of Lake Winnipeg. They were kind to their old people, who remembered and enforced the ancient customs of the tribe, but when an old person became decrepit, it was time for him to go. Sometimes he was simply abandoned, with a little food, on an island in the lake. If he deserved special honor, they held a tribal feast for him. The old man sang a death song and danced, if he could. While he was still singing, his son came from behind and brained him with a tomahawk.

That was quick, it was dignified, and I wonder whether it was any more cruel, essentially, than some of our civilized customs or inadvertences in disposing of the aged. I believe in rites and ceremonies. I believe in big parties for special occasions such as an 80th birthday. It is a sort of belated bar mitzvah, since the 80-year-old, like a Jewish adolescent, is entering a new stage of life; let him (or her) undergo a *rite de passage*, with toasts and a cantor. Seventy-year-olds, or septuas, have the illusion of being middle-aged, even if they have been pushed back on a shelf. The 80-year-old, the octo, looks at the double-dumpling figure and admits that he is old. The last act has begun, and it will be the test of the play.

He has joined a select minority that numbers, in this country, 4,842,000 persons (according to Census Bureau estimates for 1977), or about two percent of the American population. Two-thirds of the octos are women, who have retained the good habit of living longer than men. Someday you, the reader, will join that minority, if you escape hypertension and cancer, the two killers, and if you survive the dangerous years from 75 to 79, when half the survivors till then are lost. With advances in medicine, the living space taken over by octos is growing larger year by year.

To enter the country of age is a new experience, different from what you supposed it to be. Nobody, man or woman, knows the country until he has lived in it and has taken out his citizenship papers. Here is my own report, submitted as a road map and guide to some of the principal monuments.

THE new octogenarian feels as strong as ever when he is sitting back in a comfortable chair. He ruminates, he dreams, he remembers. He doesn't want to be disturbed by others. It seems to him that old age is only a costume assumed for those others; the true, the essential self is ageless. In a moment he will rise and go for a ramble in the woods, taking a gun along, or a fishing rod, if it is spring. Then he creaks to his feet, bending forward to keep his balance, and realizes that he will do nothing of the sort. The body and its surroundings have their messages for him, or only one message: "You are old." Here are some of the occasions on which he receives the message:

——when it becomes an achievement to do thoughtfully, step by step, what he once did instinctively

——when his bones ache

——when there are more and more little bottles in the medicine cabinet, with instructions for taking four times a day

——when he fumbles and drops his toothbrush (butterfingers)

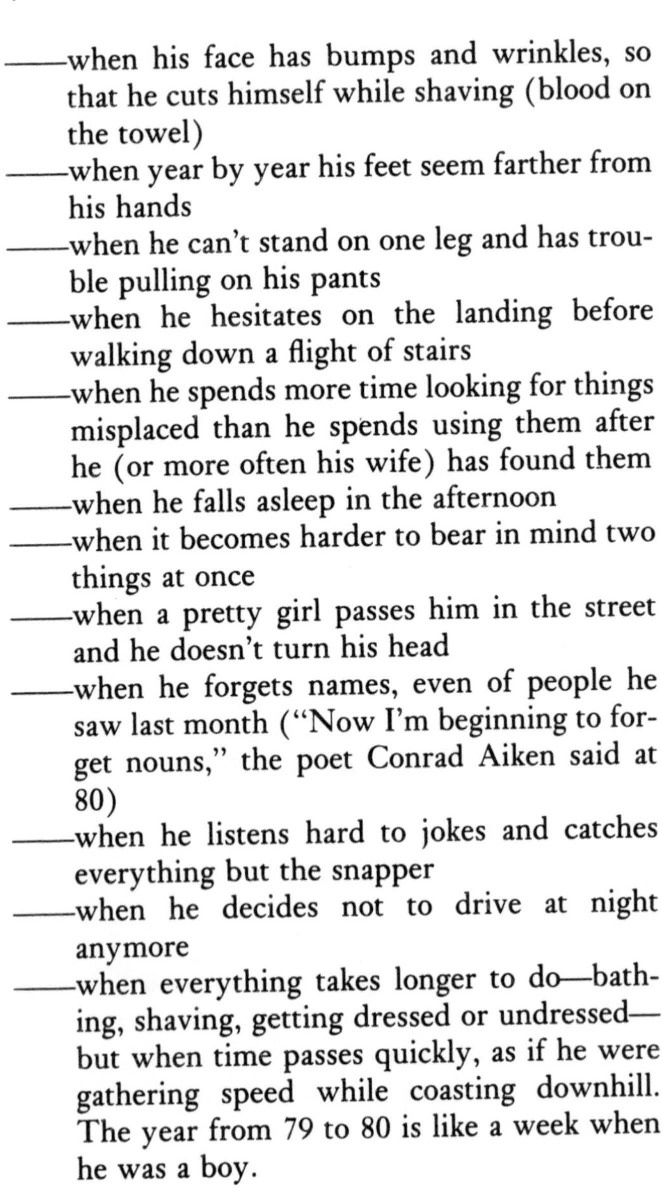

——when his face has bumps and wrinkles, so that he cuts himself while shaving (blood on the towel)
——when year by year his feet seem farther from his hands
——when he can't stand on one leg and has trouble pulling on his pants
——when he hesitates on the landing before walking down a flight of stairs
——when he spends more time looking for things misplaced than he spends using them after he (or more often his wife) has found them
——when he falls asleep in the afternoon
——when it becomes harder to bear in mind two things at once
——when a pretty girl passes him in the street and he doesn't turn his head
——when he forgets names, even of people he saw last month ("Now I'm beginning to forget nouns," the poet Conrad Aiken said at 80)
——when he listens hard to jokes and catches everything but the snapper
——when he decides not to drive at night anymore
——when everything takes longer to do—bathing, shaving, getting dressed or undressed—but when time passes quickly, as if he were gathering speed while coasting downhill. The year from 79 to 80 is like a week when he was a boy.

Those are some of the intimate messages. "Put cotton in your ears and pebbles in your shoes," said a gerontologist, a member of that new profession dedicated to alleviating all maladies of old people except the passage of years. "Pull on rubber gloves. Smear Vaseline over your glasses, and there you have it: instant aging." Not quite. His formula omits the messages from the social world, which are louder, in most cases, than those from within. We start by growing old in other people's eyes, then slowly we come to share their judgment.

I remember a morning many years ago when I was backing out of the parking lot near the railroad station in Brewster, New York. There was a near collision. The driver of the other car jumped out and started to abuse me; he had his fists ready. Then he looked hard at me and said, "Why, you're an old man." He got back into his car, slammed the door, and drove away, while I stood there fuming. "I'm only 65," I thought. "He wasn't driving carefully. I can still take care of myself in a car, or in a fight, for that matter."

My hair was whiter—it may have been in 1974—when a young woman rose and offered me her seat in a Madison Avenue bus. That message was kind and also devastating. "Can't I even stand up?" I thought as I thanked her and declined the seat. But the same thing happened twice the following year, and the second time I gratefully accepted the offer, though with a sense of having diminished myself. "People are right about me," I thought while wondering why all those kind gestures were made by women. Do men now regard themselves as the weaker sex, not called upon to show consideration? All the same it was a relief to sit down and relax.

A few days later I wrote a poem, "The Red Wagon," that belongs in the record of aging:

For his birthday they gave him a red express
  wagon
with a driver's high seat and a handle that
  steered.
His mother pulled him around the yard.
"Giddyap," he said, but she laughed and went
  off
to wash the breakfast dishes.

"I wanta ride too," his sister said,
and he pulled her to the edge of a hill.
"Now, sister, go home and wait for me,
but first give a push to the wagon."

He climbed again to the high seat,
this time grasping the handle-that-steered.
The red wagon rolled slowly down the slope,
then faster as it passed the schoolhouse
and faster as it passed the store,
the road still dropping away.
Oh, it was fun.

But would it ever stop?
Would the road always go downhill?

The red wagon rolled faster.
Now it was in strange country.
It passed a white house he must have dreamed about,
deep woods he had never seen,
a graveyard where, something told him, his sister was buried.

Far below
the sun was sinking into a broad plain.

The red wagon rolled faster.
Now he was clutching the seat, not even trying to steer.
Sweat clouded his heavy spectacles.
His white hair streamed in the wind.

EVEN before he or she is 80, the aging person may undergo another identity crisis like that of adolescence. Perhaps there had also been a middle-aged crisis, the male or the female menopause, but for the rest of adult life he had taken himself for granted, with his capabilities and failings. Now, when he looks in the mirror, he asks himself, "Is this really me?"—or he avoids the mirror out of distress at what it reveals, those bags and wrinkles. In his new makeup he is called upon to play a new role in a play that must be improvised. André Gide, that long-lived man of letters, wrote in his journal, "My heart has remained so young that I have the continual feeling of playing a part, the part of the 70-year-old that I certainly am; and the infirmities and weaknesses that remind me of my age act like a prompter, reminding me of my lines when I tend to stray. Then, like the good actor I want to be, I go back into my role, and I pride myself on playing it well."

In his new role the old person will find that he is tempted by new vices, that he receives new compensations (not so widely known), and that he may possibly achieve new virtues. Chief among these is the heroic or merely obstinate refusal to surrender in the face of time. One admires the ships that go down with all flags flying and the captain on the bridge.

Among the vices of age are avarice, untidiness, and vanity, which last takes the form of a craving to be loved or simply admired. Avarice is the worst of those three. Why do so many old persons, men and women alike, insist on hoarding money when they have no prospect of using it and even when they have no heirs? They eat the cheapest food, buy no clothes, and live in a single room when they could afford better lodging. It may be that they regard money as a form of power; there is a comfort in watching it accumulate while other powers are dwindling away. How often we read of an old person found dead in a hovel, on a mattress partly stuffed with bankbooks and stock certificates! The bankbook syndrome, we call it in our family, which has never succumbed.

Untidiness we call the Langley Collyer syndrome. To explain, Langley Collyer was a former concert pianist who lived alone with his 70-year-old brother in a brownstone house on upper Fifth Avenue. The once fashionable neighborhood had become part of Harlem. Homer, the brother, had been an admiralty lawyer, but was now blind and partly paralyzed; Langley played for him and fed him on buns and oranges, which he thought would restore Homer's sight. He never threw away a daily paper because Homer, he said, might want to read them all. He saved other things as well and the house became filled with rubbish from roof to basement. The halls were lined on both sides with bundled newspapers, leaving narrow passageways in which Langley had devised booby traps to catch intruders.

On March 21, 1947, some unnamed person telephoned the police to report that there was a dead body in the Collyer house. The police broke down the front door and found the hall impassable; then they hoisted a ladder to a second-story window. Behind it Homer was lying on the floor in a bathrobe; he had starved to death. Langley had disappeared. After some delay, the police broke into the basement, chopped a hole in the roof, and began throwing junk out of the house, top and bottom. It was 18 days before they found Langley's body, gnawed by rats. Caught in one of his own booby traps, he had died in a hallway just outside Homer's door. By that time the police had collected, and the Department of Sanitation had hauled away, 120 tons of rubbish, including, besides the newspapers, 14 grand pianos and the parts of a dismantled Model T Ford.

Why do so many old people accumulate junk, not on the scale of Langley Collyer, but still in a dismaying fashion? Their tables are piled high with it, their bureau drawers are stuffed with it, their closet rods bend with the weight of clothes not worn for years. I suppose that the piling up is partly from lethargy and partly from the feeling that everything once useful, including their own bodies, should be preserved. Others, though not so many, have such a fear of becoming Langley Collyers that they strive to be painfully neat. Every tool they own is in its place, though it will never be used again; every scrap of paper is filed away in alphabetical order. At last their immoderate neatness becomes another vice of age, if a milder one.

THE vanity of older people is an easier weakness to explain, and to condone. With less to look forward to, they yearn for recognition of what they have been: the reigning beauty, the athlete, the soldier, the scholar. It is the beauties who have the hardest time. A portrait of themselves at twenty hangs on the wall, and they try to resemble it by making an extravagant use of creams, powders, and dyes. Being young at heart, they think they are merely revealing their essential persons. The athletes find shelves for their silver trophies, which are polished once a year. Perhaps a letter sweater lies wrapped in a bureau drawer. I remember one evening when a no-longer athlete had guests for dinner and tried to find his sweater. "Oh, that old thing," his wife said. "The moths got into it and I threw it away." The athlete sulked and his guests went home early.

Often the yearning to be recognized appears in conversation as an innocent boast. Thus, a distinguished physician, retired at 94, remarks casually that a disease was named after him. A former judge bursts into chuckles as he repeats bright things that he said on the bench. Aging scholars complain in letters (or one of them does), "As I approach 70 I'm becoming avid of honors, and such things—medals, honorary degrees, etc.—are only passed around among academics on a *quid pro quo* basis (one hood capping another)." Or they say querulously, "Bill Underwood has ten honorary doctorates and I have only three. Why didn't they elect me to . . . ?" and they mention the name of some learned society. That search for honors is a harmless passion, though it may lead to jealousies and deformations of character, as with Robert Frost in his later years. Still, honors cost little. Why shouldn't the very old have more than their share of them?

To be admired and praised, especially by the young, is an autumnal pleasure enjoyed by the lucky ones (who are not always the most deserving). "What is more charming," Cicero observes in his famous essay *De Senectute*, "than an old age surrounded by the enthusiasm of youth! . . . Attentions which seem trivial and conventional are marks of honor—the morning call, being sought after, precedence, having people rise for you, being escorted to and from the forum. . . . What pleasures of the body can be compared to the prerogatives of influence?" But there are also pleasures of the body, or the mind, that are enjoyed by a greater number of older persons.

Those pleasures include some that younger people find hard to appreciate. One of them is simply sitting still, like a snake on a sun-warmed stone, with a delicious feeling of indolence that was seldom attained in earlier years. A leaf flutters down; a cloud moves by inches across the horizon. At such moments the older person, completely relaxed, has become a part of nature—and a living part, with blood coursing through his veins. The future does not exist for him. He thinks, if he thinks at all, that life for younger persons is still a battle royal of each against each, but that now he has nothing more to win or lose. He is not so much above as outside the battle, as if he had assumed the uniform of some small neutral country, perhaps Liechtenstein or Andorra. From a distance he notes that some of the combatants, men or women, are jostling ahead—but why do they fight so hard when the most they can hope for is a longer obituary? He can watch the scrounging and gouging, he can hear the shouts of exultation, the moans of the gravely wounded, and meanwhile he feels secure; nobody will attack him from ambush.

Age has other physical compensations besides the nirvana of dozing in the sun. A few of the simplest needs become a pleasure to satisfy. When an old woman in a nursing home was asked what she really liked to do, she answered in one word: "Eat." She might have been speaking for many of her fellows. Meals in a nursing home, however badly cooked, serve as climactic moments of the day. The physical essence of the pensioners is being renewed at an appointed hour; now they can go back to meditating or to watching TV while looking forward to the next meal. They can also look forward to sleep, which has become a definite pleasure, not the mere interruption it once had been.

Here I am thinking of old persons under nursing care. Others ferociously guard their independence, and some of them suffer less than one might expect from being lonely and impoverished. They can be rejoiced by visits and meetings, but they also have company inside their heads. Some of them are busiest when their hands are still. What passes through the minds of many is a stream of persons, images, phrases, and familiar tunes. For some that stream has continued since childhood, but now it is deeper; it is their present and their past combined. At times they conduct silent dialogues with a vanished friend, and these are less tiring—often more rewarding—than spoken conversations. If inner resources are lacking, old persons living alone may seek comfort and a kind of companionship in the bottle. I should judge from the gossip of various neighborhoods that the outer suburbs from Boston to San Diego are full of secretly alcoholic widows. One of those widows, an old friend, was moved from her apartment into a retirement home. She left behind her a closet in which the floor was covered wall to wall with whiskey bottles. "Oh, those empty bottles!" she explained. "They were left by a former tenant."

Not whiskey or cooking sherry but simply giving up is the greatest temptation of age. It is something different from a stoical acceptance of infirmities, which is something to be admired. At 63, when he first recognized that his powers were failing, Emerson wrote one of his best poems, "Terminus":

> It is time to be old,
> To take in sail:—
> The god of bounds,
> Who sets to seas a shore,
> Came to me in his fatal rounds,
> And said: "No more!
> No farther shoot

Thy broad ambitious branches, and thy root.
Fancy departs: no more invent;
Contract thy firmament
To compass of a tent."

Emerson lived in good health to the age of 79. Within his narrowed firmament, he continued working until his memory failed; then he consented to having younger editors and collaborators. The givers-up see no reason for working. Sometimes they lie in bed all day when moving about would still be possible, if difficult. I had a friend, a distinguished poet, who surrendered in that fashion. The doctors tried to stir him to action, but he refused to leave his room. Another friend, once a successful artist, stopped painting when his eyes began to fail. His doctor made the mistake of telling him that he suffered from a fatal disease. He then lost interest in everything except the splendid Rolls-Royce, acquired in his prosperous days, that stood in the garage. Daily he wiped the dust from its hood. He couldn't drive it on the road any longer, but he used to sit in the driver's seat, start the motor, then back the Rolls out of the garage and drive it in again, back twenty feet and forward twenty feet; that was his only distraction.

I haven't the right to blame those who surrender, not being able to put myself inside their minds or bodies. Often they must have compelling reasons, physical or moral. Not only do they suffer from a variety of ailments, but also they are made to feel that they no longer have a function in the community. Their families and neighbors don't ask them for advice, don't really listen when they speak, don't call on them for efforts. One notes that there are not a few recoveries from apparent senility when that situation changes. If it doesn't change, old persons may decide that efforts are useless. I sympathize with their problems, but the men and women I envy are those who accept old age as a series of challenges.

For such persons, every new infirmity is an enemy to be outwitted, an obstacle to be overcome by force of will. They enjoy each little victory over themselves, and sometimes they win a major success. Renoir was one of them. He continued painting, and magnificently, for years after he was crippled by arthritis; the brush had to be strapped to his arm. "You don't need your hand to paint," he said. Goya was another of the unvanquished. At 72 he retired as an official painter of the Spanish court and decided to work only for himself. His later years were those of the famous "black paintings" in which he let his imagination run (and also of the lithographs, then a new technique). At 78 he escaped a reign of terror in Spain by fleeing to Bordeaux. He was deaf and his eyes were failing; in order to work he had to wear several pairs of spectacles, one over another, and then use a magnifying glass; but he was producing splendid work in a totally new style. At 80 he drew an ancient man propped on two sticks, with a mass of white hair and beard hiding his face and with the inscription "I am still learning."

Giovanni Papini said when he was nearly blind, "I prefer martyrdom to imbecility." After writing sixty books, including his famous *Life of Christ*, he was at work on two huge projects when he was stricken with a form of muscular atrophy. He lost the use of his left leg, then of his fingers, so that he couldn't hold a pen. The two big books, though never to be finished, moved forward slowly by dictation; that in itself was a triumph. Toward the end, when his voice had become incomprehensible, he spelled out a word, tapping on the table to indicate letters of the alphabet. One hopes never to be faced with the need for such heroic measures.

"Eighty years old!" the great Catholic poet Paul Claudel wrote in his journal. "No eyes left, no ears, no teeth, no legs, no wind! And when all is said and done, how astonishingly well one does without them!"

YEATS is the great modern poet of age, though he died—I am now tempted to say—as a mere stripling of 73. His reaction to growing old was not that of a stoic like Emerson or Cicero, bent on obeying nature's laws and the edicts of Terminus, the god "Who sets to seas a shore"; it was that of a romantic rebel, the Faustian man. He was only 61 when he wrote (in "The Tower"):

> What shall I do with this absurdity—
> O heart, O troubled heart—this caricature,
> Decrepit age that has been tied to me
> As to a dog's tail?

At 68 he began to be worried because he wasn't producing many new poems. Could it be, he must have wondered, that his libido had lost its force and that it was somehow connected with his imagination? He had the Faustian desire for renewed youth, felt almost universally, but in Yeats's case with a stronger excuse, since his imagination was the center of his life. A friend told him, with gestures, about Dr. Steinach's then famous operation designed to rejuvenate men by implanting new sex glands. The operation has since fallen into such medical disfavor that Steinach's name is nowhere mentioned in the latest edition of *The Encyclopaedia Britannica.* But Yeats read a pamphlet about it in the Trinity College library, in Dublin, and was favorably impressed. After consulting a physician, who wouldn't say yes or no, he arranged to have the operation performed in a London clinic; that was in May 1934.

Back in Dublin he felt himself to be a different man. Oliver St. John Gogarty, himself a physician, reports a conversation with Yeats that took place the following summer. "I was horrified," he says, "to hear when it was too late that he had undergone such an operation. 'On both sides?' I asked.

" 'Yes,' he acknowledged.

" 'But why on earth did you not consult anyone?'

" 'I read a pamphlet.'

" 'What was wrong with you?'

" 'I used to fall asleep after lunch.' "

It was no use making a serious answer to Gogarty the jester. He tells us in his memoir of Yeats that the poet claimed to have been greatly benefited by the operation, but adds, "I have reason to believe that this was not so. He had reached the age when he would not take 'Yes' for an answer." Gogarty's judgment as a physician was probably right; the poet's physical health did not improve and in fact deteriorated. One conjectures that the operation may have put an added strain on his heart and thus may have shortened his life by years. Psychologically, however, Yeats was transformed. He began to think of himself as "the wild old wicked man," and in that character he wrote dozens of poems in a new style, direct, earthy, and passionate. One of them reads:

> You think it horrible that lust and rage
> Should dance attention upon my old age;
> They were not such a plague when I was
>   young;
> What else have I to spur me into song?

False remedies are sometimes beneficial in their own fashion. What artist would not sacrifice a few years of life in order to produce work on a level with Yeats's *Last Poems*? Early in January 1939, he wrote to his friend Lady Elizabeth Pelham:

> I know for certain that my time will not be long. . . . I am happy, and I think full of energy, of an energy I had despaired of. It seems to me that I have found what I wanted. When I try to put all into a phrase I say, "Man can embody truth but he cannot know it." I must embody it in the completion of my life.

His very last poem, and one of the best, is "The Black Tower," dated the 21st of that month. Yeats died a week after writing it.

2

One's 80th birthday is a time for thinking about the future, not the past. From Census Bureau reports I learned that in August 1978, as a white male, I had a life expectancy of 6.7 years; it would have been 8.6 years if I were a woman and 11.0 years if I were a black woman. There was something unfair in those figures, I thought in my sexist fashion. Women have generally lived longer than men (as the females of almost all the higher mammals do), but lately the difference in years has been pretty steadily growing. In 1920 there was only a 1.0-year difference between the life expectancy of a newborn male and that of a newborn female (according to the Census Bureau, whose records were incomplete at the time). By 1940 the difference had increased to 4.4 years (with more complete reporting), by 1960 to 6.5 years, and by 1977 to 7.8 years (68.7 for men, 76.5 for women). Why the disparity? It can be argued that men have been dying sooner than women partly because they were exposed to greater strains in their active lives and partly because of problems connected with retirement; housewives never retire. But now that more and more women are fighting to rise in the business world; now that more of them smoke and drink like troopers, will the difference be as great as before? I wonder.

For "Negro and Other" the life expectancy at birth has always been lower than for whites. Here the difference, largely due to lower incomes for blacks, was 9.6 years in 1900, but it has been decreasing; the Census Bureau reports that it has come down to 5.3 years. After 80, for some reason, black males and black females both live longer than their white counterparts. As I write, the oldest person in the United States is a former slave, Charlie Smith, who was kidnapped near the Liberian coast and sold in the New Orleans slave market in 1854, at the age of 12. Much later he worked in an orange grove until he was 113; then he was retired because people thought he was too old to climb trees. In the fall of 1978, when he was 136 years old by Social Security records, a television crew set up sound equipment at the retirement home where he was living in Bartow, Florida, but they reported that he couldn't be understood; he mumbled. Nature sets a limit on our effective lives, even for persons of exceptional vitality such as Charlie Smith.[1]

Vitalism—the notion that we live until we exhaust our vital energy—is medically discredited, but I'm not sure that the doctors are right. Sometimes I feel that each of us is born with a smaller or larger store of energy; the differences can be observed even in very young babies. Of course the store isn't constant; it can be renewed or diminished by circumstances; but each of us may have some voice in determining how fast the energy will be spent. One of Hemingway's heroes says of himself on his deathbed, "He had sold vitality, in one form or another, all his life." Hemingway too sold vitality, or tossed it away. Before he was 62, the shelves in his store were empty. Many years ago the younger partners of J. P. Morgan, Sr., were deciding, when they accepted the offer of partnership, that they would lead short, frenzied lives and make a lot of money. I heard that some of their widows lived in

[1] Smith died at the Bartow Convalescent Center in October 1979, when according to Social Security records he was 137. His age has been disputed by the editor of the *Guinness Book of World Records*, who asserts that Smith was only 104. That lower figure, if accepted, would make him younger than many other Americans. In June 1979 Social Security payments were being made to 11,885 persons of 100 or older.

brownstone houses near the Morgan mansion on Murray Hill.

Elihu Root, the internationalist, chose a different course. He decided at the age of 47 to last a long time (or so he afterward confided to one of his physicians, who passed along the word to me much later). From that day forward he watched his diet and refrained from activities that would strain his heart, such, for instance, as running for office (though he consented to serve as secretary of state and later as U.S. senator, in the days when senators were still appointed). He was always the wise counselor, not the harassed executive, and he lived to be just short of 92. John D. Rockefeller, Sr., appears to have made a similar decision at 58, after he had amassed his fortune; thenceforth he devoted himself to golf and philanthropy. He wasn't a philanthropist on the links. The only time of record that he tipped his caddy more than a dime was during the bank holiday of 1933, when dimes were scarcer than dollars. But his public benefactions were enormous, and he had given away $530 million before he died at 97.

The doctors haven't had much success in lengthening the maximum life span of the human species. Their immense achievement has been helping to increase the average expectancy of life—to double it, in fact—by preventing or curing the diseases of infancy and early adulthood;

that is something quite different. Once a man or woman reaches 80, the prospect of living much longer is only a little better than it might have been in the 17th century (that is, if the octo then had adequate food and care). Has modern medicine added as much as two years to his prospective span? Gerontologists are trying to add more, and they have found some promising guides to future research—for instance, the notion that brain damage in later life may be partly the result of a virus—but so far those guides have not led to practical results. Methods have been found, however, to alleviate various infirmities of age, including broken hips and blocked aortas. Perhaps in the future our active lives, or those of persons a little younger, may be lengthened almost to the end of our days on earth; that is the most we can hope for. Otherwise we remain subject to the edicts of the god Terminus.

And what are those edicts? A different one seems to govern the span of each individual, depending largely on his genes, but also on his lifestyle and his chosen profession. As for the average, if any, we can only look at past records and make a guess. My own guess would be that without grave diseases or crippling accidents or inherited defects, and with a careful diet, the normal human life span might be about 90 years—a little more for women, a little less for men. Centenarians would seem to be a breed apart, marked from their earliest days. Almost all of them come from long-lived families. In age they are more cheerful than others, so doctors report, and their clinical records show very few serious illnesses. Much as we others might like to emulate them, we cannot join their company by striving.

TURNING again to the past, we find that great artists, if they didn't die in early manhood—not womanhood, for there were few famous women in the arts before the 19th century—may have longer productive lives than those in other callings. Sophocles is one of the earliest confirmed examples. When he was 89, his oldest son brought suit against him in an Athenian court; the son claimed that Sophocles had fallen into his dotage and was unable to manage his estate. As evidence in his defense, Sophocles read aloud to the court a draft of the tragedy on which he was working; it was *Oedipus at Colonus*, one of the two great plays about age, the other being *King Lear.* The judges instantly rose, dismissed the suit, and escorted the poet to his home. "Poets die young," we hear it said, but if they survive into middle age they are likely to prove a long-resistant species. In our own century some poets have lived about as long as Sophocles and have continued working to the end; I think of Hardy, Frost, Sandburg, and my friend John Hall Wheelock, who wrote his best poems after he was 80 and had a new book half finished when he died at 91.

Painters and sculptors sometimes have very long productive lives. Here the familiar examples, besides Goya, are Titian, Michelangelo, Monet, Matisse, Chagall—and of course Picasso, who said, "Age only matters when one is aging. Now that I have arrived at a great age, I might just as well be 20." Shortly before his death at 91, he was still venturing into new fields of art. In the American Academy of Arts and Letters, the oldest member (as I write) is a sculptor, José de Creeft, 94. The second oldest is a painter, Georgia O'Keeffe, 91, who has produced some admirable work in recent years.

I have a feeling that novelists, to speak in general, are not a long-lasting breed, though I have to admit exceptions. E. M. Forster, Somerset Maugham, and P. G. Wodehouse all lived into their nineties and Rebecca West is still dispensing wisdom at 87. Many others, however, must have followed the example of Balzac and Dickens; they shortened their time on earth by living hypertensively in their imaginations. Among the truly great, a small company, Tolstoy was the only one to live beyond 80. In my World War I generation of writers, all the famous novelists have vanished, beginning with Thomas Wolfe at 37 and Scott Fitzgerald at 44 (I omit Henry Miller, now 88, who is more and less than a novelist). The other survivors are Archibald MacLeish, Lewis Mumford, Kenneth Burke, and E. B. White, all octogenarians. "We are the last leaves on the oak," MacLeish wrote me. Those last leaves are essayists or poets, two breeds that seem to outlast fiction writers.

Musicians are an even hardier breed, as note among others Toscanini, Casals, and Arthur Rubinstein, who gave a concert at 89, when his vision was so impaired that he could no longer read music or even distinguish his fingers on the keyboard. He played entirely from memory and critics said he played better than ever. Eubie Blake, the black composer, still performs in public at 96.

Scientists, mathematicians, and philosophers seem to be long-enduring: Santayana lived to be 88; John Dewey and Bertrand Russell survived well into their nineties. Doctors have a shorter life expectancy, on the average and with many exceptions (the one I mentioned, the famous internist who retired at 94, is Burrill Crohn, now of South Kent, Connecticut). Apparently most of his colleagues drove themselves too hard.

I note that many lawyers outlast the members of other professions. One of them, an octogenarian with all his buttons, said at a testimonial dinner for his senior partner, "They tell you that you'll lose your mind when you grow older. What they don't tell you is that you won't miss it very much." Often the lawyers who live longest are those who become judges. "If you want to live forever," Felix Frankfurter used to say, "get yourself appointed to the Supreme Court." Justice Frankfurter died at 83, a few years after he stepped down from the bench. Justice Holmes lived until a few days before his 94th birthday. Besides the sounder reasons for his being remembered, there is the classical remark he made on catching sight of a pretty girl: "Oh, to be 80 again!"

A general rule might be that persons called upon to give sage advice—unless they are doctors—live longer than persons who act on that advice; thus, corporation lawyers and investment bankers live longer than the presidents of corporations. The presidents, as a group, have a hard time adjusting themselves to retirement at 65. "They drink too much," a fiction writer said of them. But fiction writers as a group also drink too much.

Those matters of comparative longevity among sexes, races, and professions are not my present concern. Like many old people—or so it would seem from various reports—I think less about death than might be expected. As death comes nearer, it becomes less frightening, less a disaster, more an everyday fact to be noted and filed away. There is still what John Cowper Powys, in his book *The Art of Growing Old*, calls "the central miracle of being alive." The question that obsesses me is what to do with those 6.7 years, more or less, that the Census Bureau has grudgingly allowed me.

TO speak in general terms, old people would like to have a clearly defined place and function in American life; it is something they now lack. Their function was more widely recognized in many primitive societies, especially those which hadn't acquired the art of writing. Nothing of the past survived there unless it was remembered by old persons, those who had mastered the lore of the tribe, its rites, customs, legends, genealogies, and means of coping with sudden dangers. They were the tribal libraries, repositories of knowledge which they jealously guarded and passed along to younger persons only in return for gifts. They also served as priests and medicine men, since they were thought to be closer to the realm of spirits. Feared and honored in this role, they received still other gifts, so that they often ended with more possessions than warriors in the prime of life.

There were other tribes less bent on maintaining social stability—or simply with less to eat—in which older persons were ordinarily starved or abandoned in the wilds. Indeed, the aged enjoyed or suffered every variety of treatment in the primitive world, from being obeyed and venerated to being cast from a high rock into the sea, as among the ancient Scythians. Still, there are a few generalities to be hazarded. Older persons were usually better treated in agricultural societies, where there was some work they could do almost to the end; if they couldn't any longer plow a field, they could pull weeds or mind the children. The situation was different among hunting and food-gathering tribes, which had to move about a great deal; often they left old people behind as encumbrances. Another generality: tribes that mistreated their children also mistreated the aged, since they had never formed bonds of affection between generations. Tribes that petted children were usually kind to their older members—though sometimes that kindness took the form of putting them to death in a tender fashion. "Dear Father!" an Eskimo's daughter cried out to him after the neighbors had encouraged him to jump into the sea. "Push your head under the water. That way the road will be shorter."

Old persons lost one of their functions when tribal lore was committed to writing; their store of memories became less essential to the community. They gained in status, however—or a few of them gained—when property relations were stabilized, for the simple reason that the able or grasping ones had accumulated fortunes that were protected by law. Having the power of the purse, they often tyrannized over their wives, children, and dependents. That power might be extended to larger communities, some of which came to be ruled over by old men, by *gerontes.* Thus, in Sparta a central governing body was the gerousia, or council of elders, composed of chosen men over 60, who served for life; it proposed laws to the general assembly and conducted trials that involved capital crimes. In Rome the senate was at first a council of elders composed of former magistrates. It exercised its greatest power during the middle years of the Roman republic and declined in importance during the civil wars of the last two centuries before Christ. Its decline suggests another generality: that older persons (always of the privileged classes) are likely to be most powerful in times of social stability, and weakest in times of rapid change and civil commotion. As for slaves and artisans, they do not figure in the historical records and, it would seem, did not often attain old age.

China, with the most stable society of historic times, showed a special respect for aged persons, not excluding mothers-in-law. In Europe during the Middle Ages, the old played no great part in public life; they were few in number and society was so unsettled that boldness and a sharp sword were more important than accumulated wisdom. Venice had more stability than other European cities, and there the doges, who served as ceremonial heads of state, were almost always old men. The most famous doge, Enrico Dandolo, assumed office at 85 and retained it until his death at 97. Personal distinction gave him a degree of real power, but most of the doges simply obeyed the Council of Forty (later the secret Council of Ten), also consisting of old men. France during the restoration of the Bourbons, 1814–1830, was another gerontocracy; it had only 90,000 electors, for the most part elderly men of property, and only 8000 who were qualified to hold office—all of these, a pamphleteer asserted, "asthmatic, gouty, paralytic beings who have no wish for anything except peace and quiet."

For the middle classes, age had its comforts and compensations during the 19th century. It was an era of family businesses, often with a patriarch at the head of them, a man unwilling to share authority and waiting till the last moment before passing the business over to a middle-aged son. It was a time when there were more peasants in Europe, more small independent farmers in America, and it would seem that men (not always women) last longer in agricultural societies. Families were more cohesive then and tried to take care of their own members, including grandparents and maiden aunts; people expected to die at home. But the century was less kind to the millions without resources and without a family. In age they were "on the county" or "on the town," and what they dreaded was dying in the poorhouse.

OUR own era has a mixed record as regards its treatment of what are now called senior citizens; it takes care of them after a fashion. Government agencies, federal and state, have assumed many of the functions that used to be performed in a haphazard fashion by families and neighborhoods. Social Security, Medicare, and food stamps are fairly recent measures, and it is hard now to see how the country did without them for so many years. But meanwhile the older population keeps increasing; by 1978 there were 23.5 million Americans over 65. Under present arrangements they have to be supported by the productive labor force, or by savings accumulated during their own productive years, and the number of persons between 20 and 65 is not increasing at the same rate. Soon there will be greater burdens on the labor force, and the country is not so fabulously rich as it seemed to be in the early years after World War II; it has less to sell abroad and more to import at rising prices.

If we judge by earlier examples, this is not one of the eras when older people might expect to be honored and cherished. They have fared best, as we have seen, in agricultural or trading societies, in settled communities that remembered the past, and in periods of relative social stability. Ours is a period of frantic changes when memories have become irrelevant; when experience is less to be valued than youthful force and adaptability. It is a long time since the country might have been described as basically agricultural; now our lives, in some respects, have come to resemble those of the hunting or food-gathering tribes. Like them we wander over the face of the land; like them we regard the old as encumbrances to be left behind or sent off to die in what we think is a safe haven.

This has been an age of migrations: from countryside to city to suburb (and often back to countryside, but not to be farmers again); from Snowbelt to Sunbelt, and, for the old, from New England to Florida, from Iowa to Arizona. Once-vigorous communities have lost their sense of cohesion and their local pride. How long is it since people boasted of living in Cleveland ("Sixth City," as it used to advertise in *The Saturday Evening Post*) or Bridgeport or Detroit? Neighborliness is a fading ideal. Who would admit to being pious, in the Latin sense of being dutiful toward one's parents, relations, and native country (like *pius Aeneas*)? The household altar, *ara domestica*, has been dismantled and the family silver sold by the ounce. Family ties are coming to depend on the long-distance telephone. With childlessness and impermanent marriages, it is easy to predict that many persons now in their thirties will have a lonely old age.

To make things more difficult for those now in their sixties, or beyond, the era is one of financial confusion when thrift and foresight, those qualities of the old, are no longer sure of being rewarded. So you bought absolutely safe bonds in

1968 to prepare for your later years? At this moment the bonds are worth two-thirds or less of the dollars you paid for them, and the punctual income they yield will buy only half as much as in the beginning. Or you invested in real estate that you thought was certain to increase in value? Usually it did increase, but now you can't afford the redoubled taxes or meet payments on the mortgage. Or you (not I) moved to Florida on the assurance of what seemed a comfortable pension and now you can't live on it; you have to apply for relief in a town full of strange faces. Or again, your doctor has advised an operation and you find that Medicare stops far short of paying the hospital bill; where will the money come from? Social Security is a great help, but it doesn't offer a living wage, and the government forbids you to rejoin the working force on pain of not receiving its monthly stipend—that is, until you are 73; then the government throws up its hands and says, "All right, you've outlived our calculations. Now get a job if you can."[2]

[2] To judge from Ronald Blythe's excellent book *The View in Winter*—which appeared just as I was finishing this manuscript—old people in England have a somewhat better time of it than their American coevals. Medical care costs them nothing, or next to nothing, and the social-security system is more secure; at least the many old persons whom Blythe interviewed had few complaints about it. Even when living alone, they suffered less from the fear of break-ins and muggings. More persons in each community

To get a job of any decent sort is the ideal of many, but the working force won't take you back. Nobody over 50 is easily hired; almost everyone not in government service is retired at 65 or 70, if he hasn't been discharged sooner (and no matter if he had been producing more than the younger person hired to replace him). Older persons are our great unutilized source of labor (don't tell me that there isn't work in this country for everyone to do; it simply doesn't get done). A growing weakness of American society is that it regards the old as consumers but not producers, as mouths but not hands. They aren't even first-rank consumers in a culture largely devoted to consumption, since they have fewer wants than younger people and less money to supply them. A study by the National Council on Aging reported that for persons over 65, average incomes were roughly half as large as for persons between 45 and 55.

Many of the retired do find work for themselves, paid or unpaid. They start new businesses, often based on their hobbies, or they do odd jobs of a special sort—sharpening saws, for example—

---

seemed honestly concerned with their welfare. But England has been no more successful than the United States in finding useful occupations for persons retired from industry. Many of them—so Blythe reports—spend most of their time looking out from the crack in their curtained window or sitting on the sea wall—the "front"—and watching the waves roll in.

or they form political groups to advance the welfare of others like themselves. Such persons are to be admired—and hurrah for the Gray Panthers and Maggie Kuhn! Others, however, let themselves be isolated in retirement communities or—often too soon—in nursing homes, where they are left without an occupation to dignify their lives. Their capabilities dwindle away like their bodies, through not being used.

I remember an old man dreaming on a bench in the Florida sun, outside his daughter's tourist cabin. From across the court I used to steal glances at him when my work wasn't going well. He sat with his workingman's big hands on his knees, stirring at moments to open and reflectively drain another can of beer, then drop it into a paper bag. He didn't raise his eyes when a flight of drunken robins went staggering through the air. Though he seemed happy enough as he sat there day after day, I thought he was abusing an old man's privilege of indolence. He may have felt that, with nothing better to do, drinking beer in the sun was a convenient form of euthanasia.

I DON'T want to voice complaints about the lot of the old. As a group we compose a disadvantaged minority, but some of us are vastly more fortunate than others. Although we are all in the same boat, with tickets for the same destination, we do not enjoy the same comforts during the voyage. The boat turns out to be an old-fashioned liner with first-, second-, and third-class accommodations, not to mention a crowded steerage. Age has inequalities that are even greater than those of youth. In the matter of income, for example, most of the old are well below the national median, but others are far above it. Many of the great American fortunes are now controlled by aged men (or by their widows or lawyers). It must be added, however, that those older fortunes are melting away, from the effect of inflation on conservative investments; almost all the growth is in new speculative fortunes.

It must also be added that mere wealth becomes less important in age, except as a symbol of power and security. Things harder to measure—health, temperament, education, esteem, and self-esteem—contribute more to one's life. Thus, intellectual poverty proves to be as bad as material poverty. The educated live better than the uneducated, even on similar incomes; they have more interests and occupations (for example, reading) and are entertained by prosperous friends. They may live longer, too, though it would be hard to quote statistics, and meanwhile they enjoy more respect.

Whether old people are truly respected by their neighbors, and by the world at large, is another point at which their status differs. In our present society they are usually pushed aside—let's be frank about it—but there are stable small communities, especially in the South and New England, where some of them have a definite place. A man of 90 in our little town was widely consulted in questions having to do with titles, boundaries, wills, and family connections. He was impartial, he was truthful, and he served as the walking memory of the tribe. When he died a few years ago, his place was partly filled by a woman, also in her nineties, who was compiling a local history.

In college towns, many of which are stable communities, there may be a retired professor, one among many, or an almost-oldest living graduate who becomes a cherished figure. That happened to a former colleague of mine, Bruce Bliven, after he had a second heart attack and retired from his editorship of *The New Republic* in 1955. Editing a magazine had been his life, but he found a new one. Moving west to Stanford, his own college, he rented an apartment near the campus and there he wrote every morning, as if *The New Republic*'s printer were waiting for copy. He published three or four books, including an autobiography, *Five Million Words Later*, which appeared when he was 80. Every afternoon, on doctor's orders, he went for a walk of exactly two miles, measured by a pedometer. Almost everyone on the faculty came to know him and smiled respectfully as he passed; he was their perambulating monument.

Bruce defended himself against old age in a special way, by making fun of it each year in a Christmas letter that went out to five hundred friends. In 1972 he said, "A year ago, when I was only 82, I wrote somebody that 'I don't feel like an old man, I feel like a young man who has something the matter with him.' I have now found out what it is: it is the approach of middle age, and I don't care for it." In 1973: "I am thinking of becoming an old man; if I decide to I'll send out cards and wear a lapel pin." In 1975: "We live by the rules of the elderly. If the toothbrush is wet you have cleaned your teeth. If the bedside radio is warm in the morning you left it on all night. If you are wearing one brown and one black shoe, quite possibly there is a similar pair in the closet. . . . I stagger when I walk, and small boys follow me making bets on which way I'll go next. This upsets me; children shouldn't gamble."

At the 1976 commencement, Bruce and Rosie, his wife of 63 years, were the oldest members present from the Stanford class of 1911, which was the oldest class represented. That year's Christmas letter was to be his last. He said in part, "I am as bright as can be expected, remembering the friend who told me years ago, 'If your I.Q. ever breaks 100, *sell!*' My motto this year is from the Spanish: 'I don't want the cheese, I only want to get out of this trap.' " Bruce could afford to make fun of himself, knowing that he was respected in the community.

He also profited from a situation that prevails in the arts and the learned professions, where so many younger people are trying to be first among their peers. Everyone striving for distinction is regarded as a rival and a potential enemy by everyone else engaged in the same struggle. Ambitious writers, painters, lawyers, scientists, and politicians have lived among professional jealousies since their apprentice days; they are used to being politely stabbed in the back; but if they survive to a fairly advanced age they find that most—not all—of the old vendettas have been interred. They have ceased to be rivals and are ticketed as hors concours, like some of the famous exhibitors at a world's fair. Any honors henceforth conferred on them will be honors to the whole profession.

One can imagine a young instructor saying, or feeling in his heart, "I won't make any more cracks about the old man. He's helping the rest of us now by presenting an image of achievement and durability. But let him take warning: he had better remain an image and not engage in literary or academic politics. For that we need more vigorous persons like myself. We'll use his name, we'll put him on the platform at meetings, out front, but we'll not invite him to our parties. Let him be like Emerson in his last ten years and serve as a benevolent effigy."

Among the truly great American writers, Emerson was the only one who resigned himself to occupying that position. Though he had lost his memory, everyone admired him for what he had written in his middle years. Everyone who approached him worshiped as at a shrine. Walt Whitman visited Concord in 1881, the year before Emerson died, and recorded an evening there in *Specimen Days.* ". . . without being rude, or anything of the kind," he says, "I could just look squarely at E., which I did a good part of the two hours. On entering, he had spoken very briefly and politely to several of the company, then settled himself in his chair, a trifle push'd back, and, though a listener and apparently an alert one, remain'd silent throughout the whole talk and discussion. . . . A good color in his face, eyes clear, with the well-known expression of sweetness, and the old clear-peering aspect quite the same." Whitman was reverently gazing on the effigy of the Emerson that had been.

There have been writers high in the second rank who attained a similar position, and without losing their faculties: some names are Longfellow, Whittier, Julia Ward Howe, Robert Frost, and more recently Edmund Wilson. William Dean Howells had the position too, but was toppled from it at 70 by a revolt against the genteel tradition. At 78 he wrote to his friend Henry James, "I am a comparatively dead cult with my statues cut down and the grass growing over them in the pale moonlight." Each new generation elects its own heroes, and nobody can be certain who they will be. Besides, that Emersonian place as a revered idol is not a tempting goal for those, however ambitious, who are not much concerned with reputation. Those others don't want to be regarded as a monument to themselves, or a seemly model for the young, or a memory bank for scholars; they want to do their work—but at 80, what shall it be?

3

I turn to books and find some guidance, but not so many firsthand reports as I had hoped to find. Very old people—I wonder why—have written comparatively little about the problems of aging. One exception is Florida Scott-Maxwell, whose last book, *The Measure of My Days*, is a record of her 83d year. That wasn't a lucky year for her. It was marked by a serious operation, by a recovery that was less complete than she thought, so that she collapsed after making a round of visits, then finally by the departure of beloved grandchildren for Australia. Living alone in a London flat, she came to terms with herself. "We who are old know that age is more than a disability," she says. "It is an intense and varied experience, almost beyond our capacity at times, but something to be carried high. If it is a long defeat it is also a victory, meaningful for the initiates of time, if not for those who have come less far."

She says, "When a new disability arrives I look about me to see if death has come, and I call quietly, 'Death, is that you? Are you there?' So far the disability has answered, 'Don't be silly, it's me.' " Somehow those words have the sound of being a sincere report, not a mere self-consolation, and as much can be said about her other statements.

She says, for example, "Age puzzles me. I thought it was a quiet time. My seventies were interesting and fairly serene, but my eighties are passionate. I grow more intense with age. To my own surprise I burst out with hot conviction. . . . I must calm down. I am too frail to indulge in moral fervour."

She says, giving sound advice, "A note book might be the very thing for all the old who wave away crossword puzzles, painting, petit point, and knitting. It is more restful than conversation, and for me it has become a companion, more, a confessional. It cannot shrive me, but knowing myself better comes near to that."

Almost at the end of the book she says, "I want to tell people approaching and perhaps fearing age that it is a time of discovery. If they say—'Of what?' I can only answer, 'We must find out for ourselves, otherwise it won't be discovery.' "

Florida Scott-Maxwell had a rich life behind her; she had been an actress, a housewife, an author, and for many years a consulting psychologist. She lived to be 95, still alone in her little flat, still visited and loved by her children and grandchildren. In the field of writing about age she is an exception. The other four works I consulted were produced by men and women in their late fifties or early sixties, a time when most of them wanted to paint a bright prospect of their years to come; as yet they couldn't speak from experience.

Cicero's admired essay *De Senectute*, written when he was 62, is clearly a work of self-reassurance that praises the delights of age. At the same time it is a defense of the elder statesmen who composed the Roman senate. "The mightiest states," Cicero tells us, "have been overthrown by the young and supported and restored by the old." One might observe that his efforts and adages were wasted. Cicero was beheaded the following year, without having a chance to enjoy those promised delectations, and the senate he loved was gradually stripped of its powers. For two thousand years, however, his happily phrased maxims have been a comfort to elderly scholars. "Old age," he says in the guise of his spokesman, the aged Cato, "must be resisted and its deficiencies supplied by taking pains; we must fight it as we do disease." On memory: "I have never heard of any old man forgetting where he had hidden his money. The old remember everything that concerns them." On obeying nature (and still speaking through Cato): "I am wise in that I follow that good guide nature; it is not likely, when she has written the rest of the play well, that she should, like a lazy playwright, skimp the last act."

Emerson's essay "Old Age," written when he was 57, is still more optimistic and reassuring. He tries to make us believe that the years pour out their rewards as from a horn of plenty. "For a fourth benefit," he says, after listing three others, "age sets its house in order, and finishes its works, which to every artist is a supreme pleasure." But what if the house burns down, as Emerson's did a dozen years later, and what if the artist is left without enough strength of mind to finish the last of those inspiring essays? Emerson is one of my heroes, but often his observations lack the salt and sting of realism.

A Good Age, by Alex Comfort, appeared when its author was 56. It has the advantage of being written by a gerontologist, a man familiar with everything new in his field. "Gerontology," he says, "will not abolish old age; it will make it happen later." His book, which I recommend, is full of sound advice to the old, of a sort that wise doctors might give their patients in down-to-earth language. "What the retired need," he says, ". . . isn't 'leisure,' it's occupation. . . . Two weeks is about the ideal length of time to retire." Sometimes I suspect Alex Comfort of being too reassuring, as a tenderhearted doctor might be. Thus, he tries to banish one fear by asserting that dementia in age is neither general nor common, a statement that many would question from observation. He is cheery about the prospects for long-continuing sexual energy, this being his other special field (*The Joy of Sex*). Is he being tenderhearted about his own future, in the Ciceronian fashion?

Simone de Beauvoir is the least Ciceronian of the authors I read; she almost revels in a mood of bleak pessimism about everybody's future, including her own. *The Coming of Age*, a big book written when she was 60, presents a grim picture in almost every paragraph, except those dealing with some of her favorite artists. Even when speaking of these, she refuses to acknowledge—or hasn't yet discovered—that old age may have its inner compensations. Instead she drags existentialism out of the closet by quoting the abstruse remarks of her consort, Jean-Paul Sartre. One admires her, though, for bringing together the historical and literary records of old age as nobody else has done; here are facts to be brooded over. Incidentally, her book is a mine of fascinating anecdotes, some of which I have shamelessly borrowed. It was in *The Coming of Age* that I read about a famous 18th-century rake, the Duc de Richelieu, who at 84 took a young wife, gave her a child, and then deceived her with a bevy of actresses until he died at 92. Alex Comfort take note.

I WOULD not recommend the duke to my classmates as a model for Golden Age deportment. Harvard '19 is my class, and, as a respite from *The Coming of Age*, I took to reading what was then its latest bulletin, dated May 1978. The class had started with 722 members. When that bulletin appeared there were 208 survivors, all but a handful of them octos. Only one showed any inclination to emulate the Duc de Richelieu—"and my doctors," he said, "have forbidden me to chase women unless they are going downhill."

Some fifty classmates contributed notes about themselves to the bulletin. The general impression I gathered was one of moderate activity and moderate cheerfulness in accepting handicaps, almost the opposite of Beauvoir's grim pictures. Frederic B. Whitman reported, for example, that he and his wife of fifty years were enjoying life "with great gusto," although he was paraplegic. Whitman is a retired president of the Western Pacific; he had started his career in railroading as a freight-house trucker. It is to be noted that our class had entered the labor market during the Jazz Age, when individual success was an almost universal ideal. A few of the classmates had been grandly successful in business, and none of those who reported was destitute. As Cicero himself conceded, "Old age is impossible to bear in extreme poverty, even if one is a philosopher."

The most cheerful were those who had recently enjoyed a family celebration, usually a golden wedding. One man wrote from the West Coast, "My wife and I celebrated our 50th by assembling a dozen of our children and grandchildren, with their mates. . . . We ourselves are in better condition than might be expected, although a bit creaky in the joints." Another wrote from Illinois, "My children and grandchildren gave me a big party on my 80th birthday. Had such a good time that I am looking forward to my 85th." I should have mentioned grandchildren among the solid pleasures of age. They are valued chiefly for themselves, but partly, it would seem, as an insurance policy against loneliness. The classmates sometimes boasted of the number of their grandchildren, as they didn't boast about having several sons and daughters. Great-grandchildren, if any, are valued largely as a form of reinsurance.

The most unhappy classmate was a man whose wife had recently died, leaving him alone, without occupation, in a rather large Arizona house—"Also I have been unable to drive a car for four years," he said. "Thank goodness for good friends." The old help each other. One classmate, a New England clergyman, was spending much of his free time "visiting the elderly in the various nursing homes and retirement centers. They are the forgotten ones," but he remembered.

It was refreshing to learn how many of the classmates hadn't retired. Richard L. Strout had been with *The Christian Science Monitor* since 1921, most of that time as head of its Washington bureau; in 1977 he was given a special Pulitzer award. Morton S. Enslin, a theologian, was still teaching at Dropsie University, many years after having been retired because of age from St. Lawrence University and then Bryn Mawr. He was hoping for more invitations to preach. Jacob Davis was president of a wholesale jewelry firm. He wrote from Pittsburgh, "I work five days a week. Without a daily job I'd be hard put to maintain my sanity." Several classmates had started new businesses: manufacturing cross-country skis, semicommercial gardening, selling out-of-print books by mail. "The day of the week never seems long enough," one man complained. "Do you have the time?" a young woman whispered to another '19er while she was sitting beside him in a doctor's waiting room. He whispered back, "Time for what?"

I was impressed by the second career of a banker and foundation executive. At 70 he had resigned his chairmanships and had taken up watercolor painting. He went back to school (as Goya said, "I am still learning"), painted hard, had exhibitions, and sold pictures. Had he been happy? I distrust that word, whose meaning is summed up for me in the phrase "happy as a clam." The point is that he had been leading a sort of work-filled afterlife on earth. For all my praise of indolence, which has its place in the old man's day, work has always been the sovereign specific.

In June 1979, a year after issuing that bulletin, the class held its sixtieth reunion. About sixty of the survivors were present, in spite of problems in getting to airports, and there was perhaps an equal number of wives and widows. "I like the women," my wife said. "You men are beginning to look alike." By then all the men were octos except Louis Dolan, the baby of the class, who was born in 1900 and entered Harvard at 15. Almost all of them looked hale and vigorous until they tried walking downstairs, and then they held on to the banisters. There wasn't so much drinking as at earlier reunions; the good-time Charlies had vanished. At a cocktail party the voices were animated, but low, friendly, and without the ring of self-importance. "Are you still buying and selling corporations?" somebody asked Roy Little, who was known for having organized Textron, Inc. "Not so many as before," he answered. "I've been writing a book and I'll bet you don't know the title."

"Somebody told me it was *How to Lose a Million Dollars.*"

"That was before inflation," Little said. "No, the title is *How to Lose $100,000,000 and Other Valuable Advice.*" He ruminated. "Of course that's a rough figure and I never lost a hundred million at one time. But over the last sixty years, if you count it up, I've lost a good deal more."

There was a pleasant dinner, with speakers, and a bus took us back to the hotel. Almost everyone went to bed early. I thought as I undressed that our glow of comradeliness was not unlike the mood of castaways on a beleaguered island, happy to have survived together, but waiting for another storm.

STORMS there will be, or at least darkening skies, and this by an edict of nature. We don't have to read books in order to learn that one's eighties are a time of gradually narrowing horizons. Partly the narrowing is literal and physical, being due to a loss of peripheral vision: "Incipient cataracts," the oculist says. Trees on a not-so-distant hillside are no longer oaks or maples, but merely a blur. It is harder to distinguish faces in a crowd—and voices too, especially if several persons are speaking at once. Would you like to see or hear more by drawing closer? Your steps are less assured, your sense of balance is faulty; soon you hesitate to venture beyond your own street or your home acres. Travel becomes more difficult and you think twice before taking out the car.

Your social horizons are also narrowing. Many of your old friends have vanished and it is harder to find new ones. Entertaining visitors and making visits have both become problems. You can't have many people in to dinner and hence you are invited out less often. More and more the older person is driven back into himself; more and more he is occupied with what goes on in his mind. "I am so busy being old," Florida Scott-Maxwell tells us, "that I dread interruptions." In middle age that absorption in the self had been a weakness to be avoided, a failure to share and participate that ended by diminishing the self. For the very old it becomes a pursuit appropriate to their stage in life. It is still their duty to share affection and contribute to the world as much as possible, but they also have the task of finding and piecing together their personalities. "It has taken me all the time I've had to become myself," Mrs. Scott-Maxwell says. Later she adds, "If at the end of your life you have only yourself, it is much. Look, you will find."

Often it seems that social justice for the aged is a neglected ideal, but there may be an approximate justice for individuals. At a time when so much depends on the past, those who have led rich lives are rewarded by having richer memories. Those who have loved are more likely to be loved in return. In spite of accidents and ingratitude, those who have served others are a little more likely to be served. The selfish and heartless will suffer most from the heartlessness of others, if they live long enough; they have their punishment on earth.

Even if the old are moderately cheerful, as a majority of my classmates reported themselves to be, I suspect that most of them are haunted by fears that they prefer not to talk about. One of the fears—I wonder how many have suffered from it—is that of declining into simplified versions of themselves, of being reduced from the complexity of adult life into a single characteristic. We have seen that happen to many persons in their last years. If they were habitually kind, in age they become, like Emerson, the image of benignity, and that is a happier fate than most. If they had always insisted on having their own way, in age they become masters or mistresses without servants—except perhaps a loving daughter—and tyrants without a toady. If they had always been dissatisfied, they become whiners and scolds, the terror of nursing homes. Everything disappears from their personalities except one dominant trait. They play traditional roles: the chatterbox, the fussbudget, the invalid, the hag, the hermit, the Langley Collyer, the secret drinker, the miser, the frightened soul, the bottom pincher, the maiden aunt, or the bachelor auntie; and they almost always look the part, as if the deep lines in their faces had been drawn by a makeup artist. It is frightening to think that one might end as a caricature of oneself.

There is a sharper fear, seldom discussed, that troubles many more old persons and sometimes leads to suicide. Does it explain why the suicide rate per 100,000 is higher among the aged? Obviously the fear is not of death; it is of becoming helpless. It is the fear of being as dependent as a young child, while not being loved as a child is loved, but merely being kept alive against one's will. It is the fear of having to be dressed by a nurse, fed by a nurse, kept quiet with tranquilizers (as babies with pacifiers), and of ringing (or not being able to ring) for a nurse to change one's sheets after soiling the bed. "My only fear about death," Mrs. Scott-Maxwell says, "is that it will not come soon enough. . . . Happily I am not in such discomfort that I wish for death, I love and am loved, but please God I die before I lose my independence."

The thought of death is never far absent, but it comes to be simply accepted. Often it is less a fear than a stimulus to more intense living. John Cowper Powys says, "The one supreme advantage that Old Age possesses over Middle Age and Youth is its nearness to Death. The very thing that makes it seem pitiable to those less threatened and therefore less enlightened ages of man is the thing that deepens, heightens, and thickens out its felicity." I am quoting again from Powys's book *The Art of Growing Old*, published when he was 72 (he lived to be 90). His exclamatory style is hard for me to relish, but he says a few things worth remembering. One of them is, ". . . we poor dullards of habit and custom, we besotted and befuddled takers of life for granted, require the hell of a flaming thunderbolt to rouse us to the fact that every single second of conscious life is a miracle past reckoning, a marvel past all computation."

That "flaming thunderbolt" of imminent death sometimes rouses older persons to extraordinary efforts. I think back on a friend, the poet and scholar Ramon Guthrie, whose career was full of adventures, public rewards of a limited sort, and private frustrations. At the end he achieved a triumph, but only by force of will and only after the doctors had abandoned hope for him.

I MET Ramon Guthrie on shipboard in the summer of 1923, when he was coming back to the States with his French wife. He was a tall, loose-framed young man who carried his head bent forward and sometimes peered at you from under jutting eyebrows; later a friend described him as having "the look of a genial hawk." He also had a Dick Tracy chin and a Great War flier's clipped mustache over a wide, sensitive mouth. Marguerite, his wife, was a blue-eyed woman from Lorraine, compact and sensible, who tried not to reveal that she was terrified at starting life in a new country, with no resources except what remained of her husband's disability pay. Ramon, though, had pushed his worries aside. Someday a great poem was certain to make him famous (or might it be a novel?). Until that time he could support himself and Marguerite in one fashion or another, perhaps by finding a teaching post at some university.

I learned something about his early life in conversation. Ramon had gone to work in a New England factory at 13, after spending part of his boyhood in an orphan asylum. A benefactor sent him to Mount Hermon Academy, then rigidly Protestant and evangelical, but he rebelled against the discipline and dropped out after three years of high school; that was the end of his American schooling. In 1916 he was working at the Winchester Arms factory in New Haven, then busy with war orders. He was accepted as a volunteer by the American Field Service, which had undertaken to man and equip ambulance sections for the French Army. With a detachment of Yale undergraduates, also volunteers, he sailed for Bordeaux on Christmas Day, three weeks before his 21st birthday. That was the start of a new career for him.

Not one of his future adventures or efforts was to be unique, except the very last; all the rest can be illustrated from the lives of other American writers, famous or forgotten, who were born at about the same time. There was, for example, driving an ambulance for a foreign army and later enlisting in American aviation. There was a wound that would never let him forget his war service. There was fascination with French life and with French women. There was helping to edit a little magazine, then publishing a first book of poems (a good one, but it went unnoticed). There was trying to support himself as a novelist and having two books praised by reviewers (but failing to complete a third and a fourth because of writer's block, a problem not unknown to others). There was a career in university teaching and scholarship (other writers of his generation would embark on that career, but Ramon was a precursor). Finally there was the lifelong effort to create a work of art that might serve as a lasting testimony to all he had suffered and enjoyed. We might have learned about all those experiences in other lives—that is, if we read literary biographies—but Ramon Guthrie himself may have been unique in having undergone so many of them, and also unique in the intensity with which he confronted each new choice, as well as in the tricks of fate that followed.

Take, for example, what happened when he was still in bombing school. Fifty years later he wrote me about the adventure. "The second time," he says, "I got a chance to go up in a plane—it was a two-place Sopwith strut-and-a-half—the socket fell off the joystick at 300 meters and we spun into the ground with me in one half of the plane and the pilot in the other. I walked about three miles back to camp and came to in a hospital three days later." Ramon went on with his training, though something had changed for him. He had given himself up for dead, and I suspect that he came to regard himself as, in effect, leading a posthumous life. It would seem that many aviators who survived the Great War had the same feeling; "All the Dead Pilots" William Faulkner was to call them. In Ramon's case the first mishap was to be compounded by what amounted to a second death.

This was on September 18, 1918, in a bombing raid over the village of La Chaussée. The raid was a classical instance of military arrogance and ineptitude. Ramon had been assigned to the Eleventh Bombing Squadron, which flew slow and obsolete British planes; they were De Havilland Fours, known to aviators as "flaming coffins" from their habit of burning in the air if a bullet hit the gas tank. German fliers used them to fatten their records when they were looking for easy kills. The Eleventh Squadron had survived till then by never venturing over the lines except with a strong fighter escort. In September it received a new commanding officer, a plump major who belonged to a booster club back home and had an appetite for glory.

"You boys have been playing it safe," the major said. "Tomorrow you're going over the lines and show the Huns what American aviators are made of." He didn't order a fighter escort and, in substance, he was pronouncing a death sentence on each man in the formation.

The story of what followed I have heard from various sources, always with different details. It is safest to let Ramon speak for himself, as he was to do in that letter written fifty years later. "We had been kept on alert," the letter says, "standing by our planes since 4 a.m. Then some thirteen hours later, about 5 p.m., the raid was canceled. After we had dispersed we were called back and ordered to make this improvised raid. No time to try out our machine guns"—most of which didn't work—"or get any briefing. We didn't even know what there was to bomb at La Chaussée. About eight planes took off. Two of them got lost in the clouds and dropped out; they were the lucky ones. It's a wonder we all didn't collide in the clouds.

"The rest of us were jumped by, I think, 19 red-nosed Fokkers. They were supposed to be Von Richthofen's former outfit (the Red Baron was dead by then). It was a game of ducking into the clouds and having the Germans dive down on us as we emerged from one cloud and headed for another. All the other planes in the formation were shot down. I got two Germans; they were later confirmed, as were two others before the war was over."

When Ramon's plane got back to the field as the first (except for the two strays) and the last to return, the go-getting major came bustling out to greet him. A story I have heard more than once is that Ramon opened up on him with the machine gun and then slumped forward in a faint. Ramon's letter makes the episode less dramatic. "When we landed," he says, "I think that I did release a couple of shots in the general direction of the major. He was shortly promoted colonel and sent to the rear."

Ramon's academic career is also a story with a curious twist, considering that he was a dropout from high school. How did he get his start as a distinguished professor? The army helped him in this instance; it sent him to the Sorbonne for one term, in 1919, before sending him home to languish in a series of military hospitals (this as a delayed result of his fall in the strut-and-a-half Sopwith). From the last of the hospitals he was released with a 100-percent disability rating. He found himself a job as a waterfront detective, but after six months of sleuthing he went back to France, this time with a subvention from the Veterans Bureau. Having friends, former aviators, at the University of Toulouse, he decided to follow them. That proved to be a happy choice, since Toulouse was then eager to have American students and didn't pay close attention to their academic transcripts. Ramon studied hard and, in a little more than two years, he acquired not only the *licence* (roughly equivalent to an M.A.) but also a doctorate "of the university." The latter degree was not highly regarded in France (as opposed to the doctorate "of the state," which took many years to earn), but in America it might help him to find an academic post.

Eventually he found the post, and then a better one, after misadventures that are not essential to the story. Let me vault ahead by forty years to another crisis, the one that followed his retirement as a full professor at Dartmouth in 1963. Ramon was writing poems again, after a series of detours through fiction, translation, scholarship (two masterly introductions to modern French literature), and painting, not to mention two wartime years as a captain, then a lieutenant colonel, in the Office of Strategic Services. At Dartmouth and elsewhere he was best known for his yearly seminar on Marcel Proust, one that attracted the brightest students. "Read Proust, don't study him" was the adjuration with which he began the course each fall. Ramon had followed his own precept; he had reread *Remembrance of Things Past* each year, 31 times in all, not skipping any of its million-and-a-quarter words, and each time discovering something new that he might subtly encourage his students to rediscover; he could be proud of the achievement. He could also be proud of the new poems, which were more personal than those he had written as a young man and were finding a wider audience. Not one of them, though, was the masterpiece of which he continued to dream, and meanwhile, year by year, his health was failing disastrously.

One day (or night, he couldn't tell) he came to himself in the intensive-care unit of the Dartmouth hospital. He had undergone an emergency operation for cancer of the bladder and the doctors thought he was dying. Lying there in "this frantic bramble of glass and plastic tubes and stainless steel"—those were his words for it—he suffered from hallucinations. "I am Marsyas," he told a nurse. Marsyas was the satyr, gifted at playing the double flute, who dared to challenge the god Apollo to a musical competition. For his presumption he was flayed alive and his hide was left on a thornbush in Thessaly. Ramon felt that he too had been flayed alive, but he still had work to do and fought against slipping into a coma. In what seemed to be his final hours he was composing poems in his head; perhaps the effort was what kept him alive. Later, when his fingers were strong enough to hold a pencil, he scribbled out the poems and friends carried them away to be typed, while Ramon worked forward on others.

He was reviewing his past: the rebellion at school, his mother's suicide in the charity ward of a New Haven hospital, the adventure in the clouds over La Chaussée, his friendship with heroes of the French Resistance, his loves, his despair, his aspirations, everything that mattered. A book had taken shape, if only in his head, before he was not so much released as reprieved from the hospital. It was to be a unified work, in effect a single very long poem, but this would be composed of many shorter poems in violently contrasting moods:

Blessèd incongruities,
blends of majesty and bawdry, tenderness and horror—
and innocence.

Ramon even had a title for the book: *Maximum Security Ward.* There was actual writing still to be done—rewriting too—but the book could be hurried through the press so the author would be alive to read the reviews. Some of these were long and enthusiastic, though there were not so many of them as the book deserved. Hardly anyone mentioned that Ramon had completed a project undertaken in youth, sometimes deferred for years, but never abandoned. At the very end, as it seemed, poking among the rubble of his days, he had discovered a lasting shape, the work of art for which he had always been seeking.

When *Maximum Security Ward* was published in 1970, the poet was still believed to be on the point of death. But life has a way of blunting its climactic moments, and Ramon survived three years longer. In 1971 Dartmouth gave him the honorary doctorate he had long deserved. I congratulated him on a visit that summer, and I also said, in the fashion of old friends, "Ramon, what you should have asked for was a high-school diploma."

4

I don't propose Ramon Guthrie as a model that many of us would be able to follow, or wish to follow. He suffered vastly more than others from a feeling that some grand task was still and always to be accomplished. Even after completing his final work, he continued to struggle against nature. He couldn't bear saying to himself what most of us hope to say at the end: "It is time to rest." Still, there is a lesson in his career, one that is reinforced in a modest fashion by the testimonies of my classmates. Poet or housewife, businessman or teacher, every old person needs a work project if he wants to keep himself more alive.

It should be big enough to demand his best efforts, yet not so big as to dishearten him and let him fall back into apathy. But otherwise what sort of project? There is a wide choice within the limits of one's interests and capabilities. The project can be an old one based on the less taxing side of one's earlier career (the trial lawyer becoming a consultant), or it can be an outgrowth of some former hobby, or again it can be something completely new. Perhaps a new project is better, since it calls upon aspects of the personality that were formerly neglected and hence may release a new store of energy. It doesn't have to cost money. A man in his late eighties writes me from Iowa, "I am guilty of accumulating things —not the rubbish you speak of and not useless to me—I recycle them into works of art—even take prizes with them. But if I should go suddenly, somebody is going to have a huge bonfire. I am an artist of a sort (as I wasn't before) and really expect some useful years yet."

I like to hear about bankers who—as did my classmate—turn to painting after they are 70. And what about Grandma Moses, the housewife of Eagle Bridge, New York, who began painting in oils at 78, when she found that her fingers were too arthritic to hold a needle? Conversely, there have been painters and composers who waited till almost the same age before revealing an unexpected talent for calculation. One poet I knew, impecunious during most of a long and distinguished career, took to speculating in Wall Street. He amassed a small fortune before he died at 83.

Carl Sandburg continued writing poems well into his eighties, but he also raised goats in North Carolina. Katharine S. White, long respected as the fiction editor of *The New Yorker*, retired to

Maine with her husband, the essayist E. B. White, and grew flowers. Each fall until the last, she planned and supervised the planting of bulbs in her garden. "As the years went by and age overtook her," the husband writes in his introduction to her posthumous book, *Onward and Upward in the Garden,* "there was something comical yet touching in her bedraggled appearance on this awesome occasion—the small, hunched-over figure, her studied absorption in the implausible notion that there would be yet another spring, oblivious to the ending of her own days, which she knew perfectly well was near at hand, sitting there with her detailed chart under those dark skies in the dying October, calmly plotting the resurrection."

Very often an old person's project has to do with things that live on and are renewed: gardens, orchards, woods, or a breed of cattle. He counsels and supervises long after he has become, like Katharine White, unable to dig or harvest. "He plants trees to profit another age," Cicero quotes an earlier Latin author as saying, and himself continues, "If you ask a farmer, however old, for whom he is planting, he will reply without hesitation, 'For the immortal gods, who intended that I should not only receive these things from my ancestors, but also transmit them to my descendants.' " The welfare and renewal of the family is a very ancient project for old persons, one that has led to follies and disasters over the centuries, but also, as we often forget, to solid rewards. Families, whether illustrious or obscure, have maintained themselves in a surprising fashion.

In the present age family ties have frayed and broken, even if some of them remain stronger than many people believe. More and more old persons have transferred their hopes, in whole or part, to some other social stucture. "Colby College is my family," I heard an old bachelor say. More of the new projects (but many of the older ones too) have to do with a university, a church, a hospital, a community, or a cause. The very rich may endow museums that bear their names and testify enduringly to their love of art. A plaque in a hospital corridor attests that this wing or ward is owed to the generosity of, let us say, Mrs. Roberta Jones. Will she be remembered? At least she hopes to exert a good influence on others from beyond the grave.

Artists in general have the strongest desire to fashion something whose life will be self-contained and independent of their own mortality; that explains why so many of them work furiously at their projects to the end. But can't we all be artists, each in his own fashion?

ONE project among many, one that tempts me and might be tempting to others, is trying to find a shape or pattern in our lives. There are such patterns, I believe, even if they are hard to discern. Our lives that seemed a random and monotonous series of incidents are something more than that; each of them has a plot. Life in general (or nature, or the history of our times) is a supremely inventive novelist or playwright, but he—she?—is also wasteful beyond belief and her designs are hidden under the Langley Collyer rubbish of the years. She needs our help as collaborators. Can we clear away the bundles of old newspapers, evading the booby traps, and lay bare the outlines of ourselves?

Those outlines, if we find them, will prove to be a story, one with a beginning, a development, a climax of sorts (or more than one climax), and an epilogue. John Cowper Powys says in one of his vatic moments, ". . . in only one way can our mortal and, it may be, our immortal life be bravely, thoroughly, and absolutely justified, and that way is by *treating it as a story.*" He might better have said, ". . . as a drama for each of us in which he or she has been the protagonist." Not only that; we have been the audience too, and perhaps the critic planning his report for a morning paper: "The leading character was played by ____________" (insert your name), "who was no more than adequate in his difficult role." Or was he better than merely adequate, or worse, much worse? In age we have the privilege—which sometimes becomes a torture on sleepless nights—of passing judgment on our own performance. But before passing judgment, we have to untangle the plot of the play.

A first step in the untanglement, if we choose to make that effort, is gathering together the materials that composed our lives (including even the rubbish, which may prove to be more revealing than we had suspected). In other words, the first step is simply remembering. That seems easy in the beginning, since it always starts with our childhood, whose scenes are more vividly printed on our minds. Some of them, though, may reappear unexpectedly—for example, in my case, the picture of Jim Overman taking off his work shoes and insisting that I wear them on my bare feet before crossing the patch of nettles that barred our way to the farm lane. Jim followed me in heavy woolen socks that had been knitted for him by his older sister Maggie, who flashes across my mind as an image of blowsy kindness. What happened to dear Maggie? What happened to Jim after he went to work in a steel mill? Both of those orphans played their parts in my world.

Like many older persons, or so one suspects, I find myself leaping forward from childhood to recent years. These too are easy for most of us to remember, except in such matters as names and faces and where we mislaid our glasses. ("Thank goodness, you don't have to look for them anymore," a longtime neighbor phoned my wife to say. "I found them in the freezer compartment.") But the old, as Cicero said, end by recalling whatever really concerns them in the recent past. It is the middle years that prove hardest to recapture, so many of the persons and incidents having grown dim, but we can find the shape of these too, if we continue our efforts.

There are tangible aids to remembering, as notably letters, old snapshots, daybooks, and mementos, if we have saved them. Old tunes ring through our heads and some of them bring back pictures; this one was "our" song, Doris said, and you see the look on her face when she hummed the words. What became of Doris after she married somebody else and moved to California? And Mr. Wagner, the boss who used to dance the gazotsky at office parties? Characters crowd in on us, each making a contribution, and gradually our world takes shape. We tell stories about it, perhaps only to ourselves, and then arrange the stories in sequence: this must have been our second act and this was the third. All these efforts, if continued, might lead to an absolutely candid book of memoirs; old persons have nothing to lose by telling the truth. For others it might lead to nothing more than notebook jottings and advice to the young that might or might not be remembered. No matter: it is a fascinating pursuit in itself, and our efforts will not have been wasted if they help us to possess our own identities as an artist possesses his work. At least we can say to the world of the future, or to ourselves if nobody else will listen, "I really *was*"—or even, with greater self-confidence, "I was and am *this.*"

ı the other side. Would you find out for yourself from books? What
ıg you will need! What languages you must learn; what libraries you
·ansack; what an amount of reading must be got through! Who will
ne in such a choice? It will be hard to find the best books on the oppo-
e in any one country, and all the harder to find those on all sides; when
they would be easily answered. The absent are always in the wrong,
l arguments boldly asserted easily efface good arguments put forward
rn. Besides books are often very misleading, and scarcely express the
s of their authors. If you think you can judge the Catholic faith from
ings of Bossuet, you will find yourself greatly mistaken when you
ed among us. You will see that the doctrines with which Protestants
ered are quite different from those of the pulpit. To judge a religion
ou must not study it in the books of its partisans, you must learn it in
s; this is quite another matter. Each religion has its own traditions,
customs, prejudices, which form the spirit of its creed, and must be
onnection with it.

many great nations neither print books of their own nor read ours!
they judge of our opinions, or we of theirs? We laugh at them, they
; and if our travellers turn them into ridicule, they need only travel
to pay us back in our own coin. Are there not, in every country,
mmon-sense, honesty, and good faith, lovers of truth, who only
w what truth is that they may profess it? Yet every one finds truth
religion, and thinks the religion of other nations absurd; so all
n religions are not so absurd as they seem to us, or else the reason
our own proves nothing.

e three principal forms of religion in Europe. One accepts one
nother two, and another three. Each hates the others, showers
em, accuses them of blindness, obstinacy, hardness of heart, and
hat fair-minded man will dare to decide between them without
y weighing their evidence, without listening attentively to their
That which accepts only one revelation is the oldest and seems
blished; that which accepts three is the newest and seems the
nt; that which accepts two revelations and rejects the third may
e best, but prejudice is certainly against it; its inconsistency is

ee revelations the sacred books are written in languages un-
people who believe in them. The Jews no longer understand
hristians understand neither Hebrew nor Greek; the Turks and
t understand Arabic, and the Arabs of our time do not speak
f Mahomet. Is not it a very foolish way of teaching, to teach
known tongue? These books are translated, you say. What an
m I to know that the translations are correct, or how am I to
such a thing as a correct translation is possible? If God has
speak to men, why should he require an interpreter?
believe that every man is obliged to know what is contained

when he promised the kingdom of heaven to the simple, he was mistaken when he began his finest discourse with the praise of the poor in spirit, if so much wit is needed to understand his teaching and to get others to believe in him. When you have convinced me that submission is my duty, all will be well; but to convince me of this, come down to my level; adapt your arguments to a lowly mind, or I shall not recognise you as a true disciple of your master, and it is not his doctrine that you are teaching me.] for fear lest we should take the devil's doings for the handiwork of God. What think you of this dilemma?

"This doctrine, if it comes from God, should bear the sacred stamp of the godhead; not only should it illumine the troubled thoughts which reason imprints on our minds, but it should also offer us a form of worship, a morality, and rules of conduct in accordance with the attributes by means of which we alone conceive of God's essence. If then it teaches us what is absurd and unreasonable, if it inspires us with feelings of aversion for our fellows and terror for ourselves, if it paints us a God, angry, jealous, revengeful, partial, hating men, a God of war and battles, ever ready to strike and to destroy, ever speaking of punishment and torment, boasting even of the punishment of the innocent, my heart would not be drawn towards this terrible God, I would take good care not to quit the realm of natural religion to embrace such a religion as that; for you see plainly I must choose between them. Your God is not ours. He who begins by selecting a chosen people, and proscribing the rest of mankind, is not our common father; he who consigns to eternal punishment the greater part of his creatures, is not the merciful and gracious God revealed to me by my reason.

"Reason tells me that dogmas should be plain, clear, and striking in their simplicity. If there is something lacking in natural religion, it is with respect to the obscurity in which it leaves the great truths it teaches; revelation should teach us these truths in a way which the mind of man can understand; it should bring them within his reach, make him comprehend them, so that he may believe them. Faith is confirmed and strengthened by understanding; the best religion is of necessity the simplest. He who hides beneath mysteries and contradictions the religion that he preaches to me, teaches me at the same time to distrust that religion. The God whom I adore is not the God of darkness, he has not given me understanding in order to forbid me to use it; to tell me to submit my reason is to insult the giver of reason. The minister of truth does not tyrannise over my reason, he enlightens it.

"We have set aside all human authority, and without it I do not see how any man can convince another by preaching a doctrine contrary to reason. Let them fight it out, and let us see what they have to say with that harshness of speech which is common to both.

"INSPIRATION: Reason tells you that the whole is greater than the part; but I tell you, in God's name, that the part is greater than the whole.

"REASON: And who are you to dare to tell me that God contradicts himself? And which shall I choose to believe. God who teaches me, through my reason, the eternal truth, or you who, in his name, proclaim an absurdity?

"INSPIRATION: Believe me, for my teaching is more positive; and I will prove to you beyond all manner of doubt that he has sent me.

"REASON: What! you will convince me that God has sent you to bear witness against himself? What sort of proofs will you adduce to convince me that God speaks more surely by your mouth than through the understanding he has given me?

"INSPIRATION: The understanding he has given you! Petty, conceited creature! As if you were the first impious person who had been led astray through his reason corrupted by sin.

"REASON: Man of God, you would not be the first scoundrel who asserts his arrogance as a proof of his mission.

"INSPIRATION: What! do even philosophers call names?

"REASON: Sometimes, when the saints set them the example.

"INSPIRATION: Oh, but I have a right to do it, for I am speaking on God's behalf.

"REASON: You would do well to show your credentials before you make use of your privileges.

"INSPIRATION: My credentials are authentic, earth and heaven will bear witness on my behalf. Follow my arguments carefully, if you please.

"REASON: Your arguments! You forget what you are saying. When you teach me that my reason misleads me, do you not refute what it might have said on your behalf? He who denies the right of reason, must convince me without recourse to her aid. For suppose you have convinced me by reason, how am I to know that it is not my reason, corrupted by sin, which makes me accept what you say? besides, what proof, what demonstration, can you advance, more self-evident than the axiom it is to destroy? It is more credible that a good syllogism is a lie, than that the part is greater than the whole.

"INSPIRATION: What a difference! There is no answer to my evidence; it is of a supernatural kind.

"REASON: Supernatural! What do you mean by the word? I do not understand it.

"INSPIRATION: I mean changes in the order of nature, prophecies, signs, and wonders of every kind.

"REASON: Signs and wonders! I have never seen anything of the kind.

"INSPIRATION: Others have seen them for you. Clouds of witnesses—the witness of whole nations....

"REASON: Is the witness of nations supernatural?

"INSPIRATION: No; but when it is unanimous, it is incontestable.

"REASON: There is nothing so incontestable as the principles of reason, and one cannot accept an absurdity on human evidence. Once more, let us see your supernatural evidence, for the consent of mankind is not supernatural.

"INSPIRATION: Oh, hardened heart, grace does not speak to you.

"REASON: That is not my fault; for by your own showing, one must have already received grace before one is able to ask for it. Begin by speaking to me

in its stead.

"INSPIRATION: But that is just what I am doing, and
But what do you say to prophecy?

"REASON: In the first place, I say I have no more he
have seen a miracle. In the next, I say that no prophet
over me.

"INSPIRATION: Follower of the devil! Why should
prophets have authority over you?

"REASON: Because three things are required, three
er happen: firstly, I must have heard the prophecy; sec
its fulfilment; and thirdly, it must be clearly proved t
prophecy could not by any possibility have been a m
if it was as precise, as plain, and clear as an axior
clearness of a chance prediction does not make its f
fulfilment when it does take place does not, strictly
foretold.

"See what your so-called supernatural proofs,
ecies come to: believe all this upon the word of an
ity of men the authority of God which speaks t
truths which my mind conceives of could suffer a
sort of certainty for me; and far from being su
God's behalf, I should not even be sure that there

"My child, here are difficulties enough, but
many religions, mutually excluding and prosc
true, if indeed any one of them is true. To recog
inquire into, not one, but all; and in any que
right to condemn unheard. [Footnote: On the
the Stoics maintained, among other strange
hearing both sides; for, said they, the first ei
not prove it; if he has proved it, there is an e
condemned: if he has not proved it, he hims
should be given against him. I consider th
exclusive revelation very much like that o
claims to be the sole guardian of truth, we
choose between them without injustice.]
with the evidence; we must know what
other, and what answers they receive. Th
the more we must try to discover why s
it. We should be simple, indeed, if we t
on our own side, in order to acquaint
other. Where can you find theologians
ty? Where are those who, to refute the
begin by making out that they are of
good show among his own friends, ar
would cut a very poor figure with th

in books, and that he who is out of reach of these books, and of those who understand them, will be punished for an ignorance which is no fault of his. Books upon books! What madness! As all Europe is full of books, Europeans regard them as necessary, forgetting that they are unknown throughout three-quarters of the globe. Were not all these books written by men? Why then should a man need them to teach him his duty, and how did he learn his duty before these books were in existence? Either he must have learnt his duties for himself, or his ignorance must have been excused.

"Our Catholics talk loudly of the authority of the Church; but what is the use of it all, if they also need just as great an array of proofs to establish that authority as the other seeks to establish their doctrine? The Church decides that the Church has a right to decide. What a well-founded authority! Go beyond it, and you are back again in our discussions.

"Do you know many Christians who have taken the trouble to inquire what the Jews allege against them? If any one knows anything at all about it, it is from the writings of Christians. What a way of ascertaining the arguments of our adversaries! But what is to be done? If any one dared to publish in our day books which were openly in favour of the Jewish religion, we should punish the author, publisher, and bookseller. This regulation is a sure and certain plan for always being in the right. It is easy to refute those who dare not venture to speak.

"Those among us who have the opportunity of talking with Jews are little better off. These unhappy people feel that they are in our power; the tyranny they have suffered makes them timid; they know that Christian charity thinks nothing of injustice and cruelty; will they dare to run the risk of an outcry against blasphemy? Our greed inspires us with zeal, and they are so rich that they must be in the wrong. The more learned, the more enlightened they are, the more cautious. You may convert some poor wretch whom you have paid to slander his religion; you get some wretched old-clothes-man to speak, and he says what you want; you may triumph over their ignorance and cowardice, while all the time their men of learning are laughing at your stupidity. But do you think you would get off so easily in any place where they knew they were safe! At the Sorbonne it is plain that the Messianic prophecies refer to Jesus Christ. Among the rabbis of Amsterdam it is just as clear that they have nothing to do with him. I do not think I have ever heard the arguments of the Jews as to why they should not have a free state, schools and universities, where they can speak and argue without danger. Then alone can we know what they have to say.

"At Constantinople the Turks state their arguments, but we dare not give ours; then it is our turn to cringe. Can we blame the Turks if they require us to show the same respect for Mahomet, in whom we do not believe, as we demand from the Jews with regard to Jesus Christ in whom they do not believe? Are we right? On what grounds of justice can we answer this question?

"Two-thirds of mankind are neither Jews, Mahometans, nor Christians; and how many millions of men have never heard the name of Moses, Jesus

Christ, or Mahomet? They deny it; they maintain that our missionaries go everywhere. That is easily said. But do they go into the heart of Africa, still undiscovered, where as yet no European has ever ventured? Do they go to Eastern Tartary to follow on horseback the wandering tribes, whom no stranger approaches, who not only know nothing of the pope, but have scarcely heard tell of the Grand Lama! Do they penetrate into the vast continents of America, where there are still whole nations unaware that the people of another world have set foot on their shores? Do they go to Japan, where their intrigues have led to their perpetual banishment, where their predecessors are only known to the rising generation as skilful plotters who came with feigned zeal to take possession in secret of the empire? Do they reach the harems of the Asiatic princes to preach the gospel to those thousands of poor slaves? What have the women of those countries done that no missionary may preach the faith to them? Will they all go to hell because of their seclusion?

"If it were true that the gospel is preached throughout the world, what advantage would there be? The day before the first missionary set foot in any country, no doubt somebody died who could not hear him. Now tell me what we shall do with him? If there were a single soul in the whole world, to whom Jesus Christ had never been preached, this objection would be as strong for that man as for a quarter of the human race.

"If the ministers of the gospel have made themselves heard among far-off nations, what have they told them which might reasonably be accepted on their word, without further and more exact verification? You preach to me God, born and dying, two thousand years ago, at the other end of the world, in some small town I know not where; and you tell me that all who have not believed this mystery are damned. These are strange things to be believed so quickly on the authority of an unknown person. Why did your God make these things happen so far off, if he would compel me to know about them? Is it a crime to be unaware of what is happening half a world away? Could I guess that in another hemisphere there was a Hebrew nation and a town called Jerusalem? You might as well expect me to know what was happening in the moon. You say you have come to teach me; but why did you not come and teach my father, or why do you consign that good old man to damnation because he knew nothing of all this? Must he be punished everlastingly for your laziness, he who was so kind and helpful, he who sought only for truth? Be honest; put yourself in my place; see if I ought to believe, on your word alone, all these incredible things which you have told me, and reconcile all this injustice with the just God you proclaim to me. At least allow me to go and see this distant land where such wonders, unheard of in my own country, took place; let me go and see why the inhabitants of Jerusalem put their God to death as a robber. You tell me they did not know he was God. What then shall I do, I who have only heard of him from you? You say they have been punished, dispersed, oppressed, enslaved; that none of them dare approach that town. Indeed they richly deserved it; but what do its present inhabitants say of their crime in slaying their God! They deny him; they too refuse to recognise God as God. They are no better than the children of the original inhabitants.

"What! In the very town where God was put to death, neither the former nor the latter inhabitants knew him, and you expect that I should know him, I who was born two thousand years after his time, and two thousand leagues away? Do you not see that before I can believe this book which you call sacred, but which I do not in the least understand, I must know from others than yourself when and by whom it was written, how it has been preserved, how it came into your possession, what they say about it in those lands where it is rejected, and what are their reasons for rejecting it, though they know as well as you what you are telling me? You perceive I must go to Europe, Asia, Palestine, to examine these things for myself; it would be madness to listen to you before that.

"Not only does this seem reasonable to me, but I maintain that it is what every wise man ought to say in similar circumstances; that he ought to banish to a great distance the missionary who wants to instruct and baptise him all of a sudden before the evidence is verified. Now I maintain that there is no revelation against which these or similar objections cannot be made, and with more force than against Christianity. Hence it follows that if there is but one true religion and if every man is bound to follow it under pain of damnation, he must spend his whole life in studying, testing, comparing all these religions, in travelling through the countries in which they are established. No man is free from a man's first duty; no one has a right to depend on another's judgment. The artisan who earns his bread by his daily toil, the ploughboy who cannot read, the delicate and timid maiden, the invalid who can scarcely leave his bed, all without exception must study, consider, argue, travel over the whole world; there will be no more fixed and settled nations; the whole earth will swarm with pilgrims on their way, at great cost of time and trouble, to verify, compare, and examine for themselves the various religions to be found. Then farewell to the trades, the arts, the sciences of mankind, farewell to all peaceful occupations; there can be no study but that of religion, even the strongest, the most industrious, the most intelligent, the oldest, will hardly be able in his last years to know where he is; and it will be a wonder if he manages to find out what religion he ought to live by, before the hour of his death.

"Hard pressed by these arguments, some prefer to make God unjust and to punish the innocent for the sins of their fathers, rather than to renounce their barbarous dogmas. Others get out of the difficulty by kindly sending an angel to instruct all those who in invincible ignorance have lived a righteous life. A good idea, that angel! Not content to be the slaves of their own inventions they expect God to make use of them also!

"Behold, my son, the absurdities to which pride and intolerance bring us, when everybody wants others to think as he does, and everybody fancies that he has an exclusive claim upon the rest of mankind. I call to witness the God of Peace whom I adore, and whom I proclaim to you, that my inquiries were honestly made; but when I discovered that they were and always would be unsuccessful, and that I was embarked upon a boundless ocean, I turned back, and restricted my faith within the limits of my primitive ideas. I could never convince myself that God would require such learning of me under pain of hell. So I closed all my books. There is one book which is open to every one—the book of nature. In this good and great volume I learn to serve and adore its Author. There is no excuse for not reading this book, for it speaks to all in a language they can understand. Suppose I had been born in a desert island, suppose I had never seen any man but myself, suppose I had never heard what took place in olden days in a remote corner of the world; yet if I use my reason, if I cultivate it, if I employ rightly the innate faculties which God bestows upon me, I shall learn by myself to know and love him, to love his works, to will what he wills, and to fulfil all my duties upon earth, that I may do his pleasure. What more can all human learning teach me?

"With regard to revelation, if I were a more accomplished disputant, or a more learned person, perhaps I should feel its truth, its usefulness for those who are happy enough to perceive it; but if I find evidence for it which I cannot combat, I also find objections against it which I cannot overcome. There are so many weighty reasons for and against that I do not know what to decide, so that I neither accept nor reject it. I only reject all obligation to be convinced of its truth; for this so-called obligation is incompatible with God's justice, and far from removing objections in this way it would multiply them, and would make them insurmountable for the greater part of mankind. In this respect I maintain an attitude of reverent doubt. I do not presume to think myself infallible; other men may have been able to make up their minds though the matter seems doubtful to myself; I am speaking for myself, not for them; I neither blame them nor follow in their steps; their judgment may be superior to mine, but it is no fault of mine that my judgment does not agree with it.

"I own also that the holiness of the gospel speaks to my heart, and that this is an argument which I should be sorry to refute. Consider the books of the philosophers with all their outward show; how petty they are in comparison! Can a book at once so grand and so simple be the work of men? Is it possible that he whose history is contained in this book is no more than man? Is the tone of this book, the tone of the enthusiast or the ambitious sectary? What gentleness and purity in his actions, what a touching grace in his teaching, how lofty are his sayings, how profoundly wise are his sermons, how ready, how discriminating, and how just are his answers! What man, what sage, can live, suffer, and die without weakness or ostentation? When Plato describes his imaginary good man, overwhelmed with the disgrace of crime, and deserving of all the rewards of virtue, every feature of the portrait is that of Christ; the resemblance is so striking that it has been noticed by all the Fathers, and there can be no doubt about it. What prejudices and blindness must there be before we dare to compare the son of Sophronisca with the son of Mary. How far apart they are! Socrates dies a painless death, he is not put to open shame, and he plays his part easily to the last; and if this easy death had not done honour to his life, we might have doubted whether Socrates, with all his intellect, was more than a mere sophist. He invented morality, so they say; others before him had practised it; he only said what they had done, and made use of their example in his teaching. Aristides was just before Socrates defined justice; Leonidas died for his country before Socrates declared that patriotism was a virtue; Sparta was sober before Socrates extolled sobriety; there were plenty of virtuous men in Greece before he defined virtue. But among the men of his own time where did Jesus find that pure and lofty morality of which he is both the teacher and pattern? [Footnote: Cf. in the Sermon on the Mount the parallel he himself draws between the teaching of Moses and his own.—Matt. v.] The voice of loftiest wisdom arose among the fiercest fanaticism, the simplicity of the most heroic virtues did honour to the most degraded of nations. One could wish no easier death than that of Socrates, calmly discussing philosophy with his friends; one could fear nothing worse than that of Jesus, dying in torment, among the insults, the mockery, the curses of the whole nation. In the midst of these terrible sufferings, Jesus prays for his cruel murderers. Yes, if the life and death of Socrates are those of a philosopher, the life and death of Christ are those of a God. Shall we say that the gospel story is the work of the imagination? My friend, such things are not imagined; and the doings of Socrates, which no one doubts, are less well attested than those of Jesus Christ. At best, you only put the difficulty from you; it would be still more incredible that several persons should have agreed together to invent such a book, than that there was one man who supplied its subject matter. The tone and morality of this story are not those of any Jewish authors, and the gospel indeed contains characters so great, so striking, so entirely inimitable, that their invention would be more astonishing than their hero. With all this the same gospel is full of incredible things, things repugnant to reason, things which no natural man can understand or accept. What can you do among so many contradictions? You can be modest and wary, my child; respect in silence what you can neither reject nor understand, and humble yourself in the sight of the Divine Being who alone knows the truth.

"This is the unwilling scepticism in which I rest; but this scepticism is in no way painful to me, for it does not extend to matters of practice, and I am well assured as to the principles underlying all my duties. I serve God in the simplicity of my heart; I only seek to know what affects my conduct. As to those dogmas which have no effect upon action or morality, dogmas about which so many men torment themselves, I give no heed to them. I regard all individual religions as so many wholesome institutions which prescribe a uniform method by which each country may do honour to God in public worship; institutions which may each have its reason in the country, the government, the genius of the people, or in other local causes which make one preferable to another in a given time or place. I think them all good alike, when God is served in a fitting manner. True worship is of the heart. God rejects no homage, however offered, provided it is sincere. Called to the service of the Church in my own religion, I fulfil as scrupulously as I can all the duties prescribed to me, and my conscience would reproach me if I were knowingly wanting with regard to any point. You are aware that after being suspended for a long time, I have, through the influence of M. Mellarede, obtained permission to resume my priestly duties, as a means of livelihood. I used to say Mass with the levity that comes from long experience even of the most serious matters when they are too familiar to us; with my new principles I now celebrate it with more reverence; I dwell upon the majesty of the Supreme Being, his presence, the insufficiency of the human mind, which so little realises what concerns its Creator. When I consider how I present before him the prayers of all the people in a form laid down for me, I carry out the whole ritual exactly; I give heed to what I say, I am careful not to omit the least word, the least ceremony; when the moment of the consecration approaches, I collect my powers, that I may do all things as required by the Church and by the greatness of this sacrament; I strive to annihilate my own reason before the Supreme Mind; I say to myself, Who art thou to measure infinite power? I reverently pronounce the sacramental words, and I give to their effect all the faith I can bestow. Whatever may be this mystery which passes understanding, I am not afraid that at the day of judgment I shall be punished for having profaned it in my heart."

Honoured with the sacred ministry, though in its lowest ranks, I will never do or say anything which may make me unworthy to fulfil these sublime duties. I will always preach virtue and exhort men to well-doing; and so far as I can I will set them a good example. It will be my business to make religion attractive; it will be my business to strengthen their faith in those doctrines which are really useful, those which every man must believe; but, please God, I shall never teach them to hate their neighbour, to say to other men, You will be damned; to say, No salvation outside the Church. [Footnote: The duty of following and loving the religion of our country does not go so far as to require us to accept doctrines contrary to good morals, such as intolerance. This horrible doctrine sets men in arms against their fellow-men, and makes them all enemies of mankind. The distinction between civil toleration and theological toleration is vain and childish. These two kinds of toleration are inseparable, and we cannot accept one without the other. Even the angels could not live at peace with men whom they regarded as the enemies of God.] If I were in a more conspicuous position, this reticence might get me into trouble; but I am too obscure to have much to fear, and I could hardly sink lower than I am. Come what may, I will never blaspheme the justice of God, nor lie against the Holy Ghost.

"I have long desired to have a parish of my own; it is still my ambition, but I no longer hope to attain it. My dear friend, I think there is nothing so delightful as to be a parish priest. A good clergyman is a minister of mercy, as a good magistrate is a minister of justice. A clergyman is never called upon to do evil; if he cannot always do good himself, it is never out of place for him to beg for others, and he often gets what he asks if he knows how to gain respect. Oh! if I should ever have some poor mountain parish where I might minister to kindly folk, I should be happy indeed; for it seems to me that I should make my parishioners happy. I should not bring them riches, but I should share their poverty; I should remove from them the scorn and opprobrium which are harder to bear than poverty. I should make them love peace and equality, which often remove poverty, and always make it tolerable. When they saw that I was in no way better off than themselves, and that yet I was content with my lot, they would learn to put up with their fate and to be content like me. In my sermons I would lay more stress on the spirit of the gospel than on the spirit of the church; its teaching is simple, its morality sublime; there is little in it about the practices of religion, but much about works of charity. Before I teach them what they ought to do, I would try to practise it myself, that they might see that at least I think what I say. If there were Protestants in the neighbourhood or in my parish, I would make no difference between them and my own congregation so far as concerns Christian charity; I would get them to love one another, to consider themselves brethren, to respect all religions, and each to live peaceably in his own religion. To ask any one to abandon the religion in which he was born is, I consider, to ask him to do wrong, and therefore to do wrong oneself. While we await further knowledge, let us respect public order; in every country let us respect the laws, let us not disturb the form of worship prescribed by law; let us not lead its citizens into disobedience; for we have no certain knowledge that it is good for them to abandon their own opinions for others, and on the other hand we are quite certain that it is a bad thing to disobey the law.

"My young friend, I have now repeated to you my creed as God reads it in my heart; you are the first to whom I have told it; perhaps you will be the last. As long as there is any true faith left among men, we must not trouble quiet souls, nor scare the faith of the ignorant with problems they cannot solve, with difficulties which cause them uneasiness, but do not give them any guidance. But when once everything is shaken, the trunk must be preserved at the cost of the branches. Consciences, restless, uncertain, and almost quenched like yours, require to be strengthened and aroused; to set the feet again upon the foundation of eternal truth, we must remove the trembling supports on which they think they rest.

"You are at that critical age when the mind is open to conviction, when the heart receives its form and character, when we decide our own fate for life, either for good or evil. At a later date, the material has hardened and fresh impressions leave no trace. Young man, take the stamp of truth upon your heart which is not yet hardened, if I were more certain of myself, I should have adopted a more decided and dogmatic tone; but I am a man ignorant and liable to error; what could I do? I have opened my heart fully to you; and I have told what I myself hold for certain and sure; I have told you my doubts as doubts, my opinions as opinions; I have given you my reasons both for faith and doubt. It is now your turn to judge; you have asked for time; that is a wise precaution and it makes me think well of you. Begin by bringing your conscience into that state in which it desires to see clearly; be honest with yourself. Take to yourself such of my opinions as convince you, reject the rest. You are not yet so depraved by vice as to run the risk of choosing amiss. I would offer to argue with you, but as soon as men dispute they lose their temper; pride and obstinacy come in, and there is an end of honesty. My friend, never argue; for by arguing we gain no light for ourselves or for others. So far as I myself am concerned, I have only made up my mind after many years of meditation; here I rest, my conscience is at peace, my heart is satisfied. If I wanted to begin afresh the examination of my feelings, I should not bring to the task a purer love of truth; and my mind, which is already less active, would be less able to perceive the truth. Here I shall rest, lest the love of contemplation, developing step by step into an idle passion, should make me lukewarm in the performance of my duties, lest I should fall into my former scepticism without strength to struggle out of it. More than half my life is spent; I have barely time to make good use of what is left, to blot out my faults by my virtues. If I am mistaken, it is against my will. He who reads my inmost heart knows that I have no love for my blindness. As my own knowledge is powerless to free me from this blindness, my only way out of it is by a good life; and if God from the very stones can raise up children to Abraham, every man has a right to hope that he may be taught the truth, if he makes himself worthy of it.

"If my reflections lead you to think as I do, if you share my feelings, if we have the same creed, I give you this advice: Do not continue to expose your life to the temptations of poverty and despair, nor waste it in degradation and at the mercy of strangers; no longer eat the shameful bread of charity. Return to your own country, go back to the religion of your fathers, and follow it in sincerity of heart, and never forsake it; it is very simple and very holy; I think there is no other religion upon earth whose morality is purer, no other more satisfying to the reason. Do not trouble about the cost of the journey, that will be provided for you. Neither do you fear the false shame of a humiliating return; we should blush to commit a fault, not to repair it. You are still at an age when all is forgiven, but when we cannot go on sinning with impunity. If you desire to listen to your conscience, a thousand empty objections will disappear at her voice. You will feel that, in our present state of uncertainty, it is an inexcusable presumption to profess any faith but that we were born into, while it is treachery not to practise honestly the faith we profess. If we go astray, we deprive ourselves of a great excuse before the tribunal of the sovereign judge. Will he not pardon the errors in which we were brought up, rather than those of our own choosing?

"My son, keep your soul in such a state that you always desire that there should be a God and you will never doubt it. Moreover, whatever decision you come to, remember that the real duties of religion are independent of human institutions; that a righteous heart is the true temple of the Godhead; that in every land, in every sect, to love God above all things and to love our neighbour as ourself is the whole law; remember there is no religion which absolves us from our moral duties; that these alone are really essential, that the service of the heart is the first of these duties, and that without faith there is no such thing as true virtue.

"Shun those who, under the pretence of explaining nature, sow destructive doctrines in the heart of men, those whose apparent scepticism is a hundredfold more self-assertive and dogmatic than the firm tone of their opponents. Under the arrogant claim, that they alone are enlightened, true, honest, they subject us imperiously to their far-reaching decisions, and profess to give us, as the true principles of all things, the unintelligible systems framed by their imagination. Moreover, they overthrow, destroy, and trample under foot all that men reverence; they rob the afflicted of their last consolation in their misery; they deprive the rich and powerful of the sole bridle of their passions; they tear from the very depths of man's heart all remorse for crime, and all hope of virtue; and they boast, moreover, that they are the benefactors of the human race. Truth, they say, can never do a man harm. I think so too, and to my mind that is strong evidence that what they teach is not true. [Footnote: The rival parties attack each other with so many sophistries that it would be a rash and overwhelming enterprise to attempt to deal with all of them; it is difficult enough to note some of them as they occur. One of the commonest errors among the partisans of philosophy is to contrast a nation of good philosophers with a nation of bad Christians; as if it were easier to make a nation of good philosophers than a nation of good Christians. I know not whether in individual cases it is easier to discover one rather than the other; but I am quite certain that, as far as nations are concerned, we must assume that there will be those who misuse their philosophy without religion, just as our people misuse their religion without philosophy, and that seems to put quite a different face upon the matter.]—Bayle has proved very satisfactorily that fanaticism is more harmful than atheism, and that cannot be denied; but what he has not taken the trouble to say, though it is none the less true, is this: Fanaticism, though cruel and bloodthirsty, is still a great and powerful passion, which stirs the heart of man, teaching him to despise death, and giving him an enormous motive power, which only needs to be guided rightly to produce the noblest virtues; while irreligion, and the argumentative philosophic spirit generally, on the other hand, assaults the life and enfeebles it, degrades the soul, concentrates all the passions in the basest self-interest, in the meanness of the human self; thus it saps unnoticed the very foundations of all society, for what is common to all these private interests is so small that it will never outweigh their opposing interests.—If atheism does not lead to bloodshed, it is less from love of peace than from indifference to what is good; as if it mattered little what happened to others, provided the sage remained undisturbed in his study. His principles do not kill men, but they prevent their birth, by destroying the morals by which they were multiplied, by detaching them from their fellows, by reducing all their affections to a secret selfishness, as fatal to population as to virtue. The indifference of the philosopher is like the peace in a despotic state; it is the repose of death; war itself is not more destructive.—Thus fanaticism though its immediate results are more fatal than those of what is now called the philosophic mind, is much less fatal in its after effects. Moreover, it is an easy matter to exhibit fine maxims in books; but the real question is—Are they really in accordance with your teaching, are they the necessary consequences of it? and this has not been clearly proved so far. It remains to be seen whether philosophy, safely enthroned, could control successfully man's petty vanity, his self-interest, his ambition, all the lesser passions of mankind, and whether it would practise that sweet humanity which it boasts of, pen in hand.—In theory, there is no good which philosophy can bring about which is not equally secured by religion, while religion secures much that philosophy cannot secure.—In practice, it is another matter; but still we must put it to the proof. No man follows his religion in all things, even if his religion is true; most people have hardly any religion, and they do not in the least follow what they have; that is still more true; but still there are some people who have a religion and follow it, at least to some extent; and beyond doubt religious motives do prevent them from wrong-doing, and win from them virtues, praiseworthy actions, which would not have existed but for these motives.—A monk denies that money was entrusted to him; what of that? It only proves that the man who entrusted the money to him was a fool. If Pascal had done the same, that would have proved that Pascal was a hypocrite. But a monk! Are those who make a trade of religion religious people? All the crimes committed by the clergy, as by other men, do not prove that religion is useless, but that very few people are religious.—Most certainly our modern governments owe to Christianity their more stable authority, their less frequent revolutions; it has made those governments less bloodthirsty; this can be shown by comparing them with the governments of former times. Apart from fanaticism, the best known religion has given greater gentleness to Christian conduct. This change is not the result of learning; for wherever learning has been most illustrious humanity has been no more respected on that account; the cruelties of the Athenians, the Egyptians, the Roman emperors, the Chinese bear witness to this. What works of mercy spring from the gospel! How many acts of restitution, reparation, confession does the gospel lead to among Catholics! Among ourselves, as the times of communion draw near, do they not lead us to reconciliation and to alms-giving? Did not the Hebrew Jubilee make the grasping less greedy, did it not prevent much poverty? The brotherhood of the Law made the nation one; no beggar was found among them. Neither are there beggars among the Turks, where there are countless pious institutions; from motives of religion they even show hospitality to the foes of their religion.—"The Mahometans say, according to Chardin, that after the interrogation which will follow the general resurrection, all bodies will traverse a bridge called Poul-Serrho, which is thrown across the eternal fires, a bridge which may be called the third and last test of the great Judgment, because it is there that the good and bad will be separated, etc.—"The Persians, continues Chardin, make a great point of this bridge; and when any one suffers a wrong which he can never hope to wipe out by any means or at any time, he finds his last consolation in these words: 'By the living God, you will pay me double at the last day; you will never get across the Poul-Serrho if you do not first do me justice; I will hold the hem of your garment, I will cling about your knees.' I have seen many eminent men, of every profession, who for fear lest this hue and cry should be raised against them as they cross that fearful bridge, beg pardon of those who complained against them; it has happened to me myself on many occasions. Men of rank, who had compelled me by their importunity to do what I did not wish to do, have come to me when they thought my anger had had time to cool, and have said to me; I pray you "Halal becon antchisra," that is, "Make this matter lawful and right." Some of them have even sent gifts and done me service, so that I might forgive them and say I did it willingly; the cause of this is nothing else but this belief that they will not be able to get across the bridge of hell until they have paid the uttermost farthing to the oppressed."—Must I think that the idea of this bridge where so many iniquities are made good is of no avail? If the Persians were deprived of this idea, if they were persuaded that there was no Poul-Serrho, nor anything of the kind, where the oppressed were avenged of their tyrants after death, is it not clear that they would be very much at their ease, and they would be freed from the care of appeasing the wretched? But it is false to say that this doctrine is hurtful; yet it would not be true.—O Philosopher, your moral laws are all very fine; but kindly show me their sanction. Cease to shirk the question, and tell me plainly what you would put in the place of Poul-Serrho.

"My good youth, be honest and humble; learn how to be ignorant, then you will never deceive yourself or others. If ever your talents are so far cultivated as to enable you to speak to other men, always speak according to your conscience, without oaring for their applause. The abuse of knowledge causes incredulity. The learned always despise the opinions of the crowd; each of them must have his own opinion. A haughty philosophy leads to atheism just as blind devotion leads to fanaticism. Avoid these extremes; keep steadfastly to the path of truth, or what seems to you truth, in simplicity of heart, and never let yourself be turned aside by pride or weakness. Dare to confess God before the philosophers; dare to preach humanity to the intolerant. It may be you will stand alone, but you will bear within you a witness which will make the witness of men of no account with you. Let them love or hate, let them read your writings or despise them; no matter. Speak the truth and do the right; the one thing that really matters is to do one's duty in this world; and when we forget ourselves we are really working for ourselves. My child, self-interest misleads us; the hope of the just is the only sure guide."

I have transcribed this document not as a rule for the sentiments we should adopt in matters of religion, but as an example of the way in which we may reason with our pupil without forsaking the method I have tried to establish. So long as we yield nothing to human authority, nor to the prejudices of our native land, the light of reason alone, in a state of nature, can lead us no further than to natural religion; and this is as far as I should go with Emile. If he must have any other religion, I have no right to be his guide; he must choose for himself.

We are working in agreement with nature, and while she is shaping the physical man, we are striving to shape his moral being, but we do not make the same progress. The body is already strong and vigorous, the soul is still frail and delicate, and whatever can be done by human art, the body is always ahead of the mind. Hitherto all our care has been devoted to restrain the one and stimulate the other, so that the man might be as far as possible at one with himself. By developing his individuality, we have kept his growing susceptibilities in check; we have controlled it by cultivating his reason. Objects of thought moderate the influence of objects of sense. By going back to the causes of things, we have withdrawn him from the sway of the senses; it is an easy thing to raise him from the study of nature to the search for the author of nature.

When we have reached this point, what a fresh hold we have got over our pupil; what fresh ways of speaking to his heart! Then alone does he find a real motive for being good, for doing right when he is far from every human eye, and when he is not driven to it by law. To be just in his own eyes and in the sight of God, to do his duty, even at the cost of life itself, and to bear in his heart virtue, not only for the love of order which we all subordinate to the love of self, but for the love of the Author of his being, a love which mingles with that self-love, so that he may at length enjoy the lasting happiness which the peace of a good conscience and the contemplation of that supreme being promise him in another life, after he has used this life aright. Go beyond this, and I see nothing but injustice, hypocrisy, and falsehood among men; private interest, which in competition necessarily prevails over everything else, teaches all things to adorn vice with the outward show of virtue. Let all men do what is good for me at the cost of what is good for themselves; let everything depend on me alone; let the whole human race perish, if needs be, in suffering and want, to spare me a moment's pain or hunger. Yes, I shall always maintain that whoso says in his heart, "There is no God," while he takes the name of God upon his lips, is either a liar or a madman.

Reader, it is all in vain; I perceive that you and I shall never see Emile with the same eyes; you will always fancy him like your own young people, hasty, impetuous, flighty, wandering from fete to fete, from amusement to amusement, never able to settle to anything. You smile when I expect to make a thinker, a philosopher, a young theologian, of an ardent, lively, eager, and fiery young man, at the most impulsive period of youth. This dreamer, you say, is always in pursuit of his fancy; when he gives us a pupil of his own making, he does not merely form him, he creates him, he makes him up out of his own head; and while he thinks he is treading in the steps of nature, he is getting further and further from her. As for me, when I compare my pupil with yours, I can scarcely find anything in common between them. So differently brought up, it is almost a miracle if they are alike in any respect. As his childhood was passed in the freedom they assume in youth, in his youth he begins to bear the yoke they bore as children; this yoke becomes hateful to them, they are sick of it, and they see in it nothing but their masters' tyranny; when they escape from childhood, they think they must shake off all control, they make up for the prolonged restraint imposed upon them, as a prisoner, freed from his fetters, moves and stretches and shakes his limbs. [Footnote: There is no one who looks down upon childhood with such lofty scorn as those who are barely grown-up; just as there is no country where rank is more strictly regarded than that where there is little real inequality; everybody is afraid of being confounded with his inferiors.] Emile, however, is proud to be a man, and to submit to the yoke of his growing reason; his body, already well grown, no longer needs so much action, and begins to control itself, while his half-fledged mind tries its wings on every occasion. Thus the age of reason becomes for the one the age of licence; for the other, the age of reasoning.

Would you know which of the two is nearer to the order of nature! Consider the differences between those who are more or less removed from a state of nature. Observe young villagers and see if they are as undisciplined as your scholars. The Sieur de Beau says that savages in childhood are always active, and ever busy with sports that keep the body in motion; but scarcely do they reach adolescence than they become quiet and dreamy; they no longer devote themselves to games of skill or chance. Emile, who has been brought up in full freedom like young peasants and savages, should behave like them and change as he grows up. The whole difference is in this, that instead of merely being active in sport or for food, he has, in the course of his sports, learned to think. Having reached this stage, and by this road, he is quite ready to enter upon the next stage to which I introduce him; the subjects I suggest for his consideration rouse his curiosity, because they are fine in themselves, because they are quite new to him, and because he is able to understand them. Your young people, on the other hand, are weary and overdone with your stupid lessons, your long sermons, and your tedious catechisms; why should they not refuse to devote their minds to what has made them sad, to the burdensome precepts which have been continually piled upon them, to the thought of the Author of their being, who has been represented as the enemy of their pleasures? All this has only inspired in them aversion, disgust, and weariness; constraint has set them against it; why then should they devote themselves to it when they are beginning to choose for themselves? They require novelty, you must not repeat what they learned as children. Just so with my own pupil, when he is a man I speak to him as a man, and only tell him what is new to him; it is just because they are tedious to your pupils that he will find them to his taste.

This is how I doubly gain time for him by retarding nature to the advantage of reason. But have I indeed retarded the progress of nature? No, I have only prevented the imagination from hastening it; I have employed another sort of teaching to counterbalance the precocious instruction which the young man receives from other sources. When he is carried away by the flood of existing customs and I draw him in the opposite direction by means of other customs, this is not to remove him from his place, but to keep him in it.

Nature's due time comes at length, as come it must. Since man must die, he must reproduce himself, so that the species may endure and the order of the world continue. When by the signs I have spoken of you perceive that the critical moment is at hand, at once abandon for ever your former tone. He is still your disciple, but not your scholar. He is a man and your friend; henceforth you must treat him as such.

What! Must I abdicate my authority when most I need it? Must I abandon the adult to himself just when he least knows how to control himself, when he may fall into the gravest errors! Must I renounce my rights when it matters most that I should use them on his behalf? Who bids you renounce them; he is only just becoming conscious of them. Hitherto all you have gained has been won by force or guile; authority, the law of duty, were unknown to him, you had to constrain or deceive him to gain his obedience. But see what fresh chains you have bound about his heart. Reason, friendship, affection, gratitude, a thousand bonds of affection, speak to him in a voice he cannot fail to hear. His ears are not yet dulled by vice, he is still sensitive only to the passions of nature. Self-love, the first of these, delivers him into your hands; habit confirms this. If a passing transport tears him from you, regret restores him to you without delay; the sentiment which attaches him to you is the only lasting sentiment, all the rest are fleeting and self-effacing. Do not let him become corrupt, and he will always be docile; he will not begin to rebel till he is already perverted.

I grant you, indeed, that if you directly oppose his growing desires and foolishly treat as crimes the fresh needs which are beginning to make themselves felt in him, he will not listen to you for long; but as soon as you abandon my method I cannot be answerable for the consequences. Remember that you are nature's minister; you will never be her foe.

But what shall we decide to do? You see no alternative but either to favour his inclinations or to resist them; to tyrannise or to wink at his misconduct; and both of these may lead to such dangerous results that one must indeed hesitate between them.

The first way out of the difficulty is a very early marriage; this is undoubtedly the safest and most natural plan. I doubt, however, whether it is the best or the most useful. I will give my reasons later; meanwhile I admit that young men should marry when they reach a marriageable age. But this age comes too soon; we have made them precocious; marriage should be postponed to maturity.

If it were merely a case of listening to their wishes and following their lead it would be an easy matter; but there are so many contradictions between the rights of nature and the laws of society that to conciliate them we must continually contradict ourselves. Much art is required to prevent man in society from being altogether artificial.

For the reasons just stated, I consider that by the means I have indicated and others like them the young man's desires may be kept in ignorance and his senses pure up to the age of twenty. This is so true that among the Germans a young man who lost his virginity before that age was considered dishonoured; and the writers justly attribute the vigour of constitution and the number of children among the Germans to the continence of these nations during youth.

This period may be prolonged still further, and a few centuries ago nothing was more common even in France. Among other well-known examples, Montaigne's father, a man no less scrupulously truthful than strong and healthy, swore that his was a virgin marriage at three and thirty, and he had served for a long time in the Italian wars. We may see in the writings of his son what strength and spirit were shown by the father when he was over sixty. Certainly the contrary opinion depends rather on our own morals and our own prejudices than on the experience of the race as a whole.

I may, therefore, leave on one side the experience of our young people; it proves nothing for those who have been educated in another fashion. Considering that nature has fixed no exact limits which cannot be advanced or postponed, I think I may, without going beyond the law of nature, assume that under my care Emil has so far remained in his first innocence, but I see that this happy period is drawing to a close. Surrounded by ever-increasing perils, he will escape me at the first opportunity in spite of all my efforts, and this opportunity will not long be delayed; he will follow the blind instinct of his senses; the chances are a thousand to one on his ruin. I have considered the morals of mankind too profoundly not to be aware of the irrevocable influence of this first moment on all the rest of his life. If I dissimulate and pretend to see nothing, he will take advantage of my weakness; if he thinks he can deceive me, he will despise me, and I become an accomplice in his destruction. If I try to recall him, the time is past, he no longer heeds me, he finds me tiresome, hateful, intolerable; it will not be long before he is rid of me. There is therefore only one reasonable course open to me; I must make him accountable for his own actions, I must at least preserve him from being taken unawares, and I must show him plainly the dangers which beset his path. I have restrained him so far through his ignorance; henceforward his restraint must be his own knowledge.

This new teaching is of great importance, and we will take up our story where we left it. This is the time to present my accounts, to show him how his time and mine have been spent, to make known to him what he is and what I am; what I have done, and what he has done; what we owe to each other; all his moral relations, all the undertakings to which he is pledged, all those to which others have pledged themselves in respect to him; the stage he has reached in the development of his faculties, the road that remains to be travelled, the difficulties he will meet, and the way to overcome them; how I can still help him and how he must henceforward help himself; in a word, the critical time which he has reached, the new dangers round about him, and all the valid reasons which should induce him to keep a close watch upon himself before giving heed to his growing desires.

Remember that to guide a grown man you must reverse all that you did to guide the child. Do not hesitate to speak to him of those dangerous mysteries which you have so carefully concealed from him hitherto. Since he must become aware of them, let him not learn them from another, nor from himself, but from you alone; since he must henceforth fight against them, let him know his enemy, that he may not be taken unawares.

Young people who are found to be aware of these matters, without our knowing how they obtained their knowledge, have not obtained it with impunity. This unwise teaching, which can have no honourable object, stains the imagination of those who receive it if it does nothing worse, and it inclines them to the vices of their instructors. This is not all; servants, by this means, ingratiate themselves with a child, gain his confidence, make him regard his tutor as a gloomy and tiresome person; and one of the favourite subjects of their secret colloquies is to slander him. When the pupil has got so far, the master may abandon his task; he can do no good.

But why does the child choose special confidants? Because of the tyranny of those who control him. Why should he hide himself from them if he were not driven to it? Why should he complain if he had nothing to complain of? Naturally those who control him are his first confidants; you can see from his eagerness to tell them what he thinks that he feels he has only half thought till he has told his thoughts to them. You may be sure that when the child knows you will neither preach nor scold, he will always tell you everything, and that no one will dare to tell him anything he must conceal from you, for they will know very well that he will tell you everything.

What makes me most confident in my method is this: when I follow it out as closely as possible, I find no situation in the life of my scholar which does not leave me some pleasing memory of him. Even when he is carried away by his ardent temperament or when he revolts against the hand that guides him, when he struggles and is on the point of escaping from me, I still find his first simplicity in his agitation and his anger; his heart as pure as his body, he has no more knowledge of pretence than of vice; reproach and scorn have not made a coward of him; base fears have never taught him the art of concealment. He has all the indiscretion of innocence; he is absolutely out-spoken; he does not even know the use of deceit. Every impulse of his heart is betrayed either by word or look, and I often know what he is feeling before he is aware of it himself.

So long as his heart is thus freely opened to me, so long as he delights to tell me what he feels, I have nothing to fear; the danger is not yet at hand; but if he becomes more timid, more reserved, if I perceive in his conversation the first signs of confusion and shame, his instincts are beginning to develop, he is beginning to connect the idea of evil with these instincts, there is not a moment to lose, and if I do not hasten to instruct him, he will learn in spite of me.

Some of my readers, even of those who agree with me, will think that it is only a question of a conversation with the young man at any time. Oh, this is not the way to control the human heart. What we say has no meaning unless the opportunity has been carefully chosen. Before we sow we must till the ground; the seed of virtue is hard to grow; and a long period of preparation is required before it will take root. One reason why sermons have so little effect is that they are offered to everybody alike, without discrimination or choice. How can any one imagine that the same sermon could be suitable for so many hearers, with their different dispositions, so unlike in mind, temper, age, sex, station, and opinion. Perhaps there are not two among those to whom what is addressed to all is really suitable; and all our affections are so transitory that perhaps there are not even two occasions in the life of any man when the same speech would have the same effect on him. Judge for yourself whether the time when the eager senses disturb the understanding and tyrannise over the will, is the time to listen to the solemn lessons of wisdom. Therefore never reason with young men, even when they have reached the age of reason, unless you have first prepared the way. Most lectures miss their mark more through the master's fault than the disciple's. The pedant and the teacher say much the same; but the former says it at random, and the latter only when he is sure of its effect.

As a somnambulist, wandering in his sleep, walks along the edge of a precipice, over which he would fall if he were awake, so my Emile, in the sleep of ignorance, escapes the perils which he does not see; were I to wake him with a start, he might fall. Let us first try to withdraw him from the edge of the precipice, and then we will awake him to show him it from a distance.

Reading, solitude, idleness, a soft and sedentary life, intercourse with women and young people, these are perilous paths for a young man, and these lead him constantly into danger. I divert his senses by other objects of sense; I trace another course for his spirits by which I distract them from the course they would have taken; it is by bodily exercise and hard work that I check the activity of the imagination, which was leading him astray. When the arms are hard at work, the imagination is quiet; when the body is very weary, the passions are not easily inflamed. The quickest and easiest precaution is to remove him from immediate danger. At once I take him away from towns, away from things which might lead him into temptation. But that is not enough; in what desert, in what wilds, shall he escape from the thoughts which pursue him? It is not enough to remove dangerous objects; if I fail to remove the memory of them, if I fail to find a way to detach him from everything, if I fail to distract him from himself, I might as well have left him where he was.

Emile has learned a trade, but we do not have recourse to it; he is fond of farming and understands it, but farming is not enough; the occupations he is acquainted with degenerate into routine; when he is engaged in them he is not really occupied; he is thinking of other things; head and hand are at work on different subjects. He must have some fresh occupation which has the interest of novelty—an occupation which keeps him busy, diligent, and hard at work, an occupation which he may become passionately fond of, one to which he will devote himself entirely. Now the only one which seems to possess all these characteristics is the chase. If hunting is ever an innocent pleasure, if it is ever worthy of a man, now is the time to betake ourselves to it. Emile is well-fitted to succeed in it. He is strong, skilful, patient, unwearied. He is sure to take a fancy to this sport; he will bring to it all the ardour of youth; in it he will lose, at least for a time, the dangerous inclinations which spring from softness. The chase hardens the heart a well as the body; we get used to the sight of blood and cruelty. Diana is represented as the enemy of love; and the allegory is true to life; the languors of love are born of soft repose, and tender feelings are stifled by violent exercise. In the woods and fields, the lover and the sportsman are so diversely affected that they receive very different impressions. The fresh shade, the arbours, the pleasant resting-places of the one, to the other are but feeding grounds, or places where the quarry will hide or turn to bay. Where the lover hears the flute and the nightingale, the hunter hears the horn and the hounds; one pictures to himself the nymphs and dryads, the other sees the horses, the huntsman, and the pack. Take a country walk with one or other of these men; their different conversation will soon show you that they behold the earth with other eyes, and that the direction of their thoughts is as different as their favourite pursuit.

I understand how these tastes may be combined, and that at last men find time for both. But the passions of youth cannot be divided in this way. Give the youth a single occupation which he loves, and the rest will soon be forgotten. Varied desires come with varied knowledge, and the first pleasures we know are the only ones we desire for long enough. I would not have the whole of Emile's youth spent in killing creatures, and I do not even profess to justify this cruel passion; it is enough for me that it serves to delay a more dangerous passion, so that he may listen to me calmly when I speak of it, and give me time to describe it without stimulating it.

There are moments in human life which can never be forgotten. Such is the time when Emile receives the instruction of which I have spoken; its influence should endure all his life through. Let us try to engrave it on his memory so that it may never fade away. It is one of the faults of our age to rely too much on cold reason, as if men were all mind. By neglecting the language of expression we have lost the most forcible mode of speech. The spoken word is always weak, and we speak to the heart rather through the eyes than the ears. In our attempt to appeal to reason only, we have reduced our precepts to words, we have not embodied them in deed. Mere reason is not active; occasionally she restrains, more rarely she stimulates, but she never does any great thing. Small minds have a mania for reasoning. Strong souls speak a very different language, and it is by this language that men are persuaded and driven to action.

I observe that in modern times men only get a hold over others by force or self-interest, while the ancients did more by persuasion, by the affections of the heart; because they did not neglect the language; of symbolic expression.

All agreements were drawn up solemnly, so that they might be more inviolable; before the reign of force, the gods were the judges of mankind; in their presence, individuals made their treaties and alliances, and pledged themselves to perform their promises; the face of the earth was the book in which the archives were preserved. The leaves of this book were rocks, trees, piles of stones, made sacred by these transactions, and regarded with reverence by barbarous men; and these pages were always open before their eyes. The well of the oath, the well of the living and seeing one; the ancient oak of Mamre, the stones of witness, such were the simple but stately monuments of the sanctity of contracts; none dared to lay a sacrilegious hand on these monuments, and man's faith was more secure under the warrant of these dumb witnesses than it is to-day upon all the rigour of the law.

In government the people were over-awed by the pomp and splendour of royal power. The symbols of greatness, a throne, a sceptre, a purple robe, a crown, a fillet, these were sacred in their sight. These symbols, and the respect which they inspired, led them to reverence the venerable man whom they beheld adorned with them; without soldiers and without threats, he spoke and was obeyed. [Footnote: The Roman Catholic clergy have very wisely retained these symbols, and certain republics, such as Venice, have followed their example. Thus the Venetian government, despite the fallen condition of the state, still enjoys, under the trappings of its former greatness, all the affection, all the reverence of the people; and next to the pope in his triple crown, there is perhaps no king, no potentate, no person in the world so much respected as the Doge of Venice; he has no power, no authority, but he is rendered sacred by his pomp, and he wears beneath his ducal coronet a woman's flowing locks. That ceremony of the Bucentaurius, which stirs the laughter of fools, stirs the Venetian populace to shed its life-blood for the maintenance of this tyrannical government.] In our own day men profess to do away with these symbols. What are the consequences of this contempt? The kingly majesty makes no impression on all hearts, kings can only gain obedience by the help of troops, and the respect of their subjects is based only on the fear of punishment. Kings are spared the trouble of wearing their crowns, and our nobles escape from the outward signs of their station, but they must have a hundred thousand men at their command if their orders are to be obeyed. Though this may seem a finer thing, it is easy to see that in the long run they will gain nothing.

It is amazing what the ancients accomplished with the aid of eloquence; but this eloquence did not merely consist in fine speeches carefully prepared; and it was most effective when the orator said least. The most startling speeches were expressed not in words but in signs; they were not uttered but shown. A thing beheld by the eyes kindles the imagination, stirs the curiosity, and keeps the mind on the alert for what we are about to say, and often enough the thing tells the whole story. Thrasybulus and Tarquin cutting off the heads of the poppies, Alexander placing his seal on the lips of his favourite, Diogenes marching before Zeno, do not these speak more plainly than if they had uttered long orations? What flow of words could have expressed the ideas as clearly? Darius, in the course of the Scythian war, received from the king of the Scythians a bird, a frog, a mouse, and five arrows. The ambassador deposited this gift and retired without a word. In our days he would have been taken for a madman. This terrible speech was understood, and Darius withdrew to his own country with what speed he could. Substitute a letter for these symbols and the more threatening it was the less terror it would inspire; it would have been merely a piece of bluff, to which Darius would have paid no attention.

What heed the Romans gave to the language of signs! Different ages and different ranks had their appropriate garments, toga, tunic, patrician robes, fringes and borders, seats of honour, lictors, rods and axes, crowns of gold, crowns of leaves, crowns of flowers, ovations, triumphs, everything had its pomp, its observances, its ceremonial, and all these spoke to the heart of the citizens. The state regarded it as a matter of importance that the populace should assemble in one place rather than another, that they should or should not behold the Capitol, that they should or should not turn towards the Senate, that this day or that should be chosen for their deliberations. The accused wore a special dress, so did the candidates for election; warriors did not boast of their exploits, they showed their scars. I can fancy one of our orators at the death of Caesar exhausting all the commonplaces of rhetoric to give a pathetic description of his wounds, his blood, his dead body; Anthony was an orator, but he said none of this; he showed the murdered Caesar. What rhetoric was this!

But this digression, like many others, is drawing me unawares away from my subject; and my digressions are too frequent to be borne with patience. I therefore return to the point.

Do not reason coldly with youth. Clothe your reason with a body, if you would make it felt. Let the mind speak the language of the heart, that it may be understood. I say again our opinions, not our actions, may be influenced by cold argument; they set us thinking, not doing; they show us what we ought to think, not what we ought to do. If this is true of men, it is all the truer of young people who are still enwrapped in their senses and cannot think otherwise than they imagine.

Even after the preparations of which I have spoken, I shall take good care not to go all of a sudden to Emile's room and preach a long and heavy sermon on the subject in which he is to be instructed. I shall begin by rousing his imagination; I shall choose the time, place, and surroundings most favourable to the impression I wish to make; I shall, so to speak, summon all nature as witness to our conversations; I shall call upon the eternal God, the Creator of nature, to bear witness to the truth of what I say. He shall judge between Emile and myself; I will make the rocks, the woods, the mountains round about us, the monuments of his promises and mine; eyes, voice, and gesture shall show the enthusiasm I desire to inspire. Then I will speak and he will listen, and his emotion will be stirred by my own. The more impressed I am by the sanctity of my duties, the more sacred he will regard his own. I will enforce the voice of reason with images and figures, I will not give him long-winded speeches or cold precepts, but my overflowing feelings will break their bounds; my reason shall be grave and serious, but my heart cannot speak too warmly. Then when I have shown him all that I have done for him, I will show him how he is made for me; he will see in my tender affection the cause of all my care. How greatly shall I surprise and disturb him when I change my tone. Instead of shrivelling up his soul by always talking of his own interests, I shall henceforth speak of my own; he will be more deeply touched by this. I will kindle in his young heart all the sentiments of affection, generosity, and gratitude which I have already called into being, and it will indeed be sweet to watch their growth. I will press him to my bosom, and weep over him in my emotion; I will say to him: "You are my wealth, my child, my handiwork; my happiness is bound up in yours; if you frustrate my hopes, you rob me of twenty years of my life, and you bring my grey hairs with sorrow to the grave." This is the way to gain a hearing and to impress what is said upon the heart and memory of the young man.

Hitherto I have tried to give examples of the way in which a tutor should instruct his pupil in cases of difficulty. I have tried to do so in this instance; but after many attempts I have abandoned the task, convinced that the French language is too artificial to permit in print the plainness of speech required for the first lessons in certain subjects.

They say French is more chaste than other languages; for my own part I think it more obscene; for it seems to me that the purity of a language does not consist in avoiding coarse expressions but in having none. Indeed, if we are to avoid them, they must be in our thoughts, and there is no language in which it is so difficult to speak with purity on every subject than French. The reader is always quicker to detect than the author to avoid a gross meaning, and he is shocked and startled by everything. How can what is heard by impure ears avoid coarseness? On the other hand, a nation whose morals are pure has fit terms for everything, and these terms are always right because they are rightly used. One could not imagine more modest language than that of the Bible, just because of its plainness of speech. The same things translated into French would become immodest. What I ought to say to Emile will sound pure and honourable to him; but to make the same impression in print would demand a like purity of heart in the reader.

I should even think that reflections on true purity of speech and the sham delicacy of vice might find a useful place in the conversations as to morality to which this subject brings us; for when he learns the language of plain-spoken goodness, he must also learn the language of decency, and he must know why the two are so different. However this may be, I maintain that if instead of the empty precepts which are prematurely dinned into the ears of children, only to be scoffed at when the time comes when they might prove useful, if instead of this we bide our time, if we prepare the way for a hearing, if we then show him the laws of nature in all their truth, if we show him the sanction of these laws in the physical and moral evils which overtake those who neglect them, if while we speak to him of this great mystery of generation, we join to the idea of the pleasure which the Author of nature has given to this act the idea of the exclusive affection which makes it delightful, the idea of the duties of faithfulness and modesty which surround it, and redouble its charm while fulfilling its purpose; if we paint to him marriage, not only as the sweetest form of society, but also as the most sacred and inviolable of contracts, if we tell him plainly all the reasons which lead men to respect this sacred bond, and to pour hatred and curses upon him who dares to dishonour it; if we give him a true and terrible picture of the horrors of debauch, of its stupid brutality, of the downward road by which a first act of misconduct leads from bad to worse, and at last drags the sinner to his ruin; if, I say, we give him proofs that on a desire for chastity depends health, strength, courage, virtue, love itself, and all that is truly good for man—I maintain that this chastity will be so dear and so desirable in his eyes, that his mind will be ready to receive our teaching as to the way to preserve it; for so long as we are chaste we respect chastity; it is only when we have lost this virtue that we scorn it.

It is not true that the inclination to evil is beyond our control, and that we cannot overcome it until we have acquired the habit of yielding to it. Aurelius Victor says that many men were mad enough to purchase a night with Cleopatra at the price of their life, and this is not incredible in the madness of passion. But let us suppose the maddest of men, the man who has his senses least under control; let him see the preparations for his death, let him realise that he will certainly die in torment a quarter of an hour later; not only would that man, from that time forward, become able to resist temptation, he would even find it easy to do so; the terrible picture with which they are associated will soon distract his attention from these temptations, and when they are continually put aside they will cease to recur. The sole cause of our weakness is the feebleness of our will, and we have always strength to perform what we strongly desire. "Volenti nihil difficile!" Oh! if only we hated vice as much as we love life, we should abstain as easily from a pleasant sin as from a deadly poison in a delicious dish.

How is it that you fail to perceive that if all the lessons given to a young man on this subject have no effect, it is because they are not adapted to his age, and that at every age reason must be presented in a shape which will win his affection? Speak seriously to him if required, but let what you say to him always have a charm which will compel him to listen. Do not coldly oppose his wishes; do not stifle his imagination, but direct it lest it should bring forth monsters. Speak to him of love, of women, of pleasure; let him find in your conversation a charm which delights his youthful heart; spare no pains to make yourself his confidant; under this name alone will you really be his master. Then you need not fear he will find your conversation tedious; he will make you talk more than you desire.

If I have managed to take all the requisite precautions in accordance with these maxims, and have said the right things to Emile at the age he has now reached, I am quite convinced that he will come of his own accord to the point to which I would lead him, and will eagerly confide himself to my care. When he sees the dangers by which he is surrounded, he will say to me with all the warmth of youth, "Oh, my friend, my protector, my master! resume the authority you desire to lay aside at the very time when I most need it; hitherto my weakness has given you this power. I now place it in your hands of my own free-will, and it will be all the more sacred in my eyes. Protect me from all the foes which are attacking me, and above all from the traitors within the citadel; watch over your work, that it may still be worthy of you. I mean to obey your laws, I shall ever do so, that is my steadfast purpose; if I ever disobey you, it will be against my will; make me free by guarding me against the passions which do me violence; do not let me become their slave; compel me to be my own master and to obey, not my senses, but my reason."

When you have led your pupil so far (and it will be your own fault if you fail to do so), beware of taking him too readily at his word, lest your rule should seem too strict to him, and lest he should think he has a right to escape from it, by accusing you of taking him by surprise. This is the time for reserve and seriousness; and this attitude will have all the more effect upon him seeing that it is the first time you have adopted it towards him.

You will say to him therefore: "Young man, you readily make promises which are hard to keep; you must understand what they mean before you have a right to make them; you do not know how your fellows are drawn by their passions into the whirlpool of vice masquerading as pleasure. You are honourable, I know; you will never break your word, but how often will you repent of having given it? How often will you curse your friend, when, in order to guard you from the ills which threaten you, he finds himself compelled to do violence to your heart. Like Ulysses who, hearing the song of the Sirens, cried aloud to his rowers to unbind him, you will break your chains at the call of pleasure; you will importune me with your lamentations, you will reproach me as a tyrant when I have your welfare most at heart; when I am trying to make you happy, I shall incur your hatred. Oh, Emile, I can never bear to be hateful in your eyes; this is too heavy a price to pay even for your happiness. My dear young man, do you not see that when you undertake to obey me, you compel me to promise to be your guide, to forget myself in my devotion to you, to refuse to listen to your murmurs and complaints, to wage unceasing war against your wishes and my own. Before we either of us undertake such a task, let us count our resources; take your time, give me time to consider, and be sure that the slower we are to promise, the more faithfully will our promises be kept."

You may be sure that the more difficulty he finds in getting your promise, the easier you will find it to carry it out. The young man must learn that he is promising a great deal, and that you are promising still more. When the time is come, when he has, so to say, signed the contract, then change your tone, and make your rule as gentle as you said it would be severe. Say to him, "My young friend, it is experience that you lack; but I have taken care that you do not lack reason. You are ready to see the motives of my conduct in every respect; to do this you need only wait till you are free from excitement. Always obey me first, and then ask the reasons for my commands; I am always ready to give my reasons so soon as you are ready to listen to them, and I shall never be afraid to make you the judge between us. You promise to follow my teaching, and I promise only to use your obedience to make you the happiest of men. For proof of this I have the life you have lived hitherto. Show me any one of your age who has led as happy a life as yours, and I promise you nothing more."

When my authority is firmly established, my first care will be to avoid the necessity of using it. I shall spare no pains to become more and more firmly established in his confidence, to make myself the confidant of his heart and the arbiter of his pleasures. Far from combating his youthful tastes, I shall consult them that I may be their master; I will look at things from his point of view that I may be his guide; I will not seek a remote distant good at the cost of his present happiness. I would always have him happy always if that may be.

Those who desire to guide young people rightly and to preserve them from the snares of sense give them a disgust for love, and would willingly make the very thought of it a crime, as if love were for the old. All these mistaken lessons have no effect; the heart gives the lie to them. The young man, guided by a surer instinct, laughs to himself over the gloomy maxims which he pretends to accept, and only awaits the chance of disregarding them. All that is contrary to nature. By following the opposite course I reach the same end more safely. I am not afraid to encourage in him the tender feeling for which he is so eager, I shall paint it as the supreme joy of life, as indeed it is; when I picture it to him, I desire that he shall give himself up to it; by making him feel the charm which the union of hearts adds to the delights of sense, I shall inspire him with a disgust for debauchery; I shall make him a lover and a good man.

How narrow-minded to see nothing in the rising desires of a young heart but obstacles to the teaching of reason. In my eyes, these are the right means to make him obedient to that very teaching. Only through passion can we gain the mastery over passions; their tyranny must be controlled by their legitimate power, and nature herself must furnish us with the means to control her.

Emile is not made to live alone, he is a member of society, and must fulfil his duties as such. He is made to live among his fellow-men and he must get to know them. He knows mankind in general; he has still to learn to know individual men. He knows what goes on in the world; he has now to learn how men live in the world. It is time to show him the front of that vast stage, of which he already knows the hidden workings. It will not arouse in him the foolish admiration of a giddy youth, but the discrimination of an exact and upright spirit. He may no doubt be deceived by his passions; who is there who yields to his passions without being led astray by them? At least he will not be deceived by the passions of other people. If he sees them, he will regard them with the eye of the wise, and will neither be led away by their example nor seduced by their prejudices.

As there is a fitting age for the study of the sciences, so there is a fitting age for the study of the ways of the world. Those who learn these too soon, follow them throughout life, without choice or consideration, and although they follow them fairly well they never really know what they are about. But he who studies the ways of the world and sees the reason for them, follows them with more insight, and therefore more exactly and gracefully. Give me a child of twelve who knows nothing at all; at fifteen I will restore him to you knowing as much as those who have been under instruction from infancy; with this difference, that your scholars only know things by heart, while mine knows how to use his knowledge. In the same way plunge a young man of twenty into society; under good guidance, in a year's time, he will be more charming and more truly polite than one brought up in society from childhood. For the former is able to perceive the reasons for all the proceedings relating to age, position, and sex, on which the customs of society depend, and can reduce them to general principles, and apply them to unforeseen emergencies; while the latter, who is guided solely by habit, is at a loss when habit fails him.

Young French ladies are all brought up in convents till they are married. Do they seem to find any difficulty in acquiring the ways which are so new to them, and is it possible to accuse the ladies of Paris of awkward and embarrassed manners or of ignorance of the ways of society, because they have not acquired them in infancy! This is the prejudice of men of the world, who know nothing of more importance than this trifling science, and wrongly imagine that you cannot begin to acquire it too soon.

On the other hand, it is quite true that we must not wait too long. Any one who has spent the whole of his youth far from the great world is all his life long awkward, constrained, out of place; his manners will be heavy and clumsy, no amount of practice will get rid of this, and he will only make himself more ridiculous by trying to do so. There is a time for every kind of teaching and we ought to recognise it, and each has its own dangers to be avoided. At this age there are more dangers than at any other; but I do not expose my pupil to them without safeguards.

When my method succeeds completely in attaining one object, and when in avoiding one difficulty it also provides against another, I then consider that it is a good method, and that I am on the right track. This seems to be the case with regard to the expedient suggested by me in the present case. If I desire to be stern and cold towards my pupil, I shall lose his confidence, and he will soon conceal himself from me. If I wish to be easy and complaisant, to shut my eyes, what good does it do him to be under my care? I only give my authority to his excesses, and relieve his conscience at the expense of my own. If I introduce him into society with no object but to teach him, he will learn more than I want. If I keep him apart from society, what will he have learnt from me? Everything perhaps, except the one art absolutely necessary to a civilised man, the art of living among his fellow-men. If I try to attend to this at a distance, it will be of no avail; he is only concerned with the present. If I am content to supply him with amusement, he will acquire habits of luxury and will learn nothing.

We will have none of this. My plan provides for everything. Your heart, I say to the young man, requires a companion; let us go in search of a fitting one; perhaps we shall not easily find such a one, true worth is always rare, but we will be in no hurry, nor will we be easily discouraged. No doubt there is such a one, and we shall find her at last, or at least we shall find some one like her. With an end so attractive to himself, I introduce him into society. What more need I say? Have I not achieved my purpose?

By describing to him his future mistress, you may imagine whether I shall gain a hearing, whether I shall succeed in making the qualities he ought to love pleasing and dear to him, whether I shall sway his feelings to seek or shun what is good or bad for him. I shall be the stupidest of men if I fail to make him in love with he knows not whom. No matter that the person I describe is imaginary, it is enough to disgust him with those who might have attracted him; it is enough if it is continually suggesting comparisons which make him prefer his fancy to the real people he sees; and is not love itself a fancy, a falsehood, an illusion? We are far more in love with our own fancy than with the object of it. If we saw the object of our affections as it is, there would be no such thing as love. When we cease to love, the person we used to love remains unchanged, but we no longer see with the same eyes; the magic veil is drawn aside, and love disappears. But when I supply the object of imagination, I have control over comparisons, and I am able easily to prevent illusion with regard to realities.

For all that I would not mislead a young man by describing a model of perfection which could never exist; but I would so choose the faults of his mistress that they will suit him, that he will be pleased by them, and they may serve to correct his own. Neither would I lie to him and affirm that there really is such a person; let him delight in the portrait, he will soon desire to find the original. From desire to belief the transition is easy; it is a matter of a little skilful description, which under more perceptible features will give to this imaginary object an air of greater reality. I would go so far as to give her a name; I would say, smiling. Let us call your future mistress Sophy; Sophy is a name of good omen; if it is not the name of the lady of your choice at least she will be worthy of the name; we may honour her with it meanwhile. If after all these details, without affirming or denying, we excuse ourselves from giving an answer, his suspicions will become certainty; he will think that his destined bride is purposely concealed from him, and that he will see her in good time. If once he has arrived at this conclusion and if the characteristics to be shown to him have been well chosen, the rest is easy; there will be little risk in exposing him to the world; protect him from his senses, and his heart is safe.

But whether or no he personifies the model I have contrived to make so attractive to him, this model, if well done, will attach him none the less to everything that resembles itself, and will give him as great a distaste for all that is unlike it as if Sophy really existed. What a means to preserve his heart from the dangers to which his appearance would expose him, to repress his senses by means of his imagination, to rescue him from the hands of those women who profess to educate young men, and make them pay so dear for their teaching, and only teach a young man manners by making him utterly shameless. Sophy is so modest? What would she think of their advances! Sophy is so simple! How would she like their airs? They are too far from his thoughts and his observations to be dangerous.

Every one who deals with the control of children follows the same prejudices and the same maxima, for their observation is at fault, and their reflection still more so. A young man is led astray in the first place neither by temperament nor by the senses, but by popular opinion. If we were concerned with boys brought up in boarding schools or girls in convents, I would show that this applies even to them; for the first lessons they learn from each other, the only lessons that bear fruit, are those of vice; and it is not nature that corrupts them but example. But let us leave the boarders in schools and convents to their bad morals; there is no cure for them. I am dealing only with home training. Take a young man carefully educated in his father's country house, and examine him when he reaches Paris and makes his entrance into society; you will find him thinking clearly about honest matters, and you will find his will as wholesome as his reason. You will find scorn of vice and disgust for debauchery; his face will betray his innocent horror at the very mention of a prostitute. I maintain that no young man could make up his mind to enter the gloomy abodes of these unfortunates by himself, if indeed he were aware of their purpose and felt their necessity.

See the same young man six months later, you will not know him; from his bold conversation, his fashionable maxims, his easy air, you would take him for another man, if his jests over his former simplicity and his shame when any one recalls it did not show that it is he indeed and that he is ashamed of himself. How greatly has he changed in so short a time! What has brought about so sudden and complete a change? His physical development? Would not that have taken place in his father's house, and certainly he would not have acquired these maxims and this tone at home? The first charms of sense? On the contrary; those who are beginning to abandon themselves to these pleasures are timid and anxious, they shun the light and noise. The first pleasures are always mysterious, modesty gives them their savour, and modesty conceals them; the first mistress does not make a man bold but timid. Wholly absorbed in a situation so novel to him, the young man retires into himself to enjoy it, and trembles for fear it should escape him. If he is noisy he knows neither passion nor love; however he may boast, he has not enjoyed.

These changes are merely the result of changed ideas. His heart is the same, but his opinions have altered. His feelings, which change more slowly, will at length yield to his opinions and it is then that he is indeed corrupted. He has scarcely made his entrance into society before he receives a second education quite unlike the first, which teaches him to despise what he esteemed, and esteem what he despised; he learns to consider the teaching of his parents and masters as the jargon of pedants, and the duties they have instilled into him as a childish morality, to be scorned now that he is grown up. He thinks he is bound in honour to change his conduct; he becomes forward without desire, and he talks foolishly from false shame. He rails against morality before he has any taste for vice, and prides himself on debauchery without knowing how to set about it. I shall never forget the confession of a young officer in the Swiss Guards, who was utterly sick of the noisy pleasures of his comrades, but dared not refuse to take part in them lest he should be laughed at. "I am getting used to it," he said, "as I am getting used to taking snuff; the taste will come with practice; it will not do to be a child for ever."

So a young man when he enters society must be preserved from vanity rather than from sensibility; he succumbs rather to the tastes of others than to his own, and self-love is responsible for more libertines than love.

This being granted, I ask you. Is there any one on earth better armed than my pupil against all that may attack his morals, his sentiments, his principles; is there any one more able to resist the flood? What seduction is there against which he is not forearmed? If his desires attract him towards women, he fails to find what he seeks, and his heart, already occupied, holds him back. If he is disturbed and urged onward by his senses, where will he find satisfaction? His horror of adultery and debauch keeps him at a distance from prostitutes and married women, and the disorders of youth may always be traced to one or other of these. A maiden may be a coquette, but she will not be shameless, she will not fling herself at the head of a young man who may marry her if he believes in her virtue; besides she is always under supervision. Emile, too, will not be left entirely to himself; both of them will be under the guardianship of fear and shame, the constant companions of a first passion; they will not proceed at once to misconduct, and they will not have time to come to it gradually without hindrance. If he behaves otherwise, he must have taken lessons from his comrades, he must have learned from them to despise his self-control, and to imitate their boldness. But there is no one in the whole world so little given to imitation as Emile. What man is there who is so little influenced by mockery as one who has no prejudices himself and yields nothing to the prejudices of others. I have laboured twenty years to arm him against mockery; they will not make him their dupe in a day; for in his eyes ridicule is the argument of fools, and nothing makes one less susceptible to raillery than to be beyond the influence of prejudice. Instead of jests he must have arguments, and while he is in this frame of mind, I am not afraid that he will be carried away by young fools; conscience and truth are on my side. If prejudice is to enter into the matter at all, an affection of twenty years' standing counts for something; no one will ever convince him that I have wearied him with vain lessons; and in a heart so upright and so sensitive the voice of a tried and trusted friend will soon efface the shouts of twenty libertines. As it is therefore merely a question of showing him that he is deceived, that while they pretend to treat him as a man they are really treating him as a child, I shall choose to be always simple but serious and plain in my arguments, so that he may feel that I do indeed treat him as a man. I will say to him, You will see that your welfare, in which my own is bound up, compels me to speak; I can do nothing else. But why do these young men want to persuade you? Because they desire to seduce you; they do not care for you, they take no real interest in you; their only motive is a secret spite because they see you are better than they; they want to drag you down to their own level, and they only reproach you with submitting to control that they may themselves control you. Do you think you have anything to gain by this? Are they so much wiser than I, is the affection of a day stronger than mine? To give any weight to their jests they must give weight to their authority; and by what experience do they support their maxima above ours? They have only followed the example of other giddy youths, as they would have you follow theirs. To escape from the so-called prejudices of their fathers, they yield to those of their comrades. I cannot see that they are any the better off; but I see that they lose two things of value—the affection of their parents, whose advice is that of tenderness and truth, and the wisdom of experience which teaches us to judge by what we know; for their fathers have once been young, but the young men have never been fathers.

But you think they are at least sincere in their foolish precepts. Not so, dear Emile; they deceive themselves in order to deceive you; they are not in agreement with themselves; their heart continually revolts, and their very words often contradict themselves. This man who mocks at everything good would be in despair if his wife held the same views. Another extends his indifference to good morals even to his future wife, or he sinks to such depths of infamy as to be indifferent to his wife's conduct; but go a step further; speak to him of his mother; is he willing to be treated as the child of an adulteress and the son of a woman of bad character, is he ready to assume the name of a family, to steal the patrimony of the true heir, in a word will he bear being treated as a bastard? Which of them will permit his daughter to be dishonoured as he dishonours the daughter of another? There is not one of them who would not kill you if you adopted in your conduct towards him all the principles he tries to teach you. Thus they prove their inconsistency, and we know they do not believe what they say. Here are reasons, dear Emile; weigh their arguments if they have any, and compare them with mine. If I wished to have recourse like them to scorn and mockery, you would see that they lend themselves to ridicule as much or more than myself. But I am not afraid of serious inquiry. The triumph of mockers is soon over; truth endures, and their foolish laughter dies away.

You do not think that Emile, at twenty, can possibly be docile. How differently we think! I cannot understand how he could be docile at ten, for what hold have I on him at that age? It took me fifteen years of careful preparation to secure that hold. I was not educating him, but preparing him for education. He is now sufficiently educated to be docile; he recognises the voice of friendship and he knows how to obey reason. It is true I allow him a show of freedom, but he was never more completely under control, because he obeys of his own free will. So long as I could not get the mastery over his will, I retained my control over his person; I never left him for a moment. Now I sometimes leave him to himself because I control him continually. When I leave him I embrace him and I say with confidence: Emile, I trust you to my friend, I leave you to his honour; he will answer for you.

To corrupt healthy affections which have not been previously depraved, to efface principles which are directly derived from our own reasoning, is not the work of a moment. If any change takes place during my absence, that absence will not be long, he will never be able to conceal himself from me, so that I shall perceive the danger before any harm comes of it, and I shall be in time to provide a remedy. As we do not become depraved all at once, neither do we learn to deceive all at once; and if ever there was a man unskilled in the art of deception it is Emile, who has never had any occasion for deceit.

By means of these precautions and others like them, I expect to guard him so completely against strange sights and vulgar precepts that I would rather see him in the worst company in Paris than alone in his room or in a park left to all the restlessness of his age. Whatever we may do, a young man's worst enemy is himself, and this is an enemy we cannot avoid. Yet this is an enemy of our own making, for, as I have said again and again, it is the imagination which stirs the senses. Desire is not a physical need; it is not true that it is a need at all. If no lascivious object had met our eye, if no unclean thought had entered our mind, this so-called need might never have made itself felt, and we should have remained chaste, without temptation, effort, or merit. We do not know how the blood of youth is stirred by certain situations and certain sights, while the youth himself does not understand the cause of his uneasiness-an uneasiness difficult to subdue and certain to recur. For my own part, the more I consider this serious crisis and its causes, immediate and remote, the more convinced I am that a solitary brought up in some desert, apart from books, teaching, and women, would die a virgin, however long he lived.

But we are not concerned with a savage of this sort. When we educate a man among his fellow-men and for social life, we cannot, and indeed we ought not to, bring him up in this wholesome ignorance, and half knowledge is worse than none. The memory of things we have observed, the ideas we have acquired, follow us into retirement and people it, against our will, with images more seductive than the things themselves, and these make solitude as fatal to those who bring such ideas with them as it is wholesome for those who have never left it.

Therefore, watch carefully over the young man; he can protect himself from all other foes, but it is for you to protect him against himself. Never leave him night or day, or at least share his room; never let him go to bed till he is sleepy, and let him rise as soon as he wakes. Distrust instinct as soon as you cease to rely altogether upon it. Instinct was good while he acted under its guidance only; now that he is in the midst of human institutions, instinct is not to be trusted; it must not be destroyed, it must be controlled, which is perhaps a more difficult matter. It would be a dangerous matter if instinct taught your pupil to abuse his senses; if once he acquires this dangerous habit he is ruined. From that time forward, body and soul will be enervated; he will carry to the grave the sad effects of this habit, the most fatal habit which a young man can acquire. If you cannot attain to the mastery of your passions, dear Emile, I pity you; but I shall not hesitate for a moment, I will not permit the purposes of nature to be evaded. If you must be a slave, I prefer to surrender you to a tyrant from whom I may deliver you; whatever happens, I can free you more easily from the slavery of women than from yourself.

Up to the age of twenty, the body is still growing and requires all its strength; till that age continence is the law of nature, and this law is rarely violated without injury to the constitution. After twenty, continence is a moral duty; it is an important duty, for it teaches us to control ourselves, to be masters of our own appetites. But moral duties have their modifications, their exceptions, their rules. When human weakness makes an alternative inevitable, of two evils choose the least; in any case it is better to commit a misdeed than to contract a vicious habit.

Remember, I am not talking of my pupil now, but of yours. His passions, to which you have given way, are your master; yield to them openly and without concealing his victory. If you are able to show him it in its true light, he will be ashamed rather than proud of it, and you will secure the right to guide him in his wanderings, at least so as to avoid precipices. The disciple must do nothing, not even evil, without the knowledge and consent of his master; it is a hundredfold better that the tutor should approve of a misdeed than that he should deceive himself or be deceived by his pupil, and the wrong should be done without his knowledge. He who thinks he must shut his eyes to one thing, must soon shut them altogether; the first abuse which is permitted leads to others, and this chain of consequences only ends in the complete overthrow of all order and contempt for every law.

There is another mistake which I have already dealt with, a mistake continually made by narrow-minded persons; they constantly affect the dignity of a master, and wish to be regarded by their disciples as perfect. This method is just the contrary of what should be done. How is it that they fail to perceive that when they try to strengthen their authority they are really destroying it; that to gain a hearing one must put oneself in the place of our hearers, and that to speak to the human heart, one must be a man. All these perfect people neither touch nor persuade; people always say, "It is easy for them to fight against passions they do not feel." Show your pupil your own weaknesses if you want to cure his; let him see in you struggles like his own; let him learn by your example to master himself and let him not say like other young men, "These old people, who are vexed because they are no longer young, want to treat all young people as if they were old; and they make a crime of our passions because their own passions are dead."

Montaigne tells us that he once asked Seigneur de Langey how often, in his negotiations with Germany, he had got drunk in his king's service. I would willingly ask the tutor of a certain young man how often he has entered a house of ill-fame for his pupil's sake. How often? I am wrong. If the first time has not cured the young libertine of all desire to go there again, if he does not return penitent and ashamed, if he does not shed torrents of tears upon your bosom, leave him on the spot; either he is a monster or you are a fool; you will never do him any good. But let us have done with these last expedients, which are as distressing as they are dangerous; our kind of education has no need of them.

What precautions we must take with a young man of good birth before exposing him to the scandalous manners of our age! These precautions are painful but necessary; negligence in this matter is the ruin of all our young men; degeneracy is the result of youthful excesses, and it is these excesses which make men what they are. Old and base in their vices, their hearts are shrivelled, because their worn-out bodies were corrupted at an early age; they have scarcely strength to stir. The subtlety of their thoughts betrays a mind lacking in substance; they are incapable of any great or noble feeling, they have neither simplicity nor vigour; altogether abject and meanly wicked, they are merely frivolous, deceitful, and false; they have not even courage enough to be distinguished criminals. Such are the despicable men produced by early debauchery; if there were but one among them who knew how to be sober and temperate, to guard his heart, his body, his morals from the contagion of bad example, at the age of thirty he would crush all these insects, and would become their master with far less trouble than it cost him to become master of himself.

However little Emile owes to birth and fortune, he might be this man if he chose; but he despises such people too much to condescend to make them his slaves. Let us now watch him in their midst, as he enters into society, not to claim the first place, but to acquaint himself with it and to seek a helpmeet worthy of himself.

Whatever his rank or birth, whatever the society into which he is introduced, his entrance into that society will be simple and unaffected; God grant he may not be unlucky enough to shine in society; the qualities which make a good impression at the first glance are not his, he neither possesses them, nor desires to possess them. He cares too little for the opinions of other people to value their prejudices, and he is indifferent whether people esteem him or not until they know him. His address is neither shy nor conceited, but natural and sincere, he knows nothing of constraint or concealment, and he is just the same among a group of people as he is when he is alone. Will this make him rude, scornful, and careless of others? On the contrary; if he were not heedless of others when he lived alone, why should he be heedless of them now that he is living among them? He does not prefer them to himself in his manners, because he does not prefer them to himself in his heart, but neither does he show them an indifference which he is far from feeling; if he is unacquainted with the forms of politeness, he is not unacquainted with the attentions dictated by humanity. He cannot bear to see any one suffer; he will not give up his place to another from mere external politeness, but he will willingly yield it to him out of kindness if he sees that he is being neglected and that this neglect hurts him; for it will be less disagreeable to Emile to remain standing of his own accord than to see another compelled to stand.

Although Emile has no very high opinion of people in general, he does not show any scorn of them, because he pities them and is sorry for them. As he cannot give them a taste for what is truly good, he leaves them the imaginary good with which they are satisfied, lest by robbing them of this he should leave them worse off than before. So he neither argues nor contradicts; neither does he flatter nor agree; he states his opinion without arguing with others, because he loves liberty above all things, and freedom is one of the fairest gifts of liberty.

He says little, for he is not anxious to attract attention; for the same reason he only says what is to the point; who could induce him to speak otherwise? Emile is too well informed to be a chatter-box. A great flow of words comes either from a pretentious spirit, of which I shall speak presently, or from the value laid upon trifles which we foolishly think to be as important in the eyes of others as in our own. He who knows enough of things to value them at their true worth never says too much; for he can also judge of the attention bestowed on him and the interest aroused by what he says. People who know little are usually great talkers, while men who know much say little. It is plain that an ignorant person thinks everything he does know important, and he tells it to everybody. But a well-educated man is not so ready to display his learning; he would have too much to say, and he sees that there is much more to be said, so he holds his peace.

Far from disregarding the ways of other people, Emile conforms to them readily enough; not that he may appear to know all about them, nor yet to affect the airs of a man of fashion, but on the contrary for fear lest he should attract attention, and in order to pass unnoticed; he is most at his ease when no one pays any attention to him.

Although when he makes his entrance into society he knows nothing of its customs, this does not make him shy or timid; if he keeps in the background, it is not because he is embarrassed, but because, if you want to see, you must not be seen; for he scarcely troubles himself at all about what people think of him, and he is not the least afraid of ridicule. Hence he is always quiet and self-possessed and is not troubled with shyness. All he has to do is done as well as he knows how to do it, whether people are looking at him or not; and as he is always on the alert to observe other people, he acquires their ways with an ease impossible to the slaves of other people's opinions. We might say that he acquires the ways of society just because he cares so little about them.

But do not make any mistake as to his bearing; it is not to be compared with that of your young dandies. It is self-possessed, not conceited; his manners are easy, not haughty; an insolent look is the mark of a slave, there is nothing affected in independence. I never saw a man of lofty soul who showed it in his bearing; this affectation is more suited to vile and frivolous souls, who have no other means of asserting themselves. I read somewhere that a foreigner appeared one day in the presence of the famous Marcel, who asked him what country he came from. "I am an Englishman," replied the stranger. "You are an Englishman!" replied the dancer, "You come from that island where the citizens have a share in the government, and form part of the sovereign power? [Footnote: As if there were citizens who were not part of the city and had not, as such, a share in sovereign power! But the French, who have thought fit to usurp the honourable name of citizen which was formerly the right of the members of the Gallic cities, have degraded the idea till it has no longer any sort of meaning. A man who recently wrote a number of silly criticisms on the "Nouvelle Heloise" added to his signature the title "Citizen of Paimboeuf," and he thought it a capital joke.] No, sir, that modest bearing, that timid glance, that hesitating manner, proclaim only a slave adorned with the title of an elector."

I cannot say whether this saying shows much knowledge of the true relation between a man's character and his appearance. I have not the honour of being a dancing master, and I should have thought just the opposite. I should have said, "This Englishman is no courtier; I never heard that courtiers have a timid bearing and a hesitating manner. A man whose appearance is timid in the presence of a dancer might not be timid in the House of Commons." Surely this M. Marcel must take his fellow-countrymen for so many Romans.

He who loves desires to be loved, Emile loves his fellows and desires to please them. Even more does he wish to please the women; his age, his character, the object he has in view, all increase this desire. I say his character, for this has a great effect; men of good character are those who really adore women. They have not the mocking jargon of gallantry like the rest, but their eagerness is more genuinely tender, because it comes from the heart. In the presence of a young woman, I could pick out a young man of character and self-control from among a hundred thousand libertines. Consider what Emile must be, with all the eagerness of early youth and so many reasons for resistance! For in the presence of women I think he will sometimes be shy and timid; but this shyness will certainly not be displeasing, and the least foolish of them will only too often find a way to enjoy it and augment it. Moreover, his eagerness will take a different shape according to those he has to do with. He will be more modest and respectful to married women, more eager and tender towards young girls. He never loses sight of his purpose, and it is always those who most recall it to him who receive the greater share of his attentions.

No one could be more attentive to every consideration based upon the laws of nature, and even on the laws of good society; but the former are always preferred before the latter, and Emile will show more respect to an elderly person in private life than to a young magistrate of his own age. As he is generally one of the youngest in the company, he will always be one of the most modest, not from the vanity which apes humility, but from a natural feeling founded upon reason. He will not have the effrontery of the young fop, who speaks louder than the wise and interrupts the old in order to amuse the company. He will never give any cause for the reply given to Louis XV by an old gentleman who was asked whether he preferred this century or the last: "Sire, I spent my youth in reverence towards the old; I find myself compelled to spend my old age in reverence towards the young."

His heart is tender and sensitive, but he cares nothing for the weight of popular opinion, though he loves to give pleasure to others; so he will care little to be thought a person of importance. Hence he will be affectionate rather than polite, he will never be pompous or affected, and he will be always more touched by a caress than by much praise. For the same reasons he will never be careless of his manners or his clothes; perhaps he will be rather particular about his dress, not that he may show himself a man of taste, but to make his appearance more pleasing; he will never require a gilt frame, and he will never spoil his style by a display of wealth.

All this demands, as you see, no stock of precepts from me; it is all the result of his early education. People make a great mystery of the ways of society, as if, at the age when these ways are acquired, we did not take to them quite naturally, and as if the first laws of politeness were not to be found in a kindly heart. True politeness consists in showing our goodwill towards men; it shows its presence without any difficulty; those only who lack this goodwill are compelled to reduce the outward signs of it to an art.

"The worst effect of artificial politeness is that it teaches us how to dispense with the virtues it imitates. If our education teaches us kindness and humanity, we shall be polite, or we shall have no need of politeness.

"If we have not those qualities which display themselves gracefully we shall have those which proclaim the honest man and the citizen; we shall have no need for falsehood.

"Instead of seeking to please by artificiality, it will suffice that we are kindly; instead of flattering the weaknesses of others by falsehood, it will suffice to tolerate them.

"Those with whom we have to do will neither be puffed up nor corrupted by such intercourse; they will only be grateful and will be informed by it." [Footnote: Considerations sur les moeurs de ce siecle, par M. Duclos.]

It seems to me that if any education is calculated to produce the sort of politeness required by M. Duclos in this passage, it is the education I have already described.

Yet I admit that with such different teaching Emile will not be just like everybody else, and heaven preserve him from such a fate! But where he is unlike other people, he will neither cause annoyance nor will he be absurd; the difference will be perceptible but not unpleasant. Emile will be, if you like, an agreeable foreigner. At first his peculiarities will be excused with the phrase, "He will learn." After a time people will get used to his ways, and seeing that he does not change they will still make excuses for him and say, "He is made that way."

He will not be feted as a charming man, but every one will like him without knowing why; no one will praise his intellect, but every one will be ready to make him the judge between men of intellect; his own intelligence will be clear and limited, his mind will be accurate, and his judgment sane. As he never runs after new ideas, he cannot pride himself on his wit. I have convinced him that all wholesome ideas, ideas which are really useful to mankind, were among the earliest known, that in all times they have formed the true bonds of society, and that there is nothing left for ambitious minds but to seek distinction for themselves by means of ideas which are injurious and fatal to mankind. This way of winning admiration scarcely appeals to him; he knows how he ought to seek his own happiness in life, and how he can contribute to the happiness of others. The sphere of his knowledge is restricted to what is profitable. His path is narrow and clearly defined; as he has no temptation to leave it, he is lost in the crowd; he will neither distinguish himself nor will he lose his way. Emile is a man of common sense and he has no desire to be anything more; you may try in vain to insult him by applying this phrase to him; he will always consider it a title of honour.

Although from his wish to please he is no longer wholly indifferent to the opinion of others, he only considers that opinion so far as he himself is directly concerned, without troubling himself about arbitrary values, which are subject to no law but that of fashion or conventionality. He will have pride enough to wish to do well in everything that he undertakes, and even to wish to do it better than others; he will want to be the swiftest runner, the strongest wrestler, the cleverest workman, the readiest in games of skill; but he will not seek advantages which are not in themselves clear gain, but need to be supported by the opinion of others, such as to be thought wittier than another, a better speaker, more learned, etc.; still less will he trouble himself with those which have nothing to do with the man himself, such as higher birth, a greater reputation for wealth, credit, or public estimation, or the impression created by a showy exterior.

As he loves his fellows because they are like himself, he will prefer him who is most like himself, because he will feel that he is good; and as he will judge of this resemblance by similarity of taste in morals, in all that belongs to a good character, he will be delighted to win approval. He will not say to himself in so many words, "I am delighted to gain approval," but "I am delighted because they say I have done right; I am delighted because the men who honour me are worthy of honour; while they judge so wisely, it is a fine thing to win their respect."

As he studies men in their conduct in society, just as he formerly studied them through their passions in history, he will often have occasion to consider what it is that pleases or offends the human heart. He is now busy with the philosophy of the principles of taste, and this is the most suitable subject for his present study.

The further we seek our definitions of taste, the further we go astray; taste is merely the power of judging what is pleasing or displeasing to most people. Go beyond this, and you cannot say what taste is. It does not follow that the men of taste are in the majority; for though the majority judges wisely with regard to each individual thing, there are few men who follow the judgment of the majority in everything; and though the most general agreement in taste constitutes good taste, there are few men of good taste just as there are few beautiful people, although beauty consists in the sum of the most usual features.

It must be observed that we are not here concerned with what we like because it is serviceable, or hate because it is harmful to us. Taste deals only with things that are indifferent to us, or which affect at most our amusements, not those which relate to our needs; taste is not required to judge of these, appetite only is sufficient. It is this which makes mere decisions of taste so difficult and as it seems so arbitrary; for beyond the instinct they follow there appears to be no reason whatever for them. We must also make a distinction between the laws of good taste in morals and its laws in physical matters. In the latter the laws of taste appear to be absolutely inexplicable. But it must be observed that there is a moral element in everything which involves imitation.[Footnote: This is demonstrated in an "Essay on the Origin of Languages" which will be found in my collected works.] This is the explanation of beauties which seem to be physical, but are not so in reality. I may add that taste has local rules which make it dependent in many respects on the country we are in, its manners, government, institutions; it has other rules which depend upon age, sex, and character, and it is in this sense that we must not dispute over matters of taste.

Taste is natural to men; but all do not possess it in the same degree, it is not developed to the same extent in every one; and in every one it is liable to be modified by a variety of causes. Such taste as we may possess depends on our native sensibility; its cultivation and its form depend upon the society in which we have lived. In the first place we must live in societies of many different kinds, so as to compare much. In the next place, there must be societies for amusement and idleness, for in business relations, interest, not pleasure, is our rule. Lastly, there must be societies in which people are fairly equal, where the tyranny of public opinion may be moderate, where pleasure rather than vanity is queen; where this is not so, fashion stifles taste, and we seek what gives distinction rather than delight.

In the latter case it is no longer true that good taste is the taste of the majority. Why is this? Because the purpose is different. Then the crowd has no longer any opinion of its own, it only follows the judgment of those who are supposed to know more about it; its approval is bestowed not on what is good, but on what they have already approved. At any time let every man have his own opinion, and what is most pleasing in itself will always secure most votes.

Every beauty that is to be found in the works of man is imitated. All the true models of taste are to be found in nature. The further we get from the master, the worse are our pictures. Then it is that we find our models in what we ourselves like, and the beauty of fancy, subject to caprice and to authority, is nothing but what is pleasing to our leaders.

Those leaders are the artists, the wealthy, and the great, and they themselves follow the lead of self-interest or pride. Some to display their wealth, others to profit by it, they seek eagerly for new ways of spending it. This is how luxury acquires its power and makes us love what is rare and costly; this so-called beauty consists, not in following nature, but in disobeying her. Hence luxury and bad taste are inseparable. Wherever taste is lavish, it is bad.

Taste, good or bad, takes its shape especially in the intercourse between the two sexes; the cultivation of taste is a necessary consequence of this form of society. But when enjoyment is easily obtained, and the desire to please becomes lukewarm, taste must degenerate; and this is, in my opinion, one of the best reasons why good taste implies good morals.

Consult the women's opinions in bodily matters, in all that concerns the senses; consult the men in matters of morality and all that concerns the understanding. When women are what they ought to be, they will keep to what they can understand, and their judgment will be right; but since they have set themselves up as judges of literature, since they have begun to criticise books and to make them with might and main, they are altogether astray. Authors who take the advice of blue-stockings will always be ill-advised; gallants who consult them about their clothes will always be absurdly dressed. I shall presently have an opportunity of speaking of the real talents of the female sex, the way to cultivate these talents, and the matters in regard to which their decisions should receive attention.

These are the elementary considerations which I shall lay down as principles when I discuss with Emile this matter which is by no means indifferent to him in his present inquiries. And to whom should it be a matter of indifference? To know what people may find pleasant or unpleasant is not only necessary to any one who requires their help, it is still more necessary to any one who would help them; you must please them if you would do them service; and the art of writing is no idle pursuit if it is used to make men hear the truth.

If in order to cultivate my pupil's taste, I were compelled to choose between a country where this form of culture has not yet arisen and those in which it has already degenerated, I would progress backwards; I would begin his survey with the latter and end with the former. My reason for this choice is, that taste becomes corrupted through excessive delicacy, which makes it sensitive to things which most men do not perceive; this delicacy leads to a spirit of discussion, for the more subtle is our discrimination of things the more things there are for us. This subtlety increases the delicacy and decreases the uniformity of our touch. So there are as many tastes as there are people. In disputes as to our preferences, philosophy and knowledge are enlarged, and thus we learn to think. It is only men accustomed to plenty of society who are capable of very delicate observations, for these observations do not occur to us till the last, and people who are unused to all sorts of society exhaust their attention in the consideration of the more conspicuous features. There is perhaps no civilised place upon earth where the common taste is so bad as in Paris. Yet it is in this capital that good taste is cultivated, and it seems that few books make any impression in Europe whose authors have not studied in Paris. Those who think it is enough to read our books are mistaken; there is more to be learnt from the conversation of authors than from their books; and it is not from the authors that we learn most. It is the spirit of social life which develops a thinking mind, and carries the eye as far as it can reach. If you have a spark of genius, go and spend a year in Paris; you will soon be all that you are capable of becoming, or you will never be good for anything at all.

One may learn to think in places where bad taste rules supreme; but we must not think like those whose taste is bad, and it is very difficult to avoid this if we spend much time among them. We must use their efforts to perfect the machinery of judgment, but we must be careful not to make the same use of it. I shall take care not to polish Emile's judgment so far as to transform it, and when he has acquired discernment enough to feel and compare the varied tastes of men, I shall lead him to fix his own taste upon simpler matters.

I will go still further in order to keep his taste pure and wholesome. In the tumult of dissipation I shall find opportunities for useful conversation with him; and while these conversations are always about things in which he takes a delight, I shall take care to make them as amusing as they are instructive. Now is the time to read pleasant books; now is the time to teach him to analyse speech and to appreciate all the beauties of eloquence and diction. It is a small matter to learn languages, they are less useful than people think; but the study of languages leads us on to that of grammar in general. We must learn Latin if we would have a thorough knowledge of French; these two languages must be studied and compared if we would understand the rules of the art of speaking.

There is, moreover, a certain simplicity of taste which goes straight to the heart; and this is only to be found in the classics. In oratory, poetry, and every kind of literature, Emile will find the classical authors as he found them in history, full of matter and sober in their judgment. The authors of our own time, on the contrary, say little and talk much. To take their judgment as our constant law is not the way to form our own judgment. These differences of taste make themselves felt in all that is left of classical times and even on their tombs. Our monuments are covered with praises, theirs recorded facts.

"Sta, viator; heroem calcas."

If I had found this epitaph on an ancient monument, I should at once have guessed it was modern; for there is nothing so common among us as heroes, but among the ancients they were rare. Instead of saying a man was a hero, they would have said what he had done to gain that name. With the epitaph of this hero compare that of the effeminate Sardanapalus—

"Tarsus and Anchiales I built in a day, and now I am dead."

Which do you think says most? Our inflated monumental style is only fit to trumpet forth the praises of pygmies. The ancients showed men as they were, and it was plain that they were men indeed. Xenophon did honour to the memory of some warriors who were slain by treason during the retreat of the Ten Thousand. "They died," said he, "without stain in war and in love." That is all, but think how full was the heart of the author of this short and simple elegy. Woe to him who fails to perceive its charm. The following words were engraved on a tomb at Thermopylae—

"Go, Traveller, tell Sparta that here we fell in obedience to her laws."

It is pretty clear that this was not the work of the Academy of Inscriptions.

If I am not mistaken, the attention of my pupil, who sets so small value upon words, will be directed in the first place to these differences, and they will affect his choice in his reading. He will be carried away by the manly eloquence of Demosthenes, and will say, "This is an orator;" but when he reads Cicero, he will say, "This is a lawyer."

Speaking generally Emile will have more taste for the books of the ancients than for our own, just because they were the first, and therefore the ancients are nearer to nature and their genius is more distinct. Whatever La Motte and the Abbe Terrasson may say, there is no real advance in human reason, for what we gain in one direction we lose in another; for all minds start from the same point, and as the time spent in learning what others have thought is so much time lost in learning to think for ourselves, we have more acquired knowledge and less vigour of mind. Our minds like our arms are accustomed to use tools for everything, and to do nothing for themselves. Fontenelle used to say that all these disputes as to the ancients and the moderns came to this—Were the trees in former times taller than they are now. If agriculture had changed, it would be worth our while to ask this question.

After I have led Emile to the sources of pure literature, I will also show him the channels into the reservoirs of modern compilers; journals, translations, dictionaries, he shall cast a glance at them all, and then leave them for ever. To amuse him he shall hear the chatter of the academies; I will draw his attention to the fast that every member of them is worth more by himself than he is as a member of the society; he will then draw his own conclusions as to the utility of these fine institutions.

I take him to the theatre to study taste, not morals; for in the theatre above all taste is revealed to those who can think. Lay aside precepts and morality, I should say; this is not the place to study them. The stage is not made for truth; its object is to flatter and amuse: there is no place where one can learn so completely the art of pleasing and of interesting the human heart. The study of plays leads to the study of poetry; both have the same end in view. If he has the least glimmering of taste for poetry, how eagerly will he study the languages of the poets, Greek, Latin, and Italian! These studies will afford him unlimited amusement and will be none the less valuable; they will be a delight to him at an age and in circumstances when the heart finds so great a charm in every kind of beauty which affects it. Picture to yourself on the one hand Emile, on the other some young rascal from college, reading the fourth book of the Aeneid, or Tibollus, or the Banquet of Plato: what a difference between them! What stirs the heart of Emile to its depths, makes not the least impression on the other! Oh, good youth, stay, make a pause in your reading, you are too deeply moved; I would have you find pleasure in the language of love, but I would not have you carried away by it; be a wise man, but be a good man too. If you are only one of these, you are nothing. After this let him win fame or not in dead languages, in literature, in poetry, I care little. He will be none the worse if he knows nothing of them, and his education is not concerned with these mere words.

My main object in teaching him to feel and love beauty of every kind is to fix his affections and his taste on these, to prevent the corruption of his natural appetites, lest he should have to seek some day in the midst of his wealth for the means of happiness which should be found close at hand. I have said elsewhere that taste is only the art of being a connoisseur in matters of little importance, and this is quite true; but since the charm of life depends on a tissue of these matters of little importance, such efforts are no small thing; through their means we learn how to fill our life with the good things within our reach, with as much truth as they may hold for us. I do not refer to the morally good which depends on a good disposition of the heart, but only to that which depends on the body, on real delight, apart from the prejudices of public opinion.

The better to unfold my idea, allow me for a moment to leave Emile, whose pure and wholesome heart cannot be taken as a rule for others, and to seek in my own memory for an illustration better suited to the reader and more in accordance with his own manners.

There are professions which seem to change a man's nature, to recast, either for better or worse, the men who adopt them. A coward becomes a brave man in the regiment of Navarre. It is not only in the army that esprit de corps is acquired, and its effects are not always for good. I have thought again and again with terror that if I had the misfortune to fill a certain post I am thinking of in a certain country, before to-morrow I should certainly be a tyrant, an extortioner, a destroyer of the people, harmful to my king, and a professed enemy of mankind, a foe to justice and every kind of virtue.

In the same way, if I were rich, I should have done all that is required to gain riches; I should therefore be insolent and degraded, sensitive and feeling only on my own behalf, harsh and pitiless to all besides, a scornful spectator of the sufferings of the lower classes; for that is what I should call the poor, to make people forget that I was once poor myself. Lastly I should make my fortune a means to my own pleasures with which I should be wholly occupied; and so far I should be just like other people.

But in one respect I should be very unlike them; I should be sensual and voluptuous rather than proud and vain, and I should give myself up to the luxury of comfort rather than to that of ostentation. I should even be somewhat ashamed to make too great a show of my wealth, and if I overwhelmed the envious with my pomp I should always fancy I heard him saying, "Here is a rascal who is greatly afraid lest we should take him for anything but what he is."

In the vast profusion of good things upon this earth I should seek what I like best, and what I can best appropriate to myself.

To this end, the first use I should make of my wealth would be to purchase leisure and freedom, to which I would add health, if it were to be purchased; but health can only be bought by temperance, and as there is no real pleasure without health, I should be temperate from sensual motives.

I should also keep as close as possible to nature, to gratify the senses given me by nature, being quite convinced that, the greater her share in my pleasures, the more real I shall find them. In the choice of models for imitation I shall always choose nature as my pattern; in my appetites I will give her the preference; in my tastes she shall always be consulted; in my food I will always choose what most owes its charm to her, and what has passed through the fewest possible hands on its way to table. I will be on my guard against fraudulent shams; I will go out to meet pleasure. No cook shall grow rich on my gross and foolish greediness; he shall not poison me with fish which cost its weight in gold, my table shall not be decked with fetid splendour or putrid flesh from far-off lands. I will take any amount of trouble to gratify my sensibility, since this trouble has a pleasure of its own, a pleasure more than we expect. If I wished to taste a food from the ends of the earth, I would go, like Apicius, in search of it, rather than send for it; for the daintiest dishes always lack a charm which cannot be brought along with them, a flavour which no cook can give them—the air of the country where they are produced.

For the same reason I would not follow the example of those who are never well off where they are, but are always setting the seasons at nought, and confusing countries and their seasons; those who seek winter in summer and summer in winter, and go to Italy to be cold and to the north to be warm, do not consider that when they think they are escaping from the severity of the seasons, they are going to meet that severity in places where people are not prepared for it. I shall stay in one place, or I shall adopt just the opposite course; I should like to get all possible enjoyment out of one season to discover what is peculiar to any given country. I would have a variety of pleasures, and habits quite unlike one another, but each according to nature; I would spend the summer at Naples and the winter in St. Petersburg; sometimes I would breathe the soft zephyr lying in the cool grottoes of Tarentum, and again I would enjoy the illuminations of an ice palace, breathless and wearied with the pleasures of the dance.

In the service of my table and the adornment of my dwelling I would imitate in the simplest ornaments the variety of the seasons, and draw from each its charm without anticipating its successor. There is no taste but only difficulty to be found in thus disturbing the order of nature; to snatch from her unwilling gifts, which she yields regretfully, with her curse upon them; gifts which have neither strength nor flavour, which can neither nourish the body nor tickle the palate. Nothing is more insipid than forced fruits. A wealthy man in Paris, with all his stoves and hot-houses, only succeeds in getting all the year round poor fruit and poor vegetables for his table at a very high price. If I had cherries in frost, and golden melons in the depths of winter, what pleasure should I find in them when my palate did not need moisture or refreshment. Would the heavy chestnut be very pleasant in the heat of the dog-days; should I prefer to have it hot from the stove, rather than the gooseberry, the strawberry, the refreshing fruits which the earth takes care to provide for me. A mantelpiece covered in January with forced vegetation, with pale and scentless flowers, is not winter adorned, but spring robbed of its beauty; we deprive ourselves of the pleasure of seeking the first violet in the woods, of noting the earliest buds, and exclaiming in a rapture of delight, "Mortals, you are not forsaken, nature is living still."

To be well served I would have few servants; this has been said before, but it is worth saying again. A tradesman gets more real service from his one man than a duke from the ten gentlemen round about him. It has often struck me when I am sitting at table with my glass beside me that I can drink whenever I please; whereas, if I were dining in state, twenty men would have to call for "Wine" before I could quench my thirst. You may be sure that whatever is done for you by other people is ill done. I would not send to the shops, I would go myself; I would go so that my servants should not make their own terms with the shopkeepers, and to get a better choice and cheaper prices; I would go for the sake of pleasant exercise and to get a glimpse of what was going on out of doors; this is amusing and sometimes instructive; lastly I would go for the sake of the walk; there is always something in that. A sedentary life is the source of tedium; when we walk a good deal we are never dull. A porter and footmen are poor interpreters, I should never wish to have such people between the world and myself, nor would I travel with all the fuss of a coach, as if I were afraid people would speak to me. Shanks' mare is always ready; if she is tired or ill, her owner is the first to know it; he need not be afraid of being kept at home while his coachman is on the spree; on the road he will not have to submit to all sorts of delays, nor will he be consumed with impatience, nor compelled to stay in one place a moment longer than he chooses. Lastly, since no one serves us so well as we serve ourselves, had we the power of Alexander and the wealth of Croesus we should accept no services from others, except those we cannot perform for ourselves.

I would not live in a palace; for even in a palace I should only occupy one room; every room which is common property belongs to nobody, and the rooms of each of my servants would be as strange to me as my neighbour's. The Orientals, although very voluptuous, are lodged in plain and simply furnished dwellings. They consider life as a journey, and their house as an inn. This reason scarcely appeals to us rich people who propose to live for ever; but I should find another reason which would have the same effect. It would seem to me that if I settled myself in one place in the midst of such splendour, I should banish myself from every other place, and imprison myself, so to speak, in my palace. The world is a palace fair enough for any one; and is not everything at the disposal of the rich man when he seeks enjoyment? "Ubi bene, ibi patria," that is his motto; his home is anywhere where money will carry him, his country is anywhere where there is room for his strong-box, as Philip considered as his own any place where a mule laden with silver could enter. [Footnote: A stranger, splendidly clad, was asked in Athens what country he belonged to. "I am one of the rich," was his answer; and a very good answer in my opinion.] Why then should we shut ourselves up within walls and gates as if we never meant to leave them? If pestilence, war, or rebellion drive me from one place, I go to another, and I find my hotel there before me. Why should I build a mansion for myself when the world is already at my disposal? Why should I be in such a hurry to live, to bring from afar delights which I can find on the spot? It is impossible to make a pleasant life for oneself when one is always at war with oneself. Thus Empedocles reproached the men of Agrigentum with heaping up pleasures as if they had but one day to live, and building as if they would live for ever.

And what use have I for so large a dwelling, as I have so few people to live in it, and still fewer goods to fill it? My furniture would be as simple as my tastes; I would have neither picture-gallery nor library, especially if I was fond of reading and knew something about pictures. I should then know that such collections are never complete, and that the lack of that which is wanting causes more annoyance than if one had nothing at all. In this respect abundance is the cause of want, as every collector knows to his cost. If you are an expert, do not make a collection; if you know how to use your cabinets, you will not have any to show.

Gambling is no sport for the rich, it is the resource of those who have nothing to do; I shall be so busy with my pleasures that I shall have no time to waste. I am poor and lonely and I never play, unless it is a game of chess now and then, and that is more than enough. If I were rich I would play even less, and for very low stakes, so that I should not be disappointed myself, nor see the disappointment of others. The wealthy man has no motive for play, and the love of play will not degenerate into the passion for gambling unless the disposition is evil. The rich man is always more keenly aware of his losses than his gains, and as in games where the stakes are not high the winnings are generally exhausted in the long run, he will usually lose more than he gains, so that if we reason rightly we shall scarcely take a great fancy to games where the odds are against us. He who flatters his vanity so far as to believe that Fortune favours him can seek her favour in more exciting ways; and her favours are just as clearly shown when the stakes are low as when they are high. The taste for play, the result of greed and dullness, only lays hold of empty hearts and heads; and I think I should have enough feeling and knowledge to dispense with its help. Thinkers are seldom gamblers; gambling interrupts the habit of thought and turns it towards barren combinations; thus one good result, perhaps the only good result of the taste for science, is that it deadens to some extent this vulgar passion; people will prefer to try to discover the uses of play rather than to devote themselves to it. I should argue with the gamblers against gambling, and I should find more delight in scoffing at their losses than in winning their money.

I should be the same in private life as in my social intercourse. I should wish my fortune to bring comfort in its train, and never to make people conscious of inequalities of wealth. Showy dress is inconvenient in many ways. To preserve as much freedom as possible among other men, I should like to be dressed in such a way that I should not seem out of place among all classes, and should not attract attention in any; so that without affectation or change I might mingle with the crowd at the inn or with the nobility at the Palais Royal. In this way I should be more than ever my own master, and should be free to enjoy the pleasures of all sorts and conditions of men. There are women, so they say, whose doors are closed to embroidered cuffs, women who will only receive guests who wear lace ruffles; I should spend my days elsewhere; though if these women were young and pretty I might sometimes put on lace ruffles to spend an evening or so in their company.

Mutual affection, similarity of tastes, suitability of character; these are the only bonds between my companions and myself; among them I would be a man, not a person of wealth; the charm of their society should never be embittered by self-seeking. If my wealth had not robbed me of all humanity, I would scatter my benefits and my services broadcast, but I should want companions about me, not courtiers, friends, not proteges; I should wish my friends to regard me as their host, not their patron. Independence and equality would leave to my relations with my friends the sincerity of goodwill; while duty and self-seeking would have no place among us, and we should know no law but that of pleasure and friendship.

Neither a friend nor a mistress can be bought. Women may be got for money, but that road will never lead to love. Love is not only not for sale; money strikes it dead. If a man pays, were he indeed the most lovable of men, the mere fact of payment would prevent any lasting affection. He will soon be paying for some one else, or rather some one else will get his money; and in this double connection based on self-seeking and debauchery, without love, honour, or true pleasure, the woman is grasping, faithless, and unhappy, and she is treated by the wretch to whom she gives her money as she treats the fool who gives his money to her; she has no love for either. It would be sweet to lie generous towards one we love, if that did not make a bargain of love. I know only one way of gratifying this desire with the woman one loves without embittering love; it is to bestow our all upon her and to live at her expense. It remains to be seen whether there is any woman with regard to whom such conduct would not be unwise.

He who said, "Lais is mine, but I am not hers," was talking nonsense. Possession which is not mutual is nothing at all; at most it is the possession of the sex not of the individual. But where there is no morality in love, why make such ado about the rest? Nothing is so easy to find. A muleteer is in this respect as near to happiness as a millionaire.

Oh, if we could thus trace out the unreasonableness of vice, how often should we find that, when it has attained its object, it discovers it is not what it seemed! Why is there this cruel haste to corrupt innocence, to make, a victim of a young creature whom we ought to protect, one who is dragged by this first false step into a gulf of misery from which only death can release her? Brutality, vanity, folly, error, and nothing more. This pleasure itself is unnatural; it rests on popular opinion, and popular opinion at its worst, since it depends on scorn of self. He who knows he is the basest of men fears comparison with others, and would be the first that he may be less hateful. See if those who are most greedy in pursuit of such fancied pleasures are ever attractive young men—men worthy of pleasing, men who might have some excuse if they were hard to please. Not so; any one with good looks, merit, and feeling has little fear of his mistress' experience; with well-placed confidence he says to her, "You know what pleasure is, what is that to me? my heart assures me that this is not so."

But an aged satyr, worn out with debauchery, with no charm, no consideration, no thought for any but himself, with no shred of honour, incapable and unworthy of finding favour in the eyes of any woman who knows anything of men deserving of love, expects to make up for all this with an innocent girl by trading on her inexperience and stirring her emotions for the first time. His last hope is to find favour as a novelty; no doubt this is the secret motive of this desire; but he is mistaken, the horror he excites is just as natural as the desires he wishes to arouse. He is also mistaken in his foolish attempt; that very nature takes care to assert her rights; every girl who sells herself is no longer a maid; she has given herself to the man of her choice, and she is making the very comparison he dreads. The pleasure purchased is imaginary, but none the less hateful.

For my own part, however riches may change me, there is one matter in which I shall never change. If I have neither morals nor virtue, I shall not be wholly without taste, without sense, without delicacy; and this will prevent me from spending my fortune in the pursuit of empty dreams, from wasting my money and my strength in teaching children to betray me and mock at me. If I were young, I would seek the pleasures of youth; and as I would have them at their best I would not seek them in the guise of a rich man. If I were at my present age, it would be another matter; I would wisely confine myself to the pleasures of my age; I would form tastes which I could enjoy, and I would stifle those which could only cause suffering. I would not go and offer my grey beard to the scornful jests of young girls; I could never bear to sicken them with my disgusting caresses, to furnish them at my expense with the most absurd stories, to imagine them describing the vile pleasures of the old ape, so as to avenge themselves for what they had endured. But if habits unresisted had changed my former desires into needs, I would perhaps satisfy those needs, but with shame and blushes. I would distinguish between passion and necessity, I would find a suitable mistress and would keep to her. I would not make a business of my weakness, and above all I would only have one person aware of it. Life has other pleasures when these fail us; by hastening in vain after those that fly us, we deprive ourselves of those that remain. Let our tastes change with our years, let us no more meddle with age than with the seasons. We should be ourselves at all times, instead of struggling against nature; such vain attempts exhaust our strength and prevent the right use of life.

The lower classes are seldom dull, their life is full of activity; if there is little variety in their amusements they do not recur frequently; many days of labour teach them to enjoy their rare holidays. Short intervals of leisure between long periods of labour give a spice to the pleasures of their station. The chief curse of the rich is dullness; in the midst of costly amusements, among so many men striving to give them pleasure, they are devoured and slain by dullness; their life is spent in fleeing from it and in being overtaken by it; they are overwhelmed by the intolerable burden; women more especially, who do not know how to work or play, are a prey to tedium under the name of the vapours; with them it takes the shape of a dreadful disease, which robs them of their reason and even of their life. For my own part I know no more terrible fate than that of a pretty woman in Paris, unless it is that of the pretty manikin who devotes himself to her, who becomes idle and effeminate like her, and so deprives himself twice over of his manhood, while he prides himself on his successes and for their sake endures the longest and dullest days which human being ever put up with.

Proprieties, fashions, customs which depend on luxury and breeding, confine the course of life within the limits of the most miserable uniformity. The pleasure we desire to display to others is a pleasure lost; we neither enjoy it ourselves, nor do others enjoy it. [Footnote: Two ladies of fashion, who wished to seem to be enjoying themselves greatly, decided never to go to bed before five o'clock in the morning. In the depths of winter their servants spent the night in the street waiting for them, and with great difficulty kept themselves from freezing. One night, or rather one morning, some one entered the room where these merry people spent their hours without knowing how time passed. He found them quite alone; each of them was asleep in her armchair.] Ridicule, which public opinion dreads more than anything, is ever at hand to tyrannise, and punish. It is only ceremony that makes us ridiculous; if we can vary our place and our pleasures, to-day's impressions can efface those of yesterday; in the mind of men they are as if they had never been; but we enjoy ourselves for we throw ourselves into every hour and everything. My only set rule would be this: wherever I was I would pay no heed to anything else. I would take each day as it came, as if there were neither yesterday nor to-morrow. As I should be a man of the people, with the populace, I should be a countryman in the fields; and if I spoke of farming, the peasant should not laugh at my expense. I would not go and build a town in the country nor erect the Tuileries at the door of my lodgings. On some pleasant shady hill-side I would have a little cottage, a white house with green shutters, and though a thatched roof is the best all the year round, I would be grand enough to have, not those gloomy slates, but tiles, because they look brighter and more cheerful than thatch, and the houses in my own country are always roofed with them, and so they would recall to me something of the happy days of my youth. For my courtyard I would have a poultry-yard, and for my stables a cowshed for the sake of the milk which I love. My garden should be a kitchen-garden, and my park an orchard, like the one described further on. The fruit would be free to those who walked in the orchard, my gardener should neither count it nor gather it; I would not, with greedy show, display before your eyes superb espaliers which one scarcely dare touch. But this small extravagance would not be costly, for I would choose my abode in some remote province where silver is scarce and food plentiful, where plenty and poverty have their seat.

There I would gather round me a company, select rather than numerous, a band of friends who know what pleasure is, and how to enjoy it, women who can leave their arm-chairs and betake themselves to outdoor sports, women who can exchange the shuttle or the cards for the fishing line or the bird-trap, the gleaner's rake or grape-gatherer's basket. There all the pretensions of the town will be forgotten, and we shall be villagers in a village; we shall find all sorts of different sports and we shall hardly know how to choose the morrow's occupation. Exercise and an active life will improve our digestion and modify our tastes. Every meal will be a feast, where plenty will be more pleasing than any delicacies. There are no such cooks in the world as mirth, rural pursuits, and merry games; and the finest made dishes are quite ridiculous in the eyes of people who have been on foot since early dawn. Our meals will be served without regard to order or elegance; we shall make our dining-room anywhere, in the garden, on a boat, beneath a tree; sometimes at a distance from the house on the banks of a running stream, on the fresh green grass, among the clumps of willow and hazel; a long procession of guests will carry the material for the feast with laughter and singing; the turf will be our chairs and table, the banks of the stream our side-board, and our dessert is hanging on the trees; the dishes will be served in any order, appetite needs no ceremony; each one of us, openly putting himself first, would gladly see every one else do the same; from this warm-hearted and temperate familiarity there would arise, without coarseness, pretence, or constraint, a laughing conflict a hundredfold more delightful than politeness, and more likely to cement our friendship. No tedious flunkeys to listen to our words, to whisper criticisms on our behaviour, to count every mouthful with greedy eyes, to amuse themselves by keeping us waiting for our wine, to complain of the length of our dinner. We will be our own servants, in order to be our own masters. Time will fly unheeded, our meal will be an interval of rest during the heat of the day. If some peasant comes our way, returning from his work with his tools over his shoulder, I will cheer his heart with kindly words, and a glass or two of good wine, which will help him to bear his poverty more cheerfully; and I too shall have the joy of feeling my heart stirred within me, and I should say to myself—I too am a man.

If the inhabitants of the district assembled for some rustic feast, I and my friends would be there among the first; if there were marriages, more blessed than those of towns, celebrated near my home, every one would know how I love to see people happy, and I should be invited. I would take these good folks some gift as simple as themselves, a gift which would be my share of the feast; and in exchange I should obtain gifts beyond price, gifts so little known among my equals, the gifts of freedom and true pleasure. I should sup gaily at the head of their long table; I should join in the chorus of some rustic song and I should dance in the barn more merrily than at a ball in the Opera House.

"This is all very well so far," you will say, "but what about the shooting! One must have some sport in the country." Just so; I only wanted a farm, but I was wrong. I assume I am rich, I must keep my pleasures to myself, I must be free to kill something; this is quite another matter. I must have estates, woods, keepers, rents, seignorial rights, particularly incense and holy water.

Well and good. But I shall have neighbours about my estate who are jealous of their rights and anxious to encroach on those of others; our keepers will quarrel, and possibly their masters will quarrel too; this means altercations, disputes, ill-will, or law-suits at the least; this in itself is not very pleasant. My tenants will not enjoy finding my hares at work upon their corn, or my wild boars among their beans. As they dare not kill the enemy, every one of them will try to drive him from their fields; when the day has been spent in cultivating the ground, they will be compelled to sit up at night to watch it; they will have watch-dogs, drums, horns, and bells; my sleep will be disturbed by their racket. Do what I will, I cannot help thinking of the misery of these poor people, and I cannot help blaming myself for it. If I had the honour of being a prince, this would make little impression on me; but as I am a self-made man who has only just come into his property, I am still rather vulgar at heart.

That is not all; abundance of game attracts trespassers; I shall soon have poachers to punish; I shall require prisons, gaolers, guards, and galleys; all this strikes me as cruel. The wives of those miserable creatures will besiege my door and disturb me with their crying; they must either be driven away or roughly handled. The poor people who are not poachers, whose harvest has been destroyed by my game, will come next with their complaints. Some people will be put to death for killing the game, the rest will be punished for having spared it; what a choice of evils! On every side I shall find nothing but misery and hear nothing but groans. So far as I can see this must greatly disturb the pleasure of slaying at one's ease heaps of partridges and hares which are tame enough to run about one's feet.

If you would have pleasure without pain let there be no monopoly; the more you leave it free to everybody, the purer will be your own enjoyment. Therefore I should not do what I have just described, but without change of tastes I would follow those which seem likely to cause me least pain. I would fix my rustic abode in a district where game is not preserved, and where I can have my sport without hindrance. Game will be less plentiful, but there will be more skill in finding it, and more pleasure in securing it. I remember the start of delight with which my father watched the rise of his first partridge and the rapture with which he found the hare he had sought all day long. Yes, I declare, that alone with his dog, carrying his own gun, cartridges, and game bag together with his hare, he came home at nightfall, worn out with fatigue and torn to pieces by brambles, but better pleased with his day's sport than all your ordinary sportsmen, who on a good horse, with twenty guns ready for them, merely take one gun after another, and shoot and kill everything that comes their way, without skill, without glory, and almost without exercise. The pleasure is none the less, and the difficulties are removed; there is no estate to be preserved, no poacher to be punished, and no wretches to be tormented; here are solid grounds for preference. Whatever you do, you cannot torment men for ever without experiencing some amount of discomfort; and sooner or later the muttered curses of the people will spoil the flavour of your game.

Again, monopoly destroys pleasure. Real pleasures are those which we share with the crowd; we lose what we try to keep to ourselves alone. If the walls I build round my park transform it into a gloomy prison, I have only deprived myself, at great expense, of the pleasure of a walk; I must now seek that pleasure at a distance. The demon of property spoils everything he lays hands upon. A rich man wants to be master everywhere, and he is never happy where he is; he is continually driven to flee from himself. I shall therefore continue to do in my prosperity what I did in my poverty. Henceforward, richer in the wealth of others than I ever shall be in my own wealth, I will take possession of everything in my neighbourhood that takes my fancy; no conqueror is so determined as I; I even usurp the rights of princes; I take possession of every open place that pleases me, I give them names; this is my park, chat is my terrace, and I am their owner; henceforward I wander among them at will; I often return to maintain my proprietary rights; I make what use I choose of the ground to walk upon, and you will never convince me that the nominal owner of the property which I have appropriated gets better value out of the money it yields him than I do out of his land. No matter if I am interrupted by hedges and ditches, I take my park on my back, and I carry it elsewhere; there will be space enough for it near at hand, and I may plunder my neighbours long enough before I outstay my welcome.

This is an attempt to show what is meant by good taste in the choice of pleasant occupations for our leisure hours; this is the spirit of enjoyment; all else is illusion, fancy, and foolish pride. He who disobeys these rules, however rich he may be, will devour his gold on a dung-hill, and will never know what it is to live.

You will say, no doubt, that such amusements lie within the reach of all, that we need not be rich to enjoy them. That is the very point I was coming to. Pleasure is ours when we want it; it is only social prejudice which makes everything hard to obtain, and drives pleasure before us. To be happy is a hundredfold easier than it seems. If he really desires to enjoy himself the man of taste has no need of riches; all he wants is to be free and to be his own master. With health and daily bread we are rich enough, if we will but get rid of our prejudices; this is the "Golden Mean" of Horace. You folks with your strong-boxes may find some other use for your wealth, for it cannot buy you pleasure. Emile knows this as well as I, but his heart is purer and more healthy, so he will feel it more strongly, and all that he has beheld in society will only serve to confirm him in this opinion.

While our time is thus employed, we are ever on the look-out for Sophy, and we have not yet found her. It was not desirable that she should be found too easily, and I have taken care to look for her where I knew we should not find her.

The time is come; we must now seek her in earnest, lest Emile should mistake some one else for Sophy, and only discover his error when it is too late. Then farewell Paris, far-famed Paris, with all your noise and smoke and dirt, where the women have ceased to believe in honour and the men in virtue. We are in search of love, happiness, innocence; the further we go from Paris the better.

BOOK [illegible]

We have reached the last act of youth's drams; we are approaching its closing scene.

It is not good that man should be alone. Emile is now a man, and we must give him his promised helpmeet. That helpmeet is Sophy. Where is her dwelling-place, where shall she be found? We must know beforehand what she is, and then we can decide where to look for her. And when she is found, our task is not ended. "Since our young gentleman," says Locke, "is about to marry, it is time to leave him with his mistress." And with these words he ends his book. As I have not the honour of educating "A young gentleman," I shall take care not to follow his example.

[illegible]

Sophy should be as truly a woman as Emile is a man, i.e., she must possess all those characters of her sex which are required to enable her to play her part in the physical and moral order. Let us inquire to begin with in what respects her sex differs from our own.

But for her sex, a woman is a man; she has the same organs, the same needs, the same faculties. The machine is the same in its construction; its parts, its working, and its appearance are similar. Regard it as you will the difference is only in degree.

Yet where sex is concerned man and woman are unlike; each is the complement of the other; the difficulty in comparing them lies in our inability to decide, in either case, what is a matter of sex, and what is not. General differences present themselves to the comparative anatomist and even to the superficial observer; they seem not to be a matter of sex; yet they are really sex differences, though the connection eludes our observation. How far such differences may extend we cannot tell; all we know for certain is that where man and woman are alike we have to do with the characteristics of the species; where they are unlike, we have to do with the characteristics of sex. Considered from these two standpoints, we find so many instances of likeness and unlikeness that it is perhaps one of the greatest of marvels how nature has contrived to make two beings so like and yet so different.

These resemblances and differences must have an influence on the moral nature; this inference is obvious, and it is confirmed by experience; it shows the vanity of the disputes as to the superiority or the equality of the sexes; as if each sex, pursuing the path marked out for it by nature, were not more perfect in that very divergence than if it more closely resembled the other. A perfect man and a perfect woman should no more be alike in mind than in face, and perfection admits of neither less nor more.

In the union of the sexes each alike contributes to the common end, but in different ways. From this diversity springs the first difference which may be observed between man and woman in their moral relations. The man should be strong and active; the woman should be weak and passive; the one must have both the power and the will; it is enough that the other should offer little resistance.

When this principle is admitted, it follows that woman is specially made for man's delight. If man in his turn ought to be pleasing in her eyes, the necessity is less urgent, his virtue is in his strength, he pleases because he is strong. I grant you this is not the law of love, but it is the law of nature, which is older than love itself.

If woman is made to please and to be in subjection to man, she ought to make herself pleasing in his eyes and not provoke him to anger; her strength is in her charms, by their means she should compel him to discover and use his strength. The surest way of arousing this strength is to make it necessary by resistance. Thus pride comes to the help of desire and each exults in the other's victory. This is the origin of attack and defence, of the boldness of one sex and the timidity of the other, and even of the shame and modesty with which nature has armed the weak for the conquest of the strong.

Who can possibly suppose that nature has prescribed the same advances to the one sex as to the other, or that the first to feel desire should be the first to show it? What strange depravity of judgment! The consequences of the act being so different for the two sexes, is it natural that they should enter upon it with equal boldness? How can any one fail to see that when the share of each is so unequal, if the one were not controlled by modesty as the other is controlled by nature, the result would be the destruction of both, and the human race would perish through the very means ordained for its continuance?

Women so easily stir a man's senses and fan the ashes of a dying passion, that if philosophy ever succeeded in introducing this custom into any unlucky country, especially if it were a warm country where more women are born than men, the men, tyrannised over by the women, would at last become their victims, and would be dragged to their death without the least chance of escape.

Female animals are without this sense of shame, but what of that? Are their desires as boundless as those of women, which are curbed by this shame? The desires of the animals are the result of necessity, and when the need is satisfied, the desire ceases; they no longer make a feint of repulsing the male, they do it in earnest. Their seasons of complaisance are short and soon over. Impulse and restraint are alike the work of nature. But what would take the place of this negative instinct in women if you rob them of their modesty?

The Most High has deigned to do honour to mankind; he has endowed man with boundless passions, together with a law to guide them, so that man may be alike free and self-controlled; though swayed by these passions man is endowed with reason by which to control them. Woman is also endowed with boundless passions; God has given her modesty to restrain them. Moreover, he has given to both a present reward for the right use of their powers, in the delight which springs from that right use of them, i.e., the taste for right conduct established as the law of our behaviour. To my mind this is far higher than the instinct of the beasts.

Whether the woman shares the man's passion or not, whether she is willing or unwilling to satisfy it, she always repulses him and defends herself, though not always with the same vigour, and therefore not always with the same success. If the siege is to be successful, the besieged must permit or direct the attack. How skilfully can she stimulate the efforts of the aggressor. The freest and most delightful of activities does not permit of any real violence; reason and nature are alike against it; nature, in that she has given the weaker party strength enough to resist if she chooses; reason, in that actual violence is not only most brutal in itself, but it defeats its own ends, not only because the man thus declares war against his companion and thus gives her a right to defend her person and her liberty even at the cost of the enemy's life, but also because the woman alone is the judge of her condition, and a child would have no father if any man might usurp a father's rights.

Thus the different constitution of the two sexes leads us to a third conclusion, that the stronger party seems to be master, but is as a matter of fact dependent on the weaker, and that, not by any foolish custom of gallantry, nor yet by the magnanimity of the protector, but by an inexorable law of nature. For nature has endowed woman with a power of stimulating man's passions in excess of man's power of satisfying those passions, and has thus made him dependent on her goodwill, and compelled him in his turn to endeavour to please her, so that she may be willing to yield to his superior strength. Is it weakness which yields to force, or is it voluntary self-surrender? This uncertainty constitutes the chief charm of the man's victory, and the woman is usually cunning enough to leave him in doubt. In this respect the woman's mind exactly resembles her body; far from being ashamed of her weakness, she is proud of it; her soft muscles offer no resistance, she professes that she cannot lift the lightest weight; she would be ashamed to be strong. And why? Not only to gain an appearance of refinement; she is too clever for that; she is providing herself beforehand with excuses, with the right to be weak if she chooses.

The experience we have gained through our vices has considerably modified the views held in older times; we rarely hear of violence for which there is so little occasion that it would hardly be credited. Yet such stories are common enough among the Jews and ancient Greeks; for such views belong to the simplicity of nature, and have only been uprooted by our profligacy. If fewer deeds of violence are quoted in our days, it is not that men are more temperate, but because they are less credulous, and a complaint which would have been believed among a simple people would only excite laughter among ourselves; therefore silence is the better course. There is a law in Deuteronomy, under which the outraged maiden was punished, along with her assailant, if the crime were committed in a town; but if in the country or in a lonely place, the latter alone was punished. "For," says the law, "the maiden cried for help, and there was none to hear." From this merciful interpretation of the law, girls learnt not to let themselves be surprised in lonely places.

This change in public opinion has had a perceptible effect on our morals. It has produced our modern gallantry. Men have found that their pleasures depend, more than they expected, on the goodwill of the fair sex, and have secured this goodwill by attentions which have had their reward.

See how we find ourselves led unconsciously from the physical to the moral constitution, how from the grosser union of the sexes spring the sweet laws of love. Woman reigns, not by the will of man, but by the decrees of nature herself; she had the power long before she showed it. That same Hercules who proposed to violate all the fifty daughters of Thespis was compelled to spin at the feet of Omphale, and Samson, the strong man, was less strong than Delilah. This power cannot be taken from woman; it is hers by right; she would have lost it long ago, were it possible.

The consequences of sex are wholly unlike for man and woman. The male is only a male now and again, the female is always a female, or at least all her youth; everything reminds her of her sex; the performance of her functions requires a special constitution. She needs care during pregnancy and freedom from work when her child is born; she must have a quiet, easy life while she nurses her children; their education calls for patience and gentleness, for a zeal and love which nothing can dismay; she forms a bond between father and child, she alone can win the father's love for his children and convince him that they are indeed his own. What loving care is required to preserve a united family! And there should be no question of virtue in all this, it must be a labour of love, without which the human race would be doomed to extinction.

The mutual duties of the two sexes are not, and cannot be, equally binding on both. Women do wrong to complain of the inequality of man-made laws; this inequality is not of man's making, or at any rate it is not the result of mere prejudice, but of reason. She to whom nature has entrusted the care of the children must hold herself responsible for them to their father. No doubt every breach of faith is wrong, and every faithless husband, who robs his wife of the sole reward of the stern duties of her sex, is cruel and unjust; but the faithless wife is worse; she destroys the family and breaks the bonds of nature; when she gives her husband children who are not his own, she is false both to him and them, her crime is not infidelity but treason. To my mind, it is the source of dissension and of crime of every kind. Can any position be more wretched than that of the unhappy father who, when he clasps his child to his breast, is haunted by the suspicion that this is the child of another, the badge of his own dishonour, a thief who is robbing his own children of their inheritance. Under such circumstances the family is little more than a group of secret enemies, armed against each other by a guilty woman, who compels them to pretend to love one another.

Thus it is not enough that a wife should be faithful; her husband, along with his friends and neighbours, must believe in her fidelity; she must be modest, devoted, retiring; she should have the witness not only of a good conscience, but of a good reputation. In a word, if a father must love his children, he must be able to respect their mother. For these reasons it is not enough that the woman should be chaste, she must preserve her reputation and her good name. From these principles there arises not only a moral difference between the sexes, but also a fresh motive for duty and propriety, which prescribes to women in particular the most scrupulous attention to their conduct, their manners, their behaviour. Vague assertions as to the equality of the sexes and the similarity of their duties are only empty words; they are no answer to my argument.

It is a poor sort of logic to quote isolated exceptions against laws so firmly established. Women, you say, are not always bearing children. Granted; yet that is their proper business. Because there are a hundred or so of large towns in the world where women live licentiously and have few children, will you maintain that it is their business to have few children? And what would become of your towns if the remote country districts, with their simpler and purer women, did not make up for the barrenness of your fine ladies? There are plenty of country places where women with only four or five children are reckoned unfruitful. In conclusion, although here and there a woman may have few children, what difference does it make? [Footnote: Without this the race would necessarily diminish; all things considered, for its preservation each woman ought to have about four children, for about half the children born die before they can become parents, and two must survive to replace the father and mother. See whether the towns will supply them?] Is it any the less a woman's business to be a mother? And to not the general laws of nature and morality make provision for this state of things?

Even if there were these long intervals, which you assume, between the periods of pregnancy, can a woman suddenly change her way of life without danger? Can she be a nursing mother to-day and a soldier to-morrow? Will she change her tastes and her feelings as a chameleon changes his colour? Will she pass at once from the privacy of household duties and indoor occupations to the buffeting of the winds, the toils, the labours, the perils of war? Will she be now timid, [Footnote: Women's timidity is yet another instinct of nature against the double risk she runs during pregnancy.] now brave, now fragile, now robust? If the young men of Paris find a soldier's life too hard for them, how would a woman put up with it, a woman who has hardly ventured out of doors without a parasol and who has scarcely put a foot to the ground? Will she make a good soldier at an age when even men are retiring from this arduous business?

There are countries, I grant you, where women bear and rear children with little or no difficulty, but in those lands the men go half-naked in all weathers, they strike down the wild beasts, they carry a canoe as easily as a knapsack, they pursue the chase for 700 or 800 leagues, they sleep in the open on the bare ground, they bear incredible fatigues and go many days without food. When women become strong, men become still stronger; when men become soft, women become softer; change both the terms and the ratio remains unaltered.

I am quite aware that Plato, in the Republic, assigns the same gymnastics to women and men. Having got rid of the family there is no place for women in his system of government, so he is forced to turn them into men. That great genius has worked out his plans in detail and has provided for every contingency; he has even provided against a difficulty which in all likelihood no one would ever have raised; but he has not succeeded in meeting the real difficulty. I am not speaking of the alleged community of wives which has often been laid to his charge; this assertion only shows that his detractors have never read his works. I refer to that political promiscuity under which the same occupations are assigned to both sexes alike, a scheme which could only lead to intolerable evils; I refer to that subversion of all the tenderest of our natural feelings, which he sacrificed to an artificial sentiment which can only exist by their aid. Will the bonds of convention hold firm without some foundation in nature? Can devotion to the state exist apart from the love of those near and dear to us? Can patriotism thrive except in the soil of that miniature fatherland, the home? Is it not the good son, the good husband, the good father, who makes the good citizen?

When once it is proved that men and women are and ought to be unlike in constitution and in temperament, it follows that their education must be different. Nature teaches us that they should work together, but that each has its own share of the work; the end is the same, but the means are different, as are also the feelings which direct them. We have attempted to paint a natural man, let us try to paint a helpmeet for him.

You must follow nature's guidance if you would walk aright. The native characters of sex should be respected as nature's handiwork. You are always saying, "Women have such and such faults, from which we are free." You are misled by your vanity; what would be faults in you are virtues in them; and things would go worse, if they were without these so-called faults. Take care that they do not degenerate into evil, but beware of destroying them.

On the other hand, women are always exclaiming that we educate them for nothing but vanity and coquetry, that we keep them amused with trifles that we may be their masters; we are responsible, so they say, for the faults we attribute to them. How silly! What have men to do with the education of girls? What is there to hinder their mothers educating them as they please? There are no colleges for girls; so much the better for them! Would God there were none for the boys, their education would be more sensible and more wholesome. Who is it that compels a girl to waste her time on foolish trifles? Are they forced, against their will, to spend half their time over their toilet, following the example set them by you? Who prevents you teaching them, or having them taught, whatever seems good in your eyes? Is it our fault that we are charmed by their beauty and delighted by their airs and graces, if we are attracted and flattered by the arts they learn from you, if we love to see them prettily dressed, if we let them display at leisure the weapons by which we are subjugated? Well then, educate them like men. The more women are like men, the less influence they will have over men, and then men will be masters indeed.

All the faculties common to both sexes are not equally shared between them, but taken as a whole they are fairly divided. Woman is worth more as a woman and less as a man; when she makes a good use of her own rights, she has the best of it; when she tries to usurp our rights, she is our inferior. It is impossible to controvert this, except by quoting exceptions after the usual fashion of the partisans of the fair sex.

To cultivate the masculine virtues in women and to neglect their own is evidently to do them an injury. Women are too clear-sighted to be thus deceived; when they try to usurp our privileges they do not abandon their own; with this result: they are unable to make use of two incompatible things, so they fall below their own level as women, instead of rising to the level of men. If you are a sensible mother you will take my advice. Do not try to make your daughter a good man in defiance of nature. Make her a good woman, and be sure it will be better both for her and us.

Does this mean that she must be brought up in ignorance and kept to housework only? Is she to be man's handmaid or his help-meet? Will he dispense with her greatest charm, her companionship? To keep her a slave will he prevent her knowing and feeling? Will he make an automaton of her? No, indeed, that is not the teaching of nature, who has given women such a pleasant easy wit. On the contrary, nature means them to think, to will, to love, to cultivate their minds as well as their persons; she puts these weapons in their hands to make up for their lack of strength and to enable them to direct the strength of men. They should learn many things, but only such things as are suitable.

When I consider the special purpose of woman, when I observe her inclinations or reckon up her duties, everything combines to indicate the mode of education she requires. Men and women are made for each other, but their mutual dependence differs in degree; man is dependent on woman through his desires; woman is dependent on man through her desires and also through her needs; he could do without her better than she can do without him. She cannot fulfil her purpose in life without his aid, without his goodwill, without his respect; she is dependent on our feelings, on the price we put upon her virtue, and the opinion we have of her charms and her deserts. Nature herself has decreed that woman, both for herself and her children, should be at the mercy of man's judgment.

Worth alone will not suffice, a woman must be thought worthy; nor beauty, she must be admired; nor virtue, she must be respected. A woman's honour does not depend on her conduct alone, but on her reputation, and no woman who permits herself to be considered vile is really virtuous. A man has no one but himself to consider, and so long as he does right he may defy public opinion; but when a woman does right her task is only half finished, and what people think of her matters as much as what she really is. Hence her education must, in this respect, be different from man's education. "What will people think" is the grave of a man's virtue and the throne of a woman's.

The children's health depends in the first place on the mother's, and the early education of man is also in a woman's hands; his morals, his passions, his tastes, his pleasures, his happiness itself, depend on her. A woman's education must therefore be planned in relation to man. To be pleasing in his sight, to win his respect and love, to train him in childhood, to tend him in manhood, to counsel and console, to make his life pleasant and happy, these are the duties of woman for all time, and this is what she should be taught while she is young. The further we depart from this principle, the further we shall be from our goal, and all our precepts will fail to secure her happiness or our own.

Every woman desires to be pleasing in men's eyes, and this is right; but there is a great difference between wishing to please a man of worth, a really lovable man, and seeking to please those foppish manikins who are a disgrace to their own sex and to the sex which they imitate. Neither nature nor reason can induce a woman to love an effeminate person, nor will she win love by imitating such a person.

If a woman discards the quiet modest bearing of her sex, and adopts the airs of such foolish creatures, she is not following her vocation, she is forsaking it; she is robbing herself of the rights to which she lays claim. "If we were different," she says, "the men would not like us." She is mistaken. Only a fool likes folly; to wish to attract such men only shows her own foolishness. If there were no frivolous men, women would soon make them, and women are more responsible for men's follies than men are for theirs. The woman who loves true manhood and seeks to find favour in its sight will adopt means adapted to her ends. Woman is a coquette by profession, but her coquetry varies with her aims; let these aims be in accordance with those of nature, and a woman will receive a fitting education.

Even the tiniest little girls love finery; they are not content to be pretty, they must be admired; their little airs and graces show that their heads are full of this idea, and as soon as they can understand they are controlled by "What will people think of you?" If you are foolish enough to try this way with little boys, it will not have the same effect; give them their freedom and their sports, and they care very little what people think; it is a work of time to bring them under the control of this law.

However acquired, this early education of little girls is an excellent thing in itself. As the birth of the body must precede the birth of the mind, so the training of the body must precede the cultivation of the mind. This is true of both sexes; but the aim of physical training for boys and girls is not the same; in the one case it is the development of strength, in the other of grace; not that these qualities should be peculiar to either sex, but that their relative values should be different. Women should be strong enough to do anything gracefully; men should be skilful enough to do anything easily.

The exaggeration of feminine delicacy leads to effeminacy in men. Women should not be strong like men but for them, so that their sons may be strong. Convents and boarding-schools, with their plain food and ample opportunities for amusements, races, and games in the open air and in the garden, are better in this respect than the home, where the little girl is fed on delicacies, continually encouraged or reproved, where she is kept sitting in a stuffy room, always under her mother's eye, afraid to stand or walk or speak or breathe, without a moment's freedom to play or jump or run or shout, or to be her natural, lively, little self; there is either harmful indulgence or misguided severity, and no trace of reason. In this fashion heart and body are alike destroyed.

In Sparta the girls used to take part in military sports just like the boys, not that they might go to war, but that they might bear sons who could endure hardship. That is not what I desire. To provide the state with soldiers it is not necessary that the mother should carry a musket and master the Prussian drill. Yet, on the whole, I think the Greeks were very wise in this matter of physical training. Young girls frequently appeared in public, not with the boys, but in groups apart. There was scarcely a festival, a sacrifice, or a procession without its bands of maidens, the daughters of the chief citizens. Crowned with flowers, chanting hymns, forming the chorus of the dance, bearing baskets, vases, offerings, they presented a charming spectacle to the depraved senses of the Greeks, a spectacle well fitted to efface the evil effects of their unseemly gymnastics. Whatever this custom may have done for the Greek men, it was well fitted to develop in the Greek women a sound constitution by means of pleasant, moderate, and healthy exercise; while the desire to please would develop a keen and cultivated taste without risk to character.

When the Greek women married, they disappeared from public life; within the four walls of their home they devoted themselves to the care of their household and family. This is the mode of life prescribed for women alike by nature and reason. These women gave birth to the healthiest, strongest, and best proportioned men who ever lived, and except in certain islands of ill repute, no women in the whole world, not even the Roman matrons, were ever at once so wise and so charming, so beautiful and so virtuous, as the women of ancient Greece.

It is admitted that their flowing garments, which did not cramp the figure, preserved in men and women alike the fine proportions which are seen in their statues. These are still the models of art, although nature is so disfigured that they are no longer to be found among us. The Gothic trammels, the innumerable bands which confine our limbs as in a press, were quite unknown. The Greek women were wholly unacquainted with those frames of whalebone in which our women distort rather than display their figures. It seems to me that this abuse, which is carried to an incredible degree of folly in England, must sooner or later lead to the production of a degenerate race. Moreover, I maintain that the charm which these corsets are supposed to produce is in the worst possible taste; it is not a pleasant thing to see a woman cut in two like a wasp—it offends both the eye and the imagination. A slender waist has its limits, like everything else, in proportion and suitability, and beyond these limits it becomes a defect. This defect would be a glaring one in the nude; why should it be beautiful under the costume?

I will not venture upon the reasons which induce women to incase themselves in these coats of mail. A clumsy figure, a large waist, are no doubt very ugly at twenty, but at thirty they cease to offend the eye, and as we are bound to be what nature has made us at any given age, and as there is no deceiving the eye of man, such defects are less offensive at any age than the foolish affectations of a young thing of forty.

Everything which cramps and confines nature is in bad taste; this is as true of the adornments of the person as of the ornaments of the mind. Life, health, common-sense, and comfort must come first; there is no grace in discomfort, languor is not refinement, there is no charm in ill-health; suffering may excite pity, but pleasure and delight demand the freshness of health.

Boys and girls have many games in common, and this is as it should be; do they not play together when they are grown up? They have also special tastes of their own. Boys want movement and noise, drums, tops, toy-carts; girls prefer things which appeal to the eye, and can be used for dressing-up—mirrors, jewellery, finery, and specially dolls. The doll is the girl's special plaything; this shows her instinctive bent towards her life's work. The art of pleasing finds its physical basis in personal adornment, and this physical side of the art is the only one which the child can cultivate.

Here is a little girl busy all day with her doll; she is always changing its clothes, dressing and undressing it, trying new combinations of trimmings well or ill matched; her fingers are clumsy, her taste is crude, but there is no mistaking her bent; in this endless occupation time flies unheeded, the hours slip away unnoticed, even meals are forgotten. She is more eager for adornment than for food. "But she is dressing her doll, not herself," you will say. Just so; she sees her doll, she cannot see herself; she cannot do anything for herself, she has neither the training, nor the talent, nor the strength; as yet she herself is nothing, she is engrossed in her doll and all her coquetry is devoted to it. This will not always be so; in due time she will be her own doll.

We have here a very early and clearly-marked bent; you have only to follow it and train it. What the little girl most clearly desires is to dress her doll, to make its bows, its tippets, its sashes, and its tuckers; she is dependent on other people's kindness in all this, and it would be much pleasanter to be able to do it herself. Here is a motive for her earliest lessons, they are not tasks prescribed, but favours bestowed. Little girls always dislike learning to read and write, but they are always ready to learn to sew. They think they are grown up, and in imagination they are using their knowledge for their own adornment.

The way is open and it is easy to follow it; cutting out, embroidery, lace-making follow naturally. Tapestry is not popular; furniture is too remote from the child's interests, it has nothing to do with the person, it depends on conventional tastes. Tapestry is a woman's amusement; young girls never care for it.

This voluntary course is easily extended to include drawing, an art which is closely connected with taste in dress; but I would not have them taught landscape and still less figure painting. Leaves, fruit, flowers, draperies, anything that will make an elegant trimming for the accessories of the toilet, and enable the girl to design her own embroidery if she cannot find a pattern to her taste; that will be quite enough. Speaking generally, if it is desirable to restrict a man's studies to what is useful, this is even more necessary for women, whose life, though less laborious, should be even more industrious and more uniformly employed in a variety of duties, so that one talent should not be encouraged at the expense of others.

Whatever may be said by the scornful, good sense belongs to both sexes alike. Girls are usually more docile than boys, and they should be subjected to more authority, as I shall show later on, but that is no reason why they should be required to do things in which they can see neither rhyme nor reason. The mother's art consists in showing the use of everything they are set to do, and this is all the easier as the girl's intelligence is more precocious than the boy's. This principle banishes, both for boys and girls, not only those pursuits which never lead to any appreciable results, not even increasing the charms of those who have pursued them, but also those studies whose utility is beyond the scholar's present age and can only be appreciated in later years. If I object to little boys being made to learn to read, still more do I object to it for little girls until they are able to see the use of reading; we generally think more of our own ideas than theirs in our attempts to convince them of the utility of this art. After all, why should a little girl know how to read and write! Has she a house to manage? Most of them make a bad use of this fatal knowledge, and girls are so full of curiosity that few of them will fail to learn without compulsion. Possibly cyphering should come first; there is nothing so obviously useful, nothing which needs so much practice or gives so much opportunity for error as reckoning. If the little girl does not get the cherries for her lunch without an arithmetical exercise, she will soon learn to count.

I once knew a little girl who learnt to write before she could read, and she began to write with her needle. To begin with, she would write nothing but O's; she was always making O's, large and small, of all kinds and one within another, but always drawn backwards. Unluckily one day she caught a glimpse of herself in the glass while she was at this useful work, and thinking that the cramped attitude was not pretty, like another Minerva she flung away her pen and declined to make any more O's. Her brother was no fonder of writing, but what he disliked was the constraint, not the look of the thing. She was induced to go on with her writing in this way. The child was fastidious and vain; she could not bear her sisters to wear her clothes. Her things had been marked, they declined to mark them any more, she must learn to mark them herself; there is no need to continue the story.

Show the sense of the tasks you set your little girls, but keep them busy. Idleness and insubordination are two very dangerous faults, and very hard to cure when once established. Girls should be attentive and industrious, but this is not enough by itself; they should early be accustomed to restraint. This misfortune, if such it be, is inherent in their sex, and they will never escape from it, unless to endure more cruel sufferings. All their life long, they will have to submit to the strictest and most enduring restraints, those of propriety. They must be trained to bear the yoke from the first, so that they may not feel it, to master their own caprices and to submit themselves to the will of others. If they were always eager to be at work, they should sometimes be compelled to do nothing. Their childish faults, unchecked and unheeded, may easily lead to dissipation, frivolity, and inconstancy. To guard against this, teach them above all things self-control. Under our senseless conditions, the life of a good woman is a perpetual struggle against self; it is only fair that woman should bear her share of the ills she has brought upon man.

Beware lest your girls become weary of their tasks and infatuated with their amusements; this often happens under our ordinary methods of education, where, as Fenelon says, all the tedium is on one side and all the pleasure on the other. If the rules already laid down are followed, the first of these dangers will be avoided, unless the child dislikes those about her. A little girl who is fond of her mother or her friend will work by her side all day without getting tired; the chatter alone will make up for any loss of liberty. But if her companion is distasteful to her, everything done under her direction will be distasteful too. Children who take no delight in their mother's company are not likely to turn out well; but to judge of their real feelings you must watch them and not trust to their words alone, for they are flatterers and deceitful and soon learn to conceal their thoughts. Neither should they be told that they ought to love their mother. Affection is not the result of duty, and in this respect constraint is out of place. Continual intercourse, constant care, habit itself, all these will lead a child to love her mother, if the mother does nothing to deserve the child's ill-will. The very control she exercises over the child, if well directed, will increase rather than diminish the affection, for women being made for dependence, girls feel themselves made to obey.

Just because they have, or ought to have, little freedom, they are apt to indulge themselves too fully with regard to such freedom as they have; they carry everything to extremes, and they devote themselves to their games with an enthusiasm even greater than that of boys. This is the second difficulty to which I referred. This enthusiasm must be kept in check, for it is the source of several vices commonly found among women, caprice and that extravagant admiration which leads a woman to regard a thing with rapture to-day and to be quite indifferent to it to-morrow. This fickleness of taste is as dangerous as exaggeration; and both spring from the same cause. Do not deprive them of mirth, laughter, noise, and romping games, but do not let them tire of one game and go off to another; do not leave them for a moment without restraint. Train them to break off their games and return to their other occupations without a murmur. Habit is all that is needed, as you have nature on your side.

This habitual restraint produces a docility which woman requires all her life long, for she will always be in subjection to a man, or to man's judgment, and she will never be free to set her own opinion above his. What is most wanted in a woman is gentleness; formed to obey a creature so imperfect as man, a creature often vicious and always faulty, she should early learn to submit to injustice and to suffer the wrongs inflicted on her by her husband without complaint; she must be gentle for her own sake, not his. Bitterness and obstinacy only multiply the sufferings of the wife and the misdeeds of the husband; the man feels that these are not the weapons to be used against him. Heaven did not make women attractive and persuasive that they might degenerate into bitterness, or meek that they should desire the mastery; their soft voice was not meant for hard words, nor their delicate features for the frowns of anger. When they lose their temper they forget themselves; often enough they have just cause of complaint; but when they scold they always put themselves in the wrong. We should each adopt the tone which befits our sex; a soft-hearted husband may make an overbearing wife, but a man, unless he is a perfect monster, will sooner or later yield to his wife's gentleness, and the victory will be hers.

Daughters must always be obedient, but mothers need not always be harsh. To make a girl docile you need not make her miserable; to make her modest you need not terrify her; on the contrary, I should not be sorry to see her allowed occasionally to exercise a little ingenuity, not to escape punishment for her disobedience, but to evade the necessity for obedience. Her dependence need not be made unpleasant, it is enough that she should realise that she is dependent. Cunning is a natural gift of woman, and so convinced am I that all our natural inclinations are right, that I would cultivate this among others, only guarding against its abuse.

For the truth of this I appeal to every honest observer. I do not ask you to question women themselves, our cramping institutions may compel them to sharpen their wits; I would have you examine girls, little girls, newly-born so to speak; compare them with boys of the same age, and I am greatly mistaken if you do not find the little boys heavy, silly, and foolish, in comparison. Let me give one illustration in all its childish simplicity.

Children are commonly forbidden to ask for anything at table, for people think they can do nothing better in the way of education than to burden them with useless precepts; as if a little bit of this or that were not readily given or refused without leaving a poor child dying of greediness intensified by hope. Every one knows how cunningly a little boy brought up in this way asked for salt when he had been overlooked at table. I do not suppose any one will blame him for asking directly for salt and indirectly for meat; the neglect was so cruel that I hardly think he would have been punished had he broken the rule and said plainly that he was hungry. But this is what I saw done by a little girl of six; the circumstances were much more difficult, for not only was she strictly forbidden to ask for anything directly or indirectly, but disobedience would have been unpardonable, for she had eaten of every dish; one only had been overlooked, and on this she had set her heart. This is what she did to repair the omission without laying herself open to the charge of disobedience; she pointed to every dish in turn, saying, "I've had some of this; I've had some of this;" however she omitted the one dish so markedly that some one noticed it and said, "Have not you had some of this?" "Oh, no," replied the greedy little girl with soft voice and downcast eyes. These instances are typical of the cunning of the little boy and girl.

What is, is good, and no general law can be bad. This special skill with which the female sex is endowed is a fair equivalent for its lack of strength; without it woman would be man's slave, not his helpmeet. By her superiority in this respect she maintains her equality with man, and rules in obedience. She has everything against her, our faults and her own weakness and timidity; her beauty and her wiles are all that she has. Should she not cultivate both? Yet beauty is not universal; it may be destroyed by all sorts of accidents, it will disappear with years, and habit will destroy its influence. A woman's real resource is her wit; not that foolish wit which is so greatly admired in society, a wit which does nothing to make life happier; but that wit which is adapted to her condition, the art of taking advantage of our position and controlling us through our own strength. Words cannot tell how beneficial this is to man, what a charm it gives to the society of men and women, how it checks the petulant child and restrains the brutal husband; without it the home would be a scene of strife; with it, it is the abode of happiness. I know that this power is abused by the sly and the spiteful; but what is there that is not liable to abuse? Do not destroy the means of happiness because the wicked use them to our hurt.

The toilet may attract notice, but it is the person that wins our hearts. Our finery is not us; its very artificiality often offends, and that which is least noticeable in itself often wins the most attention. The education of our girls is, in this respect, absolutely topsy-turvy. Ornaments are promised them as rewards, and they are taught to delight in elaborate finery. "How lovely she is!" people say when she is most dressed up. On the contrary, they should be taught that so much finery is only required to hide their defects, and that beauty's real triumph is to shine alone. The love of fashion is contrary to good taste, for faces do not change with the fashion, and while the person remains unchanged, what suits it at one time will suit it always.

If I saw a young girl decked out like a little peacock, I should show myself anxious about her figure so disguised, and anxious what people would think of her; I should say, "She is over-dressed with all those ornaments; what a pity! Do you think she could do with something simpler? Is she pretty enough to do without this or that?" Possibly she herself would be the first to ask that her finery might be taken off and that we should see how she looked without it. In that case her beauty should receive such praise as it deserves. I should never praise her unless simply dressed. If she only regards fine clothes as an aid to personal beauty, and as a tacit confession that she needs their aid, she will not be proud of her finery, she will be humbled by it; and if she hears some one say, "How pretty she is," when she is smarter than usual, she will blush for shame.

Moreover, though there are figures that require adornment there are none that require expensive clothes. Extravagance in dress is the folly of the class rather than the individual, it is merely conventional. Genuine coquetry is sometimes carefully thought out, but never sumptuous, and Juno dressed herself more magnificently than Venus. "As you cannot make her beautiful you are making her fine," said Apelles to an unskilful artist who was painting Helen loaded with jewellery. I have also noticed that the smartest clothes proclaim the plainest women; no folly could be more misguided. If a young girl has good taste and a contempt for fashion, give her a few yards of ribbon, muslin, and gauze, and a handful of flowers, without any diamonds, fringes, or lace, and she will make herself a dress a hundredfold more becoming than all the smart clothes of La Duchapt.

Good is always good, and as you should always look your best, the women who know what they are about select a good style and keep to it, and as they are not always changing their style they think less about dress than those who can never settle to any one style. A genuine desire to dress becomingly does not require an elaborate toilet. Young girls rarely give much time to dress; needlework and lessons are the business of the day; yet, except for the rouge, they are generally as carefully dressed as older women and often in better taste. Contrary to the usual opinion, the real cause of the abuse of the toilet is not vanity but lack of occupation. The woman who devotes six hours to her toilet is well aware that she is no better dressed than the woman who took half an hour, but she has got rid of so many of the tedious hours and it is better to amuse oneself with one's clothes than to be sick of everything. Without the toilet how would she spend the time between dinner and supper. With a crowd of women about her, she can at least cause them annoyance, which is amusement of a kind; better still she avoids a tete-a-tete with the husband whom she never sees at any other time; then there are the tradespeople, the dealers in bric-a-brac, the fine gentlemen, the minor poets with their songs, their verses, and their pamphlets; how could you get them together but for the toilet. Its only real advantage is the chance of a little more display than is permitted by full dress, and perhaps this is less than it seems and a woman gains less than she thinks. Do not be afraid to educate your women as women; teach them a woman's business, that they be modest, that they may know how to manage their house and look after their family; the grand toilet will soon disappear, and they will be more tastefully dressed.

Growing girls perceive at once that all this outside adornment is not enough unless they have charms of their own. They cannot make themselves beautiful, they are too young for coquetry, but they are not too young to acquire graceful gestures, a pleasing voice, a self-possessed manner, a light step, a graceful bearing, to choose whatever advantages are within their reach. The voice extends its range, it grows stronger and more resonant, the arms become plumper, the bearing more assured, and they perceive that it is easy to attract attention however dressed. Needlework and industry suffice no longer, fresh gifts are developing and their usefulness is already recognised.

I know that stern teachers would have us refuse to teach little girls to sing or dance, or to acquire any of the pleasing arts. This strikes me as absurd. Who should learn these arts—our boys? Are these to be the favourite accomplishments of men or women? Of neither, say they; profane songs are simply so many crimes, dancing is an invention of the Evil One; her tasks and her prayers we all the amusement a young girl should have. What strange amusements for a child of ten! I fear that these little saints who have been forced to spend their childhood in prayers to God will pass their youth in another fashion; when they are married they will try to make up for lost time. I think we must consider age as well as sex; a young girl should not live like her grandmother; she should be lively, merry, and eager; she should sing and dance to her heart's content, and enjoy all the innocent pleasures of youth; the time will come, all too soon, when she must settle down and adopt a more serious tone.

But is this change in itself really necessary? Is it not merely another result of our own prejudices? By making good women the slaves of dismal duties, we have deprived marriage of its charm for men. Can we wonder that the gloomy silence they find at home drives them elsewhere, or inspires little desire to enter a state which offers so few attractions? Christianity, by exaggerating every duty, has made our duties impracticable and useless; by forbidding singing, dancing, and amusements of every kind, it renders women sulky, fault-finding, and intolerable at home. There is no religion which imposes such strict duties upon married life, and none in which such a sacred engagement is so often profaned. Such pains has been taken to prevent wives being amiable, that their husbands have become indifferent to them. This should not be, I grant you, but it will be, since husbands are but men. I would have an English maiden cultivate the talents which will delight her husband as zealously as the Circassian cultivates the accomplishments of an Eastern harem. Husbands, you say, care little for such accomplishments. So I should suppose, when they are employed, not for the husband, but to attract the young rakes who dishonour the home. But imagine a virtuous and charming wife, adorned with such accomplishments and devoting them to her husband's amusement; will she not add to his happiness? When he leaves his office worn out with the day's work, will she not prevent him seeking recreation elsewhere? Have we not all beheld happy families gathered together, each contributing to the general amusement? Are not the confidence and familiarity thus established, the innocence and the charm of the pleasures thus enjoyed, more than enough to make up for the more riotous pleasures of public entertainments?

Pleasant accomplishments have been made too formal an affair of rules and precepts, so that young people find them very tedious instead of a mere amusement or a merry game as they ought to be. Nothing can be more absurd than an elderly singing or dancing master frowning upon young people, whose one desire is to laugh, and adopting a more pedantic and magisterial manner in teaching his frivolous art than if he were teaching the catechism. Take the case of singing; does this art depend on reading music; cannot the voice be made true and flexible, can we not learn to sing with taste and even to play an accompaniment without knowing a note? Does the same kind of singing suit all voices alike? Is the same method adapted to every mind? You will never persuade me that the same attitudes, the same steps, the same movements, the same gestures, the same dances will suit a lively little brunette and a tall fair maiden with languishing eyes. So when I find a master giving the same lessons to all his pupils I say, "He has his own routine, but he knows nothing of his art!"

Should young girls have masters or mistresses? I cannot say; I wish they could dispense with both; I wish they could learn of their own accord what they are already so willing to learn. I wish there were fewer of these dressed-up old ballet masters promenading our streets. I fear our young people will get more harm from intercourse with such people than profit from their instruction, and that their jargon, their tone, their airs and graces, will instil a precocious taste for the frivolities which the teacher thinks so important, and to which the scholars are only too likely to devote themselves.

Where pleasure is the only end in view, any one may serve as teacher—father, mother, brother, sister, friend, governess, the girl's mirror, and above all her own taste. Do not offer to teach, let her ask; do not make a task of what should be a reward, and in these studies above all remember that the wish to succeed is the first step. If formal instruction is required I leave it to you to choose between a master and a mistress. How can I tell whether a dancing master should take a young pupil by her soft white hand, make her lift her skirt and raise her eyes, open her arms and advance her throbbing bosom? but this I know, nothing on earth would induce me to be that master.

Taste is formed partly by industry and partly by talent, and by its means the mind is unconsciously opened to the idea of beauty of every kind, till at length it attains to those moral ideas which are so closely related to beauty. Perhaps this is one reason why ideas of propriety and modesty are acquired earlier by girls than by boys, for to suppose that this early feeling is due to the teaching of the governesses would show little knowledge of their style of teaching and of the natural development of the human mind. The art of speaking stands first among the pleasing arts; it alone can add fresh charms to those which have been blunted by habit. It is the mind which not only gives life to the body, but renews, so to speak, its youth; the flow of feelings and ideas give life and variety to the countenance, and the conversation to which it gives rise arouses and sustains attention, and fixes it continuously on one object. I suppose this is why little girls so soon learn to prattle prettily, and why men enjoy listening to them even before the child can understand them; they are watching for the first gleam of intelligence and sentiment.

Women have ready tongues; they talk earlier, more easily, and more pleasantly than men. They are also said to talk more; this may be true, but I am prepared to reckon it to their credit; eyes and mouth are equally busy and for the same cause. A man says what he knows, a woman says what will please; the one needs knowledge, the other taste; utility should be the man's object; the woman speaks to give pleasure. There should be nothing in common but truth.

You should not check a girl's prattle like a boy's by the harsh question, "What is the use of that?" but by another question at least as difficult to answer, "What effect will that have?" At this early age when they know neither good nor evil, and are incapable of judging others, they should make this their rule and never say anything which is unpleasant to those about them; this rule is all the more difficult to apply because it must always be subordinated to our first rule, "Never tell a lie."

I can see many other difficulties, but they belong to a later stage. For the present it is enough for your little girls to speak the truth without grossness, and as they are naturally averse to what is gross, education easily teaches them to avoid it. In social intercourse I observe that a man's politeness is usually more helpful and a woman's more caressing. This distinction is natural, not artificial. A man seeks to serve, a woman seeks to please. Hence a woman's politeness is less insincere than ours, whatever we may think of her character; for she is only acting upon a fundamental instinct; but when a man professes to put my interests before his own, I detect the falsehood, however disguised. Hence it is easy for women to be polite, and easy to teach little girls politeness. The first lessons come by nature; art only supplements them and determines the conventional form which politeness shall take. The courtesy of woman to woman is another matter; their manner is so constrained, their attentions so chilly, they find each other so wearisome, that they take little pains to conceal the fact, and seem sincere even in their falsehood, since they take so little pains to conceal it. Still young girls do sometimes become sincerely attached to one another. At their age good spirits take the place of a good disposition, and they are so pleased with themselves that they are pleased with every one else. Moreover, it is certain that they kiss each other more affectionately and caress each other more gracefully in the presence of men, for they are proud to be able to arouse their envy without danger to themselves by the sight of favours which they know will arouse that envy.

If young boys must not be allowed to ask unsuitable questions, much more must they be forbidden to little girls; if their curiosity is satisfied or unskilfully evaded it is a much more serious matter, for they are so keen to guess the mysteries concealed from them and so skilful to discover them. But while I would not permit them to ask questions, I would have them questioned frequently, and pains should be taken to make them talk; let them be teased to make them speak freely, to make them answer readily, to loosen mind and tongue while it can be done without danger. Such conversation always leading to merriment, yet skilfully controlled and directed, would form a delightful amusement at this age and might instil into these youthful hearts the first and perhaps the most helpful lessons in morals which they will ever receive, by teaching them in the guise of pleasure and fun what qualities are esteemed by men and what is the true glory and happiness of a good woman.

If boys are incapable of forming any true idea of religion, much more is it beyond the grasp of girls; and for this reason I would speak of it all the sooner to little girls, for if we wait till they are ready for a serious discussion of these deep subjects we should be in danger of never speaking of religion at all. A woman's reason is practical, and therefore she soon arrives at a given conclusion, but she fails to discover it for herself. The social relation of the sexes is a wonderful thing. This relation produces a moral person of which woman is the eye and man the hand, but the two are so dependent on one another that the man teaches the woman what to see, while she teaches him what to do. If women could discover principles and if men had as good heads for detail, they would be mutually independent, they would live in perpetual strife, and there would be an end to all society. But in their mutual harmony each contributes to a common purpose; each follows the other's lead, each commands and each obeys.

As a woman's conduct is controlled by public opinion, so is her religion ruled by authority. The daughter should follow her mother's religion, the wife her husband's. Were that religion false, the docility which leads mother and daughter to submit to nature's laws would blot out the sin of error in the sight of God. Unable to judge for themselves they should accept the judgment of father and husband as that of the church.

While women unaided cannot deduce the rules of their faith, neither can they assign limits to that faith by the evidence of reason; they allow themselves to be driven hither and thither by all sorts of external influences, they are ever above or below the truth. Extreme in everything, they are either altogether reckless or altogether pious; you never find them able to combine virtue and piety. Their natural exaggeration is not wholly to blame; the ill-regulated control exercised over them by men is partly responsible. Loose morals bring religion into contempt; the terrors of remorse make it a tyrant; this is why women have always too much or too little religion.

As a woman's religion is controlled by authority it is more important to show her plainly what to believe than to explain the reasons for belief; for faith attached to ideas half-understood is the main source of fanaticism, and faith demanded on behalf of what is absurd leads to madness or unbelief. Whether our catechisms tend to produce impiety rather than fanaticism I cannot say, but I do know that they lead to one or other.

In the first place, when you teach religion to little girls never make it gloomy or tiresome, never make it a task or a duty, and therefore never give them anything to learn by heart, not even their prayers. Be content to say your own prayers regularly in their presence, but do not compel them to join you. Let their prayers be short, as Christ himself has taught us. Let them always be said with becoming reverence and respect; remember that if we ask the Almighty to give heed to our words, we should at least give heed to what we mean to say.

It does not much matter that a girl should learn her religion young, but it does matter that she should learn it thoroughly, and still more that she should learn to love it. If you make religion a burden to her, if you always speak of God's anger, if in the name of religion you impose all sorts of disagreeable duties, duties which she never sees you perform, what can she suppose but that to learn one's catechism and to say one's prayers is only the duty of a little girl, and she will long to be grown-up to escape, like you, from these duties. Example! Example! Without it you will never succeed in teaching children anything.

When you explain the Articles of Faith let it be by direct teaching, not by question and answer. Children should only answer what they think, not what has been drilled into them. All the answers in the catechism are the wrong way about; it is the scholar who instructs the teacher; in the child's mouth they are a downright lie, since they explain what he does not understand, and affirm what he cannot believe. Find me, if you can, an intelligent man who could honestly say his catechism. The first question I find in our catechism is as follows: "Who created you and brought you into the world?" To which the girl, who thinks it was her mother, replies without hesitation, "It was God." All she knows is that she is asked a question which she only half understands and she gives an answer she does not understand at all.

I wish some one who really understands the development of children's minds would write a catechism for them. It might be the most useful book ever written, and, in my opinion, it would do its author no little honour. This at least is certain—if it were a good book it would be very unlike our catechisms.

Such a catechism will not be satisfactory unless the child can answer the questions of its own accord without having to learn the answers; indeed the child will often ask the questions itself. An example is required to make my meaning plain and I feel how ill equipped I am to furnish such an example. I will try to give some sort of outline of my meaning.

To get to the first question in our catechism I suppose we must begin somewhat after the following fashion.

NURSE: Do you remember when your mother was a little girl?

CHILD: No, nurse.
NURSE: Why not, when you have such a good memory?
CHILD: I was not alive.
NURSE: Then you were not always alive!
CHILD: No.
NURSE: Will you live for ever!
CHILD: Yes.
NURSE: Are you young or old?
CHILD: I am young.
NURSE: Is your grandmamma old or young?
CHILD: She is old.
NURSE: Was she ever young?
CHILD: Yes.
NURSE: Why is she not young now?
CHILD: She has grown old.
NURSE: Will you grow old too?
CHILD: I don't know.
NURSE: Where are your last year's frocks?
CHILD: They have been unpicked.
NURSE: Why!
CHILD: Because they were too small for me.
NURSE: Why were they too small?
CHILD: I have grown bigger.
NURSE: Will you grow any more!
CHILD: Oh, yes.
NURSE: And what becomes of big girls?
CHILD: They grow into women.
NURSE: And what becomes of women!
CHILD: They are mothers.
NURSE: And what becomes of mothers?
CHILD: They grow old.
NURSE: Will you grow old?
CHILD: When I am a mother.
NURSE: And what becomes of old people?
CHILD: I don't know.
NURSE: What became of your grandfather?

CHILD: He died. [Footnote: The child will say this because she has heard it said; but you must make sure she knows what death is, for the idea is not so simple and within the child's grasp as people think. In that little poem "Abel" you will find an example of the way to teach them. This charming work breathes a delightful simplicity with which one should feed one's own mind so as to talk with children.]

NURSE: Why did he die?
CHILD: Because he was so old.
NURSE: What becomes of old people!

CHILD: They die.

NURSE: And when you are old— —?

CHILD: Oh nurse! I don't want to die!

NURSE: My dear, no one wants to die, and everybody dies.

CHILD: Why, will mamma die too!

NURSE: Yes, like everybody else. Women grow old as well as men, and old age ends in death.

CHILD: What must I do to grow old very, very slowly?

NURSE: Be good while you are little.

CHILD: I will always be good, nurse.

NURSE: So much the better. But do you suppose you will live for ever?

CHILD: When I am very, very old— —

NURSE: Well?

CHILD: When we are so very old you say we must die?

NURSE: You must die some day.

CHILD: Oh dear! I suppose I must.

NURSE: Who lived before you?

CHILD: My father and mother.

NURSE: And before them?

CHILD: Their father and mother.

NURSE: Who will live after you?

CHILD: My children.

NURSE: Who will live after them?

CHILD: Their children.

In this way, by concrete examples, you will find a beginning and end for the human race like everything else—that is to say, a father and mother who never had a father and mother, and children who will never have children of their own.

It is only after a long course of similar questions that we are ready for the first question in the catechism; then alone can we put the question and the child may be able to understand it. But what a gap there is between the first and the second question which is concerned with the definitions of the divine nature. When will this chasm be bridged? "God is a spirit." "And what is a spirit?" Shall I start the child upon this difficult question of metaphysics which grown men find so hard to understand? These are no questions for a little girl to answer; if she asks them, it is as much or more than we can expect. In that case I should tell her quite simply, "You ask me what God is; it is not easy to say; we can neither hear nor see nor handle God; we can only know Him by His works. To learn what He is, you must wait till you know what He has done."

If our dogmas are all equally true, they are not equally important. It makes little difference to the glory of God that we should perceive it everywhere, but it does make a difference to human society, and to every member of that society, that a man should know and do the duties which are laid upon him by the law of God, his duty to his neighbour and to himself. This is what we should always be teaching one another, and it is this which fathers and mothers are specially bound to teach their little ones. Whether a virgin became the mother of her Creator, whether she gave birth to God, or merely to a man into whom God has entered, whether the Father and the Son are of the same substance or of like substance only, whether the Spirit proceeded from one or both of these who are but one, or from both together, however important these questions may seem, I cannot see that it is any more necessary for the human race to come to a decision with regard to them than to know what day to keep Easter, or whether we should tell our beads, fast, and refuse to eat meat, speak Latin or French in church, adorn the walls with statues, hear or say mass, and have no wife of our own. Let each think as he pleases; I cannot see that it matters to any one but himself; for my own part it is no concern of mine. But what does concern my fellow-creatures and myself alike is to know that there is indeed a judge of human fate, that we are all His children, that He bids us all be just, He bids us love one another, He bids us be kindly and merciful, He bids us keep our word with all men, even with our own enemies and His; we must know that the apparent happiness of this world is naught; that there is another life to come, in which this Supreme Being will be the rewarder of the just and the judge of the unjust. Children need to be taught these doctrines and others like them and all citizens require to be persuaded of their truth. Whoever sets his face against these doctrines is indeed guilty; he is the disturber of the peace, the enemy of society. Whoever goes beyond these doctrines and seeks to make us the slaves of his private opinions, reaches the same goal by another way; to establish his own kind of order he disturbs the peace; in his rash pride he makes himself the interpreter of the Divine, and in His name demands the homage and the reverence of mankind; so far as may be, he sets himself in God's place; he should receive the punishment of sacrilege if he is not punished for his intolerance.

Give no heed, therefore, to all those mysterious doctrines which are words without ideas for us, all those strange teachings, the study of which is too often offered as a substitute for virtue, a study which more often makes men mad rather than good. Keep your children ever within the little circle of dogmas which are related to morality. Convince them that the only useful learning is that which teaches us to act rightly. Do not make your daughters theologians and casuists; only teach them such things of heaven as conduce to human goodness; train them to feel that they are always in the presence of God, who sees their thoughts and deeds, their virtue and their pleasures; teach them to do good without ostentation and because they love it, to suffer evil without a murmur, because God will reward them; in a word to be all their life long what they will be glad to have been when they appear in His presence. This is true religion; this alone is incapable of abuse, impiety, or fanaticism. Let those who will, teach a religion more sublime, but this is the only religion I know.

Moreover, it is as well to observe that, until the age when the reason becomes enlightened, when growing emotion gives a voice to conscience, what is wrong for young people is what those about have decided to be wrong. What they are told to do is good; what they are forbidden to do is bad; that is all they ought to know: this shows how important it is for girls, even more than for boys, that the right people should be chosen to be with them and to have authority over them. At last there comes a time when they begin to judge things for themselves, and that is the time to change your method of education.

Perhaps I have said too much already. To what shall we reduce the education of our women if we give them no law but that of conventional prejudice? Let us not degrade so far the set which rules over us, and which does us honour when we have not made it vile. For all mankind there is a law anterior to that of public opinion. All other laws should bend before the inflexible control of this law; it is the judge of public opinion, and only in so far as the esteem of men is in accordance with this law has it any claim on our obedience.

This law is our individual conscience. I will not repeat what has been said already; it is enough to point out that if these two laws clash, the education of women will always be imperfect. Right feeling without respect for public opinion will not give them that delicacy of soul which lends to right conduct the charm of social approval; while respect for public opinion without right feeling will only make false and wicked women who put appearances in the place of virtue.

It is, therefore, important to cultivate a faculty which serves as judge between the two guides, which does not permit conscience to go astray and corrects the errors of prejudice. That faculty is reason. But what a crowd of questions arise at this word. Are women capable of solid reason; should they cultivate it, can they cultivate it successfully? Is this culture useful in relation to the functions laid upon them? Is it compatible with becoming simplicity?

The different ways of envisaging and answering these questions lead to two extremes; some would have us keep women indoors sewing and spinning with their maids; thus they make them nothing more than the chief servant of their master. Others, not content to secure their rights, lead them to usurp ours; for to make woman our superior in all the qualities proper to her sex, and to make her our equal in all the rest, what is this but to transfer to the woman the superiority which nature has given to her husband? The reason which teaches a man his duties is not very complex; the reason which teaches a woman hers is even simpler. The obedience and fidelity which she owes to her husband, the tenderness and care due to her children, are such natural and self-evident consequences of her position that she cannot honestly refuse her consent to the inner voice which is her guide, nor fail to discern her duty in her natural inclination.

I would not altogether blame those who would restrict a woman to the labours of her sex and would leave her in profound ignorance of everything else; but that would require a standard of morality at once very simple and very healthy, or a life withdrawn from the world. In great towns, among immoral men, such a woman would be too easily led astray; her virtue would too often be at the mercy of circumstances; in this age of philosophy, virtue must be able to resist temptation; she must know beforehand what she may hear and what she should think of it.

Moreover, in submission to man's judgment she should deserve his esteem; above all she should obtain the esteem of her husband; she should not only make him love her person, she should make him approve her conduct; she should justify his choice before the world, and do honour to her husband through the honour given to the wife. But how can she set about this task if she is ignorant of our institutions, our customs, our notions of propriety, if she knows nothing of the source of man's judgment, nor the passions by which it is swayed! Since she depends both on her own conscience and on public opinion, she must learn to know and reconcile these two laws, and to put her own conscience first only when the two are opposed to each other. She becomes the judge of her own judges, she decides when she should obey and when she should refuse her obedience. She weighs their prejudices before she accepts or rejects them; she learns to trace them to their source, to foresee what they will be, and to turn them in her own favour; she is careful never to give cause for blame if duty allows her to avoid it. This cannot be properly done without cultivating her mind and reason.

I always come back to my first principle and it supplies the solution of all my difficulties. I study what is, I seek its cause, and I discover in the end that what is, is good. I go to houses where the master and mistress do the honours together. They are equally well educated, equally polite, equally well equipped with wit and good taste, both of them are inspired with the same desire to give their guests a good reception and to send every one away satisfied. The husband omits no pains to be attentive to every one; he comes and goes and sees to every one and takes all sorts of trouble; he is attention itself. The wife remains in her place; a little circle gathers round her and apparently conceals the rest of the company from her; yet she sees everything that goes on, no one goes without a word with her; she has omitted nothing which might interest anybody, she has said nothing unpleasant to any one, and without any fuss the least is no more overlooked than the greatest. Dinner is announced, they take their places; the man knowing the assembled guests will place them according to his knowledge; the wife, without previous acquaintance, never makes a mistake; their looks and bearing have already shown her what is wanted and every one will find himself where he wishes to be. I do not assert that the servants forget no one. The master of the house may have omitted no one, but the mistress perceives what you like and sees that you get it; while she is talking to her neighbour she has one eye on the other end of the table; she sees who is not eating because he is not hungry and who is afraid to help himself because he is clumsy and timid. When the guests leave the table every one thinks she has had no thought but for him, everybody thinks she has had no time to eat anything, but she has really eaten more than anybody.

When the guests are gone, husband and wife tails over the events of the evening. He relates what was said to him, what was said and done by those with whom he conversed. If the lady is not always quite exact in this respect, yet on the other hand she perceived what was whispered at the other end of the room; she knows what so-and-so thought, and what was the meaning of this speech or that gesture; there is scarcely a change of expression for which she has not an explanation in readiness, and she is almost always right.

The same turn of mind which makes a woman of the world such an excellent hostess, enables a flirt to excel in the art of amusing a number of suitors. Coquetry, cleverly carried out, demands an even finer discernment than courtesy; provided a polite lady is civil to everybody, she has done fairly well in any case; but the flirt would soon lose her hold by such clumsy uniformity; if she tries to be pleasant to all her lovers alike, she will disgust them all. In ordinary social intercourse the manners adopted towards everybody are good enough for all; no question is asked as to private likes or dislikes provided all are alike well received. But in love, a favour shared with others is an insult. A man of feeling would rather be singled out for ill-treatment than be caressed with the crowd, and the worst that can befall him is to be treated like every one else. So a woman who wants to keep several lovers at her feet must persuade every one of them that she prefers him, and she must contrive to do this in the sight of all the rest, each of whom is equally convinced that he is her favourite.

If you want to see a man in a quandary, place him between two women with each of whom he has a secret understanding, and see what a fool he looks. But put a woman in similar circumstances between two men, and the results will be even more remarkable; you will be astonished at the skill with which she cheats them both, and makes them laugh at each other. Now if that woman were to show the same confidence in both, if she were to be equally familiar with both, how could they be deceived for a moment? If she treated them alike, would she not show that they both had the same claims upon her? Oh, she is far too clever for that; so far from treating them just alike, she makes a marked difference between them, and she does it so skilfully that the man she flatters thinks it is affection, and the man she ill uses think it is spite. So that each of them believes she is thinking of him, when she is thinking of no one but herself.

A general desire to please suggests similar measures; people would be disgusted with a woman's whims if they were not skilfully managed, and when they are artistically distributed her servants are more than ever enslaved.

> *"Usa ogn'arte la donna, onde sia colto*
> *Nella sua rete alcun novello amante;*
> *Ne con tutti, ne sempre un stesso volto*
> *Serba; ma cangia a tempo atto e sembiante."*
> *Tasso, Jerus. Del., c. iv., v. 87.*

What is the secret of this art? Is it not the result of a delicate and continuous observation which shows her what is taking place in a man's heart, so that she is able to encourage or to check every hidden impulse? Can this art be acquired? No; it is born with women; it is common to them all, and men never show it to the same degree. It is one of the distinctive characters of the sex. Self-possession, penetration, delicate observation, this is a woman's science; the skill to make use of it is her chief accomplishment.

This is what is, and we have seen why it is so. It is said that women are false. They become false. They are really endowed with skill not duplicity; in the genuine inclinations of their sex they are not false even when they tell a lie. Why do you consult their words when it is not their mouths that speak? Consult their eyes, their colour, their breathing, their timid manner, their slight resistance, that is the language nature gave them for your answer. The lips always say "No," and rightly so; but the tone is not always the same, and that cannot lie. Has not a woman the same needs as a man, but without the same right to make them known? Her fate would be too cruel if she had no language in which to express her legitimate desires except the words which she dare not utter. Must her modesty condemn her to misery? Does she not require a means of indicating her inclinations without open expression? What skill is needed to hide from her lover what she would fain reveal! Is it not of vital importance that she should learn to touch his heart without showing that she cares for him? It is a pretty story that tale of Galatea with her apple and her clumsy flight. What more is needed? Will she tell the shepherd who pursues her among the willows that she only flees that he may follow? If she did, it would be a lie; for she would no longer attract him. The more modest a woman is, the more art she needs, even with her husband. Yes, I maintain that coquetry, kept within bounds, becomes modest and true, and out of it springs a law of right conduct.

One of my opponents has very truly asserted that virtue is one; you cannot disintegrate it and choose this and reject the other. If you love virtue, you love it in its entirety, and you close your heart when you can, and you always close your lips to the feelings which you ought not to allow. Moral truth is not only what is, but what is good; what is bad ought not to be, and ought not to be confessed, especially when that confession produces results which might have been avoided. If I were tempted to steal, and in confessing it I tempted another to become my accomplice, the very confession of my temptation would amount to a yielding to that temptation. Why do you say that modesty makes women false? Are those who lose their modesty more sincere than the rest? Not so, they are a thousandfold more deceitful. This degree of depravity is due to many vices, none of which is rejected, vices which owe their power to intrigue and falsehood. [Footnote: I know that women who have openly decided on a certain course of conduct profess that their lack of concealment is a virtue in itself, and swear that, with one exception, they are possessed of all the virtues; but I am sure they never persuaded any but fools to believe them. When the natural curb is removed from their sex, what is there left to restrain them? What honour will they prize when they have rejected the honour of their sex? Having once given the rein to passion they have no longer any reason for self-control. "Nec femina, amissa pudicitia, alia abnuerit." No author ever understood more thoroughly the heart of both sexes than Tacitus when he wrote those words.]

On the other hand, those who are not utterly shameless, who take no pride in their faults, who are able to conceal their desires even from those who inspire them, those who confess their passion most reluctantly, these are the truest and most sincere, these are they on whose fidelity you may generally rely.

The only example I know which might be quoted as a recognised exception to these remarks is Mlle. de L'Enclos; and she was considered a prodigy. In her scorn for the virtues of women, she practised, so they say, the virtues of a man. She is praised for her frankness and uprightness; she was a trustworthy acquaintance and a faithful friend. To complete the picture of her glory it is said that she became a man. That may be, but in spite of her high reputation I should no more desire that man as my friend than as my mistress.

This is not so irrelevant as it seems. I am aware of the tendencies of our modern philosophy which make a jest of female modesty and its so-called insincerity; I also perceive that the most certain result of this philosophy will be to deprive the women of this century of such shreds of honour as they still possess.

On these grounds I think we may decide in general terms what sort of education is suited to the female mind, and the objects to which we should turn its attention in early youth.

As I have already said, the duties of their sex are more easily recognised than performed. They must learn in the first place to love those duties by considering the advantages to be derived from them—that is the only way to make duty easy. Every age and condition has its own duties. We are quick to see our duty if we love it. Honour your position as a woman, and in whatever station of life to which it shall please heaven to call you, you will be well off. The essential thing is to be what nature has made you; women are only too ready to be what men would have them.

The search for abstract and speculative truths, for principles and axioms in science, for all that tends to wide generalisation, is beyond a woman's grasp; their studies should be thoroughly practical. It is their business to apply the principles discovered by men, it is their place to make the observations which lead men to discover those principles. A woman's thoughts, beyond the range of her immediate duties, should be directed to the study of men, or the acquirement of that agreeable learning whose sole end is the formation of taste; for the works of genius are beyond her reach, and she has neither the accuracy nor the attention for success in the exact sciences; as for the physical sciences, to decide the relations between living creatures and the laws of nature is the task of that sex which is more active and enterprising, which sees more things, that sex which is possessed of greater strength and is more accustomed to the exercise of that strength. Woman, weak as she is and limited in her range of observation, perceives and judges the forces at her disposal to supplement her weakness, and those forces are the passions of man. Her own mechanism is more powerful than ours; she has many levers which may set the human heart in motion. She must find a way to make us desire what she cannot achieve unaided and what she considers necessary or pleasing; therefore she must have a thorough knowledge of man's mind; not an abstract knowledge of the mind of man in general, but the mind of those men who are about her, the mind of those men who have authority over her, either by law or custom. She must learn to divine their feelings from speech and action, look and gesture. By her own speech and action, look and gesture, she must be able to inspire them with the feelings she desires, without seeming to have any such purpose. The men will have a better philosophy of the human heart, but she will read more accurately in the heart of men. Woman should discover, so to speak, an experimental morality, man should reduce it to a system. Woman has more wit, man more genius; woman observes, man reasons; together they provide the clearest light and the profoundest knowledge which is possible to the unaided human mind; in a word, the surest knowledge of self and of others of which the human race is capable. In this way art may constantly tend to the perfection of the instrument which nature has given us.

The world is woman's book; if she reads it ill, it is either her own fault or she is blinded by passion. Yet the genuine mother of a family is no woman of the world, she is almost as much of a recluse as the nun in her convent. Those who have marriageable daughters should do what is or ought to be done for those who are entering the cloisters: they should show them the pleasures they forsake before they are allowed to renounce them, lest the deceitful picture of unknown pleasures should creep in to disturb the happiness of their retreat. In France it is the girls who live in convents and the wives who flaunt in society. Among the ancients it was quite otherwise; girls enjoyed, as I have said already, many games and public festivals; the married women lived in retirement. This was a more reasonable custom and more conducive to morality. A girl may be allowed a certain amount of coquetry, and she may be mainly occupied at amusement. A wife has other responsibilities at home, and she is no longer on the look-out for a husband; but women would not appreciate the change, and unluckily it is they who set the fashion. Mothers, let your daughters be your companions. Give them good sense and an honest heart, and then conceal from them nothing that a pure eye may behold. Balls, assemblies, sports, the theatre itself; everything which viewed amiss delights imprudent youth may be safely displayed to a healthy mind. The more they know of these noisy pleasures, the sooner they will cease to desire them.

I can fancy the outcry with which this will be received. What girl will resist such an example? Their heads are turned by the first glimpse of the world; not one of them is ready to give it up. That may be; but before you showed them this deceitful prospect, did you prepare them to behold it without emotion? Did you tell them plainly what it was they would see? Did you show it in its true light? Did you arm them against the illusions of vanity? Did you inspire their young hearts with a taste for the true pleasures which are not to be met with in this tumult? What precautions, what steps, did you take to preserve them from the false taste which leads them astray? Not only have you done nothing to preserve their minds from the tyranny of prejudice, you have fostered that prejudice; you have taught them to desire every foolish amusement they can get. Your own example is their teacher. Young people on their entrance into society have no guide but their mother, who is often just as silly as they are themselves, and quite unable to show them things except as she sees them herself. Her example is stronger than reason; it justifies them in their own eyes, and the mother's authority is an unanswerable excuse for the daughter. If I ask a mother to bring her daughter into society, I assume that she will show it in its true light.

The evil begins still earlier; the convents are regular schools of coquetry; not that honest coquetry which I have described, but a coquetry the source of every kind of misconduct, a coquetry which turns out girls who are the most ridiculous little madams. When they leave the convent to take their place in smart society, young women find themselves quite at home. They have been educated for such a life; is it strange that they like it? I am afraid what I am going to say may be based on prejudice rather than observation, but so far as I can see, one finds more family affection, more good wives and loving mothers in Protestant than in Catholic countries; if that is so, we cannot fail to suspect that the difference is partly due to the convent schools.

The charms of a peaceful family life must be known to be enjoyed; their delights should be tasted in childhood. It is only in our father's home that we learn to love our own, and a woman whose mother did not educate her herself will not be willing to educate her own children. Unfortunately, there is no such thing as home education in our large towns. Society is so general and so mixed there is no place left for retirement, and even in the home we live in public. We live in company till we have no family, and we scarcely know our own relations, we see them as strangers; and the simplicity of home life disappears together with the sweet familiarity which was its charm. In this wise do we draw with our mother's milk a taste for the pleasures of the age and the maxims by which it is controlled.

Girls are compelled to assume an air of propriety so that men may be deceived into marrying them by their appearance. But watch these young people for a moment; under a pretence of coyness they barely conceal the passion which devours them, and already you may read in their eager eyes their desire to imitate their mothers. It is not a husband they want, but the licence of a married woman. What need of a husband when there are so many other resources; but a husband there must be to act as a screen. [Footnote: The way of a man in his youth was one of the four things that the sage could not understand; the fifth was the shamelessness of an adulteress. "Quae comedit, et tergens os suum dicit; non sum operata malum." Prov. xxx. 20.] There is modesty on the brow, but vice in the heart; this sham modesty is one of its outward signs; they affect it that they may be rid of it once for all. Women of

Paris and London, forgive me! There may be miracles everywhere, but I am not aware of them; and if there is even one among you who is really pure in heart, I know nothing of our institutions.

All these different methods of education lead alike to a taste for the pleasures of the great world, and to the passions which this taste so soon kindles. In our great towns depravity begins at birth; in the smaller towns it begins with reason. Young women brought up in the country are soon taught to despise the happy simplicity of their lives, and hasten to Paris to share the corruption of ours. Vices, cloaked under the fair name of accomplishments, are the sole object of their journey; ashamed to find themselves so much behind the noble licence of the Parisian ladies, they hasten to become worthy of the name of Parisian. Which is responsible for the evil—the place where it begins, or the place where it is accomplished?

I would not have a sensible mother bring her girl to Paris to show her these sights so harmful to others; but I assert that if she did so, either the girl has been badly brought up, or such sights have little danger for her. With good taste, good sense, and a love of what is right, these things are less attractive than to those who abandon themselves to their charm. In Paris you may see giddy young things hastening to adopt the tone and fashions of the town for some six months, so that they may spend the rest of their life in disgrace; but who gives any heed to those who, disgusted with the rout, return to their distant home and are contented with their lot when they have compared it with that which others desire. How many young wives have I seen whose good-natured husbands have taken them to Paris where they might live if they pleased; but they have shrunk from it and returned home more willingly than they went, saying tenderly, "Ah, let us go back to our cottage, life is happier there than in these palaces." We do not know how many there are who have not bowed the knee to Baal, who scorn his senseless worship. Fools make a stir; good women pass unnoticed.

If so many women preserve a judgment which is proof against temptation, in spite of universal prejudice, in spite of the bad education of girls, what would their judgment have been, had it been strengthened by suitable instruction, or rather left unaffected by evil teaching, for to preserve or restore the natural feelings is our main business? You can do this without preaching endless sermons to your daughters, without crediting them with your harsh morality. The only effect of such teaching is to inspire a dislike for the teacher and the lessons. In talking to a young girl you need not make her afraid of her duties, nor need you increase the burden laid upon her by nature. When you explain her duties speak plainly and pleasantly; do not let her suppose that the performance of these duties is a dismal thing—away with every affectation of disgust or pride. Every thought which we desire to arouse should find its expression in our pupils, their catechism of conduct should be as brief and plain as their catechism of religion, but it need not be so serious. Show them that these same duties are the source of their pleasures and the basis of their rights. Is it so hard to win love by love, happiness by an amiable disposition, obedience by worth, and honour by self-respect? How fair are these woman's rights, how worthy of reverence, how dear to the heart of man when a woman is able to show their worth! These rights are no privilege of years; a woman's empire begins with her virtues; her charms are only in the bud, yet she reigns already by the gentleness of her character and the dignity of her modesty. Is there any man so hard-hearted and uncivilised that he does not abate his pride and take heed to his manners with a sweet and virtuous girl of sixteen, who listens but says little; her bearing is modest, her conversation honest, her beauty does not lead her to forget her sex and her youth, her very timidity arouses interest, while she wins for herself the respect which she shows to others?

These external signs are not devoid of meaning; they do not rest entirely upon the charms of sense; they arise from that conviction that we all feel that women are the natural judges of a man's worth. Who would be scorned by women? not even he who has ceased to desire their love. And do you suppose that I, who tell them such harsh truths, am indifferent to their verdict? Reader, I care more for their approval than for yours; you are often more effeminate than they. While I scorn their morals, I will revere their justice; I care not though they hate me, if I can compel their esteem.

What great things might be accomplished by their influence if only we could bring it to bear! Alas for the age whose women lose their ascendancy, and fail to make men respect their judgment! This is the last stage of degradation. Every virtuous nation has shown respect to women. Consider Sparta, Germany, and Rome; Rome the throne of glory and virtue, if ever they were enthroned on earth. The Roman women awarded honour to the deeds of great generals, they mourned in public for the fathers of the country, their awards and their tears were alike held sacred as the most solemn utterance of the Republic. Every great revolution began with the women. Through a woman Rome gained her liberty, through a woman the plebeians won the consulate, through a woman the tyranny of the decemvirs was overthrown; it was the women who saved Rome when besieged by Coriolanus. What would you have said at the sight of this procession, you Frenchmen who pride yourselves on your gallantry, would you not have followed it with shouts of laughter? You and I see things with such different eyes, and perhaps we are both right. Such a procession formed of the fairest beauties of France would be an indecent spectacle; but let it consist of Roman ladies, you will all gaze with the eyes of the Volscians and feel with the heart of Coriolanus.

I will go further and maintain that virtue is no less favourable to love than to other rights of nature, and that it adds as much to the power of the beloved as to that of the wife or mother. There is no real love without enthusiasm, and no enthusiasm without an object of perfection real or supposed, but always present in the imagination. What is there to kindle the hearts of lovers for whom this perfection is nothing, for whom the loved one is merely the means to sensual pleasure? Nay, not thus is the heart kindled, not thus does it abandon itself to those sublime transports which form the rapture of lovers and the charm of love. Love is an illusion, I grant you, but its reality consists in the feelings it awakes, in the love of true beauty which it inspires. That beauty is not to be found in the object of our affections, it is the creation of our illusions. What matter! do we not still sacrifice all those baser feelings to the imaginary model? and we still feed our hearts on the virtues we attribute to the beloved, we still withdraw ourselves from the baseness of human nature. What lover is there who would not give his life for his mistress? What gross and sensual passion is there in a man who is willing to die? We scoff at the knights of old; they knew the meaning of love; we know nothing but debauchery. When the teachings of romance began to seem ridiculous, it was not so much the work of reason as of immorality.

Natural relations remain the same throughout the centuries, their good or evil effects are unchanged; prejudices, masquerading as reason, can but change their outward seeming; self-mastery, even at the behest of fantastic opinions, will not cease to be great and good. And the true motives of honour will not fail to appeal to the heart of every woman who is able to seek happiness in life in her woman's duties. To a high-souled woman chastity above all must be a delightful virtue. She sees all the kingdoms of the world before her and she triumphs over herself and them; she sits enthroned in her own soul and all men do her homage; a few passing struggles are crowned with perpetual glory; she secures the affection, or it may be the envy, she secures in any case the esteem of both sexes and the universal respect of her own. The loss is fleeting, the gain is permanent. What a joy for a noble heart—the pride of virtue combined with beauty. Let her be a heroine of romance; she will taste delights more exquisite than those of Lais and Cleopatra; and when her beauty is fled, her glory and her joys remain; she alone can enjoy the past.

The harder and more important the duties, the stronger and clearer must be the reasons on which they are based. There is a sort of pious talk about the most serious subjects which is dinned in vain into the ears of young people. This talk, quite unsuited to their ideas and the small importance they attach to it in secret, inclines them to yield readily to their inclinations, for lack of any reasons for resistance drawn from the facts themselves. No doubt a girl brought up to goodness and piety has strong weapons against temptation; but one whose heart, or rather her ears, are merely filled with the jargon of piety, will certainly fall a prey to the first skilful seducer who attacks her. A young and beautiful girl will never despise her body, she will never really deplore sins which her beauty leads men to commit, she will never lament earnestly in the sight of God that she is an object of desire, she will never be convinced that the tenderest feeling is an invention of the Evil One. Give her other and more pertinent reasons for her own sake, for these will have no effect. It will be worse to instil, as is often done, ideas which contradict each other, and after having humbled and degraded her person and her charms as the stain of sin, to bid her reverence that same vile body as the temple of Jesus Christ. Ideas too sublime and too humble are equally ineffective and they cannot both be true. A reason adapted to her age and sex is what is needed.

Considerations of duty are of no effect unless they are combined with some motive for the performance of our duty.

> *"Quae quia non liceat non facit, illa facit."*
> *OVID, Amor. I. iii. eleg. iv.*

One would not suspect Ovid of such a harsh judgment.

If you would inspire young people with a love of good conduct avoid saying, "Be good;" make it their interest to be good; make them feel the value of goodness and they will love it. It is not enough to show this effect in the distant future, show it now, in the relations of the present, in the character of their lovers. Describe a good man, a man of worth, teach them to recognise him when they see him, to love him for their own sake; convince them that such a man alone can make them happy as friend, wife, or mistress. Let reason lead the way to virtue; make them feel that the empire of their sex and all the advantages derived from it depend not merely on the right conduct, the morality, of women, but also on that of men; that they have little hold over the vile and base, and that the lover is incapable of serving his mistress unless he can do homage to virtue. You may then be sure that when you describe the manners of our age you will inspire them with a genuine disgust; when you show them men of fashion they will despise them; you will give them a distaste for their maxims, an aversion to their sentiments, and a scorn for their empty gallantry; you will arouse a nobler ambition, to reign over great and strong souls, the ambition of the Spartan women to rule over men. A bold, shameless, intriguing woman, who can only attract her lovers by coquetry and retain them by her favours, wins a servile obedience in common things; in weighty and important matters she has no influence over them. But the woman who is both virtuous, wise, and charming, she who, in a word, combines love and esteem, can send them at her bidding to the end of the world, to war, to glory, and to death at her behest. This is a fine kingdom and worth the winning.

This is the spirit in which Sophy has been educated, she has been trained carefully rather than strictly, and her taste has been followed rather than thwarted. Let us say just a word about her person, according to the description I have given to Emile and the picture he himself has formed of the wife in whom he hopes to find happiness.

I cannot repeat too often that I am not dealing with prodigies. Emile is no prodigy, neither is Sophy. He is a man and she is a woman; this is all they have to boast of. In the present confusion between the sexes it is almost a miracle to belong to one's own sex. Sophy is well born and she has a good disposition; she is very warm-hearted, and this warmth of heart sometimes makes her imagination run away with her. Her mind is keen rather than accurate, her temper is pleasant but variable, her person pleasing though nothing out of the common, her countenance bespeaks a soul and it speaks true; you may meet her with indifference, but you will not leave her without emotion. Others possess good qualities which she lacks; others possess her good qualities in a higher degree, but in no one are these qualities better blended to form a happy disposition. She knows how to make the best of her very faults, and if she were more perfect she would be less pleasing.

Sophy is not beautiful; but in her presence men forget the fairer women, and the latter are dissatisfied with themselves. At first sight she is hardly pretty; but the more we see her the prettier she is; she wins where so many lose, and what she wins she keeps. Her eyes might be finer, her mouth more beautiful, her stature more imposing; but no one could have a more graceful figure, a finer complexion, a whiter hand, a daintier foot, a sweeter look, and a more expressive countenance. She does not dazzle; she arouses interest; she delights us, we know not why.

Sophy is fond of dress, and she knows how to dress; her mother has no other maid; she has taste enough to dress herself well; but she hates rich clothes; her own are always simple but elegant. She does not like showy but becoming things. She does not know what colours are fashionable, but she makes no mistake about those that suit her. No girl seems more simply dressed, but no one could take more pains over her toilet; no article is selected at random, and yet there is no trace of artificiality. Her dress is very modest in appearance and very coquettish in reality; she does not display her charms, she conceals them, but in such a way as to enhance them. When you see her you say, "That is a good modest girl," but while you are with her, you cannot take your eyes or your thoughts off her and one might say that this very simple adornment is only put on to be removed bit by bit by the imagination.

Sophy has natural gifts; she is aware of them, and they have not been neglected; but never having had a chance of much training she is content to use her pretty voice to sing tastefully and truly; her little feet step lightly, easily, and gracefully, she can always make an easy graceful courtesy. She has had no singing master but her father, no dancing mistress but her mother; a neighbouring organist has given her a few lessons in playing accompaniments on the spinet, and she has improved herself by practice. At first she only wished to show off her hand on the dark keys; then she discovered that the thin clear tone of the spinet made her voice sound sweeter; little by little she recognised the charms of harmony; as she grew older she at last began to enjoy the charms of expression, to love music for its own sake. But she has taste rather than talent; she cannot read a simple air from notes.

Needlework is what Sophy likes best; and the feminine arts have been taught her most carefully, even those you would not expect, such as cutting out and dressmaking. There is nothing she cannot do with her needle, and nothing that she does not take a delight in doing; but lace-making is her favourite occupation, because there is nothing which requires such a pleasing attitude, nothing which calls for such grace and dexterity of finger. She has also studied all the details of housekeeping; she understands cooking and cleaning; she knows the prices of food, and also how to choose it; she can keep accounts accurately, she is her mother's housekeeper. Some day she will be the mother of a family; by managing her father's house she is preparing to manage her own; she can take the place of any of the servants and she is always ready to do so. You cannot give orders unless you can do the work yourself; that is why her mother sets her to do it. Sophy does not think of that; her first duty is to be a good daughter, and that is all she thinks about for the present. Her one idea is to help her mother and relieve her of some of her anxieties. However, she does not like them all equally well. For instance, she likes dainty food, but she does not like cooking; the details of cookery offend her, and things are never clean enough for her. She is extremely sensitive in this respect and carries her sensitiveness to a fault; she would let the whole dinner boil over into the fire rather than soil her cuffs. She has always disliked inspecting the kitchen-garden for the same reason. The soil is dirty, and as soon as she sees the manure heap she fancies there is a disagreeable smell.

This defect is the result of her mother's teaching. According to her, cleanliness is one of the most necessary of a woman's duties, a special duty, of the highest importance and a duty imposed by nature. Nothing could be more revolting than a dirty woman, and a husband who tires of her is not to blame. She insisted so strongly on this duty when Sophy was little, she required such absolute cleanliness in her person, clothing, room, work, and toilet, that use has become habit, till it absorbs one half of her time and controls the other; so that she thinks less of how to do a thing than of how to do it without getting dirty.

Yet this has not degenerated into mere affectation and softness; there is none of the over refinement of luxury. Nothing but clean water enters her room; she knows no perfumes but the scent of flowers, and her husband will never find anything sweeter than her breath. In conclusion, the attention she pays to the outside does not blind her to the fact that time and strength are meant for greater tasks; either she does not know or she despises that exaggerated cleanliness of body which degrades the soul. Sophy is more than clean, she is pure.

I said that Sophy was fond of good things. She was so by nature; but she became temperate by habit and now she is temperate by virtue. Little girls are not to be controlled, as little boys are, to some extent, through their greediness. This tendency may have ill effects on women and it is too dangerous to be left unchecked. When Sophy was little, she did not always return empty handed if she was sent to her mother's cupboard, and she was not quite to be trusted with sweets and sugar-almonds. Her mother caught her, took them from her, punished her, and made her go without her dinner. At last she managed to persuade her that sweets were bad for the teeth, and that over-eating spoiled the figure. Thus Sophy overcame her faults; and when she grew older other tastes distracted her from this low kind of self-indulgence. With awakening feeling greediness ceases to be the ruling passion, both with men and women. Sophy has preserved her feminine tastes; she likes milk and sweets; she likes pastry and made-dishes, but not much meat. She has never tasted wine or spirits; moreover, she eats sparingly; women, who do not work so hard as men, have less waste to repair. In all things she likes what is good, and knows how to appreciate it; but she can also put up with what is not so good, or can go without it.

Sophy's mind is pleasing but not brilliant, and thorough but not deep; it is the sort of mind which calls for no remark, as she never seems cleverer or stupider than oneself. When people talk to her they always find what she says attractive, though it may not be highly ornamental according to modern ideas of an educated woman; her mind has been formed not only by reading, but by conversation with her father and mother, by her own reflections, and by her own observations in the little world in which she has lived. Sophy is naturally merry; as a child she was even giddy; but her mother cured her of her silly ways, little by little, lest too sudden a change should make her self-conscious. Thus she became modest and retiring while still a child, and now that she is a child no longer, she finds it easier to continue this conduct than it would have been to acquire it without knowing why. It is amusing to see her occasionally return to her old ways and indulge in childish mirth and then suddenly check herself, with silent lips, downcast eyes, and rosy blushes; neither child nor woman, she may well partake of both.

Sophy is too sensitive to be always good humoured, but too gentle to let this be really disagreeable to other people; it is only herself who suffers. If you say anything that hurts her she does not sulk, but her heart swells; she tries to run away and cry. In the midst of her tears, at a word from her father or mother she returns at once laughing and playing, secretly wiping her eyes and trying to stifle her sobs.

Yet she has her whims; if her temper is too much indulged it degenerates into rebellion, and then she forgets herself. But give her time to come round and her way of making you forget her wrong-doing is almost a virtue. If you punish her she is gentle and submissive, and you see that she is more ashamed of the fault than the punishment. If you say nothing, she never fails to make amends, and she does it so frankly and so readily that you cannot be angry with her. She would kiss the ground before the lowest servant and would make no fuss about it; and as soon as she is forgiven, you can see by her delight and her caresses that a load is taken off her heart. In a word, she endures patiently the wrong-doing of others, and she is eager to atone for her own. This amiability is natural to her sex when unspoiled. Woman is made to submit to man and to endure even injustice at his hands. You will never bring young lads to this; their feelings rise in revolt against injustice; nature has not fitted them to put up with it.

> *"Gravem Pelidae stomachum cedere nescii."*
> *HORACE, lib. i. ode vi.*

Sophy's religion is reasonable and simple, with few doctrines and fewer observances; or rather as she knows no course of conduct but the right her whole life is devoted to the service of God and to doing good. In all her parents' teaching of religion she has been trained to a reverent submission; they have often said, "My little girl, this is too hard for you; your husband will teach you when you are grown up." Instead of long sermons about piety, they have been content to preach by their example, and this example is engraved on her heart.

Sophy loves virtue; this love has come to be her ruling passion; she loves virtue because there is nothing fairer in itself, she loves it because it is a woman's glory and because a virtuous woman is little lower than the angels; she loves virtue as the only road to real happiness, because she sees nothing but poverty, neglect, unhappiness, shame, and disgrace in the life of a bad woman; she loves virtue because it is dear to her revered father and to her tender and worthy mother; they are not content to be happy in their own virtue, they desire hers; and she finds her chief happiness in the hope of making them happy. All these feelings inspire an enthusiasm which stirs her heart and keeps all its budding passions in subjection to this noble enthusiasm. Sophy will be chaste and good till her dying day; she has vowed it in her secret heart, and not before she knew how hard it would be to keep her vow; she made this vow at a time when she would have revoked it had she been the slave of her senses.

Sophy is not so fortunate as to be a charming French woman, cold-hearted and vain, who would rather attract attention than give pleasure, who seeks amusement rather than delight. She suffers from a consuming desire for love; it even disturbs and troubles her heart in the midst of festivities; she has lost her former liveliness, and her taste for merry games; far from being afraid of the tedium of solitude she desires it. Her thoughts go out to him who will make solitude sweet to her. She finds strangers tedious, she wants a lover, not a circle of admirers. She would rather give pleasure to one good man than be a general favourite, or win that applause of society which lasts but a day and to-morrow is turned to scorn.

A woman's judgment develops sooner than a man's; being on the defensive from her childhood up, and intrusted with a treasure so hard to keep, she is earlier acquainted with good and evil. Sophy is precocious by temperament in everything, and her judgment is more formed than that of most girls of her age. There is nothing strange in that, maturity is not always reached at the same age.

Sophy has been taught the duties and rights of her own sex and of ours. She knows men's faults and women's vices; she also knows their corresponding good qualities and virtues, and has them by heart. No one can have a higher ideal of a virtuous woman, but she would rather think of a virtuous man, a man of true worth; she knows that she is made for such a man, that she is worthy of him, that she can make him as happy as he will make her; she is sure she will know him when she sees him; the difficulty is to find him.

Women are by nature judges of a man's worth, as he is of theirs; this right is reciprocal, and it is recognised as such both by men and women. Sophy recognises this right and exercises it, but with the modesty becoming her youth, her inexperience, and her position; she confines her judgment to what she knows, and she only forms an opinion when it may help to illustrate some useful precept. She is extremely careful what she says about those who are absent, particularly if they are women. She thinks that talking about each other makes women spiteful and satirical; so long as they only talk about men they are merely just. So Sophy stops there. As to women she never says anything at all about them, except to tell the good she knows; she thinks this is only fair to her sex; and if she knows no good of any woman, she says nothing, and that is enough.

Sophy has little knowledge of society, but she is observant and obliging, and all that she does is full of grace. A happy disposition does more for her than much art. She has a certain courtesy of her own, which is not dependent on fashion, and does not change with its changes; it is not a matter of custom, but it arises from a feminine desire to please. She is unacquainted with the language of empty compliment, nor does she invent more elaborate compliments of her own; she does not say that she is greatly obliged, that you do her too much honour, that you should not take so much trouble, etc. Still less does she try to make phrases of her own. She responds to an attention or a customary piece of politeness by a courtesy or a mere "Thank you;" but this phrase in her mouth is quite enough. If you do her a real service, she lets her heart speak, and its words are no empty compliment. She has never allowed French manners to make her a slave to appearances; when she goes from one room to another she does not take the arm of an old gentleman, whom she would much rather help. When a scented fop offers her this empty attention, she leaves him on the staircase and rushes into the room saying that she is not lame. Indeed, she will never wear high heels though she is not tall; her feet are small enough to dispense with them.

Not only does she adopt a silent and respectful attitude towards women, but also towards married men, or those who are much older than herself; she will never take her place above them, unless compelled to do so; and she will return to her own lower place as soon as she can; for she knows that the rights of age take precedence of those of sex, as age is presumably wiser than youth, and wisdom should be held in the greatest honour.

With young folks of her own age it is another matter; she requires a different manner to gain their respect, and she knows how to adopt it without dropping the modest ways which become her. If they themselves are shy and modest, she will gladly preserve the friendly familiarity of youth; their innocent conversation will be merry but suitable; if they become serious they must say something useful; if they become silly, she soon puts a stop to it, for she has an utter contempt for the jargon of gallantry, which she considers an insult to her sex. She feels sure that the man she seeks does not speak that jargon, and she will never permit in another what would be displeasing to her in him whose character is engraved on her heart. Her high opinion of the rights of women, her pride in the purity of her feelings, that active virtue which is the basis of her self-respect, make her indignant at the sentimental speeches intended for her amusement. She does not receive them with open anger, but with a disconcerting irony or an unexpected iciness. If a fair Apollo displays his charms, and makes use of his wit in the praise of her wit, her beauty, and her grace; at the risk of offending him she is quite capable of saying politely, "Sir, I am afraid I know that better than you; if we have nothing more interesting to talk about, I think we may put an end to this conversation." To say this with a deep courtesy, and then to withdraw to a considerable distance, is the work of a moment. Ask your lady-killers if it is easy to continue to babble to such, an unsympathetic ear.

It is not that she is not fond of praise if it is really sincere, and if she thinks you believe what you say. You must show that you appreciate her merit if you would have her believe you. Her proud spirit may take pleasure in homage which is based upon esteem, but empty compliments are always rejected; Sophy was not meant to practise the small arts of the dancing-girl.

With a judgment so mature, and a mind like that of a woman of twenty, Sophy, at fifteen, is no longer treated as a child by her parents. No sooner do they perceive the first signs of youthful disquiet than they hasten to anticipate its development, their conversations with her are wise and tender. These wise and tender conversations are in keeping with her age and disposition. If her disposition is what I fancy why should not her father speak to her somewhat after this fashion?

"You are a big girl now, Sophy, you will soon be a woman. We want you to be happy, for our own sakes as well as yours, for our happiness depends on yours. A good girl finds her own happiness in the happiness of a good man, so we must consider your marriage; we must think of it in good time, for marriage makes or mars our whole life, and we cannot have too much time to consider it.

"There is nothing so hard to choose as a good husband, unless it is a good wife. You will be that rare creature, Sophy, you will be the crown of our life and the blessing of our declining years; but however worthy you are, there are worthier people upon earth. There is no one who would not do himself honour by marriage with you; there are many who would do you even greater honour than themselves. Among these we must try to find one who suits you, we must get to know him and introduce you to him.

"The greatest possible happiness in marriage depends on so many points of agreement that it is folly to expect to secure them all. We must first consider the more important matters; if others are to be found along with them, so much the better; if not we must do without them. Perfect happiness is not to be found in this world, but we can, at least, avoid the worst form of unhappiness, that for which ourselves are to blame.

"There is a natural suitability, there is a suitability of established usage, and a suitability which is merely conventional. Parents should decide as to the two latters, and the children themselves should decide as to the former. Marriages arranged by parents only depend on a suitability of custom and convention; it is not two people who are united, but two positions and two properties; but these things may change, the people remain, they are always there; and in spite of fortune it is the personal relation that makes a happy or an unhappy marriage.

"Your mother had rank, I had wealth; this was all that our parents considered in arranging our marriage. I lost my money, she lost her position; forgotten by her family, what good did it do her to be a lady born? In the midst of our misfortunes, the union of our hearts has outweighed them all; the similarity of our tastes led us to choose this retreat; we live happily in our poverty, we are all in all to each other. Sophy is a treasure we hold in common, and we thank Heaven which has bestowed this treasure and deprived us of all others. You see, my child, whither we have been led by Providence; the conventional motives which brought about our marriage no longer exist, our happiness consists in that natural suitability which was held of no account.

"Husband and wife should choose each other. A mutual liking should be the first bond between them. They should follow the guidance of their own eyes and hearts; when they are married their first duty will be to love one another, and as love and hatred do not depend on ourselves, this duty brings another with it, and they must begin to love each other before marriage. That is the law of nature, and no power can abrogate it; those who have fettered it by so many legal restrictions have given heed rather to the outward show of order than to the happiness of marriage or the morals of the citizen. You see, my dear Sophy, we do not preach a harsh morality. It tends to make you your own mistress and to make us leave the choice of your husband to yourself.

"When we have told you our reasons for giving you full liberty, it is only fair to speak of your reasons for making a wise use of that liberty. My child, you are good and sensible, upright and pious, you have the accomplishments of a good woman and you are not altogether without charms; but you are poor; you have the gifts most worthy of esteem, but not those which are most esteemed. Do not seek what is beyond your reach, and let your ambition be controlled, not by your ideas or ours, but by the opinion of others. If it were merely a question of equal merits, I know not what limits to impose on your hopes; but do not let your ambitions outrun your fortune, and remember it is very small. Although a man worthy of you would not consider this inequality an obstacle, you must do what he would not do; Sophy must follow her mother's example and only enter a family which counts it an honour to receive her. You never saw our wealth, you were born in our poverty; you make it sweet for us, and you share it without hardship. Believe me, Sophy, do not seek those good things we indeed thank heaven for having taken from us; we did not know what happiness was till we lost our money.

"You are so amiable that you will win affection, and you are not go poor as to be a burden. You will be sought in marriage, it may be by those who are unworthy of you. If they showed themselves in their true colours, you would rate them at their real value; all their outward show would not long deceive you; but though your judgment is good and you know what merit is when you see it, you are inexperienced and you do not know how people can conceal their real selves. A skilful knave might study your tastes in order to seduce you, and make a pretence of those virtues which he does not possess.

You would be ruined, Sophy, before you knew what you were doing, and you would only perceive your error when you had cause to lament it. The most dangerous snare, the only snare which reason cannot avoid, is that of the senses; if ever you have the misfortune to fall into its toils, you will perceive nothing but fancies and illusions; your eyes will be fascinated, your judgment troubled, your will corrupted, your very error will be dear to you, and even if you were able to perceive it you would not be willing to escape from it. My child, I trust you to Sophy's own reason; I do not trust you to the fancies of your own heart. Judge for yourself so long as your heart is untouched, but when you love betake yourself to your mother's care.

"I propose a treaty between us which shows our esteem for you, and restores the order of nature between us. Parents choose a husband for their daughter and she is only consulted as a matter of form; that is the custom. We shall do just the opposite; you will choose, and we shall be consulted. Use your right, Sophy, use it freely and wisely. The husband suitable for you should be chosen by you not us. But it is for us to judge whether he is really suitable, or whether, without knowing it, you are only following your own wishes. Birth, wealth, position, conventional opinions will count for nothing with us. Choose a good man whose person and character suit you; whatever he may be in other respects, we will accept him as our son-in-law. He will be rich enough if he has bodily strength, a good character, and family affection. His position will be good enough if it is ennobled by virtue. If everybody blames us, we do not care. We do not seek the approbation of men, but your happiness."

I cannot tell my readers what effect such words would have upon girls brought up in their fashion. As for Sophy, she will have no words to reply; shame and emotion will not permit her to express herself easily; but I am sure that what was said will remain engraved upon her heart as long as she lives, and that if any human resolution may be trusted, we may rely on her determination to deserve her parent's esteem.

At worst let us suppose her endowed with an ardent disposition which will make her impatient of long delays; I maintain that her judgment, her knowledge, her taste, her refinement, and, above all, the sentiments in which she has been brought up from childhood, will outweigh the impetuosity of the senses, and enable her to offer a prolonged resistance, if not to overcome them altogether. She would rather die a virgin martyr than distress her parents by marrying a worthless man and exposing herself to the unhappiness of an ill-assorted marriage. Ardent as an Italian and sentimental as an Englishwoman, she has a curb upon heart and sense in the pride of a Spaniard, who even when she seeks a lover does not easily discover one worthy of her.

Not every one can realise the motive power to be found in a love of what is right, nor the inner strength which results from a genuine love of virtue. There are men who think that all greatness is a figment of the brain, men who with their vile and degraded reason will never recognise the power over human passions which is wielded by the very madness of virtue. You can only teach such men by examples; if they persist in denying their existence, so much the worse for them. If I told them that Sophy is no imaginary person, that her name alone is my invention, that her education, her conduct, her character, her very features, really existed, and that her loss is still mourned by a very worthy family, they would, no doubt, refuse to believe me; but indeed why should I not venture to relate word for word the story of a girl so like Sophy that this story might be hers without surprising any one. Believe it or no, it is all the same to me; call my history fiction if you will; in any case I have explained my method and furthered my purpose.

This young girl with the temperament which I have attributed to Sophy was so like her in other respects that she was worthy of the name, and so we will continue to use it. After the conversation related above, her father and mother thought that suitable husbands would not be likely to offer themselves in the hamlet where they lived; so they decided to send her to spend the winter in town, under the care of an aunt who was privately acquainted with the object of the journey; for Sophy's heart throbbed with noble pride at the thought of her self-control; and however much she might want to marry, she would rather have died a maid than have brought herself to go in search of a husband.

In response to her parents' wishes her aunt introduced her to her friends, took her into company, both private and public, showed her society, or rather showed her in society, for Sophy paid little heed to its bustle. Yet it was plain that she did not shrink from young men of pleasing appearance and modest seemly behaviour. Her very shyness had a charm of its own, which was very much like coquetry; but after talking to them once or twice she repulsed them. She soon exchanged that air of authority which seems to accept men's homage for a humbler bearing and a still more chilling politeness. Always watchful over her conduct, she gave them no chance of doing her the least service; it was perfectly plain that she was determined not to accept any one of them.

Never did sensitive heart take pleasure in noisy amusements, the empty and barren delights of those who have no feelings, those who think that a merry life is a happy life. Sophy did not find what she sought, and she felt sure she never would, so she got tired of the town. She loved her parents dearly and nothing made up for their absence, nothing could make her forget them; she went home long before the time fixed for the end of her visit.

Scarcely had she resumed her home duties when they perceived that her temper had changed though her conduct was unaltered, she was forgetful, impatient, sad, and dreamy; she wept in secret. At first they thought she was in love and was ashamed to own it; they spoke to her, but she repudiated the idea. She protested she had seen no one who could touch her heart, and Sophy always spoke the truth.

Yet her languor steadily increased, and her health began to give way. Her mother was anxious about her, and determined to know the reason for this change. She took her aside, and with the winning speech and the irresistible caresses which only a mother can employ, she said, "My child, whom I have borne beneath my heart, whom I bear ever in my affection, confide your secret to your mother's bosom. What secrets are these which a mother may not know? Who pities your sufferings, who shares them, who would gladly relieve them, if not your father and myself? Ah, my child! would you have me die of grief for your sorrow without letting me share it?"

Far from hiding her griefs from her mother, the young girl asked nothing better than to have her as friend and comforter; but she could not speak for shame, her modesty could find no words to describe a condition so unworthy of her, as the emotion which disturbed her senses in spite of all her efforts. At length her very shame gave her mother a clue to her difficulty, and she drew from her the humiliating confession. Far from distressing her with reproaches or unjust blame, she consoled her, pitied her, wept over her; she was too wise to make a crime of an evil which virtue alone made so cruel. But why put up with such an evil when there was no necessity to do so, when the remedy was so easy and so legitimate? Why did she not use the freedom they had granted her? Why did she not take a husband? Why did she not make her choice? Did she not know that she was perfectly independent in this matter, that whatever her choice, it would be approved, for it was sure to be good? They had sent her to town, but she would not stay; many suitors had offered themselves, but she would have none of them. What did she expect? What did she want? What an inexplicable contradiction?

The reply was simple. If it were only a question of the partner of her youth, her choice would soon be made; but a master for life is not so easily chosen; and since the two cannot be separated, people must often wait and sacrifice their youth before they find the man with whom they could spend their life. Such was Sophy's case; she wanted a lover, but this lover must be her husband; and to discover a heart such as she required, a lover and husband were equally difficult to find. All these dashing young men were only her equals in age, in everything else they were found lacking; their empty wit, their vanity, their affectations of speech, their ill-regulated conduct, their frivolous imitations alike disgusted her. She sought a man and she found monkeys; she sought a soul and there was none to be found.

"How unhappy I am!" said she to her mother; "I am compelled to love and yet I am dissatisfied with every one. My heart rejects every one who appeals to my senses. Every one of them stirs my passions and all alike revolt them; a liking unaccompanied by respect cannot last. That is not the sort of man for your Sophy; the delightful image of her ideal is too deeply graven in her heart. She can love no other; she can make no one happy but him, and she cannot be happy without him. She would rather consume herself in ceaseless conflicts, she would rather die free and wretched, than driven desperate by the company of a man she did not love, a man she would make as unhappy as herself; she would rather die than live to suffer."

Amazed at these strange ideas, her mother found them so peculiar that she could not fail to suspect some mystery. Sophy was neither affected nor absurd. How could such exaggerated delicacy exist in one who had been so carefully taught from her childhood to adapt herself to those with whom she must live, and to make a virtue of necessity? This ideal of the delightful man with which she was so enchanted, who appeared so often in her conversation, made her mother suspect that there was some foundation for her caprices which was still unknown to her, and that Sophy had not told her all. The unhappy girl, overwhelmed with her secret grief, was only too eager to confide it to another. Her mother urged her to speak; she hesitated, she yielded, and leaving the room without a word, she presently returned with a book in her hand. "Have pity on your unhappy daughter, there is no remedy for her grief, her tears cannot be dried. You would know the cause: well, here it is," said she, flinging the book on the table. Her mother took the book and opened it; it was The Adventures of Telemachus. At first she could make nothing of this riddle; by dint of questions and vague replies, she discovered to her great surprise that her daughter was the rival of Eucharis.

Sophy was in love with Telemachus, and loved him with a passion which nothing could cure. When her father and mother became aware of her infatuation, they laughed at it and tried to cure her by reasoning with her. They were mistaken, reason was not altogether on their side; Sophy had her own reason and knew how to use it. Many a time did she reduce them to silence by turning their own arguments against them, by showing them that it was all their own fault for not having trained her to suit the men of that century; that she would be compelled to adopt her husband's way of thinking or he must adopt hers, that they had made the former course impossible by the way she had been brought up, and that the latter was just what she wanted. "Give me," said she, "a man who holds the same opinions as I do, or one who will be willing to learn them from me, and I will marry him; but until then, why do you scold me? Pity me; I am miserable, but not mad. Is the heart controlled by the will? Did my father not ask that very question? Is it my fault if I love what has no existence? I am no visionary; I desire no prince, I seek no Telemachus, I know he is only an imaginary person; I seek some one like him. And why should there be no such person, since there is such a person as I, I who feel that my heart is like his? No, let us not wrong humanity so greatly, let us not think that an amiable and virtuous man is a figment of the imagination. He exists, he lives, perhaps he is seeking me; he is seeking a soul which is capable of love for him. But who is he, where is he? I know not; he is not among those I have seen; and no doubt I shall never see him. Oh! mother, why did you make virtue too attractive? If I can love nothing less, you are more to blame than I."

Must I continue this sad story to its close? Must I describe the long struggles which preceded it? Must I show an impatient mother exchanging her former caresses for severity? Must I paint an angry father forgetting his former promises, and treating the most virtuous of daughters as a mad woman? Must I portray the unhappy girl, more than ever devoted to her imaginary hero, because of the persecution brought upon her by that devotion, drawing nearer step by step to her death, and descending into the grave when they were about to force her to the altar? No; I will not dwell upon these gloomy scenes; I have no need to go so far to show, by what I consider a sufficiently striking example, that in spite of the prejudices arising from the manners of our age, the enthusiasm for the good and the beautiful is no more foreign to women than to men, and that there is nothing which, under nature's guidance, cannot be obtained from them as well as from us.

You stop me here to inquire whether it is nature which teaches us to take such pains to repress our immoderate desires. No, I reply, but neither is it nature who gives us these immoderate desires. Now, all that is not from nature is contrary to nature, as I have proved again and again.

Let us give Emile his Sophy; let us restore this sweet girl to life and provide her with a less vivid imagination and a happier fate. I desired to paint an ordinary woman, but by endowing her with a great soul, I have disturbed her reason. I have gone astray. Let us retrace our steps. Sophy has only a good disposition and an ordinary heart; her education is responsible for everything in which she excels other women.

In this book I intended to describe all that might be done and to leave every one free to choose what he could out of all the good things I described. I meant to train a helpmeet for Emile, from the very first, and to educate them for each other and with each other. But on consideration I thought all these premature arrangements undesirable, for it was absurd to plan the marriage of two children before I could tell whether this union was in accordance with nature and whether they were really suited to each other. We must not confuse what is suitable in a state of savagery with what is suitable in civilised life. In the former, any woman will suit any man, for both are still in their primitive and undifferentiated condition; in the latter, all their characteristics have been developed by social institutions, and each mind, having taken its own settled form, not from education alone, but by the co-operation, more or less well-regulated, of natural disposition and education, we can only make a match by introducing them to each other to see if they suit each other in every respect, or at least we can let them make that choice which gives the most promise of mutual suitability.

The difficulty is this: while social life develops character it differentiates classes, and these two classifications do not correspond, so that the greater the social distinctions, the greater the difficulty of finding the corresponding character. Hence we have ill-assorted marriages and all their accompanying evils; and we find that it follows logically that the further we get from equality, the greater the change in our natural feelings; the wider the distance between great and small, the looser the marriage tie; the deeper the gulf between rich and poor the fewer husbands and fathers. Neither master nor slave belongs to a family, but only to a class.

If you would guard against these abuses, and secure happy marriages, you must stifle your prejudices, forget human institutions, and consult nature. Do not join together those who are only alike in one given condition, those who will not suit one another if that condition is changed; but those who are adapted to one another in every situation, in every country, and in every rank in which they may be placed. I do not say that conventional considerations are of no importance in marriage, but I do say that the influence of natural relations is so much more important, that our fate in life is decided by them alone, and that there is such an agreement of taste, temper, feeling, and disposition as should induce a wise father, though he were a prince, to marry his son, without a moment's hesitation, to the woman so adapted to him, were she born in a bad home, were she even the hangman's daughter. I maintain indeed that every possible misfortune may overtake husband and wife if they are thus united, yet they will enjoy more real happiness while they mingle their tears, than if they possessed all the riches of the world, poisoned by divided hearts.

Instead of providing a wife for Emile in childhood, I have waited till I knew what would suit him. It is not for me to decide, but for nature; my task is to discover the choice she has made. My business, mine I repeat, not his father's; for when he entrusted his son to my care, he gave up his place to me. He gave me his rights; it is I who am really Emile's father; it is I who have made a man of him. I would have refused to educate him if I were not free to marry him according to his own choice, which is mine. Nothing but the pleasure of bestowing happiness on a man can repay me for the cost of making him capable of happiness.

Do not suppose, however, that I have delayed to find a wife for Emile till I sent him in search of her. This search is only a pretext for acquainting him with women, so that he may perceive the value of a suitable wife. Sophy was discovered long since; Emile may even have seen her already, but he will not recognise her till the time is come.

Although equality of rank is not essential in marriage, yet this equality along with other kinds of suitability increases their value; it is not to be weighed against any one of them, but, other things being equal, it turns the scale.

A man, unless he is a king, cannot seek a wife in any and every class; if he himself is free from prejudices, he will find them in others; and this girl or that might perhaps suit him and yet she would be beyond his reach. A wise father will therefore restrict his inquiries within the bounds of prudence. He should not wish to marry his pupil into a family above his own, for that is not within his power. If he could do so he ought not desire it; for what difference does rank make to a young man, at least to my pupil? Yet, if he rises he is exposed to all sorts of real evils which he will feel all his life long. I even say that he should not try to adjust the balance between different gifts, such as rank and money; for each of these adds less to the value of the other than the amount deducted from its own value in the process of adjustment; moreover, we can never agree as to a common denominator; and finally the preference, which each feels for his own surroundings, paves the way for discord between the two families and often to difficulties between husband and wife.

It makes a considerable difference as to the suitability of a marriage whether a man marries above or beneath him. The former case is quite contrary to reason, the latter is more in conformity with reason. As the family is only connected with society through its head, it is the rank of that head which decides that of the family as a whole. When he marries into a lower rank, a man does not lower himself, he raises his wife; if, on the other hand, he marries above his position, he lowers his wife and does not raise himself. Thus there is in the first case good unmixed with evil, in the other evil unmixed with good. Moreover, the law of nature bids the woman obey the man. If he takes a wife from a lower class, natural and civil law are in accordance and all goes well. When he marries a woman of higher rank it is just the opposite case; the man must choose between diminished rights or imperfect gratitude; he must be ungrateful or despised. Then the wife, laying claim to authority, makes herself a tyrant over her lawful head; and the master, who has become a slave, is the most ridiculous and miserable of creatures. Such are the unhappy favourites whom the sovereigns of Asia honour and torment with their alliance; people tell us that if they desire to sleep with their wife they must enter by the foot of the bed.

I expect that many of my readers will remember that I think women have a natural gift for managing men, and will accuse me of contradicting myself; yet they are mistaken. There is a vast difference between claiming the right to command, and managing him who commands. Woman's reign is a reign of gentleness, tact, and kindness; her commands are caresses, her threats are tears. She should reign in the home as a minister reigns in the state, by contriving to be ordered to do what she wants. In this sense, I grant you, that the best managed homes are those where the wife has most power. But when she despises the voice of her head, when she desires to usurp his rights and take the command upon herself, this inversion of the proper order of things leads only to misery, scandal, and dishonour.

There remains the choice between our equals and our inferiors; and I think we ought also to make certain restrictions with regard to the latter; for it is hard to find in the lowest stratum of society a woman who is able to make a good man happy; not that the lower classes are more vicious than the higher, but because they have so little idea of what is good and beautiful, and because the injustice of other classes makes its very vices seem right in the eyes of this class.

By nature man thinks but seldom. He learns to think as he acquires the other arts, but with even greater difficulty. In both sexes alike I am only aware of two really distinct classes, those who think and those who do not; and this difference is almost entirely one of education. A man who thinks should not ally himself with a woman who does not think, for he loses the chief delight of social life if he has a wife who cannot share his thoughts. People who spend their whole life in working for a living have no ideas beyond their work and their own interests, and their mind seems to reside in their arms. This ignorance is not necessarily unfavourable either to their honesty or their morals; it is often favourable; we often content ourselves with thinking about our duties, and in the end we substitute words for things. Conscience is the most enlightened philosopher; to be an honest man we need not read Cicero's De Officiis, and the most virtuous woman in the world is probably she who knows least about virtue. But it is none the less true that a cultivated mind alone makes intercourse pleasant, and it is a sad thing for a father of a family, who delights in his home, to be forced to shut himself up in himself and to be unable to make himself understood.

Moreover, if a woman is quite unaccustomed to think, how can she bring up her children? How will she know what is good for them? How can she incline them to virtues of which she is ignorant, to merit of which she has no conception? She can only flatter or threaten, she can only make them insolent or timid; she will make them performing monkeys or noisy little rascals; she will never make them intelligent or pleasing children.

Therefore it is not fitting that a man of education should choose a wife who has none, or take her from a class where she cannot be expected to have any education. But I would a thousand times rather have a homely girl, simply brought up, than a learned lady and a wit who would make a literary circle of my house and install herself as its president. A female wit is a scourge to her husband, her children, her friends, her servants, to everybody. From the lofty height of her genius she scorns every womanly duty, and she is always trying to make a man of herself after the fashion of Mlle. de L'Enclos. Outside her home she always makes herself ridiculous and she is very rightly a butt for criticism, as we always are when we try to escape from our own position into one for which we are unfitted. These highly talented women only get a hold over fools. We can always tell what artist or friend holds the pen or pencil when they are at work; we know what discreet man of letters dictates their oracles in private. This trickery is unworthy of a decent woman. If she really had talents, her pretentiousness would degrade them. Her honour is to be unknown; her glory is the respect of her husband; her joys the happiness of her family. I appeal to my readers to give me an honest answer; when you enter a woman's room what makes you think more highly of her, what makes you address her with more respect—to see her busy with feminine occupations, with her household duties, with her children's clothes about her, or to find her writing verses at her toilet table surrounded with pamphlets of every kind and with notes on tinted paper? If there were none but wise men upon earth such a woman would die an old maid.

> *"Quaeris cur nolim te ducere, galla? diserta es."*
> *Martial xi. 20.*

Looks must next be considered; they are the first thing that strikes us and they ought to be the last, still they should not count for nothing. I think that great beauty is rather to be shunned than sought after in marriage. Possession soon exhausts our appreciation of beauty; in six weeks' time we think no more about it, but its dangers endure as long as life itself. Unless a beautiful woman is an angel, her husband is the most miserable of men; and even if she were an angel he would still be the centre of a hostile crowd and she could not prevent it. If extreme ugliness were not repulsive I should prefer it to extreme beauty; for before very long the husband would cease to notice either, but beauty would still have its disadvantages and ugliness its advantages. But ugliness which is actually repulsive is the worst misfortune; repulsion increases rather than diminishes, and it turns to hatred. Such a union is a hell upon earth; better death than such a marriage.

Desire mediocrity in all things, even in beauty. A pleasant attractive countenance, which inspires kindly feelings rather than love, is what we should prefer; the husband runs no risk, and the advantages are common to husband and wife; charm is less perishable than beauty; it is a living thing, which constantly renews itself, and after thirty years of married life, the charms of a good woman delight her husband even as they did on the wedding-day.

Such are the considerations which decided my choice of Sophy. Brought up, like Emile, by Nature, she is better suited to him than any other; she will be his true mate. She is his equal in birth and character, his inferior in fortune. She makes no great impression at first sight, but day by day reveals fresh charms. Her chief influence only takes effect gradually, it is only discovered in friendly intercourse; and her husband will feel it more than any one. Her education is neither showy nor neglected; she has taste without deep study, talent without art, judgment without learning. Her mind knows little, but it is trained to learn; it is well-tilled soil ready for the sower. She has read no book but Bareme and Telemachus which happened to fall into her hands; but no girl who can feel so passionately towards Telemachus can have a heart without feeling or a mind without discernment. What charming ignorance! Happy is he who is destined to be her tutor. She will not be her husband's teacher but his scholar; far from seeking to control his tastes, she will share them. She will suit him far better than a blue-stocking and he will have the pleasure of teaching her everything. It is time they made acquaintance; let us try to plan a meeting.

When we left Paris we were sorrowful and wrapped in thought. This Babel is not our home. Emile casts a scornful glance towards the great city, saying angrily, "What a time we have wasted; the bride of my heart is not there. My friend, you knew it, but you think nothing of my time, and you pay no heed to my sufferings." With steady look and firm voice I reply, "Emile, do you mean what you say?" At once he flings his arms round my neck and clasps me to his breast without speaking. That is his answer when he knows he is in the wrong.

And now we are wandering through the country like true knights-errant; yet we are not seeking adventures when we leave Paris; we are escaping from them; now fast now slow, we wander through the country like knights-errants. By following my usual practice the taste for it has become established; and I do not suppose any of my readers are such slaves of custom as to picture us dozing in a post-chaise with closed windows, travelling, yet seeing nothing, observing nothing, making the time between our start and our arrival a mere blank, and losing in the speed of our journey, the time we meant to save.

Men say life is short, and I see them doing their best to shorten it. As they do not know how to spend their time they lament the swiftness of its flight, and I perceive that for them it goes only too slowly. Intent merely on the object of their pursuit, they behold unwillingly the space between them and it; one desires to-morrow, another looks a month ahead, another ten years beyond that. No one wants to live to-day, no one contents himself with the present hour, all complain that it passes slowly. When they complain that time flies, they lie; they would gladly purchase the power to hasten it; they would gladly spend their fortune to get rid of their whole life; and there is probably not a single one who would not have reduced his life to a few hours if he had been free to get rid of those hours he found tedious, and those which separated him from the desired moment. A man spends his whole life rushing from Paris to Versailles, from Versailles to Paris, from town to country, from country to town, from one district of the town to another; but he would not know what to do with his time if he had not discovered this way of wasting it, by leaving his business on purpose to find something to do in coming back to it; he thinks he is saving the time he spends, which would otherwise be unoccupied; or maybe he rushes for the sake of rushing, and travels post in order to return in the same fashion. When will mankind cease to slander nature? Why do you complain that life is short when it is never short enough for you? If there were but one of you, able to moderate his desires, so that he did not desire the flight of time, he would never find life too short; for him life and the joy of life would be one and the same; should he die young, he would still die full of days.

If this were the only advantage of my way of travelling it would be enough. I have brought Emile up neither to desire nor to wait, but to enjoy; and when his desires are bent upon the future, their ardour is not so great as to make time seem tedious. He will not only enjoy the delights of longing, but the delights of approaching the object of his desires; and his passions are under such restraint that he lives to a great extent in the present.

So we do not travel like couriers but like explorers. We do not merely consider the beginning and the end, but the space between. The journey itself is a delight. We do not travel sitting, dismally imprisoned, so to speak, in a tightly closed cage. We do not travel with the ease and comfort of ladies. We do not deprive ourselves of the fresh air, nor the sight of the things about us, nor the opportunity of examining them at our pleasure. Emile will never enter a post-chaise, nor will he ride post unless in a great hurry. But what cause has Emile for haste? None but the joy of life. Shall I add to this the desire to do good when he can? No, for that is itself one of the joys of life.

I can only think of one way of travelling pleasanter than travelling on horseback, and that is to travel on foot. You start at your own time, you stop when you will, you do as much or as little as you choose. You see the country, you turn off to the right or left; you examine anything which interests you,

you stop to admire every view. Do I see a stream, I wander by its banks; a leafy wood, I seek its shade; a cave, I enter it; a quarry, I study its geology. If I like a place, I stop there. As soon as I am weary of it, I go on. I am independent of horses and postillions; I need not stick to regular routes or good roads; I go anywhere where a man can go; I see all that a man can see; and as I am quite independent of everybody, I enjoy all the freedom man can enjoy. If I am stopped by bad weather and I find myself getting bored, then I take horses. If I am tired—but Emile is hardly ever tired; he is strong; why should he get tired? There is no hurry? If he stops, why should he be bored? He always finds some amusement. He works at a trade; he uses his arms to rest his feet.

To travel on foot is to travel in the fashion of Thales, Plato, and Pythagoras. I find it hard to understand how a philosopher can bring himself to travel in any other way; how he can tear himself from the study of the wealth which lies before his eyes and beneath his feet. Is there any one with an interest in agriculture, who does not want to know the special products of the district through which he is passing, and their method of cultivation? Is there any one with a taste for natural history, who can pass a piece of ground without examining it, a rock without breaking off a piece of it, hills without looking for plants, and stones without seeking for fossils?

Your town-bred scientists study natural history in cabinets; they have small specimens; they know their names but nothing of their nature. Emile's museum is richer than that of kings; it is the whole world. Everything is in its right place; the Naturalist who is its curator has taken care to arrange it in the fairest order; Dauberton could do no better.

What varied pleasures we enjoy in this delightful way of travelling, not to speak of increasing health and a cheerful spirit. I notice that those who ride in nice, well-padded carriages are always wrapped in thought, gloomy, fault-finding, or sick; while those who go on foot are always merry, light-hearted, and delighted with everything. How cheerful we are when we get near our lodging for the night! How savoury is the coarse food! How we linger at table enjoying our rest! How soundly we sleep on a hard bed! If you only want to get to a place you may ride in a post-chaise; if you want to travel you must go on foot.

If Sophy is not forgotten before we have gone fifty leagues in the way I propose, either I am a bungler or Emile lacks curiosity; for with an elementary knowledge of so many things, it is hardly to be supposed that he will not be tempted to extend his knowledge. It is knowledge that makes us curious; and Emile knows just enough to want to know more.

One thing leads on to another, and we make our way forward. If I chose a distant object for the end of our first journey, it is not difficult to find an excuse for it; when we leave Paris we must seek a wife at a distance.

A few days later we had wandered further than usual among hills and valleys where no road was to be seen and we lost our way completely. No matter, all roads are alike if they bring you to your journey's end, but if you are hungry they must lead somewhere. Luckily we came across a peasant who took up to his cottage; we enjoyed his poor dinner with a hearty appetite. When he saw how hungry and tired we were he said, "If the Lord had led you to the other side of the hill you would have had a better welcome, you would have found a good resting place, such good, kindly people! They could not wish to do more for you than I, but they are richer, though folks say they used to be much better off. Still they are not reduced to poverty, and the whole country-side is the better for what they have."

When Emile heard of these good people his heart warmed to them. "My friend," said he, looking at me, "let us visit this house, whose owners are a blessing to the district; I shall be very glad to see them; perhaps they will be pleased to see us too; I am sure we shall be welcome; we shall just suit each other."

Our host told us how to find our way to the house and we set off, but lost our way in the woods. We were caught in a heavy rainstorm, which delayed us further. At last we found the right path and in the evening we reached the house, which had been described to us. It was the only house among the cottages of the little hamlet, and though plain it had an air of dignity. We went up to the door and asked for hospitality. We were taken to the owner of the house, who questioned us courteously; without telling him the object of our journey, we told him why we had left our path. His former wealth enabled him to judge a man's position by his manners; those who have lived in society are rarely mistaken; with this passport we were admitted.

The room we were shown into was very small, but clean and comfortable; a fire was lighted, and we found linen, clothes, and everything we needed. "Why," said Emile, in astonishment, "one would think they were expecting us. The peasant was quite right; how kind and attentive, how considerate, and for strangers too! I shall think I am living in the times of Homer." "I am glad you feel this," said I, "but you need not be surprised; where strangers are scarce, they are welcome; nothing makes people more hospitable than the fact that calls upon their hospitality are rare; when guests are frequent there is an end to hospitality. In Homer's time, people rarely travelled, and travellers were everywhere welcome. Very likely we are the only people who have passed this way this year." "Never mind," said he, "to know how to do without guests and yet to give them a kind welcome, is its own praise."

Having dried ourselves and changed our clothes, we rejoined the master of the house, who introduced us to his wife; she received us not merely with courtesy but with kindness. Her glance rested on Emile. A mother, in her position, rarely receives a young man into her house without some anxiety or some curiosity at least.

Supper was hurried forward on our account. When we went into the dining-room there were five places laid; we took our seats and the fifth chair remained empty. Presently a young girl entered, made a deep courtesy, and modestly took her place without a word. Emile was busy with his supper or considering how to reply to what was said to him; he bowed to her and continued talking and eating. The main object of his journey was as far from his thoughts as he believed himself to be from the end of his journey. The conversation turned upon our losing our way. "Sir," said the master of the house to Emile, "you seem to be a pleasant well-behaved young gentleman, and that reminds me that your tutor and you arrived wet and weary like Telemachus and Mentor in the island of Calypso." "Indeed," said Emile, "we have found the hospitality of Calypso." His Mentor added, "And the charms of Eucharis." But Emile knew the Odyssey and he had not read Telemachus, so he knew nothing of Eucharis. As for the young girl, I saw she blushed up to her eyebrows, fixed her eyes on her plate, and hardly dared to breathe. Her mother, noticing her confusion, made a sign to her father to turn the conversation. When he talked of his lonely life, he unconsciously began to relate the circumstances which brought him into it; his misfortunes, his wife's fidelity, the consolations they found in their marriage, their quiet, peaceful life in their retirement, and all this without a word of the young girl; it is a pleasing and a touching story, which cannot fail to interest. Emile, interested and sympathetic, leaves off eating and listens. When finally this best of men discourses with delight of the affection of the best of women, the young traveller, carried away by his feelings, stretches one hand to the husband, and taking the wife's hand with the other, he kisses it rapturously and bathes it with his tears. Everybody is charmed with the simple enthusiasm of the young man; but the daughter, more deeply touched than the rest by this evidence of his kindly heart, is reminded of Telemachus weeping for the woes of Philoctetus. She looks at him shyly, the better to study his countenance; there is nothing in it to give the lie to her comparison.

His easy bearing shows freedom without pride; his manners are lively but not boisterous; sympathy makes his glance softer and his expression more pleasing; the young girl, seeing him weep, is ready to mingle her tears with his. With so good an excuse for tears, she is restrained by a secret shame; she blames herself already for the tears which tremble on her eyelids, as though it were wrong to weep for one's family.

Her mother, who has been watching her ever since she sat down to supper, sees her distress, and to relieve it she sends her on some errand. The daughter returns directly, but so little recovered that her distress is apparent to all. Her mother says gently, "Sophy, control yourself; will you never cease to weep for the misfortunes of your parents? Why should you, who are their chief comfort, be more sensitive than they are themselves?"

At the name of Sophy you would have seen Emile give a start. His attention is arrested by this dear name, and he awakes all at once and looks eagerly at one who dares to bear it. Sophy! Are you the Sophy whom my heart is seeking? Is it you that I love? He looks at her; he watches her with a sort of fear and self-distrust. The face is not quite what he pictured; he cannot tell whether he likes it more or less. He studies every feature, he watches every movement, every gesture; he has a hundred fleeting interpretations for them all; he would give half his life if she would but speak. He looks at me anxiously and uneasily; his eyes are full of questions and reproaches. His every glance seems to say, "Guide me while there is yet time; if my heart yields itself and is deceived, I shall never get over it."

There is no one in the world less able to conceal his feelings than Emile. How should he conceal them, in the midst of the greatest disturbance he has ever experienced, and under the eyes of four spectators who are all watching him, while she who seems to heed him least is really most occupied with him. His uneasiness does not escape the keen eyes of Sophy; his own eyes tell her that she is its cause; she sees that this uneasiness is not yet love; what matter? He is thinking of her, and that is enough; she will be very unlucky if he thinks of her with impunity.

Mothers, like daughters, have eyes; and they have experience too. Sophy's mother smiles at the success of our schemes. She reads the hearts of the young people; she sees that the time has come to secure the heart of this new Telemachus; she makes her daughter speak. Her daughter, with her native sweetness, replies in a timid tone which makes all the more impression. At the first sound of her voice, Emile surrenders; it is Sophy herself; there can be no doubt about it. If it were not so, it would be too late to deny it.

The charms of this maiden enchantress rush like torrents through his heart, and he begins to drain the draughts of poison with which he is intoxicated. He says nothing; questions pass unheeded; he sees only Sophy, he hears only Sophy; if she says a word, he opens his mouth; if her eyes are cast down, so are his; if he sees her sigh, he sighs too; it is Sophy's heart which seems to speak in his. What a change have these few moments wrought in her heart! It is no longer her turn to tremble, it is Emile's. Farewell liberty, simplicity, frankness. Confused, embarrassed, fearful, he dare not look about him for fear he should see that we are watching him. Ashamed that we should read his secret, he would fain become invisible to every one, that he might feed in secret on the sight of Sophy. Sophy, on the other hand, regains her confidence at the sight of Emile's fear; she sees her triumph and rejoices in it.

> *"No'l mostra gia, ben che in suo cor ne rida."*
> *Tasso, Jerus. Del., c. iv. v. 33.*

Her expression remains unchanged; but in spite of her modest look and downcast eyes, her tender heart is throbbing with joy, and it tells her that she has found Telemachus.

If I relate the plain and simple tale of their innocent affections you will accuse me of frivolity, but you will be mistaken. Sufficient attention is not given to the effect which the first connection between man and woman is bound to produce on the future life of both. People do not see that a first impression so vivid as that of love, or the liking which takes the place of love, produces lasting effects whose influence continues till death. Works on education are crammed with wordy and unnecessary accounts of the imaginary duties of children; but there is not a word about the most important and most difficult part of their education, the crisis which forms the bridge between the child and the man. If any part of this work is really useful, it will be because I have dwelt at great length on this matter, so essential in itself and so neglected by other authors, and because I have not allowed myself to be discouraged either by false delicacy or by the difficulties of expression. The story of human nature is a fair romance. Am I to blame if it is not found elsewhere? I am trying to write the history of mankind. If my book is a romance, the fault lies with those who deprave mankind.

This is supported by another reason; we are not dealing with a youth given over from childhood to fear, greed, envy, pride, and all those passions which are the common tools of the schoolmaster; we have to do with a youth who is not only in love for the first time, but with one who is also experiencing his first passion of any kind; very likely it will be the only strong passion he will ever know, and upon it depends the final formation of his character. His mode of thought, his feelings, his tastes, determined by a lasting passion, are about to become so fixed that they will be incapable of further change.

You will easily understand that Emile and I do not spend the whole of the night which follows after such an evening in sleep. Why! Do you mean to tell me that a wise man should be so much affected by a mere coincidence of name! Is there only one Sophy in the world? Are they all alike in heart and in name? Is every Sophy he meets his Sophy? Is he mad to fall in love with a person of whom he knows so little, with whom he has scarcely exchanged a couple of words? Wait, young man; examine, observe. You do not even know who our hosts may be, and to hear you talk one would think the house was your own.

This is no time for teaching, and what I say will receive scant attention. It only serves to stimulate Emile to further interest in Sophy, through his desire to find reasons for his fancy. The unexpected coincidence in the name, the meeting which, so far as he knows, was quite accidental, my very caution itself, only serve as fuel to the fire. He is so convinced already of Sophy's excellence, that he feels sure he can make me fond of her.

Next morning I have no doubt Emile will make himself as smart as his old travelling suit permits. I am not mistaken; but I am amused to see how eager he is to wear the clean linen put out for us. I know his thoughts, and I am delighted to see that he is trying to establish a means of intercourse, through the return and exchange of the linen; so that he may have a right to return it and so pay another visit to the house.

I expected to find Sophy rather more carefully dressed too; but I was mistaken. Such common coquetry is all very well for those who merely desire to please. The coquetry of true love is a more delicate matter; it has quite another end in view. Sophy is dressed, if possible, more simply than last night, though as usual her frock is exquisitely clean. The only sign of coquetry is her self-consciousness. She knows that an elaborate toilet is a sign of love, but she does not know that a careless toilet is another of its signs; it shows a desire to be like not merely for one's clothes but for oneself. What does a lover care for her clothes if he knows she is thinking of him? Sophy is already sure of her power over Emile, and she is not content to delight his eyes if his heart is not hers also; he must not only perceive her charms, he must divine them; has he not seen enough to guess the rest?

We may take it for granted that while Emile and I were talking last night, Sophy and her mother were not silent; a confession was made and instructions given. The morning's meeting is not unprepared. Twelve hours ago our young people had never met; they have never said a word to each other; but it is clear that there is already an understanding between them. Their greeting is formal, confused, timid; they say nothing, their downcast eyes seem to avoid each other, but that is in itself a sign that they understand, they avoid each other with one consent; they already feel the need of concealment, though not a word has been uttered. When we depart we ask leave to come again to return the borrowed clothes in person, Emile's words are addressed to the father and mother, but his eyes seek Sophy's, and his looks are more eloquent than his words. Sophy says nothing by word or gesture; she seems deaf and blind, but she blushes, and that blush is an answer even plainer than that of her parents.

We receive permission to come again, though we are not invited to stay. This is only fitting; you offer shelter to benighted travellers, but a lover does not sleep in the house of his mistress.

We have hardly left the beloved abode before Emile is thinking of taking rooms in the neighbourhood; the nearest cottage seems too far; he would like to sleep in the next ditch. "You young fool!" I said in a tone of pity, "are you already blinded by passion? Have you no regard for manners or for reason? Wretched youth, you call yourself a lover and you would bring disgrace upon her you love! What would people say of her if they knew that a young man who has been staying at her house was sleeping close by? You say you love her! Would you ruin her reputation? Is that the price you offer for her parents' hospitality? Would you bring disgrace on her who will one day make you the happiest of men?" "Why should we trouble ourselves about the empty words and unjust suspicions of other people?" said he eagerly. "Have you not taught me yourself to make light of them? Who knows better than I how greatly I honour Sophy, what respect I desire to show her? My attachment will not cause her shame, it will be her glory, it shall be worthy of her. If my heart and my actions continually give her the homage she deserves, what harm can I do her?" "Dear Emile," I said, as I clasped him to my heart, "you are thinking of yourself alone; learn to think for her too. Do not compare the honour of one sex with that of the other, they rest on different foundations. These foundations are equally firm and right, because they are both laid by nature, and that same virtue which makes you scorn what men say about yourself, binds you to respect what they say of her you love. Your honour is in your own keeping, her honour depends on others. To neglect it is to wound your own honour, and you fail in what is due to yourself if you do not give her the respect she deserves."

Then while I explain the reasons for this difference, I make him realise how wrong it would be to pay no attention to it. Who can say if he will really be Sophy's husband? He does not know how she feels towards him; her own heart or her parents' will may already have formed other engagements; he knows nothing of her, perhaps there are none of those grounds of suitability which make a happy marriage. Is he not aware that the least breath of scandal with regard to a young girl is an indelible stain, which not even marriage with him who has caused the scandal can efface? What man of feeling would ruin the woman he loves? What man of honour would desire that a miserable woman should for ever lament the misfortune of having found favour in his eyes?

Always prone to extremes, the youth takes alarm at the consequences which I have compelled him to consider, and now he thinks that he cannot be too far from Sophy's home; he hastens his steps to get further from it; he glances round to make sure that no one is listening; he would sacrifice his own happiness a thousand times to the honour of her whom he loves; he would rather never see her again than cause her the least unpleasantness. This is the first result of the pains I have taken ever since he was a child to make him capable of affection.

We must therefore seek a lodging at a distance, but not too far. We look about us, we make inquiries; we find that there is a town at least two leagues away. We try and find lodgings in this town, rather than in the nearer villages, where our presence might give rise to suspicion. It is there that the new lover takes up his abode, full of love, hope, joy, above all full of right feeling. In this way, I guide his rising passion towards all that is honourable and good, so that his inclinations unconsciously follow the same bent.

My course is drawing to a close; the end is in view. All the chief difficulties are vanquished, the chief obstacles overcome; the hardest thing left to do is to refrain from spoiling my work by undue haste to complete it. Amid the uncertainty of human life, let us shun that false prudence which seeks to sacrifice the present to the future; what is, is too often sacrificed to what will never be. Let us make man happy at every age lest in spite of our care he should die without knowing the meaning of happiness. Now if there is a time to enjoy life, it is undoubtedly the close of adolescence, when the powers of mind and body have reached their greatest strength, and when man in the midst of his course is furthest from those two extremes which tell him "Life is short." If the imprudence of youth deceives itself it is not in its desire for enjoyment, but because it seeks enjoyment where it is not to be found, and lays up misery for the future, while unable to enjoy the present.

Consider my Emile over twenty years of age, well formed, well developed in mind and body, strong, healthy, active, skilful, robust, full of sense, reason, kindness, humanity, possessed of good morals and good taste, loving what is beautiful, doing what is good, free from the sway of fierce passions, released from the tyranny of popular prejudices, but subject to the law of wisdom, and easily guided by the voice of a friend; gifted with so many useful and pleasant accomplishments, caring little for wealth, able to earn a living with his own hands, and not afraid of want, whatever may come. Behold him in the intoxication of a growing passion; his heart opens to the first beams of love; its pleasant fancies reveal to him a whole world of new delights and enjoyments; he loves a sweet woman, whose character is even more delightful than her person; he hopes, he expects the reward which he deserves.

Their first attachment took its rise in mutual affection, in community of honourable feelings; therefore this affection is lasting. It abandons itself, with confidence, with reason, to the most delightful madness, without fear, regret, remorse, or any other disturbing thought, but that which is inseparable from all happiness. What lacks there yet? Behold, inquire, imagine what still is lacking, that can be combined with present joys. Every happiness which can exist in combination is already present; nothing could be added without taking away from what there is; he is as happy as man can be. Shall I choose this time to cut short so sweet a period? Shall I disturb such pure enjoyment? The happiness he enjoys is my life's reward. What could I give that could outweigh what I should take away? Even if I set the crown to his happiness I should destroy its greatest charm. That supreme joy is a hundredfold greater in anticipation than in possession; its savour is greater while we wait for it than when it is ours. O worthy Emile! love and be loved! prolong your enjoyment before it is yours; rejoice in your love and in your innocence, find your paradise upon earth, while you await your heaven. I shall not cut short this happy period of life. I will draw out its enchantments, I will prolong them as far as possible. Alas! it must come to an end and that soon; but it shall at least linger in your memory, and you will never repent of its joys.

Emile has not forgotten that we have something to return. As soon as the things are ready, we take horse and set off at a great pace, for on this occasion he is anxious to get there. When the heart opens the door to passion, it becomes conscious of the slow flight of time. If my time has not been wasted he will not spend his life like this.

Unluckily the road is intricate and the country difficult. We lose our way; he is the first to notice it, and without losing his temper, and without grumbling, he devotes his whole attention to discovering the path; he wanders for a long time before he knows where he is and always with the same self-control. You think nothing of that; but I think it a matter of great importance, for I know how eager he is; I see the results of the care I have taken from his infancy to harden him to endure the blows of necessity.

We are there at last! Our reception is much simpler and more friendly than on the previous occasion; we are already old acquaintances. Emile and Sophy bow shyly and say nothing; what can they say in our presence? What they wish to say requires no spectators. We walk in the garden; a well-kept kitchen-garden takes the place of flower-beds, the park is an orchard full of fine tall fruit trees of every kind, divided by pretty streams and borders full of flowers. "What a lovely place!" exclaims Emile, still thinking of his Homer, and still full of enthusiasm, "I could fancy myself in the garden of Alcinous." The daughter wishes she knew who Alcinous was; her mother asks. "Alcinous," I tell them, "was a king of Coreyra. Homer describes his garden and the critics think it too simple and unadorned. [Footnote: "'When you leave the palace you enter a vast garden, four acres in extent, walled in on every side, planted with tall trees in blossom, and yielding pears, pomegranates, and other goodly fruits, fig-trees with their luscious burden and green olives. All the year round these fair trees are heavy with fruit; summer and winter the soft breath of the west wind sways the trees and ripens the fruit. Pears and apples wither on the branches, the fig on the fig-tree, and the clusters of grapes on the vine. The inexhaustible stock bears fresh grapes, some are baked, some are spread out on the threshing floor to dry, others are made into wine, while flowers, sour grapes, and those which are beginning to wither are left upon the tree. At either end is a square garden filled with flowers which bloom throughout the year, these gardens are adorned by two fountains, one of these streams waters the garden, the other passes through the palace and is then taken to a lofty tower in the town to provide drinking water for its citizens.' Such is the description of the royal garden of Alcinous in the 7th book of the Odyssey, a garden in which, to the lasting disgrace of that old dreamer Homer and the princes of his day, there were neither trellises, statues, cascades, nor bowling-greens."] This Alcinous had a charming daughter who dreamed the night before her father received a stranger at his board that she would soon have a husband." Sophy, taken unawares, blushed, hung her head, and bit her lips; no one could be more confused. Her father, who was enjoying her confusion, added that the young princess bent herself to wash the linen in the river. "Do you think," said he, "she would have scorned to touch the dirty clothes, saying, that they smelt of grease?" Sophy, touched to the quick, forgot her natural timidity and defended herself eagerly. Her papa knew very well all the smaller things would have had no other laundress if she had been allowed to wash them, and she would gladly have done more had she been set to do it. [Footnote: I own I feel grateful to Sophy's mother for not letting her spoil such pretty hands with soap, hands which Emile will kiss so often.] Meanwhile she watched me secretly with such anxiety that I could not suppress a smile, while I read the terrors of her simple heart which urged her to speak. Her father was cruel enough to continue this foolish sport, by asking her, in jest, why she spoke on her own behalf and what had she in common with the daughter of Alcinous. Trembling and ashamed she dared hardly breathe or look at us. Charming girl! This is no time for feigning, you have shown your true feelings in spite of yourself.

To all appearance this little scene is soon forgotten; luckily for Sophy, Emile, at least, is unaware of it. We continue our walk, the young people at first keeping close beside us; but they find it hard to adapt themselves to our slower pace, and presently they are a little in front of us, they are walking side by side, they begin to talk, and before long they are a good way ahead. Sophy seems to be listening quietly, Emile is talking and gesticulating vigorously; they seem to find their conversation interesting. When we turn homewards a full hour later, we call them to us and they return slowly enough now, and we can see they are making good use of their time. Their conversation ceases suddenly before they come within earshot, and they hurry up to us. Emile meets us with a frank affectionate expression; his eyes are sparkling with joy; yet he looks anxiously at Sophy's mother to see how she takes it. Sophy is not nearly so much at her ease; as she approaches us she seems covered with confusion at finding herself tete-a-tete with a young man, though she has met so many other young men frankly enough, and without being found fault with for it. She runs up to her mother, somewhat out of breath, and makes some trivial remark, as if to pretend she had been with her for some time.

From the happy expression of these dear children we see that this conversation has taken a load off their hearts. They are no less reticent in their intercourse, but their reticence is less embarrassing, it is only due to Emile's reverence and Sophy's modesty, to the goodness of both. Emile ventures to say a few words to her, she ventures to reply, but she always looks at her mother before she dares to answer. The most remarkable change is in her attitude towards me. She shows me the greatest respect, she watches me with interest, she takes pains to please me; I see that I am honoured with her esteem, and that she is not indifferent to mine. I understand that Emile has been talking to her about me; you might say they have been scheming to win me over to their side; yet it is not so, and Sophy herself is not so easily won. Perhaps Emile will have more need of my influence with her than of hers with me. What a charming pair! When I consider that the tender love of my young friend has brought my name so prominently into his first conversation with his lady-love, I enjoy the reward of all my trouble; his affection is a sufficient recompense.

Our visit is repeated. There are frequent conversations between the young people. Emile is madly in love and thinks that his happiness is within his grasp. Yet he does not succeed in winning any formal avowal from Sophy; she listens to what he says and answers nothing. Emile knows how modest she is, and is not surprised at her reticence; he feels sure that she likes him; he knows that parents decide whom their daughters shall marry; he supposes that Sophy is awaiting her parents' commands; he asks her permission to speak to them, and she makes no objection. He talks to me and I speak on his behalf and in his presence. He is immensely surprised to hear that Sophy is her own mistress, that his happiness depends on her alone. He begins to be puzzled by her conduct. He is less self-confident, he takes alarm, he sees that he has not made so much progress as he expected, and then it is that his love appeals to her in the tenderest and most moving language.

Emile is not the sort of man to guess what is the matter; if no one told him he would never discover it as long as he lived, and Sophy is too proud to tell him. What she considers obstacles, others would call advantages. She has not forgotten her parents' teaching. She is poor; Emile is rich; so much she knows. He must win her esteem; his deserts must be great indeed to remove this inequality. But how should he perceive these obstacles? Is Emile aware that he is rich? Has he ever condescended to inquire? Thank heaven, he has no need of riches, he can do good without their aid. The good he does comes from his heart, not his purse. He gives the wretched his time, his care, his affection, himself; and when he reckons up what he has done, he hardly dares to mention the money spent on the poor.

As he does not know what to make of his disgrace, he thinks it is his own fault; for who would venture to accuse the adored one of caprice. The shame of humiliation adds to the pangs of disappointed love. He no longer approaches Sophy with that pleasant confidence of his own worth; he is shy and timid in her presence. He no longer hopes to win her affections, but to gain her pity. Sometimes he loses patience and is almost angry with her. Sophy seems to guess his angry feelings and she looks at him. Her glance is enough to disarm and terrify him; he is more submissive than he used to be.

Disturbed by this stubborn resistance, this invincible silence, he pours out his heart to his friend. He shares with him the pangs of a heart devoured by sorrow; he implores his help and counsel. "How mysterious it is, how hard to understand! She takes an interest in me, that I am sure; far from avoiding me she is pleased to see me; when I come she shows signs of pleasure, when I go she shows regret; she receives my attentions kindly, my services seem to give her pleasure, she condescends to give me her advice and even her commands. Yet she rejects my requests and my prayers. When I venture to speak of marriage, she bids me be silent; if I say a word, she leaves me at once. Why on earth should she wish me to be hers but refuse to be mine? She respects and loves you, and she will not dare to refuse to listen to you. Speak to her, make her answer. Come to your friend's help, and put the coping stone to all you have done for him; do not let him fall a victim to your care! If you fail to secure his happiness, your own teaching will have been the cause of his misery."

I speak to Sophy, and have no difficulty in getting her to confide her secret to me, a secret which was known to me already. It is not so easy to get permission to tell Emile; but at last she gives me leave and I tell him what is the matter. He cannot get over his surprise at this explanation. He cannot understand this delicacy; he cannot see how a few pounds more or less can affect his character or his deserts. When I get him to see their effect on people's prejudices he begins to laugh; he is so wild with delight that he wants to be off at once to tear up his title deeds and renounce his money, so as to have the honour of being as poor as Sophy, and to return worthy to be her husband.

"Why," said I, trying to check him, and laughing in my turn at his impetuosity, "will this young head never grow any older? Having dabbled all your life in philosophy, will you never learn to reason? Do not you see that your wild scheme would only make things worse, and Sophy more obstinate? It is a small superiority to be rather richer than she, but to give up all for her would be a very great superiority; if her pride cannot bear to be under the small obligation, how will she make up her mind to the greater? If she cannot bear to think that her husband might taunt her with the fact that he has enriched her, would she permit him to blame her for having brought him to poverty? Wretched boy, beware lest she suspects you of such a plan! On the contrary, be careful and economical for her sake, lest she should accuse you of trying to gain her by cunning, by sacrificing of your own free will what you are really wasting through carelessness.

"Do you really think that she is afraid of wealth, and that she is opposed to great possessions in themselves? No, dear Emile; there are more serious and substantial grounds for her opinion, in the effect produced by wealth on its possessor. She knows that those who are possessed of fortune's gifts are apt to place them first. The rich always put wealth before merit. When services are reckoned against silver, the latter always outweighs the former, and those who have spent their life in their master's service are considered his debtors for the very bread they eat. What must you do, Emile, to calm her fears? Let her get to know you better; that is not done in a day. Show her the treasures of your heart, to counterbalance the wealth which is unfortunately yours. Time and constancy will overcome her resistance; let your great and noble feelings make her forget your wealth. Love her, serve her, serve her worthy parents. Convince her that these attentions are not the result of a foolish fleeting passion, but of settled principles engraved upon your heart. Show them the honour deserved by worth when exposed to the buffets of Fortune; that is the only way to reconcile it with that worth which basks in her smiles."

The transports of joy experienced by the young man at these words may easily be imagined; they restore confidence and hope, his good heart rejoices to do something to please Sophy, which he would have done if there had been no such person, or if he had not been in love with her. However little his character has been understood, anybody can see how he would behave under such circumstances.

Here am I, the confidant of these two young people and the mediator of their affection. What a fine task for a tutor! So fine that never in all my life have I stood so high in my own eyes, nor felt so pleased with myself. Moreover, this duty is not without its charms. I am not unwelcome in the home; it is my business to see that the lovers behave themselves; Emile, ever afraid of offending me, was never so docile. The little lady herself overwhelms me with a kindness which does not deceive me, and of which I only take my proper share. This is her way of making up for her severity towards Emile. For his sake she bestows on me a hundred tender caresses, though she would die rather than bestow them on him; and he, knowing that I would never stand in his way, is delighted that I should get on so well with her. If she refuses his arm when we are out walking, he consoles himself with the thought that she has taken mine. He makes way for me without a murmur, he clasps my hand, and voice and look alike whisper, "My friend, plead for me!" and his eyes follow us with interest; he tries to read our feelings in our faces, and to interpret our conversation by our gestures; he knows that everything we are saying concerns him. Dear Sophy, how frank and easy you are when you can talk to Mentor without being overheard by Telemachus. How freely and delightfully you permit him to read what is passing in your tender little heart! How delighted you are to show him how you esteem his pupil! How cunningly and appealingly you allow him to divine still tenderer sentiments. With what a pretence of anger you dismiss Emile when his impatience leads him to interrupt you? With what pretty vexation you reproach his indiscretion when he comes and prevents you saying something to his credit, or listening to what I say about him, or finding in my words some new excuse to love him!

Having got so far as to be tolerated as an acknowledged lover, Emile takes full advantage of his position; he speaks, he urges, he implores, he demands. Hard words or ill treatment make no difference, provided he gets a hearing. At length Sophy is persuaded, though with some difficulty, to assume the authority of a betrothed, to decide what he shall do, to command instead of to ask, to accept instead of to thank, to control the frequency and the hours of his visits, to forbid him to come till such a day or to stay beyond such an hour. This is not done in play, but in earnest, and if it was hard to induce her to accept these rights, she uses them so sternly that Emile is often ready to regret that he gave them to her. But whatever her commands, they are obeyed without question, and often when at her bidding he is about to leave her, he glances at me his eyes full of delight, as if to say, "You see she has taken possession of me." Yet unknown to him, Sophy, with all her pride, is observing him closely, and she is smiling to herself at the pride of her slave.

Oh that I had the brush of an Alban or a Raphael to paint their bliss, or the pen of the divine Milton to describe the pleasures of love and innocence! Not so; let such hollow arts shrink back before the sacred truth of nature. In tenderness and pureness of heart let your imagination freely trace the raptures of these young lovers, who under the eyes of parents and tutor, abandon themselves to their blissful illusions; in the intoxication of passion they are advancing step by step to its consummation; with flowers and garlands they are weaving the bonds which are to bind them till death do part. I am carried away by this succession of pictures, I am so happy that I cannot group them in any sort of order or scheme; any one with a heart in his breast can paint the charming picture for himself and realise the different experiences of father, mother, daughter, tutor, and pupil, and the part played by each and all in the union of the most delightful couple whom love and virtue have ever led to happiness.

Now that he is really eager to please, Emile begins to feel the value of the accomplishments he has acquired. Sophy is fond of singing, he sings with her; he does more, he teaches her music. She is lively and light of foot, she loves skipping; he dances with her, he perfects and develops her untrained movements into the steps of the dance. These lessons, enlivened by the gayest mirth, are quite delightful, they melt the timid respect of love; a lover may enjoy teaching his betrothed—he has a right to be her teacher.

There is an old spinet quite out of order. Emile mends and tunes it; he is a maker and mender of musical instruments as well as a carpenter; it has always been his rule to learn to do everything he can for himself. The house is picturesquely situated and he makes several sketches of it, in some of which

Sophy does her share, and she hangs them in her father's study. The frames are not gilded, nor do they require gilding. When she sees Emile drawing, she draws too, and improves her own drawing; she cultivates all her talents, and her grace gives a charm to all she does. Her father and mother recall the days of their wealth, when they find themselves surrounded by the works of art which alone gave value to wealth; the whole house is adorned by love; love alone has enthroned among them, without cost or effort, the very same pleasures which were gathered together in former days by dint of toil and money.

As the idolater gives what he loves best to the shrine of the object of his worship, so the lover is not content to see perfection in his mistress, he must be ever trying to add to her adornment. She does not need it for his pleasure, it is he who needs the pleasure of giving, it is a fresh homage to be rendered to her, a fresh pleasure in the joy of beholding her. Everything of beauty seems to find its place only as an accessory to the supreme beauty. It is both touching and amusing to see Emile eager to teach Sophy everything he knows, without asking whether she wants to learn it or whether it is suitable for her. He talks about all sorts of things and explains them to her with boyish eagerness; he thinks he has only to speak and she will understand; he looks forward to arguing, and discussing philosophy with her; everything he cannot display before her is so much useless learning; he is quite ashamed of knowing more than she.

So he gives her lessons in philosophy, physics, mathematics, history, and everything else. Sophy is delighted to share his enthusiasm and to try and profit by it. How pleased Emile is when he can get leave to give these lessons on his knees before her! He thinks the heavens are open. Yet this position, more trying to pupil than to teacher, is hardly favourable to study. It is not easy to know where to look, to avoid meeting the eyes which follow our own, and if they meet so much the worse for the lesson.

Women are no strangers to the art of thinking, but they should only skim the surface of logic and metaphysics. Sophy understands readily, but she soon forgets. She makes most progress in the moral sciences and aesthetics; as to physical science she retains some vague idea of the general laws and order of this world. Sometimes in the course of their walks, the spectacle of the wonders of nature bids them not fear to raise their pure and innocent hearts to nature's God; they are not afraid of His presence, and they pour out their hearts before him.

What! Two young lovers spending their time together talking of religion! Have they nothing better to do than to say their catechism! What profit is there in the attempt to degrade what is noble? Yes, no doubt they are saying their catechism in their delightful land of romance; they are perfect in each other's eyes; they love one another, they talk eagerly of all that makes virtue worth having. Their sacrifices to virtue make her all the dearer to them. Their struggles after self-control draw from them tears purer than the dew of heaven, and these sweet tears are the joy of life; no human heart has ever experienced a sweeter intoxication. Their very renunciation adds to their happiness, and their sacrifices increase their self-respect. Sensual men, bodies without souls, some day they will know your pleasures, and all their life long they will recall with regret the happy days when they refused the cup of pleasure.

In spite of this good understanding, differences and even quarrels occur from time to time; the lady has her whims, the lover has a hot temper; but these passing showers are soon over and only serve to strengthen their union. Emile learns by experience not to attach too much importance to them, he always gains more by the reconciliation than he lost by the quarrel. The results of the first difference made him expect a like result from all; he was mistaken, but even if he does not make any appreciable step forward, he has always the satisfaction of finding Sophy's genuine concern for his affection more firmly established. "What advantage is this to him?" you would ask. I will gladly tell you; all the more gladly because it will give me an opportunity to establish clearly a very important principle, and to combat a very deadly one.

Emile is in love, but he is not presuming; and you will easily understand that the dignified Sophy is not the sort of girl to allow any kind of familiarity. Yet virtue has its bounds like everything else, and she is rather to be blamed for her severity than for indulgence; even her father himself is sometimes afraid lest her lofty pride should degenerate into a haughty spirit. When most alone, Emile dare not ask for the slightest favour, he must not even seem to desire it; and if she is gracious enough to take his arm when they are out walking, a favour which she will never permit him to claim as a right, it is only occasionally that he dare venture with a sigh to press her hand to his heart. However, after a long period of self-restraint, he ventured secretly to kiss the hem of her dress, and several times he was lucky enough to find her willing at least to pretend she was not aware of it. One day he attempts to take the same privilege rather more openly, and Sophy takes it into her head to be greatly offended. He persists, she gets angry and speaks sharply to him; Emile will not put up with this without reply; the rest of the day is given over to sulks, and they part in a very ill temper.

Sophy is ill at ease; her mother is her confidant in all things, how can she keep this from her? It is their first misunderstanding, and the misunderstanding of an hour is such a serious business. She is sorry for what she has done, she has her mother's permission and her father's commands to make reparation.

The next day Emile returns somewhat earlier than usual and in a state of some anxiety. Sophy is in her mother's dressing-room and her father is also present. Emile enters respectfully but gloomily. Scarcely have her parents greeted him than Sophy turns round and holding out her hand asks him in an affectionate tone how he is. That pretty hand is clearly held out to be kissed; he takes it but does not kiss it. Sophy, rather ashamed of herself, withdraws her hand as best she may. Emile, who is not used to a woman's whims, and does not know how far caprice may be carried, does not forget so easily or make friends again all at once. Sophy's father, seeing her confusion, completes her discomfiture by his jokes. The poor girl, confused and ashamed, does not know what to do with herself and would gladly have a good cry. The more she tries to control herself the worse she feels; at last a tear escapes in spite of all she can do to prevent it. Emile, seeing this tear, rushes towards her, falls on his knees, takes her hand and kisses it again and again with the greatest devotion. "My word, you are too kind to her," says her father, laughing; "if I were you, I should deal more severely with these follies, I should punish the mouth that wronged me." Emboldened by these words, Emile turns a suppliant eye towards her mother, and thinking she is not unwilling, he tremblingly approaches Sophy's face; she turns away her head, and to save her mouth she exposes a blushing cheek. The daring young man is not content with this; there is no great resistance. What a kiss, if it were not taken under her mother's eyes. Have a care, Sophy, in your severity; he will be ready enough to try to kiss your dress if only you will sometimes say "No."

After this exemplary punishment, Sophy's father goes about his business, and her mother makes some excuse for sending her out of the room; then she speaks to Emile very seriously. "Sir," she says, "I think a young man so well born and well bred as yourself, a man of feeling and character, would never reward with dishonour the confidence reposed in him by the friendship of this family. I am neither prudish nor over strict; I know how to make excuses for youthful folly, and what I have permitted in my own presence is sufficient proof of this. Consult your friend as to your own duty, he will tell you there is all the difference in the world between the playful kisses sanctioned by the presence of father and mother, and the same freedom taken in their absence and in betrayal of their confidence, a freedom which makes a snare of the very favours which in the parents' presence were wholly innocent. He will tell you, sir, that my daughter is only to blame for not having perceived from the first what she ought never to have permitted; he will tell you that every favour, taken as such, is a favour, and that it is unworthy of a man of honour to take advantage of a young girl's innocence, to usurp in private the same freedom which she may permit in the presence of others. For good manners teach us what is permitted in public; but we do not know what a man will permit to himself in private, if he makes himself the sole judge of his conduct."

After this well-deserved rebuke, addressed rather to me than to my pupil, the good mother leaves us, and I am amazed by her rare prudence, in thinking it a little thing that Emile should kiss her daughter's lips in her presence, while fearing lest he should venture to kiss her dress when they are alone. When I consider the folly of worldly maxims, whereby real purity is continually sacrificed to a show of propriety, I understand why speech becomes more refined while the heart becomes more corrupt, and why etiquette is stricter while those who conform to it are most immoral.

While I am trying to convince Emile's heart with regard to these duties which I ought to have instilled into him sooner, a new idea occurs to me, an idea which perhaps does Sophy all the more credit, though I shall take care not to tell her lover; this so-called pride, for which she has been censured, is clearly only a very wise precaution to protect her from herself. Being aware that, unfortunately, her own temperament is inflammable, she dreads the least spark, and keeps out of reach so far as she can. Her sternness is due not to pride but to humility. She assumes a control over Emile because she doubts her control of herself; she turns the one against the other. If she had more confidence in herself she would be much less haughty. With this exception is there anywhere on earth a gentler, sweeter girl? Is there any who endures an affront with greater patience, any who is more afraid of annoying others? Is there any with less pretension, except in the matter of virtue? Moreover, she is not proud of her virtue, she is only proud in order to preserve her virtue, and if she can follow the guidance of her heart without danger, she caresses her lover himself. But her wise mother does not confide all this even to her father; men should not hear everything.

Far from seeming proud of her conquest, Sophy has grown more friendly and less exacting towards everybody, except perhaps the one person who has wrought this change. Her noble heart no longer swells with the feeling of independence. She triumphs modestly over a victory gained at the price of her freedom. Her bearing is more restrained, her speech more timid, since she has begun to blush at the word "lover"; but contentment may be seen beneath her outward confusion and this very shame is not painful. This change is most noticeable in her behaviour towards the young men she meets. Now that she has ceased to be afraid of them, much of her extreme reserve has disappeared. Now that her choice is made, she does not hesitate to be gracious to those to whom she is quite indifferent; taking no more interest in them, she is less difficult to please, and she always finds them pleasant enough for people who are of no importance to her.

If true love were capable of coquetry, I should fancy I saw traces of it in the way Sophy behaves towards other young men in her lover's presence. One would say that not content with the ardent passion she inspires by a mixture of shyness and caresses, she is not sorry to rouse this passion by a little anxiety; one would say that when she is purposely amusing her young guests she means to torment Emile by the charms of a freedom she will not allow herself with him; but Sophy is too considerate, too kindly, too wise to really torment him. Love and honour take the place of prudence and control the use of this dangerous weapon. She can alarm and reassure him just as he needs it; and if she sometimes makes him uneasy she never really gives him pain. The anxiety she causes to her beloved may be forgiven because of her fear that he is not sufficiently her own.

But what effect will this little performance have upon Emile? Will he be jealous or not? That is what we must discover; for such digressions form part of the purpose of my book, and they do not lead me far from my main subject.

I have already shown how this passion of jealousy in matters of convention finds its way into the heart of man. In love it is another matter; then jealousy is so near akin to nature, that it is hard to believe that it is not her work; and the example of the very beasts, many of whom are madly jealous, seems to prove this point beyond reply. Is it man's influence that has taught cooks to tear each other to pieces or bulls to fight to the death?

No one can deny that the aversion to everything which may disturb or interfere with our pleasures is a natural impulse. Up to a certain point the desire for the exclusive possession of that which ministers to our pleasure is in the same case. But when this desire has become a passion, when it is transformed into madness, or into a bitter and suspicious fancy known as jealousy, that is quite another matter; such a passion may be natural or it may not; we must distinguish between these different cases.

I have already analysed the example of the animal world in my Discourse on Inequality, and on further consideration I think I may refer my readers to that analysis as sufficiently thorough. I will only add this further point to those already made in that work, that the jealousy which springs from nature depends greatly on sexual power, and that when sexual power is or appears to be boundless, that jealousy is at its height; for then the male, measuring his rights by his needs, can never see another male except as an unwelcome rival. In such species the females always submit to the first comer, they only belong to the male by right of conquest, and they are the cause of unending strife.

Among the monogamous species, where intercourse seems to give rise to some sort of moral bond, a kind of marriage, the female who belongs by choice to the male on whom she has bestowed herself usually denies herself to all others; and the male, having this preference of affection as a pledge of her fidelity, is less uneasy at the sight of other males and lives more peaceably with them. Among these species the male shares the care of the little ones; and by one of those touching laws of nature it seems as if the female rewards the father for his love for his children.

Now consider the human species in its primitive simplicity; it is easy to see, from the limited powers of the male, and the moderation of his desires, that nature meant him to be content with one female; this is confirmed by the numerical equality of the two sexes, at any rate in our part of the world; an equality which does not exist in anything like the same degree among those species in which several females are collected around one male. Though a man does not brood like a pigeon, and though he has no milk to suckle the young, and must in this respect be classed with the quadrupeds, his children are feeble and helpless for so long a time, that mother and children could ill dispense with the father's affection, and the care which results from it.

All these observations combine to prove that the jealous fury of the males of certain animals proves nothing with regard to man; and the exceptional case of those southern regions were polygamy is the established custom, only confirms the rule, since it is the plurality of wives that gives rise to the tyrannical precautions of the husband, and the consciousness of his own weakness makes the man resort to constraint to evade the laws of nature.

Among ourselves where these same laws are less frequently evaded in this respect, but are more frequently evaded in another and even more detestable manner, jealousy finds its motives in the passions of society rather than in those of primitive instinct. In most irregular connections the hatred of the lover for his rivals far exceeds his love for his mistress; if he fears a rival in her affections it is the effect of that self-love whose origin I have already traced out, and he is moved by vanity rather than affection. Moreover, our clumsy systems of education have made women so deceitful, [Footnote: The kind of deceit referred to here is just the opposite of that deceit becoming in a woman, and taught her by nature; the latter consists in concealing her real feelings, the former in feigning what she does not feel. Every society lady spends her life in boasting of her supposed sensibility, when in reality she cares for no one but herself.] and have so over-stimulated their appetites, that you cannot rely even on the most clearly proved affection; they can no longer display a preference which secures you against the fear of a rival.

True love is another matter. I have shown, in the work already referred to, that this sentiment is not so natural as men think, and that there is a great difference between the gentle habit which binds a man with cords of love to his helpmeet, and the unbridled passion which is intoxicated by the fancied charms of an object which he no longer sees in its true light. This passion which is full of exclusions and preferences, only differs from vanity in this respect, that vanity demands all and gives nothing, so that it is always harmful, while love, bestowing as much as it demands, is in itself a sentiment full of equity. Moreover, the more exacting it is, the more credulous; that very illusion which gave rise to it, makes it easy to persuade. If love is suspicious, esteem is trustful; and love will never exist in an honest heart without esteem, for every one loves in another the qualities which he himself holds in honour.

When once this is clearly understood, we can predict with confidence the kind of jealousy which Emile will be capable of experiencing; as there is only the smallest germ of this passion in the human heart, the form it takes must depend solely upon education: Emile, full of love and jealousy, will not be angry, sullen, suspicious, but delicate, sensitive, and timid; he will be more alarmed than vexed; he will think more of securing his lady-love than of threatening his rival; he will treat him as an obstacle to be removed if possible from his path, rather than as a rival to be hated; if he hates him, it is not because he presumes to compete with him for Sophy's affection, but because Emile feels that there is a real danger of losing that affection; he will not be so unjust and foolish as to take offence at the rivalry itself; he understands that the law of preference rests upon merit only, and that honour depends upon success; he will redouble his efforts to make himself acceptable, and he will probably succeed. His generous Sophy, though she has given alarm to his love, is well able to allay that fear, to atone for it; and the rivals who were only suffered to put him to the proof are speedily dismissed.

But whither am I going? O Emile! what art thou now? Is this my pupil? How art thou fallen! Where is that young man so sternly fashioned, who braved all weathers, who devoted his body to the hardest tasks and his soul to the laws of wisdom; untouched by prejudice or passion, a lover of truth, swayed by reason only, unheeding all that was not hers? Living in softness and idleness he now lets himself be ruled by women; their amusements are the business of his life, their wishes are his laws; a young girl is the arbiter of his fate, he cringes and grovels before her; the earnest Emile is the plaything of a child.

So shift the scenes of life; each age is swayed by its own motives, but the man is the same. At ten his mind was set upon cakes, at twenty it is set upon his mistress; at thirty it will be set upon pleasure; at forty on ambition, at fifty on avarice; when will he seek after wisdom only? Happy is he who is compelled to follow her against his will! What matter who is the guide, if the end is attained. Heroes and sages have themselves paid tribute to this human weakness; and those who handled the distaff with clumsy fingers were none the less great men.

If you would prolong the influence of a good education through life itself, the good habits acquired in childhood must be carried forward into adolescence, and when your pupil is what he ought to be you must manage to keep him what he ought to be. This is the coping-stone of your work. This is why it is of the first importance that the tutor should remain with young men; otherwise there is little doubt they will learn to make love without him. The great mistake of tutors and still more of fathers is to think that one way of living makes another impossible, and that as soon as the child is grown up, you must abandon everything you used to do when he was little. If that were so, why should we take such pains in childhood, since the good or bad use we make of it will vanish with childhood itself; if another way of life were necessarily accompanied by other ways of thinking?

The stream of memory is only interrupted by great illnesses, and the stream of conduct, by great passions. Our tastes and inclinations may change, but this change, though it may be sudden enough, is rendered less abrupt by our habits. The skilful artist, in a good colour scheme, contrives so to mingle and blend his tints that the transitions are imperceptible; and certain colour washes are spread over the whole picture so that there may be no sudden breaks. So should it be with our likings. Unbalanced characters are always changing their affections, their tastes, their sentiments; the only constant factor is the habit of change; but the man of settled character always returns to his former habits and preserves to old age the tastes and the pleasures of his childhood.

If you contrive that young people passing from one stage of life to another do not despise what has gone before, that when they form new habits, they do not forsake the old, and that they always love to do what is right, in things new and old; then only are the fruits of your toil secure, and you are sure of your scholars as long as they live; for the revolution most to be dreaded is that of the age over which you are now watching. As men always look back to this period with regret so the tastes carried forward into it from childhood are not easily destroyed; but if once interrupted they are never resumed.

Most of the habits you think you have instilled into children and young people are not really habits at all; they have only been acquired under compulsion, and being followed reluctantly they will be cast off at the first opportunity. However long you remain in prison you never get a taste for prison life; so aversion is increased rather than diminished by habit. Not so with Emile; as a child he only did what he could do willingly and with pleasure, and as a man he will do the same, and the force of habit will only lend its help to the joys of freedom. An active life, bodily labour, exercise, movement, have become so essential to him that he could not relinquish them without suffering. Reduce him all at once to a soft and sedentary life and you condemn him to chains and imprisonment, you keep him in a condition of thraldom and constraint; he would suffer, no doubt, both in health and temper. He can scarcely breathe in a stuffy room, he requires open air, movement, fatigue. Even at Sophy's feet he cannot help casting a glance at the country and longing to explore it in her company. Yet he remains if he must; but he is anxious and ill at ease; he seems to be struggling with himself; he remains because he is a captive. "Yes," you will say, "these are necessities to which you have subjected him, a yoke which you have laid upon him." You speak truly, I have subjected him to the yoke of manhood.

Emile loves Sophy; but what were the charms by which he was first attracted? Sensibility, virtue, and love for things pure and honest. When he loves this love in Sophy, will he cease to feel it himself? And what price did she put upon herself? She required all her lover's natural feelings—esteem of what is really good, frugality, simplicity, generous unselfishness, a scorn of pomp and riches. These virtues were Emile's before love claimed them of him. Is he really changed? He has all the more reason to be himself; that is the only difference. The careful reader will not suppose that all the circumstances in which he is placed are the work of chance. There were many charming girls in the town; is it chance that his choice is discovered in a distant retreat? Is their meeting the work of chance? Is it chance that makes them so suited to each other? Is it chance that they cannot live in the same place, that he is compelled to find a lodging so far from her? Is it chance that he can see her so seldom and must purchase the pleasure of seeing her at the price of such fatigue? You say he is becoming effeminate. Not so, he is growing stronger; he must be fairly robust to stand the fatigue he endures on Sophy's account.

He lives more than two leagues away. That distance serves to temper the shafts of love. If they lived next door to each other, or if he could drive to see her in a comfortable carriage, he would love at his ease in the Paris fashion. Would Leander have braved death for the sake of Hero if the sea had not lain between them? Need I say more; if my reader is able to take my meaning, he will be able to follow out my principles in detail.

The first time we went to see Sophy, we went on horseback, so as to get there more quickly. We continue this convenient plan until our fifth visit. We were expected; and more than half a league from the house we see people on the road. Emile watches them, his pulse quickens as he gets nearer, he recognises Sophy and dismounts quickly; he hastens to join the charming family. Emile is fond of good horses; his horse is fresh, he feels he is free, and gallops off across the fields; I follow and with some difficulty I succeed in catching him and bringing him back. Unluckily Sophy is afraid of horses, and I dare not approach her. Emile has not seen what happened, but Sophy whispers to him that he is giving his friend a great deal of trouble. He hurries up quite ashamed of himself, takes the horses, and follows after the party. It is only fair that each should take his turn and he rides on to get rid of our mounts. He has to leave Sophy behind him, and he no longer thinks riding a convenient mode of travelling. He returns out of breath and meets us half-way.

The next time, Emile will not hear of horses. "Why," say I, "we need only take a servant to look after them." "Shall we put our worthy friends to such expense?" he replies. "You see they would insist on feeding man and horse." "That is true," I reply; "theirs is the generous hospitality of the poor. The rich man in his niggardly pride only welcomes his friends, but the poor find room for their friends' horses." "Let us go on foot," says he; "won't you venture on the walk, when you are always so ready to share the toilsome pleasures of your child?" "I will gladly go with you," I reply at once, "and it seems to me that love does not desire so much show."

As we draw near, we meet the mother and daughter even further from home than on the last occasion. We have come at a great pace. Emile is very warm; his beloved condescends to pass her handkerchief over his cheeks. It would take a good many horses to make us ride there after this.

But it is rather hard never to be able to spend an evening together. Midsummer is long past and the days are growing shorter. Whatever we say, we are not allowed to return home in the dark, and unless we make a very early start, we have to go back almost as soon as we get there. The mother is sorry for us and uneasy on our account, and it occurs to her that, though it would not be proper for us to stay in the house, beds might be found for us in the village, if we liked to stay there occasionally. Emile claps his hands at this idea and trembles with joy; Sophy, unwittingly, kisses her mother rather oftener than usual on the day this idea occurs to her.

Little by little the charm of friendship and the familiarity of innocence take root and grow among us. I generally accompany my young friend on the days appointed by Sophy or her mother, but sometimes I let him go alone. The heart thrives in the sunshine of confidence, and a man must not be treated as a child; and what have I accomplished so far, if my pupil is unworthy of my esteem? Now and then I go without him; he is sorry, but he does not complain; what use would it be? And then he knows I shall not interfere with his interests. However, whether we go together or separately you will understand that we are not stopped by the weather; we are only too proud to arrive in a condition which calls for pity. Unluckily Sophy deprives us of this honour and forbids us to come in bad weather. This is the only occasion on which she rebels against the rules which I laid down for her in private.

One day Emile had gone alone and I did not expect him back till the following day, but he returned the same evening. "My dear Emile," said I, "have you come back to your old friend already?" But instead of responding to my caresses he replied with some show of temper, "You need not suppose I came back so soon of my own accord; she insisted on it; it is for her sake not yours that I am here." Touched by his frankness I renewed my caresses, saying, "Truthful heart and faithful friend, do not conceal from me anything I ought to know. If you came back for her sake, you told me so for my own; your return is her doing, your frankness is mine. Continue to preserve the noble candour of great souls; strangers may think what they will, but it is a crime to let our friends think us better than we are."

I take care not to let him underrate the cost of his confession by assuming that there is more love than generosity in it, and by telling him that he would rather deprive himself of the honour of this return, than give it to Sophy. But this is how he revealed to me, all unconsciously, what were his real feelings; if he had returned slowly and comfortably, dreaming of his sweetheart, I should know he was merely her lover; when he hurried back, even if he was a little out of temper, he was the friend of his Mentor.

You see that the young man is very far from spending his days with Sophy, and seeing as much of her as he wants. One or two visits a week are all that is permitted, and these visits are often only for the afternoon and are rarely extended to the next day. He spends much more of his time in longing to see her, or in rejoicing that he has seen her, than he actually spends in her presence. Even when he goes to see her, more time is spent in going and returning than by her side. His pleasures, genuine, pure, delicious, but more imaginary than real, serve to kindle his love but not to make him effeminate.

On the days when he does not see Sophy he is not sitting idle at home. He is Emile himself and quite unchanged. He usually scours the country round in pursuit of its natural history; he observes and studies the soil, its products, and their mode of cultivation; he compares the methods he sees with those with which he is already familiar; he tries to find the reasons for any differences; if he thinks other methods better than those of the locality, he introduces them to the farmers' notice; if he suggests a better kind of plough, he has one made from his own drawings; if he finds a lime pit he teaches them how to use the lime on the land, a process new to them; he often lends a hand himself; they are surprised to find him handling all manner of tools more easily than they can themselves; his furrows are deeper and straighter than theirs, he is a more skilful sower, and his beds for early produce are more cleverly planned. They do not scoff at him as a fine talker, they see he knows what he is talking about. In a word, his zeal and attention are bestowed on everything that is really useful to everybody; nor does he stop there. He visits the peasants in their homes; inquires into their circumstances, their families, the number of their children, the extent of their holdings, the nature of their produce, their markets, their rights, their burdens, their debts, etc. He gives away very little money, for he knows it is usually ill spent; but he himself directs the use of his money, and makes it helpful to them without distributing it among them. He supplies them with labourers, and often pays them for work done by themselves, on tasks for their own benefit. For one he has the falling thatch repaired or renewed; for another he clears a piece of land which had gone out of cultivation for lack of means; to another he gives a cow, a horse, or stock of any kind to replace a loss; two neighbours are ready to go to law, he wins them over, and makes them friends again; a peasant falls ill, he has him cared for, he looks after him himself; [Footnote: To look after a sick peasant is not merely to give him a pill, or medicine, or to send a surgeon to him. That is not what these poor folk require in sickness; what they want is more and better food. When you have fever, you will do well to fast, but when your peasants have it, give them meat and wine; illness, in their case, is nearly always due to poverty and exhaustion; your cellar will supply the best draught, your butchers will be the best apothecary.] another is harassed by a rich and powerful neighbor, he protects him and speaks on his behalf; young people are fond of one another, he helps forward their marriage; a good woman has lost her beloved child, he goes to see her, he speaks words of comfort and sits a while with her; he does not despise the poor, he is in no hurry to avoid the unfortunate; he often takes his dinner with some peasant he is helping, and he will even accept a meal from those who have no need of his help; though he is the benefactor of some and the friend of all, he is none the less their equal. In conclusion, he always does as much good by his personal efforts as by his money.

Sometimes his steps are turned in the direction of the happy abode; he may hope to see Sophy without her knowing, to see her out walking without being seen. But Emile is always quite open in everything he does; he neither can nor would deceive. His delicacy is of that pleasing type in which pride rests on the foundation of a good conscience. He keeps strictly within bounds, and never comes near enough to gain from chance what he only desires to win from Sophy herself. On the other hand, he delights to roam about the neighbourhood, looking for the trace of Sophy's steps, feeling what pains she has taken and what a distance she has walked to please him.

The day before his visit, he will go to some neighbouring farm and order a little feast for the morrow. We shall take our walk in that direction without any special object, we shall turn in apparently by chance; fruit, cakes, and cream are waiting for us. Sophy likes sweets, so is not insensible to these attentions, and she is quite ready to do honour to what we have provided; for I always have my share of the credit even if I have had no part in the trouble; it is a girl's way of returning thanks more easily. Her father and I have cakes and wine; Emile keeps the ladies company and is always on the look-out to secure a dish of cream in which Sophy has dipped her spoon.

The cakes lead me to talk of the races Emile used to run. Every one wants to hear about them; I explain amid much laughter; they ask him if he can run as well as ever. "Better," says he; "I should be sorry to forget how to run." One member of the company is dying to see him run, but she dare not say so; some one else undertakes to suggest it; he agrees and we send for two or three young men of the neighbourhood; a prize is offered, and in imitation of our earlier games a cake is placed on the goal. Every one is ready, Sophy's father gives the signal by clapping his hands. The nimble Emile flies like lightning and reaches the goal almost before the others have started. He receives his prize at Sophy's hands, and no less generous than Aeneas, he gives gifts to all the vanquished.

In the midst of his triumph, Sophy dares to challenge the victor, and to assert that she can run as fast as he. He does not refuse to enter the lists with her, and while she is getting ready to start, while she is tucking up her skirt at each side, more eager to show Emile a pretty ankle than to vanquish him in the race, while she is seeing if her petticoats are short enough, he whispers a word to her mother who smiles and nods approval. Then he takes his place by his competitor; no sooner is the signal given than she is off like a bird.

Women were not meant to run; they flee that they may be overtaken. Running is not the only thing they do ill, but it is the only thing they do awkwardly; their elbows glued to their sides and pointed backwards look ridiculous, and the high heels on which they are perched make them look like so many grasshoppers trying to run instead of to jump.

Emile, supposing that Sophy runs no better than other women, does not deign to stir from his place and watches her start with a smile of mockery. But Sophy is light of foot and she wears low heels; she needs no pretence to make her foot look smaller; she runs so quickly that he has only just time to overtake this new Atalanta when he sees her so far ahead. Then he starts like an eagle dashing upon its prey; he pursues her, clutches her, grasps her at last quite out of breath, and gently placing his left arm about her, he lifts her like a feather, and pressing his sweet burden to his heart, he finishes the race, makes her touch the goal first, and then exclaiming, "Sophy wins!" he sinks on one knee before her and owns himself beaten.

Along with such occupations there is also the trade we learnt. One day a week at least, and every day when the weather is too bad for country pursuits, Emile and I go to work under a master-joiner. We do not work for show, like people above our trade; we work in earnest like regular workmen. Once when Sophy's father came to see us, he found us at work, and did not fail to report his wonder to his wife and daughter. "Go and see that young man in the workshop," said he, "and you will soon see if he despises the condition of the poor." You may fancy how pleased Sophy was at this! They talk it over, and they decide to surprise him at his work. They question me, apparently without any special object, and having made sure of the time, mother and daughter take a little carriage and come to town on that very day.

On her arrival, Sophy sees, at the other end of the shop, a young man in his shirt sleeves, with his hair all untidy, so hard at work that he does not see her; she makes a sign to her mother. Emile, a chisel in one hand and a hammer in the other, is just finishing a mortise; then he saws a piece of wood and places it in the vice in order to polish it. The sight of this does not set Sophy laughing; it affects her greatly; it wins her respect. Woman, honour your master; he it is who works for you, he it is who gives you bread to eat; this is he!

While they are busy watching him, I perceive them and pull Emile by the sleeve; he turns round, drops his tools, and hastens to them with an exclamation of delight. After he has given way to his first raptures, he makes them take a seat and he goes back to his work. But Sophy cannot keep quiet; she gets up hastily, runs about the workshop, looks at the tools, feels the polish of the boards, picks up shavings, looks at our hands, and says she likes this trade, it is so clean. The merry girl tries to copy Emile. With her delicate white hand she passes a plane over a bit of wood; the plane slips and makes no impression. It seems to me that Love himself is hovering over us and beating his wings; I think I can hear his joyous cries, "Hercules is avenged."

Yet Sophy's mother questions the master. "Sir, how much do you pay these two men a day?" "I give them each tenpence a day and their food; but if that young fellow wanted he could earn much more, for he is the best workman in the country." "Tenpence a day and their food," said she looking at us tenderly. "That is so, madam," replied the master. At these words she hurries up to Emile, kisses him, and clasps him to her breast with tears; unable to say more she repeats again and again, "My son, my son!"

When they had spent some time chatting with us, but without interrupting our work, "We must be going now," said the mother to her daughter, "it is getting late and we must not keep your father waiting." Then approaching Emile she tapped him playfully on the cheek, saying, "Well, my good workman, won't you come with us?" He replied sadly, "I am at work, ask the master." The master is asked if he can spare us. He replies that he cannot. "I have work on hand," said he, "which is wanted the day after to-morrow, so there is not much time. Counting on these gentlemen I refused other workmen who came; if they fail me I don't know how to replace them and I shall not be able to send the work home at the time promised." The mother said nothing, she was waiting to hear what Emile would say. Emile hung his head in silence. "Sir," she said, somewhat surprised at this, "have you nothing to say to that?" Emile looked tenderly at her daughter and merely said, "You see I am bound to stay." Then the ladies left us. Emile went with them to the door, gazed after them as long as they were in sight, and returned to his work without a word.

On the way home, the mother, somewhat vexed at his conduct, spoke to her daughter of the strange way in which he had behaved. "Why," said she, "was it so difficult to arrange matters with the master without being obliged to stay. The young man is generous enough and ready to spend money when there is no need for it, could not he spend a little on such a fitting occasion?" "Oh, mamma," replied Sophy, "I trust Emile will never rely so much on money as to use it to break an engagement, to fail to keep his own word, and to make another break his! I know he could easily give the master a trifle to make up for the slight inconvenience caused by his absence; but his soul would become the slave of riches, he would become accustomed to place wealth before duty, and he would think that any duty might be neglected provided he was ready to pay. That is not Emile's way of thinking, and I hope he will never change on my account. Do you think it cost him nothing to stay?

You are quite wrong, mamma; it was for my sake that he stayed; I saw it in his eyes."

It is not that Sophy is indifferent to genuine proofs of love; on the contrary she is imperious and exacting; she would rather not be loved at all than be loved half-heartedly. Hers is the noble pride of worth, conscious of its own value, self-respecting and claiming a like honour from others. She would scorn a heart that did not recognise the full worth of her own; that did not love her for her virtues as much and more than for her charms; a heart which did not put duty first, and prefer it to everything. She did not desire a lover who knew no will but hers. She wished to reign over a man whom she had not spoilt. Thus Circe, having changed into swine the comrades of Ulysses, bestowed herself on him over whom she had no power.

Except for this sacred and inviolable right, Sophy is very jealous of her own rights; she observes how carefully Emile respects them, how zealously he does her will; how cleverly he guesses her wishes, how exactly he arrives at the appointed time; she will have him neither late nor early; he must arrive to the moment. To come early is to think more of himself than of her; to come late is to neglect her. To neglect Sophy, that could not happen twice. An unfounded suspicion on her part nearly ruined everything, but Sophy is really just and knows how to atone for her faults.

They were expecting us one evening; Emile had received his orders. They came to meet us, but we were not there. What has become of us? What accident have we met with? No message from us! The evening is spent in expectation of our arrival. Sophy thinks we are dead; she is miserable and in an agony of distress; she cries all the night through. In the course of the evening a messenger was despatched to inquire after us and bring back news in the morning. The messenger returns together with another messenger sent by us, who makes our excuses verbally and says we are quite well. Then the scene is changed; Sophy dries her tears, or if she still weeps it is for anger. It is small consolation to her proud spirit to know that we are alive; Emile lives and he has kept her waiting.

When we arrive she tries to escape to her own room; her parents desire her to remain, so she is obliged to do so; but deciding at once what course she will take she assumes a calm and contented expression which would deceive most people. Her father comes forward to receive us saying, "You have made your friends very uneasy; there are people here who will not forgive you very readily." "Who are they, papa," said Sophy with the most gracious smile she could assume. "What business is that of yours," said her father, "if it is not you?" Sophy bent over her work without reply. Her mother received us coldly and formally. Emile was so confused he dared not speak to Sophy. She spoke first, inquired how he was, asked him to take a chair, and pretended so cleverly that the poor young fellow, who as yet knew nothing of the language of angry passions, was quite deceived by her apparent indifference, and ready to take offence on his own account.

To undeceive him I was going to take Sophy's hand and raise it to my lips as I sometimes did; she drew it back so hastily, with the word, "Sir," uttered in such a strange manner that Emile's eyes were opened at once by this involuntary movement.

Sophy herself, seeing that she had betrayed herself, exercised less control over herself. Her apparent indifference was succeeded by scornful irony. She replied to everything he said in monosyllables uttered slowly and hesitatingly as if she were afraid her anger should show itself too plainly. Emile half dead with terror stared at her full of sorrow, and tried to get her to look at him so that his eyes might read in hers her real feelings. Sophy, still more angry at his boldness, gave him one look which removed all wish for another. Luckily for himself, Emile, trembling and dumbfounded, dared neither look at her nor speak to her again; for had he not been guilty, had he been able to endure her wrath, she would never have forgiven him.

Seeing that it was my turn now, and that the time was ripe for explanation, I returned to Sophy. I took her hand and this time she did not snatch it away; she was ready to faint. I said gently, "Dear Sophy, we are the victims of misfortune; but you are just and reasonable; you will not judge us unheard; listen to what we have to say." She said nothing and I proceeded—

"We set out yesterday at four o'clock; we were told to be here at seven, and we always allow ourselves rather more time than we need, so as to rest a little before we get here. We were more than half way here when we heard lamentable groans, which came from a little valley in the hillside, some distance off. We hurried towards the place and found an unlucky peasant who had taken rather more wine than was good for him; on his way home he had fallen heavily from his horse and broken his leg. We shouted and called for help; there was no answer; we tried to lift the injured man on his horse, but without success; the least movement caused intense agony. We decided to tie up the horse in a quiet part of the wood; then we made a chair of our crossed arms and carried the man as gently as possible, following his directions till we got him home. The way was long, and we were constantly obliged to stop and rest. At last we got there, but thoroughly exhausted. We were surprised and sorry to find that it was a house we knew already and that the wretched creature we had carried with such difficulty was the very man who received us so kindly when first we came. We had all been so upset that until that moment we had not recognised each other.

"There were only two little children. His wife was about to present him with another, and she was so overwhelmed at the sight of him brought home in such a condition, that she was taken ill and a few hours later gave birth to another little one. What was to be done under such circumstances in a lonely cottage far from any help? Emile decided to fetch the horse we had left in the wood, to ride as fast as he could into the town and fetch a surgeon. He let the surgeon have the horse, and not succeeding in finding a nurse all at once, he returned on foot with a servant, after having sent a messenger to you; meanwhile I hardly knew what to do between a man with a broken leg and a woman in travail, but I got ready as well as I could such things in the house as I thought would be needed for the relief of both.

"I will pass over the rest of the details; they are not to the point. It was two o'clock in the morning before we got a moment's rest. At last we returned before daybreak to our lodging close at hand, where we waited till you were up to let you know what had happened to us."

That was all I said. But before any one could speak Emile, approaching Sophy, raised his voice and said with greater firmness than I expected, "Sophy, my fate is in your hands, as you very well know. You may condemn me to die of grief; but do not hope to make me forget the rights of humanity; they are even more sacred in my eyes than your own rights; I will never renounce them for you."

For all answer, Sophy rose, put her arm round his neck, and kissed him on the cheek; then offering him her hand with inimitable grace she said to him, "Emile, take this hand; it is yours. When you will, you shall be my husband and my master; I will try to be worthy of that honour."

Scarcely had she kissed him, when her delighted father clapped his hands calling, "Encore, encore," and Sophy without further ado, kissed him twice on the other cheek; but afraid of what she had done she took refuge at once in her mother's arms and hid her blushing face on the maternal bosom.

I will not describe our happiness; everybody will feel with us. After dinner Sophy asked if it were too far to go and see the poor invalids. It was her wish and it was a work of mercy. When we got there we found them both in bed—Emile had sent for a second bedstead; there were people there to look after them—Emile had seen to it. But in spite of this everything was so untidy that they suffered almost as much from discomfort as from their condition. Sophy asked for one of the good wife's aprons and set to work to make her more comfortable in her bed; then she did as much for the man; her soft and gentle hand seemed to find out what was hurting them and how to settle them into less painful positions. Her very presence seemed to make them more comfortable; she seemed to guess what was the matter. This fastidious girl was not disgusted by the dirt or smells, and she managed to get rid of both without disturbing the sick people. She who had always appeared so modest and sometimes so disdainful, she who would not for all the world have touched a man's bed with her little finger, lifted the sick man and changed his linen without any fuss, and placed him to rest in a more comfortable position. The zeal of charity is of more value than modesty. What she did was done so skilfully and with such a light touch that he felt better almost without knowing she had touched him. Husband and wife mingled their blessings upon the kindly girl who tended, pitied, and consoled them. She was an angel from heaven come to visit them; she was an angel in face and manner, in gentleness and goodness. Emile was greatly touched by all this and he watched her without speaking. O man, love thy helpmeet. God gave her to relieve thy sufferings, to comfort thee in thy troubles. This is she!

The new-born baby was baptised. The two lovers were its god-parents, and as they held it at the font they were longing, at the bottom of their hearts, for the time when they should have a child of their own to be baptised. They longed for their wedding day; they thought it was close at hand; all Sophy's scruples had vanished, but mine remained. They had not got so far as they expected; every one must have his turn.

One morning when they had not seen each other for two whole days, I entered Emile's room with a letter in my hands, and looking fixedly at him I said to him, "What would you do if some one told you Sophy were dead?" He uttered a loud cry, got up and struck his hands together, and without saying a single word, he looked at me with eyes of desperation. "Answer me," I continued with the same calmness. Vexed at my composure, he then approached me with eyes blazing with anger; and checking himself in an almost threatening attitude, "What would I do? I know not; but this I do know, I would never set eyes again upon the person who brought me such news." "Comfort yourself," said I, smiling, "she lives, she is well, and they are expecting us this evening. But let us go for a short walk and we can talk things over."

The passion which engrosses him will no longer permit him to devote himself as in former days to discussions of pure reason; this very passion must be called to our aid if his attention is to be given to my teaching. That is why I made use of this terrible preface; I am quite sure he will listen to me now.

"We must be happy, dear Emile; it is the end of every feeling creature; it is the first desire taught us by nature, and the only one which never leaves us. But where is happiness? Who knows? Every one seeks it, and no one finds it. We spend our lives in the search and we die before the end is attained. My young friend, when I took you, a new-born infant, in my arms, and called God himself to witness to the vow I dared to make that I would devote my life to the happiness of your life, did I know myself what I was undertaking? No; I only knew that in making you happy, I was sure of my own happiness. By making this useful inquiry on your account, I made it for us both.

"So long as we do not know what to do, wisdom consists in doing nothing. Of all rules there is none so greatly needed by man, and none which he is less able to obey. In seeking happiness when we know not where it is, we are perhaps getting further and further from it, we are running as many risks as there are roads to choose from. But it is not every one that can keep still. Our passion for our own well-being makes us so uneasy, that we would rather deceive ourselves in the search for happiness than sit still and do nothing; and when once we have left the place where we might have known happiness, we can never return.

"In ignorance like this I tried to avoid a similar fault. When I took charge of you I decided to take no useless steps and to prevent you from doing so too. I kept to the path of nature, until she should show me the path of happiness. And lo! their paths were the same, and without knowing it this was the path I trod.

"Be at once my witness and my judge; I will never refuse to accept your decision. Your early years have not been sacrificed to those that were to follow, you have enjoyed all the good gifts which nature bestowed upon you. Of the ills to which you were by nature subject, and from which I could shelter you, you have only experienced such as would harden you to bear others. You have never suffered any evil, except to escape a greater. You have known neither hatred nor servitude. Free and happy, you have remained just and kindly; for suffering and vice are inseparable, and no man ever became bad until he was unhappy. May the memory of your childhood remain with you to old age! I am not afraid that your kind heart will ever recall the hand that trained it without a blessing upon it.

"When you reached the age of reason, I secured you from the influence of human prejudice; when your heart awoke I preserved you from the sway of passion. Had I been able to prolong this inner tranquillity till your life's end, my work would have been secure, and you would have been as happy as man can be; but, my dear Emile, in vain did I dip you in the waters of Styx, I could not make you everywhere invulnerable; a fresh enemy has appeared, whom you have not yet learnt to conquer, and from whom I cannot save you. That enemy is yourself. Nature and fortune had left you free. You could face poverty, you could bear bodily pain; the sufferings of the heart were unknown to you; you were then dependent on nothing but your position as a human being; now you depend on all the ties you have formed for yourself; you have learnt to desire, and you are now the slave of your desires. Without any change in yourself, without any insult, any injury to yourself, what sorrows may attack your soul, what pains may you suffer without sickness, how many deaths may you die and yet live! A lie, an error, a suspicion, may plunge you in despair.

"At the theatre you used to see heroes, abandoned to depths of woe, making the stage re-echo with their wild cries, lamenting like women, weeping like children, and thus securing the applause of the audience. Do you remember how shocked you were by those lamentations, cries, and groans, in men from whom one would only expect deeds of constancy and heroism. 'Why,' said you, 'are those the patterns we are to follow, the models set for our imitation! Are they afraid man will not be small enough, unhappy enough, weak enough, if his weakness is not enshrined under a false show of virtue.' My young friend, henceforward you must be more merciful to the stage; you have become one of those heroes.

"You know how to suffer and to die; you know how to bear the heavy yoke of necessity in ills of the body, but you have not yet learnt to give a law to the desires of your heart; and the difficulties of life arise rather from our affections than from our needs. Our desires are vast, our strength is little better than nothing. In his wishes man is dependent on many things; in himself he is dependent on nothing, not even on his own life; the more his connections are multiplied, the greater his sufferings. Everything upon earth has an end; sooner or later all that we love escapes from our fingers, and we behave as if it would last for ever. What was your terror at the mere suspicion of Sophy's death? Do you suppose she will live for ever? Do not young people of her age die? She must die, my son, and perhaps before you. Who knows if she is alive at this moment? Nature meant you to die but once; you have prepared a second death for yourself.

"A slave to your unbridled passions, how greatly are you to be pitied! Ever privations, losses, alarms; you will not even enjoy what is left. You will possess nothing because of the fear of losing it; you will never be able to satisfy your passions, because you desired to follow them continually. You will ever be seeking that which will fly before you; you will be miserable and you will become wicked. How can you be otherwise, having no care but your unbridled passions! If you cannot put up with involuntary privations how will you voluntarily deprive yourself? How can you sacrifice desire to duty, and resist your heart in order to listen to your reason? You would never see that man again who dared to bring you word of the death of your mistress; how would you behold him who would deprive you of her living self, him who would dare to tell you, 'She is dead to you, virtue puts a gulf between you'? If you must live with her whatever happens, whether Sophy is married or single, whether you are free or not, whether she loves or hates you, whether she is given or refused to you, no matter, it is your will and you must have her at any price. Tell me then what crime will stop a man who has no law but his heart's desires, who knows not how to resist his own passions.

"My son, there is no happiness without courage, nor virtue without a struggle. The word virtue is derived from a word signifying strength, and strength is the foundation of all virtue. Virtue is the heritage of a creature weak by nature but strong by will; that is the whole merit of the righteous man; and though we call God good we do not call Him virtuous, because He does good without effort. I waited to explain the meaning of this word, so often profaned, until you were ready to understand me. As long as virtue is quite easy to practise, there is little need to know it. This need arises with the awakening of the passions; your time has come.

"When I brought you up in all the simplicity of nature, instead of preaching disagreeable duties, I secured for you immunity from the vices which make such duties disagreeable; I made lying not so much hateful as unnecessary in your sight; I taught you not so much to give others their due, as to care little about your own rights; I made you kindly rather than virtuous. But the kindly man is only kind so long as he finds it pleasant; kindness falls to pieces at the shook of human passions; the kindly man is only kind to himself.

"What is meant by a virtuous man? He who can conquer his affections; for then he follows his reason, his conscience; he does his duty; he is his own master and nothing can turn him from the right way. So far you have had only the semblance of liberty, the precarious liberty of the slave who has not received his orders. Now is the time for real freedom; learn to be your own master; control your heart, my Emile, and you will be virtuous.

"There is another apprenticeship before you, an apprenticeship more difficult than the former; for nature delivers us from the evils she lays upon us, or else she teaches us to submit to them; but she has no message for us with regard to our self-imposed evils; she leaves us to ourselves; she leaves us, victims of our own passions, to succumb to our vain sorrows, to pride ourselves on the tears of which we should be ashamed.

"This is your first passion. Perhaps it is the only passion worthy of you. If you can control it like a man, it will be the last; you will be master of all the rest, and you will obey nothing but the passion for virtue.

"There is nothing criminal in this passion; I know it; it is as pure as the hearts which experience it. It was born of honour and nursed by innocence. Happy lovers! for you the charms of virtue do but add to those of love; and the blessed union to which you are looking forward is less the reward of your goodness than of your affection. But tell me, O truthful man, though this passion is pure, is it any the less your master? Are you the less its slave? And if to-morrow it should cease to be innocent, would you strangle it on the spot? Now is the time to try your strength; there is no time for that in hours of danger. These perilous efforts should be made when danger is still afar. We do not practise the use of our weapons when we are face to face with the enemy, we do that before the war; we come to the battle-field ready prepared.

"It is a mistake to classify the passions as lawful and unlawful, so as to yield to the one and refuse the other. All alike are good if we are their masters; all alike are bad if we abandon ourselves to them. Nature forbids us to extend our relations beyond the limits of our strength; reason forbids us to want what we cannot get, conscience forbids us, not to be tempted, but to yield to temptation. To feel or not to feel a passion is beyond our control, but we can control ourselves. Every sentiment under our own control is lawful; those which control us are criminal. A man is not guilty if he loves his neighbour's wife, provided he keeps this unhappy passion under the control of the law of duty; he is guilty if he loves his own wife so greatly as to sacrifice everything to that love.

"Do not expect me to supply you with lengthy precepts of morality, I have only one rule to give you which sums up all the rest. Be a man; restrain your heart within the limits of your manhood. Study and know these limits; however narrow they may be, we are not unhappy within them; it is only when we wish to go beyond them that we are unhappy, only when, in our mad passions, we try to attain the impossible; we are unhappy when we forget our manhood to make an imaginary world for ourselves, from which we are always slipping back into our own. The only good things, whose loss really affects us, are those which we claim as our rights. If it is clear that we cannot obtain what we want, our mind turns away from it; wishes without hope cease to torture us. A beggar is not tormented by a desire to be a king; a king only wishes to be a god when he thinks himself more than man.

"The illusions of pride are the source of our greatest ills; but the contemplation of human suffering keeps the wise humble. He keeps to his proper place and makes no attempt to depart from it; he does not waste his strength in getting what he cannot keep; and his whole strength being devoted to the right employment of what he has, he is in reality richer and more powerful in proportion as he desires less than we. A man, subject to death and change, shall I forge for myself lasting chains upon this earth, where everything changes and disappears, whence I myself shall shortly vanish! Oh, Emile! my son! if I were to lose you, what would be left of myself? And yet I must learn to lose you, for who knows when you may be taken from me?

"Would you live in wisdom and happiness, fix your heart on the beauty that is eternal; let your desires be limited by your position, let your duties take precedence of your wishes; extend the law of necessity into the region of morals; learn to lose what may be taken from you; learn to forsake all things at the command of virtue, to set yourself above the chances of life, to detach your heart before it is torn in pieces, to be brave in adversity so that you may never be wretched, to be steadfast in duty that you may never be guilty of a crime. Then you will be happy in spite of fortune, and good in spite of your passions. You will find a pleasure that cannot be destroyed, even in the possession of the most fragile things; you will possess them, they will not possess you, and you will realise that the man who loses everything, only enjoys what he knows how to resign. It is true you will not enjoy the illusions of imaginary pleasures, neither will you feel the sufferings which are their result. You will profit greatly by this exchange, for the sufferings are real and frequent, the pleasures are rare and empty. Victor over so many deceitful ideas, you will also vanquish the idea that attaches such an excessive value to life. You will spend your life in peace, and you will leave it without terror; you will detach yourself from life as from other things. Let others, horror-struck, believe that when this life is ended they cease to be; conscious of the nothingness of life, you will think that you are but entering upon the true life. To the wicked, death is the close of life; to the just it is its dawn."

Emile heard me with attention not unmixed with anxiety. After such a startling preface he feared some gloomy conclusion. He foresaw that when I showed him how necessary it is to practise the strength of the soul, I desired to subject him to this stern discipline; he was like a wounded man who shrinks from the surgeon, and fancies he already feels the painful but healing touch which will cure the deadly wound.

Uncertain, anxious, eager to know what I am driving at, he does not answer, he questions me but timidly. "What must I do?" says he almost trembling, not daring to raise his eyes. "What must you do?" I reply firmly. "You must leave Sophy." "What are you saying?" he exclaimed angrily. "Leave Sophy, leave Sophy, deceive her, become a traitor, a villain, a perjurer!" "Why!" I continue, interrupting him; "does Emile suppose I shall teach him to deserve such titles?" "No," he continued with the same vigour. "Neither you nor any one else; I am capable of preserving your work; I shall not deserve such reproaches."

I was prepared for this first outburst; I let it pass unheeded. If I had not the moderation I preach it would not be much use preaching it! Emile knows me too well to believe me capable of demanding any wrong action from him, and he knows that it would be wrong to leave Sophy, in the sense he attaches to the phrase. So he waits for an explanation. Then I resume my speech.

"My dear Emile, do you think any man whatsoever can be happier than you have been for the last three months? If you think so, undeceive yourself. Before tasting the pleasures of life you have plumbed the depths of its happiness. There is nothing more than you have already experienced. The joys of sense are soon over; habit invariably destroys them. You have tasted greater joys through hope than you will ever enjoy in reality. The imagination which adorns what we long for, deserts its possession. With the exception of the one self-existing Being, there is nothing beautiful except that which is not. If that state could have lasted for ever, you would have found perfect happiness. But all that is related to man shares his decline; all is finite, all is fleeting in human life, and even if the conditions which make us happy could be prolonged for ever, habit would deprive us of all taste for that happiness. If external circumstances remain unchanged, the heart changes; either happiness forsakes us, or we forsake her.

"During your infatuation time has passed unheeded. Summer is over, winter is at hand. Even if our expeditions were possible, at such a time of year they would not be permitted. Whether we wish it or no, we shall have to change our way of life; it cannot continue. I read in your eager eyes that this does not disturb you greatly; Sophy's confession and your own wishes suggest a simple plan for avoiding the snow and escaping the journey. The plan has its advantages, no doubt; but when spring returns, the snow will melt and the marriage will remain; you must reckon for all seasons.

"You wish to marry Sophy and you have only known her five months! You wish to marry her, not because she is a fit wife for you, but because she pleases you; as if love were never mistaken as to fitness, as if those, who begin with love, never ended with hatred! I know she is virtuous; but is that enough? Is fitness merely a matter of honour? It is not her virtue I misdoubt, it is her disposition. Does a woman show her real character in a day? Do you know how often you must have seen her and under what varying conditions to really know her temper? Is four months of liking a sufficient pledge for the rest of your life? A couple of months hence you may have forgotten her; as soon as you are gone another may efface your image in her heart; on your return you may find her as indifferent as you have hitherto found her affectionate. Sentiments are not a matter of principle; she may be perfectly virtuous and yet cease to love you. I am inclined to think she will be faithful and true; but who will answer for her, and who will answer for you if you are not put to the proof? Will you postpone this trial till it is too late, will you wait to know your true selves till parting is no longer possible?

"Sophy is not eighteen, and you are barely twenty-two; this is the age for love, but not for marriage. What a father and mother for a family! If you want to know how to bring up children, you should at least wait till you yourselves are children no longer. Do you not know that too early motherhood has weakened the constitution, destroyed the health, and shortened the life of many young women? Do you not know that many children have always been weak and sickly because their mother was little more than a child herself? When mother and child are both growing, the strength required for their growth is divided, and neither gets all that nature intended; are not both sure to suffer? Either I know very little of Emile, or he would rather wait and have a healthy wife and children, than satisfy his impatience at the price of their life and health.

"Let us speak of yourself. You hope to be a husband and a father; have you seriously considered your duties? When you become the head of a family you will become a citizen of your country. And what is a citizen of the state? What do you know about it? You have studied your duties as a man, but what do you know of the duties of a citizen? Do you know the meaning of such terms as government, laws, country? Do you know the price you must pay for life, and for what you must be prepared to die? You think you know everything, when you really know nothing at all. Before you take your place in the civil order, learn to perceive and know what is your proper place.

"Emile, you must leave Sophy; I do not bid you forsake her; if you were capable of such conduct, she would be only too happy not to have married you; you must leave her in order to return worthy of her. Do not be vain enough to think yourself already worthy. How much remains to be done! Come and fulfil this splendid task; come and learn to submit to absence; come and earn the prize of fidelity, so that when you return you may indeed deserve some honour, and may ask her hand not as a favour but as a reward."

Unaccustomed to struggle with himself, untrained to desire one thing and to will another, the young man will not give way; he resists, he argues. Why should he refuse the happiness which awaits him? Would he not despise the hand which is offered him if he hesitated to accept it? Why need he leave her to learn what he ought to know? And if it were necessary to leave her why not leave her as his wife with a certain pledge of his return? Let him be her husband, and he is ready to follow me; let them be married and he will leave her without fear. "Marry her in order to leave her, dear Emile! what a contradiction! A lover who can leave his mistress shows himself capable of great things; a husband should never leave his wife unless through necessity. To cure your scruples, I see the delay must be involuntary on your part; you must be able to tell Sophy you leave her against your will. Very well, be content, and since you will not follow the commands of reason, you must submit to another master. You have not forgotten your promise. Emile, you must leave Sophy; I will have it."

For a moment or two he was downcast, silent, and thoughtful, then looking me full in the face he said, "When do we start?" "In a week's time," I replied; "Sophy must be prepared for our going. Women are weaker than we are, and we must show consideration for them; and this parting is not a duty for her as it is for you, so she may be allowed to bear it less bravely."

The temptation to continue the daily history of their love up to the time of their separation is very great; but I have already presumed too much upon the good nature of my readers; let us abridge the story so as to bring it to an end. Will Emile face the situation as bravely at his mistress' feet as he has done in conversation with his friend? I think he will; his confidence is rooted in the sincerity of his love. He would be more at a loss with her, if it cost him less to leave her; he would leave her feeling himself to blame, and that is a difficult part for a man of honour to play; but the greater the sacrifice, the more credit he demands for it in the sight of her who makes it so difficult. He has no fear that she will misunderstand his motives. Every look seems to say, "Oh, Sophy, read my heart and be faithful to me; your lover is not without virtue."

Sophy tries to bear the unforeseen blow with her usual pride and dignity. She tries to seem as if she did not care, but as the honours of war are not hers, but Emile's, her strength is less equal to the task. She weeps, she sighs against her will, and the fear of being forgotten embitters the pain of parting. She does not weep in her lover's sight, she does not let him see her terror; she would die rather than utter a sigh in his presence. I am the recipient of her lamentations, I behold her tears, it is I who am supposed to be her confidant. Women are very clever and know how to conceal their cleverness; the more she frets in private, the more pains she takes to please me; she feels that her fate is in my hands.

I console and comfort her; I make myself answerable for her lover, or rather for her husband; let her be as true to him as he to her and I promise they shall be married in two years' time. She respects me enough to believe that I do not want to deceive her. I am guarantor to each for the other. Their hearts, their virtue, my honesty, the confidence of their parents, all combine to reassure them. But what can reason avail against weakness? They part as if they were never to meet again.

Then it is that Sophy recalls the regrets of Eucharis, and fancies herself in her place. Do not let us revive that fantastic affection during his absence "Sophy," say I one day, "exchange books with Emile; let him have your Telemachus that he may learn to be like him, and let him give you his Spectator which you enjoy reading. Study the duties of good wives in it, and remember that in two years' time you will undertake those duties." The exchange gave pleasure to both and inspired them with confidence. At last the sad day arrived and they must part.

Sophy's worthy father, with whom I had arranged the whole business, took affectionate leave of me, and taking me aside, he spoke seriously and somewhat emphatically, saying, "I have done everything to please you; I knew I had to do with a man of honour; I have only one word to say. Remembering your pupil has signed his contract of marriage on my daughter's lips."

What a difference in the behaviour of the two lovers! Emile, impetuous, eager, excited, almost beside himself, cries aloud and sheds torrents of tears upon the hands of father, mother, and daughter; with sobs he embraces every one in the house and repeats the same thing over and over again in a way that would be ludicrous at any other time. Sophy, pale, sorrowful, doleful, and heavy-eyed, remains quiet without a word or a tear, she sees no one, not even Emile. In vain he takes her hand, and clasps her in his arms; she remains motionless, unheeding his tears, his caresses, and everything he does; so far as she is concerned, he is gone already. A sight more moving than the prolonged lamentations and noisy regrets of her lover! He sees, he feels, he is heartbroken. I drag him reluctantly away; if I left him another minute, he would never go. I am delighted that he should carry this touching picture with him. If he should ever be tempted to forget what is due to Sophy, his heart must have strayed very far indeed if I cannot bring it back to her by recalling her as he saw her last.

O? ??????

Is it good for young people to travel? The question is often asked and as often hotly disputed. If it were stated otherwise—Are men the better for having travelled?—perhaps there would be less difference of opinion.

The misuse of books is the death of sound learning. People think they know what they have read, and take no pains to learn. Too much reading only produces a pretentious ignoramus. There was never so much reading in any age as the present, and never was there less learning; in no country of Europe are so many histories and books of travel printed as in France, and nowhere is there less knowledge of the mind and manners of other nations. So many books lead us to neglect the book of the world; if we read it at all, we keep each to our own page. If the phrase, "Can one become a Persian," were unknown to me, I should suspect on hearing it that it came from the country where national prejudice is most prevalent and from the sex which does most to increase it.

A Parisian thinks he has a knowledge of men and he knows only Frenchmen; his town is always full of foreigners, but he considers every foreigner as a strange phenomenon which has no equal in the universe. You must have a close acquaintance with the middle classes of that great city, you must have lived among them, before you can believe that people could be at once so witty and so stupid. The strangest thing about it is that probably every one of them has read a dozen times a description of the country whose inhabitants inspire him with such wonder.

To discover the truth amidst our own prejudices and those of the authors is too hard a task. I have been reading books of travels all my life, but I never found two that gave me the same idea of the same nation. On comparing my own scanty observations with what I have read, I have decided to abandon the travellers and I regret the time wasted in trying to learn from their books; for I am quite convinced that for that sort of study, seeing not reading is required. That would be true enough if every traveller were honest, if he only said what he saw and believed, and if truth were not tinged with false colours from his own eyes. What must it be when we have to disentangle the truth from the web of lies and ill-faith?

Let us leave the boasted resources of books to those who are content to use them. Like the art of Raymond Lully they are able to set people chattering about things they do not know. They are able to set fifteen-year-old Platos discussing philosophy in the clubs, and teaching people the customs of Egypt and the Indies on the word of Paul Lucas or Tavernier.

I maintain that it is beyond dispute that any one who has only seen one nation does not know men; he only knows those men among whom he has lived. Hence there is another way of stating the question about travel: "Is it enough for a well-educated man to know his fellow-countrymen, or ought he to know mankind in general?" Then there is no place for argument or uncertainty. See how greatly the solution of a difficult problem may depend on the way in which it is stated.

But is it necessary to travel the whole globe to study mankind? Need we go to Japan to study Europeans? Need we know every individual before we know the species? No, there are men so much alike that it is not worth while to study them individually. When you have seen a dozen Frenchmen you have seen them all. Though one cannot say as much of the English and other nations, it is, however, certain that every nation has its own specific character, which is derived by induction from the study, not of one, but many of its members. He who has compared a dozen nations knows men, just he who has compared a dozen Frenchmen knows the French.

To acquire knowledge it is not enough to travel hastily through a country. Observation demands eyes, and the power of directing them towards the object we desire to know. There are plenty of people who learn no more from their travels than from their books, because they do not know how to think; because in reading their mind is at least under the guidance of the author, and in their travels they do not know how to see for themselves. Others learn nothing, because they have no desire to learn. Their object is so entirely different, that this never occurs to them; it is very unlikely that you will see clearly what you take no trouble to look for. The French travel more than any other nation, but they are so taken up with their own customs, that everything else is confused together. There are Frenchmen in every corner of the globe. In no country of the world do you find more people who have travelled than in France. And yet of all the nations of Europe, that which has seen most, knows least. The English are also travellers, but they travel in another fashion; these two nations must always be at opposite extremes. The English nobility travels, the French stays at home; the French people travel, the English stay at home. This difference does credit, I think, to the English. The French almost always travel for their own ends; the English do not seek their fortune in other lands, unless in the way of commerce and with their hands full; when they travel it is to spend their money, not to live by their wits; they are too proud to cringe before strangers. This is why they learn more abroad than the French who have other fish to fry. Yet the English have their national prejudices; but these prejudices are not so much the result of ignorance as of feeling. The Englishman's prejudices are the result of pride, the Frenchman's are due to vanity.

Just as the least cultivated nations are usually the best, so those travel best who travel least; they have made less progress than we in our frivolous pursuits, they are less concerned with the objects of our empty curiosity, so that they give their attention to what is really useful. I hardly know any but the Spaniards who travel in this fashion. While the Frenchman is running after all the artists of the country, while the Englishman is getting a copy of some antique, while the German is taking his album to every man of science, the Spaniard is silently studying the government, the manners of the country, its police, and he is the only one of the four who from all that he has seen will carry home any observation useful to his own country.

The ancients travelled little, read little, and wrote few books; yet we see in those books that remain to us, that they observed each other more thoroughly than we observe our contemporaries. Without going back to the days of Homer, the only poet who transports us to the country he describes, we cannot deny to Herodotus the glory of having painted manners in his history, though he does it rather by narrative than by comment; still he does it better than all our historians whose books are overladen with portraits and characters. Tacitus has described the Germans of his time better than any author has described the Germans of to-day. There can be no doubt that those who have devoted themselves to ancient history know more about the Greeks, Carthaginians, Romans, Gauls, and Persians than any nation of to-day knows about its neighbours.

It must also be admitted that the original characteristics of different nations are changing day by day, and are therefore more difficult to grasp. As races blend and nations intermingle, those national differences which formerly struck the observer at first sight gradually disappear. Before our time every nation remained more or less cut off from the rest; the means of communication were fewer; there was less travelling, less of mutual or conflicting interests, less political and civil intercourse between nation and nation; those intricate schemes of royalty, miscalled diplomacy, were less frequent; there were no permanent ambassadors resident at foreign courts; long voyages were rare, there was little foreign trade, and what little there was, was either the work of princes, who employed foreigners, or of people of no account who had no influence on others and did nothing to bring the nations together. The relations between Europe and Asia in the present century are a hundredfold more numerous than those between Gaul and Spain in the past; Europe alone was less accessible than the whole world is now.

Moreover, the peoples of antiquity usually considered themselves as the original inhabitants of their country; they had dwelt there so long that all record was lost of the far-off times when their ancestors settled there; they had been there so long that the place had made a lasting impression on them; but in modern Europe the invasions of the barbarians, following upon the Roman conquests, have caused an extraordinary confusion. The Frenchmen of to-day are no longer the big fair men of old; the Greeks are no longer beautiful enough to serve as a sculptor's model; the very face of the Romans has changed as well as their character; the Persians, originally from Tartary, are daily losing their native ugliness through the intermixture of Circassian blood. Europeans are no longer Gauls, Germans, Iberians, Allobroges; they are all Scythians, more or less degenerate in countenance, and still more so in conduct.

This is why the ancient distinctions of race, the effect of soil and climate, made a greater difference between nation and nation in respect of temperament, looks, manners, and character than can be distinguished in our own time, when the fickleness of Europe leaves no time for natural causes to work, when the forests are cut down and the marshes drained, when the earth is more generally, though less thoroughly, tilled, so that the same differences between country and country can no longer be detected even in purely physical features.

If they considered these facts perhaps people would not be in such a hurry to ridicule Herodotus, Ctesias, Pliny for having described the inhabitants of different countries each with its own peculiarities and with striking differences which we no longer see. To recognise such types of face we should need to see the men themselves; no change must have passed over them, if they are to remain the same. If we could behold all the people who have ever lived, who can doubt that we should find greater variations between one century and another, than are now found between nation and nation.

At the same time, while observation becomes more difficult, it is more carelessly and badly done; this is another reason for the small success of our researches into the natural history of the human race. The information acquired by travel depends upon the object of the journey. If this object is a system of philosophy, the traveller only sees what he desires to see; if it is self-interest, it engrosses the whole attention of those concerned. Commerce and the arts which blend and mingle the nations at the same time prevent them from studying each other. If they know how to make a profit out of their neighbours, what more do they need to know?

It is a good thing to know all the places where we might live, so as to choose those where we can live most comfortably. If every one lived by his own efforts, all he would need to know would be how much land would keep him in food. The savage, who has need of no one, and envies no one, neither knows nor seeks to know any other country but his own. If he requires more land for his subsistence he shuns inhabited places; he makes war upon the wild beasts and feeds on them. But for us, to whom civilised life has become a necessity, for us who must needs devour our fellow-creatures, self-interest prompts each one of us to frequent those districts where there are most people to be devoured. This is why we all flock to Rome, Paris, and London. Human flesh and blood are always cheapest in the capital cities. Thus we only know the great nations, which are just like one another.

They say that men of learning travel to obtain information; not so, they travel like other people from interested motives. Philosophers like Plato and Pythagoras are no longer to be found, or if they are, it must be in far-off lands. Our men of learning only travel at the king's command; they are sent out, their expenses are paid, they receive a salary for seeing such and such things, and the object of that journey is certainly not the study of any question of morals. Their whole time is required for the object of their journey, and they are too honest not to earn their pay. If in any country whatsoever there are people travelling at their own expense, you may be sure it is not to study men but to teach them. It is not knowledge they desire but ostentation. How should their travels teach them to shake off the yoke of prejudice? It is prejudice that sends them on their travels.

To travel to see foreign lands or to see foreign nations are two very different things. The former is the usual aim of the curious, the latter is merely subordinate to it. If you wish to travel as a philosopher you should reverse this order. The child observes things till he is old enough to study men. Man should begin by studying his fellows; he can study things later if time permits.

It is therefore illogical to conclude that travel is useless because we travel ill. But granting the usefulness of travel, does it follow that it is good for all of us? Far from it; there are very few people who are really fit to travel; it is only good for those who are strong enough in themselves to listen to the voice of error without being deceived, strong enough to see the example of vice without being led away by it. Travelling accelerates the progress of nature, and completes the man for good or evil. When a man returns from travelling about the world, he is what he will be all his life; there are more who return bad than good, because there are more who start with an inclination towards evil. In the course of their travels, young people, ill-educated and ill-behaved, pick up all the vices of the nations among whom they have sojourned, and none of the virtues with which those vices are associated; but those who, happily for themselves, are well-born, those whose good disposition has been well cultivated, those who travel with a real desire to learn, all such return better and wiser than they went. Emile will travel in this fashion; in this fashion there travelled another young man, worthy of a nobler age; one whose worth was the admiration of Europe, one who died for his country in the flower of his manhood; he deserved to live, and his tomb, ennobled by his virtues only, received no honour till a stranger's hand adorned it with flowers.

Everything that is done in reason should have its rules. Travel, undertaken as a part of education, should therefore have its rules. To travel for travelling's sake is to wander, to be a vagabond; to travel to learn is still too vague; learning without some definite aim is worthless. I would give a young man a personal interest in learning, and that interest, well-chosen, will also decide the nature of the instruction. This is merely the continuation of the method I have hitherto practised.

Now after he has considered himself in his physical relations to other creatures, in his moral relations with other men, there remains to be considered his civil relations with his fellow-citizens. To do this he must first study the nature of government in general, then the different forms of government, and lastly the particular government under which he was born, to know if it suits him to live under it; for by a right which nothing can abrogate, every man, when he comes of age, becomes his own master, free to renounce the contract by which he forms part of the community, by leaving the country in which that contract holds good. It is only by sojourning in that country, after he has come to years of discretion, that he is supposed to have tacitly confirmed the pledge given by his ancestors. He acquires the right to renounce his country, just as he has the right to renounce all claim to his father's lands; yet his place of birth was a gift of nature, and in renouncing it, he renounces what is his own. Strictly speaking, every man remains in the land of his birth at his own risk unless he voluntarily submits to its laws in order to acquire a right to their protection.

For example, I should say to Emile, "Hitherto you have lived under my guidance, you were unable to rule yourself. But now you are approaching the age when the law, giving you the control over your property, makes you master of your person. You are about to find yourself alone in society, dependent on everything, even on your patrimony. You mean to marry; that is a praiseworthy intention, it is one of the duties of man; but before you marry you must know what sort of man you want to be, how you wish to spend your life, what steps you mean to take to secure a living for your family and for yourself; for although we should not make this our main business, it must be definitely considered. Do you wish to be dependent on men whom you despise? Do you wish to establish your fortune and determine your position by means of civil relations which will make you always dependent on the choice of others, which will compel you, if you would escape from knaves, to become a knave yourself?"

In the next place I would show him every possible way of using his money in trade, in the civil service, in finance, and I shall show him that in every one of these there are risks to be taken, every one of them places him in a precarious and dependent position, and compels him to adapt his morals, his sentiments, his conduct to the example and the prejudices of others.

"There is yet another way of spending your time and money; you may join the army; that is to say, you may hire yourself out at very high wages to go and kill men who never did you any harm. This trade is held in great honour among men, and they cannot think too highly of those who are fit for nothing better. Moreover, this profession, far from making you independent of other resources, makes them all the more necessary; for it is a point of honour in this profession to ruin those who have adopted it. It is true they are not all ruined; it is even becoming fashionable to grow rich in this as in other professions; but if I told you how people manage to do it, I doubt whether you would desire to follow their example.

"Moreover, you must know that, even in this trade, it is no longer a question of courage or valour, unless with regard to the ladies; on the contrary, the more cringing, mean, and degraded you are, the more honour you obtain; if you have decided to take your profession seriously, you will be despised, you will be hated, you will very possibly be driven out of the service, or at least you will fall a victim to favouritism and be supplanted by your comrades, because you have been doing your duty in the trenches, while they have been attending to their toilet."

We can hardly suppose that any of these occupations will be much to Emile's taste. "Why," he will exclaim, "have I forgotten the amusements of my childhood? Have I lost the use of my arms? Is my strength failing me? Do I not know how to work? What do I care about all your fine professions and all the silly prejudices of others? I know no other pride than to be kindly and just; no other happiness than to live in independence with her I love, gaining health and a good appetite by the day's work. All these difficulties you speak of do not concern me. The only property I desire is a little farm in some quiet corner. I will devote all my efforts after wealth to making it pay, and I will live without a care. Give me Sophy and my land, and I shall be rich."

"Yes, my dear friend, that is all a wise man requires, a wife and land of his own; but these treasures are scarcer than you think. The rarest you have found already; let us discuss the other.

"A field of your own, dear Emile! Where will you find it, in what remote corner of the earth can you say, 'Here am I master of myself and of this estate which belongs to me?' We know where a man may grow rich; who knows where he can do without riches? Who knows where to live free and independent, without ill-treating others and without fear of being ill-treated himself! Do you think it is so easy to find a place where you can always live like an honest man? If there is any safe and lawful way of living without intrigues, without lawsuits, without dependence on others, it is, I admit, to live by the labour of our hands, by the cultivation of our own land; but where is the state in which a man can say, 'The earth which I dig is my own?' Before choosing this happy spot, be sure that you will find the peace you desire; beware lest an unjust government, a persecuting religion, and evil habits should disturb you in your home. Secure yourself against the excessive taxes which devour the fruits of your labours, and the endless lawsuits which consume your capital. Take care that you can live rightly without having to pay court to intendents, to their deputies, to judges, to priests, to powerful neighbours, and to knaves of every kind, who are always ready to annoy you if you neglect them. Above all, secure yourself from annoyance on the part of the rich and great; remember that their estates may anywhere adjoin your Naboth's vineyard. If unluckily for you some great man buys or builds a house near your cottage, make sure that he will not find a way, under some pretence or other, to encroach on your lands to round off his estate, or that you do not find him at once absorbing all your resources to make a wide highroad. If you keep sufficient credit to ward off all these disagreeables, you might as well keep your money, for it will cost you no more to keep it. Riches and credit lean upon each other, the one can hardly stand without the other.

"I have more experience than you, dear Emile; I see more clearly the difficulties in the way of your scheme. Yet it is a fine scheme and honourable; it would make you happy indeed. Let us try to carry it out. I have a suggestion to make; let us devote the two years from now till the time of your return to choosing a place in Europe where you could live happily with your family, secure from all the dangers I have just described. If we succeed, you will have discovered that true happiness, so often sought for in vain; and you will not have to regret the time spent in its search. If we fail, you will be cured of a mistaken idea; you will console yourself for an inevitable ill, and you will bow to the law of necessity."

I do not know whether all my readers will see whither this suggested inquiry will lead us; but this I do know, if Emile returns from his travels, begun and continued with this end in view, without a full knowledge of questions of government, public morality, and political philosophy of every kind, we are greatly lacking, he in intelligence and I in judgment.

The science of politics is and probably always will be unknown. Grotius, our leader in this branch of learning, is only a child, and what is worse an untruthful child. When I hear Grotius praised to the skies and Hobbes overwhelmed with abuse, I perceive how little sensible men have read or understood these authors. As a matter of fact, their principles are exactly alike, they only differ in their mode of expression. Their methods are also different: Hobbes relies on sophism; Grotius relies on the poets; they are agreed in everything else. In modern times the only man who could have created this vast and useless science was the illustrious Montesquieu. But he was not concerned with the principles of political law; he was content to deal with the positive laws of settled governments; and nothing could be more different than these two branches of study.

Yet he who would judge wisely in matters of actual government is forced to combine the two; he must know what ought to be in order to judge what is. The chief difficulty in the way of throwing light upon this important matter is to induce an individual to discuss and to answer these two questions. "How does it concern me; and what can I do?" Emile is in a position to answer both.

The next difficulty is due to the prejudices of childhood, the principles in which we were brought up; it is due above all to the partiality of authors, who are always talking about truth, though they care very little about it; it is only their own interests that they care for, and of these they say nothing. Now the nation has neither professorships, nor pensions, nor membership of the academies to bestow. How then shall its rights be established by men of that type? The education I have given him has removed this difficulty also from Emile's path. He scarcely knows what is meant by government; his business is to find the best; he does not want to write books; if ever he did so, it would not be to pay court to those in authority, but to establish the rights of humanity.

There is a third difficulty, more specious than real; a difficulty which I neither desire to solve nor even to state; enough that I am not afraid of it; sure I am that in inquiries of this kind, great talents are less necessary than a genuine love of justice and a sincere reverence for truth. If matters of government can ever be fairly discussed, now or never is our chance.

Before beginning our observations we must lay down rules of procedure; we must find a scale with which to compare our measurements. Our principles of political law are our scale. Our actual measurements are the civil law of each country.

Our elementary notions are plain and simple, being taken directly from the nature of things. They will take the form of problems discussed between us, and they will not be formulated into principles, until we have found a satisfactory solution of our problems.

For example, we shall begin with the state of nature, we shall see whether men are born slaves or free, in a community or independent; is their association the result of free will or of force? Can the force which compels them to united action ever form a permanent law, by which this original force becomes binding, even when another has been imposed upon it, so that since the power of King Nimrod, who is said to have been the first conqueror, every other power which has overthrown the original power is unjust and usurping, so that there are no lawful kings but the descendants of Nimrod or their representatives; or if this original power has ceased, has the power which succeeded it any right over us, and does it destroy the binding force of the former power, so that we are not bound to obey except under compulsion, and we are free to rebel as soon as we are capable of resistance? Such a right is not very different from might; it is little more than a play upon words.

We shall inquire whether man might not say that all sickness comes from God, and that it is therefore a crime to send for the doctor.

Again, we shall inquire whether we are bound by our conscience to give our purse to a highwayman when we might conceal it from him, for the pistol in his hand is also a power.

Does this word power in this context mean something different from a power which is lawful and therefore subject to the laws to which it owes its being?

Suppose we reject this theory that might is right and admit the right of nature, or the authority of the father, as the foundation of society; we shall inquire into the extent of this authority; what is its foundation in nature? Has it any other grounds but that of its usefulness to the child, his weakness, and the natural love which his father feels towards him? When the child is no longer feeble, when he is grown-up in mind as well as in body, does not he become the sole judge of what is necessary for his preservation? Is he not therefore his own master, independent of all men, even of his father himself? For is it not still more certain that the son loves himself, than that the father loves the son?

The father being dead, should the children obey the eldest brother, or some other person who has not the natural affection of a father? Should there always be, from family to family, one single head to whom all the family owe obedience? If so, how has power ever come to be divided, and how is it that there is more than one head to govern the human race throughout the world?

Suppose the nations to have been formed each by its own choice; we shall then distinguish between right and fact; being thus subjected to their brothers, uncles, or other relations, not because they were obliged, but because they choose, we shall inquire whether this kind of society is not a sort of free and voluntary association?

Taking next the law of slavery, we shall inquire whether a man can make over to another his right to himself, without restriction, without reserve, without any kind of conditions; that is to say, can he renounce his person, his life, his reason, his very self, can he renounce all morality in his actions; in a word, can he cease to exist before his death, in spite of nature who places him directly in charge of his own preservation, in spite of reason and conscience which tell him what to do and what to leave undone?

If there is any reservation or restriction in the deed of slavery, we shall discuss whether this deed does not then become a true contract, in which both the contracting powers, having in this respect no common master, [Footnote: If they had such a common master, he would be no other than the sovereign, and then the right of slavery resting on the right of sovereignty would not be its origin.] remain their own judge as to the conditions of the contract, and therefore free to this extent, and able to break the contract as soon as it becomes hurtful.

If then a slave cannot convey himself altogether to his master, how can a nation convey itself altogether to its head? If a slave is to judge whether his master is fulfilling his contract, is not the nation to judge whether its head is fulfilling his contract?

Thus we are compelled to retrace our steps, and when we consider the meaning of this collective nation we shall inquire whether some contract, a tacit contract at the least, is not required to make a nation, a contract anterior to that which we are assuming.

Since the nation was a nation before it chose a king, what made it a nation, except the social contract? Therefore the social contract is the foundation of all civil society, and it is in the nature of this contract that we must seek the nature of the society formed by it.

We will inquire into the meaning of this contract; may it not be fairly well expressed in this formula? As an individual every one of us contributes his goods, his person, his life, to the common stock, under the supreme direction of the general will; while as a body we receive each member as an indivisible part of the whole.

Assuming this, in order to define the terms we require, we shall observe that, instead of the individual person of each contracting party, this deed of association produces a moral and collective body, consisting of as many members as there are votes in the Assembly. This public personality is usually called the body politic, which is called by its members the State when it is passive, and the Sovereign when it is active, and a Power when compared with its equals. With regard to the members themselves, collectively they are known as the nation, and individually as citizens as members of the city or partakers in the sovereign power, and subjects as obedient to the same authority.

We shall note that this contract of association includes a mutual pledge on the part of the public and the individual; and that each individual, entering, so to speak, into a contract with himself, finds himself in a twofold capacity, i.e., as a member of the sovereign with regard to others, as member of the state with regard to the sovereign.

We shall also note that while no one is bound by any engagement to which he was not himself a party, the general deliberation which may be binding on all the subjects with regard to the sovereign, because of the two different relations under which each of them is envisaged, cannot be binding on the state with regard to itself. Hence we see that there is not, and cannot be, any other fundamental law, properly so called, except the social contract only. This does not mean that the body politic cannot, in certain respects, pledge itself to others; for in regard to the foreigner, it then becomes a simple creature, an individual.

Thus the two contracting parties, i.e., each individual and the public, have no common superior to decide their differences; so we will inquire if each of them remains free to break the contract at will, that is to repudiate it on his side as soon as he considers it hurtful.

To clear up this difficulty, we shall observe that, according to the social pact, the sovereign power is only able to act through the common, general will; so its decrees can only have a general or common aim; hence it follows that a private individual cannot be directly injured by the sovereign, unless all are injured, which is impossible, for that would be to want to harm oneself. Thus the social contract has no need of any warrant but the general power, for it can only be broken by individuals, and they are not therefore freed from their engagement, but punished for having broken it.

To decide all such questions rightly, we must always bear in mind that the nature of the social pact is private and peculiar to itself, in that the nation only contracts with itself, i.e., the people as a whole as sovereign, with the individuals as subjects; this condition is essential to the construction and working of the political machine, it alone makes pledges lawful, reasonable, and secure, without which it would be absurd, tyrannical, and liable to the grossest abuse.

Individuals having only submitted themselves to the sovereign, and the sovereign power being only the general will, we shall see that every man in obeying the sovereign only obeys himself, and how much freer are we under the social part than in the state of nature.

Having compared natural and civil liberty with regard to persons, we will compare them as to property, the rights of ownership and the rights of sovereignty, the private and the common domain. If the sovereign power rests upon the right of ownership, there is no right more worthy of respect; it is inviolable and sacred for the sovereign power, so long as it remains a private individual right; as soon as it is viewed as common to all the citizens, it is subject to the common will, and this will may destroy it. Thus the sovereign has no right to touch the property of one or many; but he may lawfully take possession of the property of all, as was done in Sparta in the time of Lycurgus; while the abolition of debts by Solon was an unlawful deed.

Since nothing is binding on the subjects except the general will, let us inquire how this will is made manifest, by what signs we may recognise it with certainty, what is a law, and what are the true characters of the law? This is quite a fresh subject; we have still to define the term law.

As soon as the nation considers one or more of its members, the nation is divided. A relation is established between the whole and its part which makes of them two separate entities, of which the part is one, and the whole, minus that part, is the other. But the whole minus the part is not the whole; as long as this relation exists, there is no longer a whole, but two unequal parts.

On the other hand, if the whole nation makes a law for the whole nation, it is only considering itself; and if a relation is set up, it is between the whole community regarded from one point of view, and the whole community regarded from another point of view, without any division of that whole. Then the object of the statute is general, and the will which makes that statute is general too. Let us see if there is any other kind of decree which may bear the name of law.

If the sovereign can only speak through laws, and if the law can never have any but a general purpose, concerning all the members of the state, it follows that the sovereign never has the power to make any law with regard to particular cases; and yet it is necessary for the preservation of the state that particular oases should also be dealt with; let us see how this can be done.

The decrees of the sovereign can only be decrees of the general will, that is laws; there must also be determining decrees, decrees of power or government, for the execution of those laws; and these, on the other hand, can only have particular aims. Thus the decrees by which the sovereign decides that a chief shall be elected is a law; the decree by which that chief is elected, in pursuance of the law, is only a decree of government.

This is a third relation in which the assembled people may be considered, i.e., as magistrates or executors of the law which it has passed in its capacity as sovereign. [Footnote: These problems and theorems are mostly taken from the Treatise on the Social Contract, itself a summary of a larger work, undertaken without due consideration of my own powers, and long since abandoned.]

We will now inquire whether it is possible for the nation to deprive itself of its right of sovereignty, to bestow it on one or more persons; for the decree of election not being a law, and the people in this decree not being themselves sovereign, we do not see how they can transfer a right which they do not possess.

The essence of sovereignty consisting in the general will, it is equally hard to see how we can be certain that an individual will shall always be in agreement with the general will. We should rather assume that it will often be opposed to it; for individual interest always tends to privileges, while the common interest always tends to equality, and if such an agreement were possible, no sovereign right could exist, unless the agreement were either necessary or indestructible.

We will inquire if, without violating the social pact, the heads of the nation, under whatever name they are chosen, can ever be more than the officers of the people, entrusted by them with the duty of carrying the law into execution. Are not these chiefs themselves accountable for their administration, and are not they themselves subject to the laws which it is their business to see carried out?

If the nation cannot alienate its supreme right, can it entrust it to others for a time? Cannot it give itself a master, cannot it find representatives? This is an important question and deserves discussion.

If the nation can have neither sovereign nor representatives we will inquire how it can pass its own laws; must there be many laws; must they be often altered; is it easy for a great nation to be its own lawgiver?

Was not the Roman people a great nation?

Is it a good thing that there should be great nations?

It follows from considerations already established that there is an intermediate body in the state between subjects and sovereign; and this intermediate body, consisting of one or more members, is entrusted with the public administration, the carrying out of the laws, and the maintenance of civil and political liberty.

The members of this body are called magistrates or kings, that is to say, rulers. This body, as a whole, considered in relation to its members, is called the prince, and considered in its actions it is called the government.

If we consider the action of the whole body upon itself, that is to say, the relation of the whole to the whole, of the sovereign to the state, we can compare this relation to that of the extremes in a proportion of which the government is the middle term. The magistrate receives from the sovereign the commands which he gives to the nation, and when it is reckoned up his product or his power is in the same degree as the product or power of the citizens who are subjects on one side of the proportion and sovereigns on the other. None of the three terms can be varied without at once destroying this proportion. If the sovereign tries to govern, and if the prince wants to make the laws, or if the subject refuses to obey them, disorder takes the place of order, and the state falls to pieces under despotism or anarchy.

Let us suppose that this state consists of ten thousand citizens. The sovereign can only be considered collectively and as a body, but each individual, as a subject, has his private and independent existence. Thus the sovereign is as ten thousand to one; that is to say, every member of the state has, as his own share, only one ten-thousandth part of the sovereign power, although he is subject to the whole. Let the nation be composed of one hundred thousand men, the position of the subjects is unchanged, and each continues to bear the whole weight of the laws, while his vote, reduced to the one hundred-thousandth part, has ten times less influence in the making of the laws. Thus the subject being always one, the sovereign is relatively greater as the number of the citizens is increased. Hence it follows that the larger the state the less liberty.

Now the greater the disproportion between private wishes and the general will, i.e., between manners and laws, the greater must be the power of repression. On the other side, the greatness of the state gives the depositaries of public authority greater temptations and additional means of abusing that authority, so that the more power is required by the government to control the people, the more power should there be in the sovereign to control the government.

From this twofold relation it follows that the continued proportion between the sovereign, the prince, and the people is not an arbitrary idea, but a consequence of the nature of the state. Moreover, it follows that one of the extremes, i.e., the nation, being constant, every time the double ratio increases or decreases, the simple ratio increases or diminishes in its turn; which cannot be unless the middle term is as often changed. From this we may conclude that there is no single absolute form of government, but there must be as many different forms of government as there are states of different size.

If the greater the numbers of the nation the less the ratio between its manners and its laws, by a fairly clear analogy, we may also say, the more numerous the magistrates, the weaker the government.

To make this principle clearer we will distinguish three essentially different wills in the person of each magistrate; first, his own will as an individual, which looks to his own advantage only; secondly, the common will of the magistrates, which is concerned only with the advantage of the prince, a will which may be called corporate, and one which is general in relation to the government and particular in relation to the state of which the government forms part; thirdly, the will of the people, or the sovereign will, which is general, as much in relation to the state viewed as the whole as in relation to the government viewed as a part of the whole. In a perfect legislature the private individual will should be almost nothing; the corporate will belonging to the government should be quite subordinate, and therefore the general and sovereign will is the master of all the others. On the other hand, in the natural order, these different wills become more and more active in proportion as they become centralised; the general will is always weak, the corporate will takes the second place, the individual will is preferred to all; so that every one is himself first, then a magistrate, and then a citizen; a series just the opposite of that required by the social order.

Having laid down this principle, let us assume that the government is in the hands of one man. In this case the individual and the corporate will are absolutely one, and therefore this will has reached the greatest possible degree of intensity. Now the use of power depends on the degree of this intensity, and as the absolute power of the government is always that of the people, and therefore invariable, it follows that the rule of one man is the most active form of government.

If, on the other hand, we unite the government with the supreme power, and make the prince the sovereign and the citizens so many magistrates, then the corporate will is completely lost in the general will, and will have no more activity than the general will, and it will leave the individual will in full vigour. Thus the government, though its absolute force is constant, will have the minimum of activity.

These rules are incontestable in themselves, and other considerations only serve to confirm them. For example, we see the magistrates as a body far more active than the citizens as a body, so that the individual will always counts for more. For each magistrate usually has charge of some particular duty of government; while each citizen, in himself, has no particular duty of sovereignty. Moreover, the greater the state the greater its real power, although its power does not increase because of the increase in territory; but the state remaining unchanged, the magistrates are multiplied in vain, the government acquires no further real strength, because it is the depositary of that of the state, which I have assumed to be constant. Thus, this plurality of magistrates decreases the activity of the government without increasing its power.

Having found that the power of the government is relaxed in proportion as the number of magistrates is multiplied, and that the more numerous the people, the more the controlling power must be increased, we shall infer that the ratio between the magistrates and the government should be inverse to that between subjects and sovereign, that is to say, that the greater the state, the smaller the government, and that in like manner the number of chiefs should be diminished because of the increased numbers of the people.

In order to make this diversity of forms clearer, and to assign them their different names, we shall observe in the first place that the sovereign may entrust the care of the government to the whole nation or to the greater part of the nation, so that there are more citizen magistrates than private citizens. This form of government is called Democracy.

Or the sovereign may restrict the government in the hands of a lesser number, so that there are more plain citizens than magistrates; and this form of government is called Aristocracy.

Finally, the sovereign may concentrate the whole government in the hands of one man. This is the third and commonest form of government, and is called Monarchy or royal government.

We shall observe that all these forms, or the first and second at least, may be less or more, and that within tolerably wide limits. For the democracy may include the whole nation, or may be confined to one half of it. The aristocracy, in its turn, may shrink from the half of the nation to the smallest number. Even royalty may be shared, either between father and son, between two brothers, or in some other fashion. There were always two kings in Sparta, and in the Roman empire there were as many as eight emperors at once, and yet it cannot be said that the empire was divided. There is a point where each form of government blends with the next; and under the three specific forms there may be really as many forms of government as there are citizens in the state.

Nor is this all. In certain respects each of these governments is capable of subdivision into different parts, each administered in one of these three ways. From these forms in combination there may arise a multitude of mixed forms, since each may be multiplied by all the simple forms.

In all ages there have been great disputes as to which is the best form of government, and people have failed to consider that each is the best in some cases and the worst in others. For ourselves, if the number of magistrates [Footnote: You will remember that I mean, in this context, the supreme magistrates or heads of the nation, the others being only their deputies in this or that respect.] in the various states is to be in inverse ratio to the number of the citizens, we infer that generally a democratic government is adapted to small states, an aristocratic government to those of moderate size, and a monarchy to large states.

These inquiries furnish us with a clue by which we may discover what are the duties and rights of citizens, and whether they can be separated one from the other; what is our country, in what does it really consist, and how can each of us ascertain whether he has a country or no?

Having thus considered every kind of civil society in itself, we shall compare them, so as to note their relations one with another; great and small, strong and weak, attacking one another, insulting one another, destroying one another; and in this perpetual action and reaction causing more misery and loss of life than if men had preserved their original freedom. We shall inquire whether too much or too little has not been accomplished in the matter of social institutions; whether individuals who are subject to law and to men, while societies preserve the independence of nature, are not exposed to the ills of both conditions without the advantages of either, and whether it would not be better to have no civil society in the world rather than to have many such societies. Is it not that mixed condition which partakes of both and secures neither?

> *"Per quem neutrum licet, nec tanquam in bello paratum esse, nec tanquam in pace securum." – Seneca De Trang: Animi, cap. I.*

Is it not this partial and imperfect association which gives rise to tyranny and war? And are not tyranny and war the worst scourges of humanity?

Finally we will inquire how men seek to get rid of these difficulties by means of leagues and confederations, which leave each state its own master in internal affairs, while they arm it against any unjust aggression. We will inquire how a good federal association may be established, what can make it lasting, and how far the rights of the federation may be stretched without destroying the right of sovereignty.

The Abbe de Saint-Pierre suggested an association of all the states of Europe to maintain perpetual peace among themselves. Is this association practicable, and supposing that it were established, would it be likely to last? These inquiries lead us straight to all the questions of international law which may clear up the remaining difficulties of political law. Finally we shall lay down the real principles of the laws of war, and we shall see why Grotius and others have only stated false principles.

I should not be surprised if my pupil, who is a sensible young man, should interrupt me saying, "One would think we were building our edifice of wood and not of men; we are putting everything so exactly in its place!" That is true; but remember that the law does not bow to the passions of men, and that we have first to establish the true principles of political law. Now that our foundations are laid, come and see what men have built upon them; and you will see some strange sights!

Then I set him to read Telemachus, and we pursue our journey; we are seeking that happy Salentum and the good Idomeneus made wise by misfortunes. By the way we find many like Protesilas and no Philocles, neither can Adrastes, King of the Daunians, be found. But let our readers picture our travels for themselves, or take the same journeys with Telemachus in their hand; and let us not suggest to them painful applications which the author himself avoids or makes in spite of himself.

Moreover, Emile is not a king, nor am I a god, so that we are not distressed that we cannot imitate Telemachus and Mentor in the good they did; none know better than we how to keep to our own place, none have less desire to leave it. We know that the same task is allotted to all; that whoever loves what is right with all his heart, and does the right so far as it is in his power, has fulfilled that task. We know that Telemachus and Mentor are creatures of the imagination. Emile does not travel in idleness and he does more good than if he were a prince. If we were kings we should be no greater benefactors. If we were kings and benefactors we should cause any number of real evils for every apparent good we supposed we were doing. If we were kings and sages, the first good deed we should desire to perform, for ourselves and for others, would be to abdicate our kingship and return to our present position.

I have said why travel does so little for every one. What makes it still more barren for the young is the way in which they are sent on their travels. Tutors, more concerned to amuse than to instruct, take them from town to town, from palace to palace, where if they are men of learning and letters, they make them spend their time in libraries, or visiting antiquaries, or rummaging among old buildings transcribing ancient inscriptions. In every country they are busy over some other century, as if they were living in another country; so that after they have travelled all over Europe at great expense, a prey to frivolity or tedium, they return, having seen nothing to interest them, and having learnt nothing that could be of any possible use to them.

All capitals are just alike, they are a mixture of all nations and all ways of living; they are not the place in which to study the nations. Paris and London seem to me the same town. Their inhabitants have a few prejudices of their own, but each has as many as the other, and all their rules of conduct are the same. We know the kind of people who will throng the court. We know the way of living which the crowds of people and the unequal distribution of wealth will produce. As soon as any one tells me of a town with two hundred thousand people, I know its life already. What I do not know about it is not worth going there to learn.

To study the genius and character of a nation you should go to the more remote provinces, where there is less stir, less commerce, where strangers seldom travel, where the inhabitants stay in one place, where there are fewer changes of wealth and position. Take a look at the capital on your way, but go and study the country far away from that capital. The French are not in Paris, but in Touraine; the English are more English in Mercia than in London, and the Spaniards more Spanish in Galicia than in Madrid. In these remoter provinces a nation assumes its true character and shows what it really is; there the good or ill effects of the government are best perceived, just as you can measure the arc more exactly at a greater radius.

The necessary relations between character and government have been so clearly pointed out in the book of L'Esprit des Lois, that one cannot do better than have recourse to that work for the study of those relations. But speaking generally, there are two plain and simple standards by which to decide whether governments are good or bad. One is the population. Every country in which the population is decreasing is on its way to ruin; and the countries in which the population increases most rapidly, even were they the poorest countries in the world, are certainly the best governed. [Footnote: I only know one exception to this rule—it is China.] But this population must be the natural result of the government and the national character, for if it is caused by colonisation or any other temporary and accidental cause, then the remedy itself is evidence of the disease. When Augustus passed laws against celibacy, those laws showed that the Roman empire was already beginning to decline. Citizens must be induced to marry by the goodness of the government, not compelled to marry by law; you must not examine the effects of force, for the law which strives against the constitution has little or no effect; you should study what is done by the influence of public morals and by the natural inclination of the government, for these alone produce a lasting effect. It was the policy of the worthy Abbe de Saint-Pierre always to look for a little remedy for every individual ill, instead of tracing them to their common source and seeing if they could not all be cured together. You do not need to treat separately every sore on a rich man's body; you should purify the blood which produces them. They say that in England there are prizes for agriculture; that is enough for me; that is proof enough that agriculture will not flourish there much longer.

The second sign of the goodness or badness of the government and the laws is also to be found in the population, but it is to be found not in its numbers but in its distribution. Two states equal in size and population may be very unequal in strength; and the more powerful is always that in which the people are more evenly distributed over its territory; the country which has fewer large towns, and makes less show on this account, will always defeat the other. It is the great towns which exhaust the state and are the cause of its weakness; the wealth which they produce is a sham wealth, there is much money and few goods. They say the town of Paris is worth a whole province to the King of France; for my own part I believe it costs him more than several provinces. I believe that Paris is fed by the provinces in more senses than one, and that the greater part of their revenues is poured into that town and stays there, without ever returning to the people or to the king. It is inconceivable that in this age of calculators there is no one to see that France would be much more powerful if Paris were destroyed. Not only is this ill-distributed population not advantageous to the state, it is more ruinous than depopulation itself, because depopulation only gives as produce nought, and the ill-regulated addition of still more people gives a negative result. When I hear an Englishman and a Frenchman so proud of the size of their capitals, and disputing whether London or Paris has more inhabitants, it seems to me that they are quarrelling as to which nation can claim the honour of being the worst governed.

Study the nation outside its towns; thus only will you really get to know it. It is nothing to see the apparent form of a government, overladen with the machinery of administration and the jargon of the administrators, if you have not also studied its nature as seen in the effects it has upon the people, and in every degree of administration. The difference of form is really shared by every degree of the administration, and it is only by including every degree that you really know the difference. In one country you begin to feel the spirit of the minister in the manoeuvres of his underlings; in another you must see the election of members of parliament to see if the nation is really free; in each and every country, he who has only seen the towns cannot possibly know what the government is like, as its spirit is never the same in town and country. Now it is the agricultural districts which form the country, and the country people who make the nation.

This study of different nations in their remoter provinces, and in the simplicity of their native genius, gives a general result which is very satisfactory, to my thinking, and very consoling to the human heart; it is this: All the nations, if you observe them in this fashion, seem much better worth observing; the nearer they are to nature, the more does kindness hold sway in their character; it is only when they are cooped up in towns, it is only when they are changed by cultivation, that they become depraved, that certain faults which were rather coarse than injurious are exchanged for pleasant but pernicious vices.

From this observation we see another advantage in the mode of travel I suggest; for young men, sojourning less in the big towns which are horribly corrupt, are less likely to catch the infection of vice; among simpler people and less numerous company, they will preserve a surer judgment, a healthier taste, and better morals. Besides this contagion of vice is hardly to be feared for Emile; he has everything to protect him from it. Among all the precautions I have taken, I reckon much on the love he bears in his heart.

We do not know the power of true love over youthful desires, because we are ourselves as ignorant of it as they are, and those who have control over the young turn them from true love. Yet a young man must either love or fall into bad ways. It is easy to be deceived by appearances. You will quote any number of young men who are said to live very chastely without love; but show me one grown man, a real man, who can truly say that his youth was thus spent? In all our virtues, all our duties, people are content with appearances; for my own part I want the reality, and I am much mistaken if there is any other way of securing it beyond the means I have suggested.

The idea of letting Emile fall in love before taking him on his travels is not my own. It was suggested to me by the following incident.

I was in Venice calling on the tutor of a young Englishman. It was winter and we were sitting round the fire. The tutor's letters were brought from the post office. He glanced at them, and then read them aloud to his pupil. They were in English; I understood not a word, but while he was reading I saw the young man tear some fine point lace ruffles which he was wearing, and throw them in the fire one after another, as quietly as he could, so that no one should see it. Surprised at this whim, I looked at his face and thought I perceived some emotion; but the external signs of passion, though much alike in all men, have national differences which may easily lead one astray. Nations have a different language of facial expression as well as of speech. I waited till the letters were finished and then showing the tutor the bare wrists of his pupil, which he did his best to hide, I said, "May I ask the meaning of this?"

The tutor seeing what had happened began to laugh; he embraced his pupil with an air of satisfaction and, with his consent, he gave me the desired explanation.

"The ruffles," said he, "which Mr. John has just torn to pieces, were a present from a lady in this town, who made them for him not long ago. Now you must know that Mr. John is engaged to a young lady in his own country, with whom he is greatly in love, and she well deserves it. This letter is from the lady's mother, and I will translate the passage which caused the destruction you beheld.

"'Lucy is always at work upon Mr. John's ruffles. Yesterday Miss Betty Roldham came to spend the afternoon and insisted on doing some of her work. I knew that Lucy was up very early this morning and I wanted to see what she was doing; I found her busy unpicking what Miss Betty had done. She would not have a single stitch in her present done by any hand but her own.'"

Mr. John went to fetch another pair of ruffles, and I said to his tutor: "Your pupil has a very good disposition; but tell me is not the letter from Miss Lucy's mother a put up job? Is it not an expedient of your designing against the lady of the ruffles?" "No," said he, "it is quite genuine; I am not so artful as that; I have made use of simplicity and zeal, and God has blessed my efforts."

This incident with regard to the young man stuck in my mind; it was sure to set a dreamer like me thinking.

But it is time we finished. Let us take Mr. John back to Miss Lucy, or rather Emile to Sophy. He brings her a heart as tender as ever, and a more enlightened mind, and he returns to his native land all the bettor for having made acquaintance with foreign governments through their vices and foreign nations through their virtues. I have even taken care that he should associate himself with some man of worth in every nation, by means of a treaty of hospitality after the fashion of the ancients, and I shall not be sorry if this acquaintance is kept up by means of letters. Not only may this be useful, not only is it always pleasant to have a correspondent in foreign lands, it is also an excellent antidote against the sway of patriotic prejudices, to which we are liable all through our life, and to which sooner or later we are more or less enslaved. Nothing is better calculated to lessen the hold of such prejudices than a friendly interchange of opinions with sensible people whom we respect; they are free from our prejudices and we find ourselves face to face with theirs, and so we can set the one set of prejudices against the other and be safe from both. It is not the same thing to have to do with strangers in our own country and in theirs. In the former case there is always a certain amount of politeness which either makes them conceal their real opinions, or makes them think more favourably of our country while they are with us; when they get home again this disappears, and they merely do us justice. I should be very glad if the foreigner I consult has seen my country, but I shall not ask what he thinks of it till he is at home again.

When we have spent nearly two years travelling in a few of the great countries and many of the smaller countries of Europe, when we have learnt two or three of the chief languages, when we have seen what is really interesting in natural history, government, arts, or men, Emile, devoured by impatience, reminds me that our time is almost up. Then I say, "Well, my friend, you remember the main object of our journey; you have seen and observed; what is the final result of your observations? What decision have you come to?" Either my method is wrong, or he will answer me somewhat after this fashion—

"What decision have I come to? I have decided to be what you made me; of my own free will I will add no fetters to those imposed upon me by nature and the laws. The more I study the works of men in their institutions, the more clearly I see that, in their efforts after independence, they become slaves, and that their very freedom is wasted in vain attempts to assure its continuance. That they may not be carried away by the flood of things, they form all sorts of attachments; then as soon as they wish to move forward they are surprised to find that everything drags them back. It seems to me that to set oneself free we need do nothing, we need only continue to desire freedom. My master, you have made me free by teaching me to yield to necessity. Let her come when she will, I follow her without compulsion; I lay hold of nothing to keep me back. In our travels I have sought for some corner of the earth where I might be absolutely my own; but where can one dwell among men without being dependent on their passions? On further consideration I have discovered that my desire contradicted itself; for were I to hold to nothing else, I should at least hold to the spot on which I had settled; my life would be attached to that spot, as the dryads were attached to their trees. I have discovered that the words liberty and empire are incompatible; I can only be master of a cottage by ceasing to be master of myself.

> *"'Hoc erat in votis, modus agri non ita magnus.'*
> *Horace, lib. ii., sat. vi.*

"I remember that my property was the origin of our inquiries. You argued very forcibly that I could not keep both my wealth and my liberty; but when you wished me to be free and at the same time without needs, you desired two incompatible things, for I could only be independent of men by returning to dependence on nature. What then shall I do with the fortune bequeathed to me by my parents? To begin with, I will not be dependent on it; I will cut myself loose from all the ties which bind me to it; if it is left in my hands, I shall keep it; if I am deprived of it, I shall not be dragged away with it. I shall not trouble myself to keep it, but I shall keep steadfastly to my own place. Rich or poor, I shall be free. I shall be free not merely in this country or in that; I shall be free in any part of the world. All the chains of prejudice are broken; as far as I am concerned I know only the bonds of necessity. I have been trained to endure them from my childhood, and I shall endure them until death, for I am a man; and why should I not wear those chains as a free man, for I should have to wear them even if I were a slave, together with the additional fetters of slavery?

"What matters my place in the world? What matters it where I am? Wherever there are men, I am among my brethren; wherever there are none, I am in my own home. So long as I may be independent and rich, and have wherewithal to live, and I shall live. If my wealth makes a slave of me, I shall find it easy to renounce it. I have hands to work, and I shall get a living. If my hands fail me, I shall live if others will support me; if they forsake me I shall die; I shall die even if I am not forsaken, for death is not the penalty of poverty, it is a law of nature. Whensoever death comes I defy it; it shall never find me making preparations for life; it shall never prevent me having lived.

"My father, this is my decision. But for my passions, I should be in my manhood independent as God himself, for I only desire what is and I should never fight against fate. At least, there is only one chain, a chain which I shall ever wear, a chain of which I may be justly proud. Come then, give me my Sophy, and I am free."

"Dear Emile, I am glad indeed to hear you speak like a man, and to behold the feelings of your heart. At your age this exaggerated unselfishness is not unpleasing. It will decrease when you have children of your own, and then you will be just what a good father and a wise man ought to be. I knew what the result would be before our travels; I knew that when you saw our institutions you would be far from reposing a confidence in them which they do not deserve. In vain do we seek freedom under the power of the laws. The laws! Where is there any law? Where is there any respect for law? Under the name of law you have everywhere seen the rule of self-interest and human passion. But the eternal laws of nature and of order exist. For the wise man they take the place of positive law; they are written in the depths of his heart by conscience and reason; let him obey these laws and be free; for there is no slave but the evil-doer, for he always does evil against his will. Liberty is not to be found in any form of government, she is in the heart of the free man, he bears her with him everywhere. The vile man bears his slavery in himself; the one would be a slave in Geneva, the other free in Paris.

"If I spoke to you of the duties of a citizen, you would perhaps ask me, 'Which is my country?' And you would think you had put me to confusion. Yet you would be mistaken, dear Emile, for he who has no country has, at least, the land in which he lives. There is always a government and certain so-called laws under which he has lived in peace. What matter though the social contract has not been observed, if he has been protected by private interest against the general will, if he has been secured by public violence against private aggressions, if the evil he has beheld has taught him to love the good, and if our institutions themselves have made him perceive and hate their own iniquities? Oh, Emile, where is the man who owes nothing to the land in which he lives? Whatever that land may be, he owes to it the most precious thing possessed by man, the morality of his actions and the love of virtue. Born in the depths of a forest he would have lived in greater happiness and freedom; but being able to follow his inclinations without a struggle there would have been no merit in his goodness, he would not have been virtuous, as he may be now, in spite of his passions. The mere sight of order teaches him to know and love it. The public good, which to others is a mere pretext, is a real motive for him. He learns to fight against himself and to prevail, to sacrifice his own interest to the common weal. It is not true that he gains nothing from the laws; they give him courage to be just, even in the midst of the wicked. It is not true that they have failed to make him free; they have taught him to rule himself.

"Do not say therefore, 'What matter where I am?' It does matter that you should be where you can best do your duty; and one of these duties is to love your native land. Your fellow-countrymen protected you in childhood; you should love them in your manhood. You should live among them, or at least you should live where you can serve them to the best of your power, and where they know where to find you if ever they are in need of you. There are circumstances in which a man may be of more use to his fellow-countrymen outside his country than within it. Then he should listen only to his own zeal and should bear his exile without a murmur; that exile is one of his duties. But you, dear Emile, you have not undertaken the painful task of telling men the truth, you must live in the midst of your fellow-creatures, cultivating their friendship in pleasant intercourse; you must be their benefactor, their pattern; your example will do more than all our books, and the good they see you do will touch them more deeply than all our empty words.

"Yet I do not exhort you to live in a town; on the contrary, one of the examples which the good should give to others is that of a patriarchal, rural life, the earliest life of man, the most peaceful, the most natural, and the most attractive to the uncorrupted heart. Happy is the land, my young friend, where one need not seek peace in the wilderness! But where is that country? A man of good will finds it hard to satisfy his inclinations in the midst of towns, where he can find few but frauds and rogues to work for. The welcome given by the towns to those idlers who flock to them to seek their fortunes only completes the ruin of the country, when the country ought really to be repopulated at the cost of the towns. All the men who withdraw from high society are useful just because of their withdrawal, since its vices are the result of its numbers. They are also useful when they can bring with them into the desert places life, culture, and the love of their first condition. I like to think what benefits Emile and Sophy, in their simple home, may spread about them, what a stimulus they may give to the country, how they may revive the zeal of the unlucky villagers.

"In fancy I see the population increasing, the land coming under cultivation, the earth clothed with fresh beauty. Many workers and plenteous crops transform the labours of the fields into holidays; I see the young couple in the midst of the rustic sports which they have revived, and I hear the shouts of joy and the blessings of those about them. Men say the golden age is a fable; it always will be for those whose feelings and taste are depraved. People do not really regret the golden age, for they do nothing to restore it. What is needed for its restoration? One thing only, and that is an impossibility; we must love the golden age.

"Already it seems to be reviving around Sophy's home; together you will only complete what her worthy parents have begun. But, dear Emile, you must not let so pleasant a life give you a distaste for sterner duties, if every they are laid upon you; remember that the Romans sometimes left the plough to become consul. If the prince or the state calls you to the service of your country, leave all to fulfil the honourable duties of a citizen in the post assigned to you. If you find that duty onerous, there is a sure and honourable means of escaping from it; do your duty so honestly that it will not long be left in your hands. Moreover, you need not fear the difficulties of such a test; while there are men of our own time, they will not summon you to serve the state."

Why may I not paint the return of Emile to Sophy and the end of their love, or rather the beginning of their wedded love! A love founded on esteem which will last with life itself, on virtues which will not fade with fading beauty, on fitness of character which gives a charm to intercourse, and prolongs to old age the delights of early love. But all such details would be pleasing but not useful, and so far I have not permitted myself to give attractive details unless I thought they would be useful. Shall I abandon this rule when my task is nearly ended? No, I feel that my pen is weary. Too feeble for such prolonged labours, I should abandon this if it were not so nearly completed; if it is not to be left imperfect it is time it were finished.

At last I see the happy day approaching, the happiest day of Emile's life and my own; I see the crown of my labours, I begin to appreciate their results. The noble pair are united till death do part; heart and lips confirm no empty vows; they are man and wife. When they return from the church, they follow where they are led; they know not where they are, whither they are going, or what is happening around them. They heed nothing, they answer at random; their eyes are troubled and they see nothing. Oh, rapture! Oh, human weakness! Man is overwhelmed by the feeling of happiness, he is not strong enough to bear it.

There are few people who know how to talk to the newly-married couple. The gloomy propriety of some and the light conversation of others seem to me equally out of place. I would rather their young hearts were left to themselves, to abandon themselves to an agitation which is not without its charm, rather than that they should be so cruelly distressed by a false modesty, or annoyed by coarse witticisms which, even if they appealed to them at other times, are surely out of place on such a day.

I behold our young people, wrapped in a pleasant languor, giving no heed to what is said. Shall I, who desire that they should enjoy all the days of their life, shall I let them lose this precious day? No, I desire that they shall taste its pleasures and enjoy them. I rescue them from the foolish crowd, and walk with them in some quiet place; I recall them to themselves by speaking of them I wish to speak, not merely to their ears, but to their hearts, and I know that there is only one subject of which they can think to-day.

"My children," say I, taking a hand of each, "it is three years since I beheld the birth of the pure and vigorous passion which is your happiness to-day. It has gone on growing; your eyes tell me that it has reached its highest point; it must inevitably decline." My readers can fancy the raptures, the anger, the vows of Emile, and the scornful air with which Sophy withdraws her hand from mine; how their eyes protest that they will adore each other till their latest breath. I let them have their way; then I continue:

"I have often thought that if the happiness of love could continue in marriage, we should find a Paradise upon earth. So far this has never been. But if it were not quite impossible, you two are quite worthy to set an example you have not received, an example which few married couples could follow. My children, shall I tell you what I think is the way, and the only way, to do it?"

They look at one another and smile at my simplicity. Emile thanks me curtly for my prescription, saying that he thinks Sophy has a better, at any rate it is good enough for him. Sophy agrees with him and seems just as certain. Yet in spite of her mockery, I think I see a trace of curiosity. I study Emile; his eager eyes are fixed upon his wife's beauty; he has no curiosity for anything else; and he pays little heed to what I say. It is my turn to smile, and I say to myself, "I will soon get your attention."

The almost imperceptible difference between these two hidden impulses is characteristic of a real difference between the two sexes; it is that men are generally less constant than women, and are sooner weary of success in love. A woman foresees man's future inconstancy, and is anxious; it is this which makes her more jealous. [Footnote: In France it is the wives who first emancipate themselves; and necessarily so, for having very little heart, and only desiring attention, when a husband ceases to pay them attention they care very little for himself. In other countries it is not so; it is the husband who first emancipates himself; and necessarily so, for women, faithful, but foolish, importune men with their desires and only disgust them. There may be plenty of exceptions to these general truths; but I still think they are truths.] When his passion begins to cool she is compelled to pay him the attentions he used to bestow on her for her pleasure; she weeps, it is her turn to humiliate herself, and she is rarely successful. Affection and kind deeds rarely win hearts, and they hardly ever win them back. I return to my prescription against the cooling of love in marriage.

"It is plain and simple," I continue. "It consists in remaining lovers when you are husband and wife."

"Indeed," said Emile, laughing at my secret, "we shall not find that hard."

"Perhaps you will find it harder than you think. Pray give me time to explain.

"Cords too tightly stretched are soon broken. This is what happens when the marriage bond is subjected to too great a strain. The fidelity imposed by it upon husband and wife is the most sacred of all rights; but it gives to each too great a power over the other. Constraint and love do not agree together, and pleasure is not to be had for the asking. Do not blush, Sophy, and do not try to run away. God forbid that I should offend your modesty! But your fate for life is at stake. For so great a cause, permit a conversation between your husband and your father which you would not permit elsewhere.

"It is not so much possession as mastery of which people tire, and affection is often more prolonged with regard to a mistress than a wife. How can people make a duty of the tenderest caresses, and a right of the sweetest pledges of love? It is mutual desire which gives the right, and nature knows no other. The law may restrict this right, it cannot extend it. The pleasure is so sweet in itself! Should it owe to sad constraint the power which it cannot gain from its own charms? No, my children, in marriage the hearts are bound, but the bodies are not enslaved. You owe one another fidelity, but not complaisance. Neither of you may give yourself to another, but neither of you belongs to the other except at your own will.

"If it is true, dear Emile, that you would always be your wife's lover, that she should always be your mistress and her own, be a happy but respectful lover; obtain all from love and nothing from duty, and let the slightest favours never be of right but of grace. I know that modesty shuns formal confessions and requires to be overcome; but with delicacy and true love, will the lover ever be mistaken as to the real will? Will not he know when heart and eyes grant what the lips refuse? Let both for ever be master of their person and their caresses, let them have the right to bestow them only at their own will. Remember that even in marriage this pleasure is only lawful when the desire is mutual. Do not be afraid, my children, that this law will keep you apart; on the contrary, it will make both more eager to please, and will prevent satiety. True to one another, nature and love will draw you to each other."

Emile is angry and cries out against these and similar suggestions. Sophy is ashamed, she hides her face behind her fan and says nothing. Perhaps while she is saying nothing, she is the most annoyed. Yet I insist, without mercy; I make Emile blush for his lack of delicacy; I undertake to be surety for Sophy that she will undertake her share of the treaty. I incite her to speak, you may guess she will not dare to say I am mistaken. Emile anxiously consults the eyes of his young wife; he beholds them, through all her confusion, filled with a, voluptuous anxiety which reassures him against the dangers of trusting her. He flings himself at her feet, kisses with rapture the hand extended to him, and swears that beyond the fidelity he has already promised, he will renounce all other rights over her. "My dear wife," said he, "be the arbiter of my pleasures as you are already the arbiter of my life and fate. Should your cruelty cost me life itself I would yield to you my most cherished rights. I will owe nothing to your complaisance, but all to your heart."

Dear Emile, be comforted; Sophy herself is too generous to let you fall a victim to your generosity.

In the evening, when I am about to leave them, I say in the most solemn tone, "Remember both of you, that you are free, that there is no question of marital rights; believe me, no false deference. Emile will you come home with me? Sophy permits it." Emile is ready to strike me in his anger. "And you, Sophy, what do you say? Shall I take him away?" The little liar, blushing, answers, "Yes." A tender and delightful falsehood, better than truth itself!

The next day. ... Men no longer delight in the picture of bliss; their taste is as much depraved by the corruption of vice as their hearts. They can no longer feel what is touching or perceive what is truly delightful. You who, as a picture of voluptuous joys, see only the happy lovers immersed in pleasure, your picture is very imperfect; you have only its grosser part, the sweetest charms of pleasure are not there. Which of you has seen a young couple, happily married, on the morrow of their marriage? their chaste yet languid looks betray the intoxication of the bliss they have enjoyed, the blessed security of innocence, and the delightful certainty that they will spend the rest of their life together. The heart of man can behold no more rapturous sight; this is the real picture of happiness; you have beheld it a hundred times without heeding it; your hearts are so hard that you cannot love it. Sophy, peaceful and happy, spends the day in the arms of her tender mother; a pleasant resting place, after a night spent in the arms of her husband.

The day after I am aware of a slight change. Emile tries to look somewhat vexed; but through this pretence I notice such a tender eagerness, and indeed so much submission, that I do not think there is much amiss. As for Sophy she is merrier than she was yesterday; her eyes are sparkling and she looks very well pleased with herself; she is charming to Emile; she ventures to tease him a little and vexes him still more.

These changes are almost imperceptible, but they do not escape me; I am anxious and I question Emile in private, and I learn that, to his great regret, and in spite of all entreaties, he was not permitted last night to share Sophy's bed. That haughty lady had made haste to assert her right. An explanation takes place. Emile complains bitterly, Sophy laughs; but at last, seeing that Emile is really getting angry, she looks at him with eyes full of tenderness and love, and pressing my hand, she only says these two words, but in a tone that goes to his heart, "Ungrateful man!" Emile is too stupid to understand. But I understand, and I send Emile away and speak to Sophy privately in her turn.

"I see," said I, "the reason for this whim. No one could be more delicate, and no one could use that delicacy so ill. Dear Sophy, do not be anxious, I have given you a man; do not be afraid to treat him as such. You have had the first fruits of his youth; he has not squandered his manhood and it will endure for you. My dear child, I must explain to you why I said what I did in our conversation of the day before yesterday. Perhaps you only understood it as a way of restraining your pleasures to secure their continuance. Oh, Sophy, there was another object, more worthy of my care. When Emile became your husband, he became your head, it is yours to obey; this is the will of nature. When the wife is like Sophy, it is, however, good for the man to be led by her; that is another of nature's laws, and it is to give you as much authority over his heart, as his sex gives him over your person, that I have made you the arbiter of his pleasures. It will be hard for you, but you will control him if you can control yourself, and what has already happened shows me that this difficult art is not beyond your courage. You will long rule him by love if you make your favours scarce and precious, if you know how to use them aright. If you want to have your husband always in your power, keep him at a distance. But let your sternness be the result of modesty not caprice; let him find you modest not capricious; beware lest in controlling his love you make him doubt your own. Be all the dearer for your favours and all the more respected when you refuse them; let him honour his wife's chastity, without having to complain of her coldness.

"Thus, my child, he will give you his confidence, he will listen to your opinion, will consult you in his business, and will decide nothing without you. Thus you may recall him to wisdom, if he strays, and bring him back by a gentle persuasion, you may make yourself lovable in order to be useful, you may employ coquetry on behalf of virtue, and love on behalf of reason.

"Do not think that with all this, your art will always serve your purpose. In spite of every precaution pleasures are destroyed by possession, and love above all others. But when love has lasted long enough, a gentle habit takes its place and the charm of confidence succeeds the raptures of passion. Children form a bond between their parents, a bond no less tender and a bond which is sometimes stronger than love itself. When you cease to be Emile's mistress you will be his friend and wife; you will be the mother of his children. Then instead of your first reticence let there be the fullest intimacy between you; no more separate beds, no more refusals, no more caprices. Become so truly his better half that he can no longer do without you, and if he must leave you, let him feel that he is far from himself. You have made the charms of home life so powerful in your father's home, let them prevail in your own. Every man who is happy at home loves his wife. Remember that if your husband is happy in his home, you will be a happy wife.

"For the present, do not be too hard on your lover; he deserves more consideration; he will be offended by your fears; do not care for his health at the cost of his happiness, and enjoy your own happiness. You must neither wait for disgust nor repulse desire; you must not refuse for the sake of refusing, but only to add to the value of your favours."

Then, taking her back to Emile, I say to her young husband, "One must bear the yoke voluntarily imposed upon oneself. Let your deserts be such that the yoke may be lightened. Above all, sacrifice to the graces, and do not think that sulkiness will make you more amiable." Peace is soon made, and everybody can guess its terms. The treaty is signed with a kiss, after which I say to my pupil, "Dear Emile, all his life through a man needs a guide and counsellor. So far I have done my best to fulfil that duty; my lengthy task is now ended, and another will undertake this duty. To-day I abdicate the authority which you gave me; henceforward Sophy is your guardian."

Little by little the first raptures subside and they can peacefully enjoy the delights of their new condition. Happy lovers, worthy husband and wife! To do honour to their virtues, to paint their felicity, would require the history of their lives. How often does my heart throb with rapture when I behold in them the crown of my life's work! How often do I take their hands in mine blessing God with all my heart! How often do I kiss their clasped hands! How often do their tears of joy fall upon mine! They are touched by my joy and they share my raptures. Their worthy parents see their own youth renewed in that of their children; they begin to live, as it were, afresh in them; or rather they perceive, for the first time, the true value of life; they curse their former wealth, which prevented them from enjoying so delightful a lot when they were young. If there is such a thing as happiness upon earth, you must seek it in our abode.

One morning a few months later Emile enters my room and embraces me, saying, "My master, congratulate your son; he hopes soon to have the honour of being a father. What a responsibility will be ours, how much we shall need you! Yet God forbid that I should let you educate the son as you educated the father. God forbid that so sweet and holy a task should be fulfilled by any but myself, even though I should make as good a choice for my child as was made for me! But continue to be the teacher of the young teachers. Advise and control us; we shall be easily led; as long as I live I shall need you. I need you more than ever now that I am taking up the duties of manhood. You have done your own duty; teach me to follow your example, while you enjoy your well-earned leisure."

CPSIA information can be obtained at www.ICGtesting.com
Printed in the USA
LVOW11s2300190516

489052LV00001BA/51/P

9 781508 537977